SCIENCE FICTION
THE BEST OF 2004

KAREN HABER
and JONATHAN STRAHAN
Editors

ibooks
new york
www.ibooks.net

DISTRIBUTED BY SIMON & SCHUSTER, INC.

KAREN HABER and JONATHAN STRAHAN

SCIENCE FICTION
THE BEST OF 2004

KAREN HABER is the acclaimed editor of the Hugo Award-nominated *Meditations on Middle Earth*, a collection of essays by some of fantasy's best-known writers. Most recently, she edited *Exploring the Matrix*, an examination of the popular film series by some of science fiction's top writers. She also created the bestselling *The Mutant Season* series of novels, of which she co-authored the first volume with her husband, Robert Silverberg. She is a respected journalist and an accomplished fiction writer. Her short fiction has appeared in *Asimov's The Magazine of Fantasy and Science Fiction, and many other publications.*

JONATHAN STRAHAN is the award-winning editor of *The Year's Best Australian Science Fiction and Fantasy* anthology series, co-founder and editor of *Eidolon: The Journal of Australian Science Fiction and Fantasy*, and publisher of *The Coode Street Press.* He has won the Australian National Science Fiction Achievement Award on several occasions and is the recipient of the William Atheling, Jr Award for Criticism and Review. He is the Reviews Editor for *Locus: The Magazine of the Science Fiction and Fantasy Field,* and is co-editor of *The Locus Awards: 30 Years of the Best in Science Fiction and Fantasy.*

FANTASY AND SCIENCE FICTION
published by ibooks, inc.:

Science Fiction: The Best of 2001
Fantasy: The Best of 2001
Science Fiction: The Best of 2002
Fantasy: The Best of 2002
Robert Silverberg & Karen Haber, Editors

Science Fiction: The Best of 2003
Karen Haber & Jonathan Strahan, Editors

The Ultimate Cyberpunk
Pat Cadigan, Editor

My Favorite Fantasy Story
Martin H. Greenberg, Editor

ACKNOWLEDGMENTS

Our thanks to Robert Silverberg, Marianne Jablon, and Charles N. Brown for services above and beyond the call of duty. We'd also like to thank Justin Ackroyd, John Joseph Adams, Brian Bienkowski, Bill Congreve, Jack Dann, Ellen Datlow, Nick Gevers, Gavin J. Grant, John Helfers, Rich Horton, Jay Lake, Deborah Layne, Kelly Link, Robin Pen, Tim Pratt, Larry Segriff, Gordon Van Gelder, Jeff VanderMeer, and Sean Williams for their invaluable assistance with this book.

CONTENTS

INTRODUCTION

2004 was another solid year for the SF short story with new and upcoming writers producing strong work in a staggering variety of publications. But the biggest noise made this year came from the editorial side of the field, with startling announcements regarding personnel changes at two major magazines. Dell Magazines announced that Gardner Dozois, long-time editor of *Asimov'sScience Fiction*, would leave the magazine and be replaced by Managing Editor Sheila Williams, beginning in 2005. During his tenure, Dozois, who began editing Asimov's in March 1986, established himself as the most important magazine editor to enter the field since John W. Campbell, and developed *Asimov's* into the leading science fiction magazine in the world. While at *Asimov's*, Dozois was instrumental in redefining and invigorating the science fiction short story, and the field itself. He introduced, developed and/or championed some of the most famous writers working in the field and shifted the focus of the field firmly toward the kind of literate SF he favored. His departure has sent shockwaves through the science fiction and fantasy publishing world.

Similarly, David Pringle, editor and publisher of the British magazine *Interzone* stepped down after 22 years with the magazine. His duties were assumed by Andy Cox of *The Third Alternative*. Under Pringle's editorship, *Interzone* became the most important English language SF magazine published outside the United States, and at one time was the go-to source for some of the most exciting fiction being published in the field. It not only championed many important new writers, including Stephen Baxter, Greg Egan, Paul McAuley and Alastair Reynolds, but was instrumentally important in pioneering 'radical hard SF', or the "new space opera." The first issues of the new *Interzone* appeared late in 2004 and indicate a significant change in direction for the magazine, away from hard sf and towards the darker kind of fiction more in sync with *The Third Alternative*.

With *Asimov's* and *Interzone* in transition, Ellen Datlow's *SciFiction* had its best year since it debuted and was clearly the best magazine in the field with fine work by Walter Jon Williams, Carol Emshwiller, James Patrick Kelly and newcomers like Christopher Rowe. Gordon Van Gelder's *The Magazine of Fantasy and Science Fiction* also had a good year, with major work from Paolo Bacigalupi, Robert Reed, Bradley Denton, and others. *Asimov's* had, by it's very high standards, an average year with important work from Charles Stross, Nancy Kress and James Patrick Kelly amongst many others, while Stanley Schmidt's *Analog Science Fiction and Fact* continued to be a reliable source of good traditional science fiction with a number of interesting serialized works and outstanding stories by Stephen Baxter and Michael Flynn.

While it was a disappointing year for science fiction anthologies—with Gregory Benford's *Microcosms* being a rare stand-out—we can unreservedly recommend *Between Worlds*, an anthology edited by Robert Silverberg featuring top quality novellas by James Patrick Kelly, Walter Jon Williams, Nancy Kress, Stephen Baxter and Silverberg himself.

The novella seems to be emerging as the form-of-choice for many writers, and many of the field's biggest names delivered major work at lengths beyond what this book could accommodate, a sign of the continuing commercial viability of the short novel. All of the major magazines published several of these excellent longer stories. Fine novellas by Robert Reed, Steven Erikson, Stephen Baxter, Mary Gentle, Paul Park, and others were published as stand-alone books by PS Publishing, Golden Gryphon and other small presses.

So, 2004 was a good year for fiction, if one of transition for editors. And just as it was year of transition for science fiction, it was also a year of transition for this anthology series. As readers of last year's volume know, founding editor Robert Silverberg stepped down and a new editorial team (founding co-editor Karen Haber and Jonathan Strahan) took up the task of decoding the runes, combing the books, magazines, semiprozines, fanzines, chapbooks, pamphlets, and websites for exciting new original fiction to bring together in these pages. Last year's *Science Fiction: Best of 2003* featured *all* of the Hugo Award winners for short fiction, as well as stories that won or were nominated for the Nebula, Locus, and Theodore Sturgeon Memorial Awards. While we can't expect to do that every year, it was gratifying to see that our view of the best in science fiction was right in step with readers, critics, and commentators. Here, then, is another's year's worth of stories. We hope you'll find much in these pages to reward, stimulate and intrigue. We know we did.

—Karen Haber and Jonathan Strahan
November 2004

The Best Christmas Ever
James Patrick Kelly

James Patrick Kelly graduated from Notre Dame in 1972 and has been a full-time writer since 1977. He attended Clarion in 1974 and 1976, and his first story, "Death Therapy," appeared in 1978. He has published four novels, Planet of Whispers, Freedom Beach *(with John Kessel),* Looking into the Sun, *and* Wildlife, *but is best known for his more than fifty published short stories, which have been collected in* Heroines, Think Like a Dinosaur *and* Strange But Not a Stranger, *and include classics like "Mr. Boy," "Think Like a Dinosaur," "Itsy Bitsy Spider," "10^{16} to 1," and "Undone." His story "Bernardo's House" appeared in* Science Fiction: Best of 2003.

Kelly has won the Hugo Award twice, the Locus Award, and has been nominated for the Nebula Award eight times. He lives in New Hampshire with his wife and children, is chairman of the New Hampshire Council on the Arts, and writes a regular column for Asimov's Science Fiction. *The poignant, mordant story that follows considers just what makes life worth living.*

Anty Em's man was not doing well at all. He had been droopy and gray ever since the neighbor Mr. Kimura had died, shuffling around the house in nothing but socks and bathrobe. He had even lost interest in the model train layout that he and the neighbor were building in the garage. Sometimes he stayed in bed until eleven in the morning and had ancient Twinkies for lunch. He had a sour, vinegary smell. By midafternoon he'd be asking her to mix strange ethanol concoctions like Brave Little Toasters and Tin Honeymoons. After he had drunk five or six, he would stagger around the house mumbling about the big fires he'd fought with Ladder Company No. 3 or the wife he had lost in the Boston plague. Sometimes he would just cry.

Begin Interaction 4022932

"Do you want to watch *Annie Hall*?" Aunty Em asked.

The man perched on the edge of the Tyvola sofa in the living room, elbows propped on knees, head sunk into hands.

"*The General*? *Monty Python and the Holy Grail*? *Spaced Out*?"

"I hate that robot." He tugged at his thinning hair and snarled. "I hate robots."

Aunty Em did not take this personally—she was a biop, not a robot. "I could call Lola. She's been asking after you."

2

"I'll bet." Still, he looked up from damp hands. "I'd rather have Kathy."

This was a bad sign. Kathy was the lost wife. The girlfriend biop could certainly assume that body; she could look like anyone the man wanted. But while the girlfriend biop could pretend, she could never be the wife that the man missed. His reactions to the Kathy body were always erratic and sometimes dangerous.

"I'll nose around town," said Aunty Em. "I heard Kathy was off on a business trip, but maybe she's back."

"Nose around," he said and then reached for the glass on the original Noguchi coffee table with spread fingers, as if he thought it might try to leap from his grasp. "You do that." He captured it on the second attempt.

End Interaction 4022932

The man was fifty-six years old and in good health, considering. His name was Albert Paul Hopkins, but none of the biops called him that. Aunty Em called him Bertie. The girlfriend called him sweetie or Al. The pal biops called him Al or Hoppy or Sport. The stranger biops called him Mr. Hopkins or sir. The animal biops didn't speak much, but the dog called him Buddy and the cat called him Mario.

When Aunty Em beamed a summary of the interaction to the girlfriend biop, the girlfriend immediately volunteered to try the Kathy body again. The girlfriend had been desperate of late, since the man didn't want anything to do with her. His slump had been hard on her, hard on Aunty Em too. Taking care of the man had changed the biops. They were all so much more emotional than they had been when they were first budded.

But Aunty Em told the girlfriend to hold off. Instead she decided to throw a Christmas. She hadn't done Christmas in almost eight months. She'd given him a *Gone With The Wind* Halloween and a Fourth of July with whistling busters, panoramas, phantom balls, and double-break shells, but those were only stopgaps. The man needed cookies, he needed presents, he was absolutely aching for a sleigh filled with Christmas cheer. So she beamed an alert to all of her biops and assigned roles. She warned them that if this wasn't the best Christmas ever, they might lose the last man on earth.

Aunty Em spent three days baking cookies. She dumped eight sticks of fatty acid triglycerides, four cups of $C_{12}H_{22}O_{11}$, four vat-grown ova, four teaspoons of flavor potentiator, twelve cups of milled grain endosperm, and five teaspoons each of $NaHCO_3$ and $KHC_4H_4O_6$ into the bathtub and then trod on the mixture with her best baking boots. She rolled the dough and then pulled cookie cutters off the top shelf of the pantry: the mitten and the dollar sign and the snake and the double-bladed ax. She dusted the cookies with red nutriceutical sprinkles, baked them at 190°C, and brought a plate to the man while they were still warm.

The poor thing was melting into the recliner in the television room. He clutched a half-full tumbler of Sins-of-the-Mother, as if it were the anchor that was keeping him from floating out of the window. He had done nothing but watch classic commercials with the sound off since he had fallen out of bed. The cat was curled on the man's lap, pretending to be asleep.

Begin Interaction 4022947

"Cookies, Bertie," said Aunty Em. "Fresh from the oven, oven fresh." She set the plate down on the end table next to the Waterford lead crystal vase filled with silk daffodils.

"Not hungry," he said. On the mint-condition 34-inch Sony Hi-Scan television Ronald McDonald was dancing with some kids.

Aunty Em stepped in front of the screen, blocking his view. "Have you decided what you want for Christmas, dear?"

"It isn't Christmas." He waved her away from the set, but she didn't budge. He did succeed in disturbing the cat, which stood, arched its back, and then dropped to the floor.

"No, of course it isn't." She laughed. "Christmas isn't until next week."

He aimed the remote at the set and turned up the sound. A man was talking very fast. "Two all beef patties, special sauce, lettuce, cheese..."

Aunty Em pressed the off button with her knee. "I'm talking to you, Bertie."

The man lowered the remote. "What's today?"

"Today is Friday." She considered. "Yes, Friday."

"No, I mean the date."

"The date is... let me see. The twenty-first."

His skin temperature had risen from 33°C to 37°. "The twenty-first of what?" he said.

She stepped away from the screen. "Have another cookie, Bertie."

"All right." He turned the television on and muted it. "You win." A morose Maytag repairman slouched at his desk, waiting for the phone to ring. "I know what I want," said the man. "I want a Glock 17."

"And what is that, dear?"

"It's a nine millimeter handgun."

"A handgun, oh my." Aunty Em was so flustered that she ate one of her own cookies, even though she had extinguished her digestive track for the day. "For shooting? What would you shoot?"

"I don't know." He broke the head off a gingerbread man. "A reindeer. The TV. Maybe one of you."

"Us? Oh, Bertie—one of us?"

He made a gun out of his thumb and forefinger and aimed. "Maybe just the cat." His thumb came down.

The cat twitched. "Mario," it said and nudged the man's bare foot with its head. "No, Mario."

On the screen the Jolly Green Giant rained peas down on capering elves.

End Interaction 4022947

Begin Interaction 4023013

The man stepped onto the front porch of his house and squinted at the sky, blinking. It was late spring and the daffodils were nodding in a warm breeze. Aunty Em pulled the sleigh to the bottom of the steps and honked the horn. It played the first three notes of "Jingle Bells." The man turned to go back into the house but the girlfriend biop took him by the arm. "Come on now, sweetie," she said and steered him toward the steps.

The girlfriend had assumed the Donna Reed body the day before, but unlike previous Christmases, the man had taken no sexual interest in her. She was wearing the severe black dress with the white lace collar from the last scene of *It's A Wonderful Life*. The girlfriend looked as worried about the man as Mary had been about despairing George Bailey. All the biops were worried, thought Aunty Em. They would be just devastated if anything happened to him. She waved gaily and hit the horn again. *Beep-beep-BEEP!*

The dog and the cat had transformed themselves into reindeer for the outing. The cat got the red nose. Three of the animal biops had assumed reindeer bodies too. They were all harnessed to the sleigh, which hovered about a foot off the ground. As the man stumped down the steps, Aunty Em discouraged the antigrav, and the runners crunched against gravel. The girlfriend bundled the man aboard.

"Do you see who we have guiding the way?" said Aunty Em. She beamed the cat and it lit up its nose. "See?"

"Is that the fake cop?" The man coughed. "Or the fake pizza guy? I can't keep them straight."

"On Dasher, now Dancer, now Comet and Nixon," cried Aunty Em as she encouraged the antigrav. "To the mall, Rudolf, and don't bother to slow down for yellow lights!" She cracked the whip and away they went, down the driveway and out into the world.

The man lived at the edge of the biop compound, away from the bustle of the spaceport and the accumulatorium with its bulging galleries of authentic human artifacts and the vat where new biops were budded off the master template. They drove along the perimeter road. The biops were letting the forest take over here, and saplings of birch and hemlock sprouted from the ruins of the town.

The sleigh floated across a bridge and Aunty Em started to sing. "Over the river and through the woods..." But when she glanced over her shoulder and saw the look on the man's face, she stopped. "Is something wrong, Bertie dear?"

"Where are you taking me?" he said. "I don't recognize this road."

"It's a secret," said Aunty Em. "A Christmas secret."

His blood pressure had dropped to 93/60. "Have I been there before?"

"I wouldn't think so. No."

The girlfriend clutched the man's shoulder. "Look," she said. "Sheep."

Four ewes had gathered at the river's edge to drink, their stumpy tails twitching. They were big animals; their long, tawny fleeces made them look like walking couches. A brown man on a dromedary camel watched over them. He was wearing a satin robe in royal purple with gold trim at the neck. When Aunty Em beamed him the signal, he tapped the line attached to the camel's nose peg and the animal turned to face the road.

"One of the wise men," said Aunty Em.

"The king of the shepherds," said the girlfriend.

As the sleigh drove by, the wise man tipped his crown to them. The sheep looked up from the river and bleated, "Happy holidays."

"They're so cute," said the girlfriend. "I wish we had sheep."

The man sighed. "I could use a drink."

"Not just yet, Bertie," said Aunty Em. "But I bet Mary packed your candy."

The girlfriend pulled a plastic pumpkin from underneath the seat. It was filled with leftovers from the Easter they'd had last month. She held it out to the man and shook it. It was filled with peeps and candy corn and squirtgum and chocolate crosses. He pulled a peep from the pumpkin and sniffed it suspiciously.

"It's safe, sweetie," said the girlfriend. "I irradiated everything just before we left."

There were no cars parked in the crumbling lot of the Wal-Mart. They pulled up to the entrance where a Salvation Army Santa stood over a black plastic pot holding a bell. The man didn't move.

"We're here, Al." The girlfriend nudged him. "Let's go."

"What is this?" said the man.

"Christmas shopping," said Aunty Em. "Time to shop."

"Who the hell am I supposed to shop for?"

"Whoever you want," said Aunty Em. "You could shop for us. You could shop for yourself. You could shop for Kathy."

"Aunty Em!" said the girlfriend.

"No," said the man. "Not Kathy."

"Then how about Mrs. Marelli?"

The man froze. "Is that what this is about?"

"It's about Christmas, Al," said the girlfriend. "It's about getting out of the god-damned sleigh and going into the store." She climbed over him and jumped down to the pavement before Aunty Em could discourage the antigrav. She stalked by the Santa and through the entrance without looking back. Aunty Em beamed her a request to come back but she went dark.

"All right," said the man. "You win."

The Santa rang his bell at them as they approached. The man stopped and grasped Aunty Em's arm. "Just a minute," he said and ran back to the sleigh to fetch the plastic pumpkin. He emptied the candy into the Santa's pot.

"God bless you, young man." The Santa knelt and sifted the candy through his red suede gloves as if it were gold.

"Yeah," said the man. "Merry Christmas."

Aunty Em twinkled at the two of them. She thought the man might finally be getting into the spirit of the season.

The store was full of biops, transformed into shoppers. They had stocked the shelves with artifacts authenticated by the accumulatorium: Barbies and Sonys and Goodyears and Dockers; patio furniture and towels and microwave ovens and watches. At the front of the store was an array of polyvinyl chloride spruce trees predecorated with bubble lights and topped with glass penguins. Some of the merchandise was new, some used, some broken. The man paid attention to none of it, not even the array of genuine Lionel "O" Scale locomotives and freight cars Aunty Em had ordered specially for this interaction. He passed methodically down the aisles, eyes bright, searching. He strode right by the girlfriend, who was sulking in Cosmetics.

Aunty Em paused to touch her shoulder and beam an encouragement, but the girlfriend shook her off.

Aunty Em thought she would have to do something about the girlfriend, but she didn't know what exactly. If she sent her back to the vat and replaced her with a new biop, the man would surely notice. The girl-friend and the man had been quite close before the man had slipped into his funk. She knew things about him that even Aunty Em didn't know.

The man found Mrs. Marelli sitting on the floor in the hardware section. She was opening packages of GE Soft White 100-watt light bulbs and then smashing them with a Stanley Workmaster claw hammer. The biop shoppers paid no attention. Only the lead biop of her team, Dr. Watson, seemed to worry about her. He waited with a broom, and whenever she tore into a new box of light bulbs he swept the shards of glass away.

Aunty Em was shocked at the waste. How many pre-extinction light bulbs were left on this world? Twenty thousand? Ten? She wanted to beam a rebuke to Dr. Watson, but she knew he was doing a difficult job as best he could.

"Hello, Ellen." The man knelt next to the woman. "How are you doing?"

She glanced at him, hammer raised. "Dad?" She blinked. "Is that you, Dad?"

"No, it's Albert Hopkins. Al—you know, your neighbor. We've met before. These… people introduced us. Remember the picnic? The trip to the spaceport?"

"Picnic?" She shook her head as if to clear it. Ellen Theresa Marelli was eleven years older than the man. She was wearing Bruno Magli black leather flats and a crinkly light blue Land's End dress with a pattern of small dark blue and white flowers. Her hair was gray and a little thin but was nicely cut and permed into tight curls. She was much better groomed than the man, but that was because she couldn't take care of herself anymore and so her biops did everything for her. "I like picnics."

"What are you doing here, Ellen?"

She stared at the hammer as if she were surprised to see it. "Practicing."

"Practicing for what?" He held out his hand for the hammer and she gave it to him.

"Just practicing." She gave him a sly look. "What are *you* doing here?"

"I was hoping to do a little Christmas shopping."

"Oh, is it Christmas?" Her eyes went wide.

"In a couple of days," said the man. "Do you want to tag along?"

She turned to Dr. Watson. "Can I?"

"By all means." Dr. Watson swept the space in front of her.

"Oh goody!" She clapped her hands. "This is just the best." She tried to get up but couldn't until the man and Dr. Watson helped her to her feet. "We'll need a shopping cart," she said.

She tottered to the fashion aisles and tried on sweaters. The man helped her pick out a Ralph Lauren blue cable cardigan that matched her dress. In the housewares section, she decided that she needed a Zyliss garlic press. She spent the most time in the toy aisle, lingering at the Barbies. She didn't care much for the late models, still in their packaging. Instead she made straight for the vintage Barbies and Kens and Francies and Skippers posed around the Barbie Dream House and the Barbie Motor Home. Dr. Watson watched her nervously.

"Look, they even have talking Barbies," she said, picking up a doll in an orange flowered dress. "I had one just like this. With all the blond hair and everything. See the little necklace? You press the button and..."

But the Barbie didn't speak. The woman's mouth set in a grim line and she smashed it against the shelf.

"Ellie," said Dr. Watson. "I wish you wouldn't..."

The woman threw the doll at him and picked up another. This was a brunette that was wearing only the top of her hot pink bathing suit. The woman jabbed at the button.

"It's time to get ready for my date with Ken," said the doll in a raspy voice.

"That's better," said the woman.

She pressed the button again and the doll said, "Let's invite the gang over!"

The woman turned to the man and the two biops, clearly excited. "Here." She thrust the doll at Aunty Em, who was nearest to her. "You try." Aunty Em pressed the button.

"I can't wait to meet my friends," said the doll.

"What a lovely toy!" Aunty Em smiled. "She certainly has the Christmas spirit, don't you think, Bertie?"

The man frowned and Aunty Em could tell from the slump of his shoulders that his good mood was slipping away. His heart rate jumped and his eyes were distant, a little misty. The woman must have noticed the change too, because she pointed a finger at Aunty Em.

"You," she said. "You ruin everything."

"Now Mrs. Marelli," she said, "I..."

"You're following us." The woman snatched the Barbie away from her. "Who are you?"

"You know me, Mrs. Marelli. I'm Aunty Em."

"That's crazy." The woman's laugh was like a growl. "I'm not crazy."

Dr. Watson beamed a general warning that he was terminating the interaction; seeing the man always upset the woman. "That's enough, Ellen." He grasped her forearm, and Aunty Em was relieved to see him paint relaxant onto her skin with his med finger. "I think it's time to go."

The woman shivered. "Wait," she said. "He said it was Christmas." She pointed at the man. "Daddy said."

"We'll talk about that when we get home, Ellen."

Daddy. She shook herself free and flung herself at the man.

The man shook his head. "This isn't…"

"Ssh. It's okay." The woman hugged him. "Just pretend. That's all we can do, isn't it?" Reluctantly, he returned her embrace. "Daddy." She spoke into his chest. "What are you getting me for Christmas?"

"Can't tell," he said. "It's a secret."

"A Barbie?" She giggled and pulled away from him. "You'll just have to wait."

"I already know that's what it is."

"But you might forget." The man held out his hand and she gave him the doll. "Now close your eyes."

She shut them so tight that Aunty Em could see her *orbicularis oculi* muscles tremble.

The man touched her forehead. "Daddy says forget." He handed the doll to Dr. Watson, who mouthed *Thank you.* Dr. Watson beamed a request for Aunty Em to hide, and she sidled behind the

14

bicycles where the woman couldn't see her. "Okay, Ellen," said the man. "Daddy says open your eyes."

She blinked at him. "Daddy," she said softly, "when are you coming home?"

The man was clearly taken aback; there was a beta wave spike in his EEG. "I... ah..." He scratched the back of his neck. "I don't know," he said. "Our friends here keep me pretty busy."

"I'm so lonely, Daddy." The last woman on earth began to cry.

The man opened his arms to her and they clung to each other, rocking back and forth. "I know," said the man, over and over. "I know."

End Interaction 4023013

Aunty Em, the dog, and the cat gathered in the living room of the house, waiting for the man to wake up. She had scheduled the pals, Jeff and Bill, to drop by around noon for sugar cookies and eggnog. The girl-friend was upstairs fuming. She had been Katie Couric, Anna Kournikova, and Jacqueline Kennedy since the Wal-Mart trip but the man had never even blinked at her.

The music box was playing "Blue Christmas." The tree was decorated with strings of pinlights and colored packing peanuts. Baseball cards and silver glass balls and plastic army men hung from the branches. Beneath the tree was a modest pile of presents. Aunty Em had picked out one each for the inner circle of biops and signed the man's name to the cards. The rest were gifts for him from them.

Begin Interaction 4023064

"'Morning, Mario," said the cat.

Aunty Em was surprised; it was only eight-thirty. But there was the man propped in the doorway, yawning.

"Merry Christmas, Bertie!" she said.

The dog scrabbled across the room to him. "Buddy, open now, Buddy, open, Buddy, open, open!" It went up on hind legs and pawed his knee.

"Later." The man pushed it away. "What's for breakfast?" he said. "I feel like waffles."

"You want waffles?" said Aunty Em. "Waffles you get."

End Interaction 4023064

She bustled into the kitchen as the man closed the bathroom door behind him. A few minutes later she heard the pipes clang as he turned on the shower. She beamed a revised schedule to the pals, calling for them to arrive within the hour.

Aunty Em could not help but be pleased. This Christmas was already a great success. The man's attitude had changed dramatically after the shopping trip. He was keeping regular hours and drinking much less. He had stopped by the train layout in the garage, although all he had done was look at it. Instead he had taken an interest in the garden in the backyard and had spent yesterday weeding the flowerbeds and digging a new vegetable patch. He had sent the pal Jeff to find seeds he could plant. The biops reported that they had found some peas and corn and string beans—but they were possibly contaminated and might not germinate. She had already warned some of the lesser animal biops that they might have to assume the form of corn stalks and pea vines if the crop failed.

Now if only he would pay attention to the girlfriend.

Begin Interaction 4023066

The doorbell gonged the first eight notes of "Silent Night." "Would you get that, Bertie dear?" Aunty Em was pouring freshly-budded ova into a pitcher filled with Pet Evaporated Milk.

"It's the pals," the man called from the front hall. "Jeff and... I'm sorry, I've forgotten your name."

"Bill."

"Bill, of course. Come in, come in."

A few minutes later, Aunty Em found them sitting on the sofa in the living room. Each of the pals balanced a present on his lap, wrapped in identical green and red paper. They were listening uncomfortably as the cat recited "'Twas the Night Before Christmas." The man was busy playing Madden NFL 2007 on his Game Boy.

"It's time for sweets and presents, Bertie." Aunty Em set the pitcher of eggnog next to the platter of cookies. She was disturbed that the girlfriend hadn't joined the party yet. She beamed a query but the girlfriend was dark. "Presents and sweets."

The man opened Jeff's present first. It was filled with hand tools for his new garden: a dibbler and a trowel and a claw hoe and a genuine Felco10 Professional Pruner. The dog gave the man a chewable rubber fire hydrant that squeeked when squeezed. The cat gave him an "O" Scale Western Pacific Steam Locomotive that had belonged to the dead neighbor, Mr. Kimura. The man and the cat exchanged looks briefly and then the cat yawned. The dog nudged his head under all the discarded wrapping paper and the man reached down with the claw hoe and scratched its back. Everyone but the cat laughed.

Next came Bill's present. In keeping with the garden theme of this Christmas, it was a painting of a balding old farmer and a middle-aged woman standing in front of a white house with an odd gothic window. Aunty Em could tell the man was a farmer because he was holding a pitchfork. The farmer stared out of the painting with a glum intensity; the woman looked at him askance. The curator biop claimed that it was one of the most copied images in the inventory, so Aunty Em was not surprised that the man seemed to recognize it.

"This looks like real paint," he said.

"Yes," said Bill. "Oil on beaverboard."

"What's beaverboard?" said the cat.

"A light, semirigid building material of compressed wood pulp," Bill said. "I looked it up."

The man turned the painting over and brushed his finger across the back. "Where did you get this?" His face was pale.

"From the accumulatorium."

"No, I mean where before then?"

Aunty Em eavesdropped as the pal beamed the query. "It was salvaged from the Chicago Art Institute."

"You're giving me the original *American Gothic*?" His voice fell into a hole.

"Is something the matter, Bertie?"

He fell silent for a moment. "No, I suppose not." He shook his head. "It's a very thoughtful gift." He propped the painting on the mantle, next to his scuffed leather fireman's helmet that the biops had retrieved from the ruins of the Ladder Company No. 3 Firehouse two Christmases ago.

Aunty Em wanted the man to open his big present, but the girlfriend had yet to make her entrance. So instead, she gave the pals their presents from the man. Jeff got the October 1937 issue of *Spicy Adventure Stories*. On the cover a brutish sailor carried a terrified woman in a shredded red dress out of the surf as their ship sank in the background. Aunty Em pretended to be shocked and the man actually chuckled. Bill got a chrome Model 1B14 Toastmaster two-slice toaster. The man took it from him and traced the triple loop logo etched in the side. "My mom had one of these."

Finally there was nothing left to open but the present wrapped in the blue paper with the Santa-in-space print. The man took the Glock 17 out of the box cautiously, as if he were afraid it might go off. It was black with a polymer grip and a four-and-a-half-inch steel barrel. Aunty Em had taken a calculated risk with the pistol. She always tried to give him whatever he asked for, as long as it wasn't too dangerous. He wasn't their captive after all. He was their master.

"Don't worry," she said. "It's not loaded. I looked but couldn't find the right bullets."

"But I did," said the girlfriend, sweeping into the

room in the Kathy body. "I looked harder and found hundreds of thousands of bullets."

"Kathy," said Aunty Em, as she beamed a request for her to terminate this unauthorized interaction. "What a nice surprise."

"9 millimeter Parabellum," said the girlfriend. Ten rounds clattered onto the glass top of the Noguchi coffee table. "115 grain. Full metal jacket."

"What are you doing?" said the man.

"You want to shoot someone?" The girlfriend glared at the man and swung her arms wide.

"Kathy," said Aunty Em. "You sound upset, dear. Maybe you should go lie down."

The man returned the girlfriend's stare. "You're not Kathy."

"No," said the girlfriend. "I'm nobody you know."

"Kathy's dead," said the man. "Everybody's dead except for me and poor Ellen Marelli. That's right, isn't it?"

The girlfriend sank to her knees, rested her head on the coffee table, and began to cry. Only biops didn't cry, or at least no biop that Aunty Em had ever heard of. The man glanced around the room for an answer. The pals looked at their shoes and said nothing. "Jingle Bell Rock" tinkled on the music box. Aunty Em felt something swell inside of her and climb her throat until she thought she might burst. If this was what the man felt all the time, it was no wonder he was tempted to drink himself into insensibility.

"Well?" he said.

"Yes," Aunty Em blurted. "Yes, dead, Bertie. All dead."

The man took a deep breath. "Thank you," he said. "Sometimes I can't believe that it really happened. Or else I forget. You make it easy to forget. Maybe you think that's good for me. But I need to know who I am."

"Buddy," said the dog, brushing against him. "Buddy, my Buddy."

The man patted the dog absently. "I could give up. But I won't. I've had a bad spell the last couple of weeks, I know. That's not your fault." He heaved himself off the couch, came around the coffee table and knelt beside the girlfriend. "I really appreciate that you trust me with this gun. And these bullets too. That's got to be scary, after what I said." The girlfriend watched him scoop up the bullets. "Kathy, I don't need these just now. Would you please keep them for me?"

She nodded.

"Do you know the movie, *Miracle On 34th Street*?" He poured the bullets into her cupped hands. "Not the remakes. The first one, with Maureen O'Hara?"

She nodded again.

He leaned close and whispered into her ear. His pulse soared to 93.

She sniffed and then giggled.

"You go ahead," he said to her. "I'll come up in a little while." He gave her a pat on the rear and stood up. The other biops watched him nervously.

"What's with all the long faces?" He tucked the Glock into the waistband of his pants. "You look like them." He waved at the painting of the somber farm folk, whose mood would never, ever change. "It's Christmas Day, people. Let's live it up!"

End Interaction 4023066

Over the years, Aunty Em gave the man many more Christmases, not to mention Thanksgivings, Easters, Halloweens, April Fools, and Valentine Days. But she always said—and no one contradicted her: not the man, not even the girlfriend—that this Christmas was the best ever.

The Voluntary State
Christopher Rowe

*Christopher Rowe was born in Kentucky and attended
Clarion West in 1996 and had his first story, "Kin to
Crows," published in 1998. Since then he was written
short fiction, poetry and essays which have appeared
in* Realms of Fantasy, The Journal of Pulse Pounding
Narratives, Sci Fiction, *and in the anthologies* Beyond
the Last Star, Swan Sister: Fairy Tales Retold, *and*
Trampoline. *The best of his short fiction was collected
in the chapbook* Bittersweet Creek *in 2003. Rowe lives
in Lexington, Kentucky, runs the small press The Fort-
ress of Words with his wife Gwenda Bond, edits the
magazine* Say..., *and is currently working on a novel.*

*Rowe's stories often center around fantastic happen-
ings in the American South—he is currently writing
the "Uncommonwealth" series of short stories, one for
each of the 120 counties that make up the Common-
wealth of Kentucky—and the story that follows grows
out of that. A tour-de-force, it marks Rowe as one of
the writers to watch.*

Soma had parked his car in the trailhead lot above Governor's Beach. A safe place, usually, checked regularly by the Tennessee Highway Patrol and surrounded on three sides by the limestone cliffs that plunged down into the Gulf of Mexico.

But today, after his struggle up the trail from the beach, he saw that his car had been attacked. The driver's side window had been kicked in.

Soma dropped his pack and rushed to his car's side. The car shied away from him, backed to the limit of its tether before it recognized him and turned, let out a low, pitiful moan.

"Oh, car," said Soma, stroking the roof and opening the passenger door, "Oh, car, you're hurt." Then Soma was rummaging through the emergency kit, tossing aside flares and bandages, finally, *finally* finding the glass salve. Only after he'd spread the ointment over the shattered window and brushed the glass shards out onto the gravel, only after he'd sprayed the whole door down with analgesic aero, only then did he close his eyes, access call signs, drop shields. He opened his head and used it to call the police.

In the scant minutes before he saw the cadre of blue and white bicycles angling in from sunward, their bubblewings pumping furiously, he gazed down the beach at Nashville. The cranes the Governor had ordered grown to dredge the harbor would go dormant for the winter soon—already their acres-broad leaves were tinged with orange and gold.

"Soma-With-The-Paintbox-In-Printer's-Alley," said voices from above. Soma turned to watch the policemen land. They all spoke simultaneously in the sing-song chant of law enforcement. "Your car will be healed at taxpayers' expense." Then the ritual words, "And the wicked will be brought to justice."

Efficiency and order took over the afternoon as the threatened rain began to fall. One of the 144 Detectives manifested, Soma and the policemen all looking about as they felt the weight of the Governor's servant inside their heads. It brushed aside the thoughts of one of the Highway Patrolmen and rode him, the man's movements becoming slightly less fluid as he was mounted and steered. The Detective filmed Soma's statement.

"I came to sketch the children in the surf," said Soma. He opened his daypack for the soapbubble lens, laid out the charcoal and pencils, the sketchbook of boughten paper bound between the rusting metal plates he'd scavenged along the middenmouth of the Cumberland River.

"Show us, show us," sang the Detective.

Soma flipped through the sketches. In black and gray, he'd drawn the floating lures that crowded the shallows this time of year. Tiny, naked babies most of them, but also some little girls in one-piece bathing suits and even one fat prepubescent boy clinging desperately to a deflating beach ball and turning horrified, pleading eyes on the viewer.

"Tssk, tssk," sang the Detective, percussive. "Draw filaments on those babies, Soma Painter. Show the lines at their heels."

Soma was tempted to show the Detective the artistic licenses tattooed around his wrists in delicate salmon inks, to remind the intelligence which authorities had purview over which aspects of civic life, but bit his tongue, fearful of a For-the-Safety-of-the-Public proscription. As if there were a living soul in all of Tennessee who didn't know that the children who splashed in the surf were nothing but extremities, nothing but lures growing from the snouts of alligators crouching on the sandy bottoms.

The Detective summarized. "You were here at your work, you parked legally, you paid the appropriate fee to the meter, you saw nothing, you informed the authorities in a timely fashion. Soma-With-The-Paintbox-In-Printer's-Alley, the Tennessee Highway Patrol applauds your citizenship."

The policemen had spread around the parking lot, casting cluenets and staring back through time. But they all heard their cue, stopped what they were doing, and broke into a raucous cheer for Soma. He accepted their adulation graciously.

Then the Detective popped the soapbubble camera and plucked the film from the air before it could fall. It rolled up the film, chewed it up thoughtfully, then dismounted the policeman, who shuddered and fell against Soma. So Soma did not at first hear what the others had begun to chant, didn't decipher it until he saw what they were encircling. Something was caught on the wispy thorns of a nodding thistle growing at the edge of the lot.

"Crow's feather," the policemen chanted. "Crow's feather Crow's feather Crow's feather."

And even Soma, licensed for art instead of justice, knew what the fluttering bit of black signified. His car had been assaulted by Kentuckians.

Soma had never, so far as he recalled, painted a self-portrait. But his disposition was melancholy, so he might have taken a few visual notes of his trudge back to Nashville if he'd thought he could have shielded the paper from the rain.

Soma Between the Sea and the City, he could call a painting like that. Or, if he'd decided to choose that one clear moment when the sun had shown through the towering slate clouds, *Soma Between Storms*.

Either image would have shown a tall young man in a broad-brimmed hat, black pants cut off at the calf, yellow jersey unsealed to show a thin chest. A young man, sure, but not a young man used to long walks. No helping that; his car would stay in the trailhead lot for at least three days.

The mechanic had arrived as the policemen were leaving, galloping up the gravel road on a white mare marked with red crosses. She'd swung from the saddle and made sympathetic clucking noises at the car even before she greeted Soma, endearing herself to auto and owner simultaneously.

Scratching the car at the base of its aerial, sussing out the very spot the car best liked attention, she'd introduced herself. "I am Jenny-With-Grease-Beneath-Her-Fingernails," she'd said, but didn't seem to be worried about it because she ran her free hand through unfashionably short cropped blond hair as she spoke.

She'd whistled for her horse and began unpacking the saddlebags. "I have to build a larger garage than normal for your car, Soma Painter, for it must house me and my horse during the convalescence. But don't worry, my licenses are in good order. I'm bonded by the city and the state. This is all at taxpayers' expense."

Which was a very great relief to Soma, poor as he was. With friends even poorer, none of them with cars, and so no one to hail out of the Alley to his rescue, and now this long, wet trudge back to the city.

Soma and his friends did not live uncomfortable lives, of course. They had dry spaces to sleep above their studios, warm or cool in response to the season and even clean if that was the proclivity of the individual artist, as was the case with Soma. A clean, warm or cool, dry space to sleep. A good space to work and a more than ample opportunity to sell his paintings and drawings, the Alley being one of the *other* things the provincials did when they visited Nashville. Before they went to the great vaulted Opera House or after.

All that and even a car, sure, freedom of the road. Even if it wasn't so free because the car was not *really* his, gift of his family, product of their ranch. Both of them, car and artist, product of that ranching life Soma did his best to forget.

If he'd been a little closer in time to that ranching youth, his legs might not have ached so. He might not have been quite so miserable to be lurching down the gravel road toward the city, might have been sharp-eyed enough to still *see* a city so lost in the fog, maybe sharp-eared enough to have heard the low hoots and caws that his assailants used to organize themselves before they sprang from all around him—down from tree branches, up from ditches, out from the undergrowth.

And there was a Crow raiding party, the sight stunning Soma motionless. "This only happens on television," he said.

The caves and hills these Kentuckians haunted

unopposed were a hundred miles and more north and east, across the shifting skirmish line of a border. Kentuckians couldn't be here, so far from the frontier stockades at Fort Clarksville and Barren Green.

But here they definitely were, hopping and calling, scratching the gravel with their clawed boots, blinking away the rain when it trickled down behind their masks and into their eyes.

A Crow clicked his tongue twice and suddenly Soma was the center of much activity. Muddy hands forced his mouth open and a paste that first stung then numbed was swabbed around his mouth and nose. His wrists were bound before him with rough hemp twine. Even frightened as he was, Soma couldn't contain his astonishment. "Smoke rope!" he said.

The squad leader grimaced, shook his head in disgust and disbelief. "Rope and cigarettes come from two completely different varieties of plants," he said, his accent barely decipherable. "Vols are so fucking stupid."

Then Soma was struggling through the undergrowth himself, alternately dragged and pushed and even half-carried by a succession of Crow Brothers. The boys were running hard, and if he was a burden to them, then their normal speed must have been terrifying. Someone finally called a halt, and Soma collapsed.

The leader approached, pulling his mask up and wiping his face. Deep red lines angled down from his temples, across his cheekbones, ending at his snub nose. Soma would have guessed the man was forty if he'd seen him in the Alley dressed like a normal person in jersey and shorts.

Even so exhausted, Soma wished he could dig his notebook and a bit of charcoal out of the daypack he still wore, so that he could capture some of the savage countenances around him.

The leader was just staring at Soma, not speaking, so Soma broke the silence. "Those scars"—the painter brought up his bound hands, traced angles down either side of his own face—"are they ceremonial? Do they indicate your rank?"

The Kentuckians close enough to hear snorted and laughed. The man before Soma went through a quick, exaggerated pantomime of disgust. He spread his hands, why-me-lording, then took the beaked mask off the top of his head and showed Soma its back. Two leather bands crisscrossed its interior, supporting the elaborate superstructure of the mask and preventing the full weight of it, Soma saw, from bearing down on the wearer's nose. He looked at the leader again, saw him rubbing at the fading marks.

"Sorry," said the painter.

"It's okay," said the Crow. "It's the fate of the noble savage to be misunderstood by effete city dwellers."

Soma stared at the man for a minute. He said, "You guys must watch a lot of the same TV programs as me."

The leader was looking around, counting his boys. He lowered his mask and pulled Soma to his feet. "That could be. We need to go."

It developed that the leader's name was Japheth Sapp. At least that's what the other Crow Brothers called out to him from where they loped along ahead or behind, circled farther out in the brush, scrambled from limb to branch to trunk high above.

Soma descended into a reverie space, singsonging subvocally and supervocally (and being hushed down by Japheth hard then). He guessed in a lucid moment that the paste the Kentuckians had dosed him with must have some sort of will-sapping effect. He didn't feel like he could open his head and call for help; he didn't even want to. But "*I will take care of you,*" Athena was always promising. He held onto that and believed that he wasn't panicking because of the Crows' drugs, sure, but also because he would be rescued by the police soon. "*I will take care of you.*" After all, wasn't that one of the Governor's slogans, clarifying out of the advertising flocks in the skies over Nashville during Campaign?

It was good to think of these things. It was good to think of the sane capital and forget that he was being kidnapped by aliens, by Indians, by toughs in the employ of a rival Veronese merchant family.

But then the warchief of the marauding band was throwing him into a gully, whistling and gesturing, calling in all his boys to dive into the wash, to gather close and throw their cloaks up and over their huddle.

"What's up, boss?" asked the blue-eyed boy Soma had noticed earlier, crouched in the mud with one elbow somehow dug into Soma's ribs.

Japheth Sapp didn't answer but another of the younger Crow Brothers hissed, "THP even got a bear in the air!"

Soma wondered if a bear meant rescue from this improbable aside. Not that parts of the experience weren't enjoyable. It didn't occur to Soma to fear for his health, even when Japheth knocked him down with a light kick to the back of the knees after the painter stood and brushed aside feathered cloaks for a glimpse of the sky.

There *was* a bear up there. And yes, it was wearing the blue and white.

"I want to see the bear, Japheth," said a young Crow. Japheth shook his head, said, "I'll take you to Willow Ridge and show you the black bears that live above the Green River when we get back home, Lowell. That bear up there is just a robot made out of balloons and possessed by a demon, not worth looking at unless you're close enough to cut her."

With all his captors concentrating on their leader or on the sky, Soma wondered if he might be able to open his head. As soon as he thought it, Japheth Sapp wheeled on him, stared him down.

Not looking at any one of them, Japheth addressed his whole merry band. "Give this one some more paste. But be careful with him; we'll still need this vol's head to get across the Cumberland, even after we bribe the bundle bugs."

Soma spoke around the viscous stuff the owl-feathered endomorph was spackling over the lower half of his face. "Bundle bugs work for the city and are above reproach. Your plans are ill-laid if they depend on corrupting the servants of the Governor."

More hoots, more hushings, then Japheth said, "If bundle bugs had mothers, they'd sell them to me for half a cask of Kentucky bourbon. And we brought more than half a cask."

Soma knew Japheth was lying—this was a known tactic of neo-anarchist agitator hero figures. "I know you're lying," said Soma. "It's a known tactic of—"

"Hush hush, Soma Painter. I like you—this you—but we've all read the Governor's curricula. You'll see that we're too sophisticated for your models." Japheth gestured and the group broke huddle. Outrunners ran out and the main body shook off cramps. "And I'm not an anarchist agitator. I'm a lot of things, but not that."

"Singer!" said a young Crow, scampering past.

"I play out some weekends, he means; I don't have a record contract or anything," Japheth said, pushing Soma along himself now.

"Welder!" said another man.

"Union-certified," said Japheth. "That's my day job, working at the border."

More lies, knew Soma. "I suppose Kentuckians built the Girding Wall, then?"

Everything he said amused these people greatly. "Not just Kentuckians, vol, the whole rest of the world. Only we call it the containment field."

"Agitator, singer, welder," said the painter, the numbness spreading deeper than it had before, affecting the way he said words and the way he chose them.

"Assassin," rumbled the Owl, the first thing Soma had heard the burly man say.

Japheth was scrambling up a bank before Soma. He stopped and twisted. His foot corkscrewed through the leaf mat and released a humid smell. He looked at the Owl, then hard at Soma, reading him.

"You're doped up good now, Soma Painter. No way to open that head until we open it for you. So, sure, here's some truth for you. We're not just here to steal her things. We're here to break into her mansion. We're here to kill Athena Parthenus, Queen of Logic and Governor of the Voluntary State of Tennessee."

Jenny-With-Grease-Beneath-Her-Fingernails spread fronds across the parking lot, letting the high green fern leaves dry out before she used the mass to make her bed. Her horse watched from above the half-door of its stall. Inside the main body of the garage, Soma's car slept, lightly anesthetized.

"Just enough for a soft cot, horse," said Jenny. "All of us we'll sleep well after this hard day."

Then she saw that little flutter. One of the fronds had a bit of feather caught between some leaves, and yes, it was coal black, midnight blue, reeking of the north. Jenny sighed, because her citizenship was less faultless than Soma's, and policemen disturbed her. But she opened her head and stared at the feather.

A telephone leapt off a tulip poplar a little ways down the road to Nashville. It squawked through its brief flight and landed with inelegant weight in front of Jenny. It turned its beady eyes on her.

"Ring," said the telephone.

"Hello," said Jenny.

Jenny's Operator sounded just like Jenny, something else that secretly disturbed her. Other people's Operators sounded like television stars or famous Legislators or like happy cartoon characters, but Jenny was in that minority of people whose Operators and Teachers always sounded like themselves. Jenny remembered a slogan from Campaign, "My voice is yours."

"The Tennessee Highway Patrol has plucked one already, Jenny Healer." The voice from the telephone thickened around Jenny and began pouring through her ears like cold syrup. "But we want a sample of this one as well. Hold that feather, Jenny, and open your head a little wider."

Now, here's the secret of those feathers. The one Jenny gave to the police and the one the cluenets had caught already. The secret of those feathers, and the feathers strung like look-here flags along the trails down from the Girding Wall, and even of the Owl feathers that had pushed through that fence and let the outside in. All of them were oily with intrigue. Each had been dipped in potent *math*, the autonomous software developed by the Owls of the Bluegrass.

Those feathers were hacks. They were lures and fal’go attacks. Those feathers marked the way the Kentuckians didn't go.

The math kept quiet and still as it floated through Jenny's head, through the ignorable defenses of the telephone and the more considerable, but still avoidable, rings of barbed wire around Jenny's Operator. The math went looking for a Detective or even a Legislator if one were to be found not braying in a pack of its brethren, an unlikely event.

The math stayed well clear of the Commodores in the Great Salt Lick ringing the Parthenon. It was sly math. Its goals were limited, realizable. It marked the way they didn't go.

The Crows made Soma carry things. "You're stronger than you think," one said and loaded him up with a sloshing keg made from white oak staves. A lot of the Crows carried such, Soma saw, and others carried damp, muddy burlap bags flecked with old root matter and smelling of poor people's meals.

Japheth Sapp carried only a piece of paper. He referred to it as he huddled with the Owl and the blue-eyed boy, crouched in a dry stream bed a few yards from where the rest of the crew were hauling out their goods.

Soma had no idea where they were at this point, though he had a vague idea that they'd described an arc above the northern suburbs and the conversations indicated that they were now heading toward the capital, unlikely as that sounded. His head was still numb and soft inside, not an unpleasant situation, but not one that helped his already shaky geographical sense.

He knew what time it was, though, when the green fall of light speckling the hollow they rested in shifted toward pink. Dull as his mind was, he recognized that and smiled.

The clouds sounded the pitch note, then suddenly a great deal was happening around him. For the first time that day, the Crows' reaction to what they perceived to be a crisis didn't involve Soma being poked somewhere or shoved under something. So he was free to sing the anthem while the Crows went mad with activity.

The instant the rising bell tone fell out of the sky, Japheth flung his mask to the ground, glared at a rangy redheaded man, and bellowed, "Where's my timekeeper? You were supposed to remind us!"

The man didn't have time to answer though, because like all of them he was digging through his pack, wrapping an elaborate crenellated set of ear-muffs around his head.

The music struck up, and Soma began.

"Tonight we'll remake Tennessee, every night we remake Tennessee…"

It was powerfully odd that the Kentuckians didn't join in the singing, and that none of them were moving into the roundel lines that a group this size would normally be forming during the anthem.

Still, it might have been stranger if they had joined in.

"Tonight we'll remake Tennessee, every night we remake Tennessee…"

There was a thicket of trumpet flowers tucked amongst a stand of willow trees across the dry creek, so the brass was louder than Soma was used to. Maybe they were farther from the city than he thought. Aficionados of different musical sections tended to find places like this and frequent them during anthem.

"Tonight we'll remake Tennessee, every night we remake Tennessee…"

Soma was happily shuffling through a solo dance, keeping one eye on a fat raccoon that was bobbing its head in time with the music as it turned over stones in the stream bed, when he saw that the young Crow who wanted to see a bear had started keeping time as well, raising and lowering a clawed boot. The Owl was the first of the outlanders who spied the tapping foot.

"Tonight we'll remake Tennessee, every night we remake Tennessee …"

Soma didn't feel the real connection with the citizenry that anthem usually provided on a daily basis, didn't feel his confidence and vigor improve, but he blamed that on the drugs the Kentuckians had given him. He wondered if those were the same drugs they were using on the Crow who now feebly twitched beneath the weight of the Owl, who had wrestled him to the ground. Others pinned down the dancing Crow's arms and legs and Japheth brought out a needle and injected the poor soul with a vast syringe full of some milky brown substance that had the consistency of honey. Soma remembered that he knew the dancing Crow's name. Japheth Sapp had called the boy Lowell.

"Tonight we'll remake Tennessee, every night we remake Tennessee..."

The pink light faded. The raccoon waddled into the woods. The trumpet flowers fell quiet and Soma completed the execution of a pirouette.

The redheaded man stood before Japheth wearing a stricken and haunted look. He kept glancing to one side, where the Owl stood over the Crow who had danced. "Japheth, I just lost track," he said. "It's so hard here, to keep track of things."

Japheth's face flashed from anger through disappointment to something approaching forgiveness. "It is. It's hard to keep track. Everybody fucks up sometime. And I think we got the dampeners in him in time."

Then the Owl said, "Second shift now, Japheth. Have to wait for the second round of garbage drops to catch our bundle bug."

Japheth grimaced, but nodded. "We can't move anyway, not until we know what's going to happen with Lowell," he said, glancing at the unconscious boy. "Get the whiskey and the food back into the cache. Set up the netting. We're staying here for the night."

Japheth stalked over to Soma, fists clenched white.

"Things are getting clearer and clearer to you, Soma Painter, even if you think things are getting harder and harder to understand. Our motivations will open up things inside you."

He took Soma's chin in his left hand and tilted Soma's face up. He waved his hand to indicate Lowell.

"There's one of mine. There's one of my motivations for all of this."

Slowly, but with loud lactic cracks, Japheth spread his fingers wide.

"I fight her, Soma, in the hope that she'll not clench up another mind. I fight her so that minds already bound might come unbound."

In the morning, the dancing Crow boy was dead.

Jenny woke near dark, damp and cold, curled up in the gravel of the parking lot. Her horse nickered. She was dimly aware that the horse had been neighing and otherwise emanating concern for some time now, and it was this that had brought her up to consciousness.

She rolled over and climbed to her feet, spitting to rid her mouth of the metal Operator taste. A dried froth of blood coated her nostrils and upper lip, and she could feel the flaky stuff in her ears as well. She looked toward the garage and saw that she wasn't the only one rousing.

"Now, you get back to bed," she told the car.

Soma's car had risen up on its back wheels and was

peering out the open window, its weight resting against the force-grown wall, bulging it outward.

Jenny made a clucking noise, hoping to reassure her horse, and walked up to the car. She was touched by its confusion and concern.

She reached for the aerial. "You should sleep some more," she said, "and not worry about me. The Operators can tell when you're being uncooperative is all, even when *you* didn't know you were being uncooperative. Then they have to root about a bit more than's comfortable to find the answers they want."

Jenny coaxed the car down from the window, wincing a little at the sharp echo pains that flashed in her head and ears. "Don't tell your owner, but this isn't the first time I've been called to question. Now, to bed."

The car looked doubtful, but obediently rolled back to the repair bed that grew from the garage floor. It settled in, grumbled a bit, then switched off its headlights.

Jenny walked around to the door and entered. She found that the water sacs were full and chilled and drew a long drink. The water tasted faintly of salt. She took another swallow, then dampened a rag with a bit more of the tangy stuff to wipe away the dried blood. Then she went to work.

The bundle bugs crawled out of the city, crossed Distinguished Opposition Bridge beneath the watching eye of bears floating overhead, then described a right-angle turn along the levy to their dumping grounds. Soma and the Kentuckians lay hidden in the brushy wasteland at the edge of the grounds, waiting.

The Owl placed a hand on Japheth's shoulder, pointing at a bundle bug just entering the grounds. Then the Owl rose to his knees and began worming his way between the bushes and dead appliances.

"Soma Painter," whispered Japheth. "I'm going to have to break your jaw in a few minutes and cut out as many of her tentacles as we can get at, but we'll knit it back up as soon as we cross the river."

Soma was too far gone in the paste to hold both of the threats in his mind at the same time. A broken jaw, Crows in the capital. He concentrated on the second.

"The bears will scoop you up and drop you in the Salt Lick," Soma said. "Children will climb on you during Campaign and Legislators will stand on your shoulders to make their stump speeches."

"The bears will not see us, Soma."

"The bears watch the river and the bridges, and—"

"'—and their eyes never close,'" finished Japheth. "Yes, we've seen the commercials."

A bundle bug, a large one at forty meters in length, reared up over them, precariously balanced on its rearmost set of legs. Soma said, "They're very good commercials," and the bug crashed down over them all.

Athena's data realm mirrored her physical realm. One-to-one constructs mimicked the buildings and the citizenry, showed who was riding and who was being ridden.

In that numerical space, the Kentuckians' math

found the bridge. The harsh light of the bears floated above. Any bear represented a statistically significant portion of the Governor herself, and from the point of view of the math, the pair above Distinguished Opposition Bridge looked like miniature suns, casting probing rays at the marching bundle bugs, the barges floating along the Cumberland, and even into the waters of the river itself, illuminating the numerical analogs of the dangerous things that lived in the muddy bottom.

Bundle bugs came out of the city, their capacious abdomens distended with the waste they'd ingested along their routes. The math could see that the bug crossing through the bears' probes right now had a lot of restaurants on its itinerary. The beams pierced the dun-colored carapace and showed a riot of uneaten jellies, crumpled cups, soiled napkins.

The bugs marching in the opposite direction, emptied and ready for reloading, were scanned even more carefully than their outward-bound kin. The beam scans were withering, complete, and exceedingly precise.

The math knew that precision and accuracy are not the same thing.

"Lowell's death has set us back further than we thought," said Japheth, talking to the four Crows, the Owl, and, Soma guessed, to the bundle bug they inhabited. Japheth had detailed off the rest of the raiding party to carry the dead boy back north, so there was plenty of room where they crouched.

The interior of the bug's abdomen was larger than Soma's apartment by a factor of two and smelled of flowers instead of paint thinner. Soma's apartment, however, was not an alcoholic.

"This is good, though, good good." The bug's voice rang from every direction at once. "I'm scheduled down for a rest shift. You-uns was late and missed my last run, and now we can all rest and drink good whiskey. Good good."

But none of the Kentuckians drank any of the whiskey from the casks they'd cracked once they'd crawled down the bug's gullet. Instead, every half hour or so, they poured another gallon into one of the damp fissures that ran all through the interior. Bundle bugs abdomens weren't designed for digestion, just evacuation, and it was the circulatory system that was doing the work of carrying the bourbon to the bug's brain.

Soma dipped a finger into an open cask and touched finger to tongue. "Bourbon burns!" he said, pulling his finger from his mouth.

"Burns good!" said the bug. "Good good."

"We knew that not all of us were going to be able to actually enter the city—we don't have enough outfits, for one thing—but six is a bare minimum. And since we're running behind, we'll have to wait out tonight's anthem in our host's apartment."

"Printer's Alley is two miles from the Parthenon," said the Owl, nodding at Soma.

Japheth nodded. "I know. And I know that those might be the two longest miles in the world. But we expected hard walking."

He banged the curving gray wall he leaned against with his elbow. "Hey! Bundle bug! How long until you start your shift?"

A vast and disappointed sigh shuddered through

the abdomen. "Two more hours, bourbon man," said the bug.

"Get out your gear, cousin," Japheth said to the Owl. He stood and stretched, motioned for the rest of the Crows to do the same. He turned toward Soma. "The rest of us will hold him down."

Jenny had gone out midmorning, when the last of the fog was still burning off the bluffs, searching for low moisture organics to feed the garage. She'd run its reserves very low, working on one thing and another until quite late in the night.

As she suspected from the salty taste of the water supply, the filters in the housings between the tap roots and the garage's plumbing array were clogged with silt. She'd blown them out with pressurized air—no need to replace what you can fix—and reinstalled them one, two, three. But while she was blowing out the filters, she'd heard a whine she didn't like in the air compressor, and when she'd gone to check it she found it panting with effort, tongue hanging out onto the workbench top where it sat.

And then things went as these things go, and she moved happily from minor maintenance problem to minor maintenance problem—wiping away the air compressor's crocodile tears while she stoned the motor brushes in its A/C motor, then replacing the fusible link in the garage itself. "Links are so easily fusible," she joked to her horse when she rubbed it down with handfuls of the sweet-smelling fern fronds she'd intended for her own bed.

And all the while, of course, she watched the little car, monitoring the temperatures at its core points and doing what she could to coax the broken window to reknit in a smooth, steady fashion. Once, when the car awoke in the middle of the night making colicky noises, Jenny had to pop the hood, where she found that the points needed to be pulled and regapped. They were fouled with the viscous residue of the analgesic aero the owner had spread about so liberally.

She tsked. The directions on the labels clearly stated that the nozzle was to be pointed *away* from the engine compartment. Still, hard to fault Soma Painter's goodhearted efforts. It was an easy fix, and she would have pulled the plugs during the tune-up she had planned for the morning anyway.

So, repairings and healings, lights burning and tools turning, and when she awoke to the morning tide sounds the garage immediately began flashing amber lights at her wherever she turned. The belly-grumble noises it floated from the speakers worried the horse, so she set out looking for something to put in the hoppers of the hungry garage.

When she came back, bearing a string-tied bundle of dried wood and a half bucket of old walnuts some gatherer had wedged beneath an overhang and forgotten at least a double handful of autumns past, the car was gone.

Jenny hurried to the edge of the parking lot and looked down the road, though she couldn't see much. This time of year the morning fog turned directly into the midday haze. She could see the city, and bits of road between trees and bluff line, but no sign of the car.

The garage pinged at her, and she shoved its breakfast into the closest intake. She didn't open her head to call the police—she hadn't yet fully recovered from yesterday afternoon's interview. She was even hesitant to open her head the little bit she needed to access her own garage's security tapes. But she'd built the garage, and either built or rebuilt everything in it, so she risked it.

She stood at her workbench, rubbing her temple, as a see-through Jenny and a see-through car built themselves up out of twisted light. Light Jenny put on a light rucksack, scratched the light car absently on the roof as she walked by, and headed out the door. Light Jenny did not tether the car. Light Jenny did not lock the door.

"Silly light Jenny," said Jenny.

As soon as light Jenny was gone, the little light car rolled over to the big open windows. It popped a funny little wheelie and caught itself on the sash, the way it had yesterday when it had watched real Jenny swim up out of her government dream.

The light car kept one headlight just above the sash for a few minutes, then lowered itself back to the floor with a bounce (real Jenny had aired up the tires first thing, even before she grew the garage).

The light car revved its motor excitedly. Then, just a gentle tap on the door, and it was out in the parking lot. It drove over to the steps leading down to the beach, hunching its grill down to the ground. It circled the lot a bit, snuffling here and there, until it found whatever it was looking for. Before it zipped down the road toward Nashville, it circled back round and stopped outside the horse's stall. The light car opened its passenger door and waggled it back and forth a time or two. The real horse neighed and tossed its head at the light car in a friendly fashion.

Jenny-With-Grease-Beneath-Her-Fingernails visited her horse with the meanest look that a mechanic can give a horse. The horse snickered. "You laugh, horse," she said, opening the tack locker, "but we still have to go after it."

Inside the bundle bug, there was some unpleasantness with a large glass-and-pewter contraption of the Owl's. The Crow Brothers held Soma as motionless as they could, and Japheth seemed genuinely sorry when he forced the painter's mouth open much wider than Soma had previously thought possible. "You should have drunk more of the whiskey," said Japheth. There was a loud, wet, popping sound, and Soma shuddered, stiffened, fainted.

"Well, that'll work best for all of us," said Japheth. He looked up at the Owl, who was peering through a lens polished out of a semiprecious gemstone, staring down into the painter's gullet.

"Have you got access?"

The Owl nodded.

"Talk to your math," said the Crow.

The math had been circling beneath the bridge, occasionally dragging a curiosity-begat string of numbers into the water. Always low test numbers, because invariably whatever lived beneath the water snatched at the lines and sucked them down.

The input the math was waiting for finally arrived in the form of a low hooting sound rising up from the dumping grounds. It was important that the math not know which bundle bug the sound emanated from. There were certain techniques the bears had developed for teasing information out of recalcitrant math.

No matter. The math knew the processes. It had the input. It spread itself out over the long line of imagery the bundle bugs yielded up to the bears. It affected its changes. It lent clarity.

Above, the bears did their work with great precision.

Below, the Kentuckians slipped into Nashville undetected.

Soma woke to find the Kentuckians doing something terrible. When he tried to speak, he found that his face was immobilized by a mask of something that smelled of the docks but felt soft and gauzy.

The four younger Crows were dressed in a gamut of jerseys and shorts colored in the hotter hues of the spectrum. Japheth was struggling into a long, jangly coat hung with seashells and old capacitors. But it was the Owl that frightened Soma the most. The broad-chested man was dappled with opal stones from collarbones to ankles and wore nothing else save a breechcloth cut from an old newspaper. Soma moaned, trying to attract their attention again.

The blue-eyed boy said, "Your painter stirs, Japheth."

But it was the Owl who leaned over Soma, placed his hand on Soma's chin and turned his head back and forth with surprising gentleness. The Owl nodded, to himself Soma guessed, for none of the Crows reacted, then peeled the bandages off Soma's face.

Soma took a deep breath, then said, "Nobody's

worn opals for months! And those shorts," he gestured at the others, "Too much orange! Too much orange!"

Japheth laughed. "Well, we'll be tourists in from the provinces, then, not princes of Printer's Alley. Do *I* offend?" He wriggled his shoulders, set the shells and circuits to clacking.

Soma pursed his lips, shook his head. "Seashells and capacitors are timeless," he said.

Japheth nodded. "That's what it said on the box." Then, "Hey! Bug! Are we to market yet?"

"It's hard to say, whiskey man," came the reply. "My eyes are funny."

"Close enough. Open up."

The rear of the beast's abdomen cracked, and yawned wide. Japheth turned to his charges. "You boys ready to play like vols?"

The younger Crows started gathering burlap bundles. The Owl hoisted a heavy rucksack, adjusted the flowers in his hat, and said, "Wacka wacka ho."

In a low place, horizon bounded by trees in every direction, Jenny and her horse came on the sobbing car. From the ruts it had churned up in the mud, Jenny guessed it had been there for some time, driving back and forth along the northern verge.

"Now what have you done to yourself?" she asked, dismounting. The car turned to her and shuddered. Its front left fender was badly dented, and its hood and windshield were a mess of leaves and small branches.

"Trying to get into the woods? Cars are for roads, car." She brushed some muck off the damaged fender.

"Well, that's not too bad, though. This is all cosmetic. Why would a car try to go where trees are? See what happens?"

The horse called. It had wandered a little way into the woods and was standing at the base of a vast poplar. Jenny reached in through the passenger's window of the car, avoiding the glassy knitting blanket on the other side, and set the parking brake. "You wait here."

She trotted out to join her horse. It was pawing at a small patch of ground. Jenny was a mechanic and had no woodscraft, but she could see the outline of a cleft-toed sandal. Who would be in the woods with such impractical footwear?

"The owner's an artist. An artist looking for a shortcut to the Alley, I reckon," said Jenny. "Wearing funny artist shoes."

She walked back to the car, considering. The car was pining. Not unheard of, but not common. It made her think better of Soma Painter that his car missed him so.

"Say, horse. Melancholy slows car repair. I think this car will convalesce better in its own parking space."

The car revved.

"But there's the garage still back at the beach," said Jenny.

She turned things over and over. "Horse," she said, "you're due three more personal days this month. If I release you for them now, will you go fold up the garage and bring it to me in the city?"

The horse tossed its head enthusiastically.

"Good. I'll drive with this car back to the Alley, then—" But the horse was already rubbing its flanks against her.

"Okay, okay." She drew a tin of salve from her tool belt, dipped her fingers in it, then ran her hands across the horse's back. The red crosses came away in her hands, wriggling. "The cases for these are in my cabinet," she said, and then inspiration came.

"Here, car," she said, and laid the crosses on its hood. They wriggled around until they were at statute-specified points along the doors and roof. "Now you're an ambulance! Not a hundred percent legal, maybe, but this way you can drive fast and whistle siren-like."

The car spun its rear wheels but couldn't overcome the parking brake. Jenny laughed. "Just a minute more. I need you to give me a ride into town."

She turned to speak to the horse, only to see it already galloping along the coast road. "Don't forget to drain the water tanks before you fold it up!" she shouted.

The bundles that were flecked with root matter, Soma discovered, were filled with roots. Carrots and turnips, a half dozen varieties of potatoes, beets. The Kentuckians spread out through the Farmer's Market, trading them by the armload for the juices and gels that the rock monkeys brought in from their gardens.

"This is our secondary objective," said Japheth. "We do this all the time, trading doped potatoes for that shit y'all eat."

"You're poisoning us?" Soma was climbing out of the paste a little, or something. His thoughts were shifting around some.

"Doped with nutrients, friend. Forty ain't old outside Tennessee. Athena doesn't seem to know any more about human nutrition than she does human psychology. Hey, we're trying to *help* you people."

Then they were in the very center of the market, and the roar of the crowds drowned out any reply Soma might make.

Japheth kept a grip on Soma's arm as he spoke to a gray old monkey. "Ten pounds, right?" The monkey was weighing a bundle of carrots on a scale.

"Okay," grunted the monkey. "Okay, man. Ten pounds I give you … four blue jellies."

Soma was incredulous. He'd never developed a taste for them himself, but he knew that carrots were popular. Four blue jellies was an insulting trade. But Japheth said, "Fair enough," and pocketed the plastic tubes the monkey handed over.

"You're no trader," said Soma, or started to, but heard the words slur out of him in an unintelligible mess of vowels. *One spring semester, when he'd already been a TA for a year, he was tapped to work on the interface. No more need for scholarships.*

"Painter!" shouted Japheth.

Soma looked up. There was a Crow dressed in Alley haute couture standing in front of him. He tried to open his head to call the Tennessee Highway Patrol. He couldn't find his head.

"Give him one of these yellow ones," said a monkey. "They're good for fugues."

"Painter!" shouted Japheth again. The grip on Soma's shoulder was like a vise.

Soma struggled to stand under his own power. "I'm forgetting something."

"Hah!" said Japheth, "You're remembering. Too soon for my needs, though. Listen to me. Rock monkeys are full voluntary citizens of Tennessee."

The outlandishness of the statement shocked Soma out of his reverie and brought the vendor up short.

"Fuck you, man!" said the monkey.

"No, no," said Soma, then said by rote, "Tennessee is a fully realized postcolonial state. The land of the rock monkeys is an autonomous partner-principality within our borders, and while the monkeys are our staunch allies, their allegiance is not to our Governor, but to their king."

"Yah," said the monkey. "Long as we get our licenses and pay the tax machine. Plus, who the jelly cubes going to listen to besides the monkey king, huh?"

Soma marched Japheth to the next stall. "Lot left in there to wash out yet," Japheth said.

"I wash every day," said Soma, then fell against a sloshing tray of juice containers. *The earliest results were remarkable.*

A squat man covered with black gems came up to them. The man who'd insulted the monkey said, "You might have killed too much of it; he's getting kind of wonky."

The squat man looked into Soma's eyes. "We can stabilize him easy enough. There are televisions in the food court."

Then Soma and Japheth were drinking hot rum punches and watching a newsfeed. There was a battle out over the Gulf somewhere, Commodores mounted on bears darted through the clouds, lancing Cuban zeppelins.

"The Cubans will never achieve air superiority," said Soma, and it felt right saying it.

Japheth eyed him wearily. "I need you to keep thinking that for now, Soma Painter," he said quietly.

"But I hope sometime soon you'll know that Cubans don't live in a place called the Appalachian Archipelago, and that the salty reach out there isn't the Gulf of Mexico."

The bicycle race results were on then, and Soma scanned the lists, hoping to see his favorites' names near the top of the general classifications.

"That's the Tennessee River, dammed up by your Governor's hubris."

Soma saw that his drink was nearly empty and heard that his friend Japheth was still talking. "What?" he asked, smiling.

"I asked if you're ready to go to the Alley," said Japheth.

"Good good," said Soma.

The math was moving along minor avenues, siphoning data from secondary and tertiary ports when it sensed her looming up. It researched ten thousand thousand escapes but rejected them all when it perceived that it had been subverted, that it was inside her now, becoming part of her, that it *is primitive in materials but clever clever in architecture and there have been blindings times not seen places to root out root out all of it check again check one thousand more times all told all told eat it all up all the little bluegrass math is absorbed*

"The Alley at night!" shouted Soma. "Not like where you're from, eh, boys?"

A lamplighter's stalk legs eased through the little group. Soma saw that his friends were staring up at the civil servant's welding mask head, gaping open-mouthed as it turned a spigot at the top of a tree and lit the gas with a flick of its tongue.

"Let's go to my place!" said Soma. "When it's time for anthem we can watch the parade from my balcony. I live in one of the lofts above the Tyranny of the Anecdote."

"Above what?" asked Japheth.

"It's a tavern. They're my landlords," said Soma. "Vols are so fucking stupid."

But that wasn't right.

Japheth's Owl friend fell to his knees and vomited right in the street. Soma stared at the jiggling spheres in the gutter as the man choked some words out. "She's taken the feathers. She's looking for us now."

Too much rum punch, thought Soma, thought it about the Owl man and himself and about all of Japheth's crazy friends.

"Soma, how far now?" asked Japheth.

Soma remembered his manners. "Not far," he said.

And it wasn't, just a few more struggling yards, Soma leading the way and Japheth's friends half-carrying, half-dragging their drunken friend down the Alley. Nothing unusual there. Every night in the Alley was Carnival.

Then a wave at the bouncer outside the Anecdote, then up the steps, then sing "Let me in, let me in!" to the door, and finally all of them packed into the cramped space.

"There," said the sick man, pointing at the industrial sink Soma had installed himself to make brush cleaning easier. *Brushes... where were his brushes, his pencils, his notes for the complexity seminar?*

"Towels, Soma?"

"What? Oh, here let me get them." Soma bustled

around, finding towels, pulling out stools for the now silent men who filled his room.

He handed the towels to Japheth. "Was it something he ate?" Soma asked.

Japheth shrugged. "Ate a long time ago, you could say. Owls are as much numbers as they are meat. He's divesting himself. Those are ones and zeroes washing down your drain."

The broad man—hadn't he been broad?—the scrawny man with opals falling off him said, "We can only take a few minutes. There are unmounted Detectives swarming the whole city now. What I've left in me is too deep for their little minds, but the whole sphere is roused and things will only get tighter. Just let me—" He turned and retched into the sink again. "Just a few minutes more until the singing."

Japheth moved to block Soma's view of the Owl. He nodded at the drawings on the wall. "Yours?"

The blue-eyed boy moved over to the sink, helped the Owl ease to the floor. Soma looked at the pictures. "Yes, mostly. I traded for a few."

Japheth was studying one charcoal piece carefully, a portrait. "What's this one?"

The drawing showed a tall, thin young man dressed in a period costume, leaning against a mechanical of some kind, staring intently out at the viewer. Soma didn't remember drawing it, specifically, but knew what it must be.

"That's a caricature. I do them during Campaign for the provincials who come into the city to vote. Someone must have asked me to draw him and then never come back to claim it."

And he remembered trying to remember. He

remembered asking his hand to remember when his head wouldn't.

"I'm… what did you put in me?" Soma asked. There was moisture on his cheeks, and he hoped it was tears.

The Owl was struggling up to his feet. A bell tone sounded from the sky and he said, "Now, Japheth. There's no time."

"Just a minute more," snapped the Crow. "What did *we* put in you? You…" Japheth spat. "While you're remembering, try and remember this. You *chose* this! All of you chose it!"

The angry man wouldn't have heard any reply Soma might have made, because it was then that all of the Kentuckians clamped their ears shut with their odd muffs. To his surprise, they forced a pair onto Soma as well.

Jenny finally convinced the car to stop wailing out its hee-haw pitch when they entered the maze of streets leading to Printer's Alley. The drive back had been long, the car taking every northern side road, backtracking, looping, even trying to enter the dumping grounds at one point before the bundle bugs growled them away. During anthem, while Jenny drummed her fingers and forced out the words, the car still kept up its search, not even pretending to dance.

So Jenny had grown more and more fascinated by the car's behavior. She had known cars that were slavishly attached to their owners before, and she had known cars that were smart—almost as smart as bundle bugs, some of them—but the two traits never seemed to go together. "Cars are dogs or cars are cats," her Teacher had said to explain the phenomenon, another of the long roll of enigmatic statements that constituted formal education in the Voluntary State.

But here, now, here was a bundle bug that didn't seem to live up to those creatures' reputations for craftiness. The car had been following the bug for a few blocks—Jenny only realized that after the car, for the first time since they entered the city proper, made a turn *away* from the address painted on its nametag.

The bug was a big one, and was describing a gentle career down Commerce Street, drifting from side to side and clearly ignoring the traffic signals that flocked around its head in an agitated cloud.

"Car, we'd better get off this street. Rogue bugs are too much for the THP. If it doesn't self-correct, a Commodore is likely to be rousted out from the Parthenon." Jenny sometimes had nightmares about Commodores.

The car didn't listen—though it was normally an excellent listener—but accelerated toward the bug. The bug, Jenny now saw, had stopped in front of a restaurant and cracked its abdomen. Dumpster feelers had started creeping out of the interstices between thorax and head when the restaurateur charged out, beating at the feelers with a broom. "Go now!" the man shouted, face as red as his vest and leggings, "I told you twice already! You pick up here Chaseday! Go! I already called your supervisor, bug!"

The bug's voice echoed along the street. "No load? Good good." Its sigh was pure contentment, but Jenny had no time to appreciate it. The car sped up, and Jenny covered her eyes, anticipating a collision. But the car slid to a halt with bare inches to spare, peered into the empty cavern of the bug's belly, then sighed, this one not content at all.

"Come on, car," Jenny coaxed. "He must be at home by now. Let's just try your house, okay?"

The car beeped and executed a precise three-point turn. As they turned off Commerce and climbed the viaduct that arced above the Farmer's Market, Jenny caught a hint of motion in the darkening sky. "THP bicycles, for sure," she said. "Tracking your bug friend."

At the highest point on the bridge, Jenny leaned out and looked down into the controlled riot of the Market. Several stalls were doing brisk business, and when Jenny saw why, she asked the car to stop, then let out a whistle.

"Oi! Monkey!" she shouted. "Some beets up here!"

Jenny loved beets.

signals from the city center subsidiaries routing reports and recommendations increase percentages dedicated to observation and prediction dispatch commodore downcycle biological construct extra-parametrical lower authority

"It's funny that I don't know what it means, though, don't you think, friends?" Soma was saying this for perhaps the fifth time since they began their walk. "*Church* Street. *Church*. Have you ever heard that word anywhere else?"

"No," said the blue-eyed boy.

The Kentuckians were less and less talkative the farther the little group advanced west down Church Street. It was a long, broad avenue, but rated for pedestrians and emergency vehicles only. Less a street, really, than a linear park, for there were neither businesses nor apartments on either side, just low gray government buildings, slate-colored in the sunset.

The sunset. That was why the boulevard was crowded, as it was every night. As the sun dropped down, down, down it dropped behind the Parthenon. At the very instant the disc disappeared behind the sand-colored edifice, the Great Salt Lick self-illuminated and the flat acres of white surrounding the Parthenon shone with a vast, icy light.

The Lick itself was rich with the minerals that fueled the Legislators and Bears, but the white light emanating from it was sterile. Soma noticed that the Crows faces grew paler and paler as they all got closer to its source. *His work was fascinating, and grew more so as more and more disciplines began finding ways to integrate their fields of study into a meta-architecture of science. His department chair co-authored a paper with an expert in animal husbandry, of all things.*

The Owl held Soma's head as the painter vomited up the last of whatever was in his stomach. Japheth and the others were making reassuring noises to passersby. "Too much monkey wine!" they said, and, "We're in from the provinces, he's not used to such rich food!" and, "He's overcome by the sight of the Parthenon!"

Japheth leaned over next to the Owl. "Why's it hitting him so much harder than the others?"

The Owl said, "Well, we've always taken them back north of the border. This poor fool we're dragging ever closer to the glory of his owner. I couldn't even guess what's trying to fill up the empty spaces I left in him—but I'm pretty sure whatever's rushing in isn't all from her."

Japheth cocked an eyebrow at his lieutenant. "I think that's the most words I've ever heard you say all together at once."

The Owl smiled, another first, if that sad little half grin counted as a smile. "Not a lot of time left for talking. Get up now, friend painter."

The Owl and Japheth pulled Soma to his feet. "What did you mean," Soma asked, wiping his mouth with the back of his hand, "'the glory of his owner?'"

"Governor," said Japheth. "He said, 'the glory of his Governor,'" and Japheth swept his arm across, and yes, there it was, the glory of the Governor.

Church Street had a slight downward grade in its last few hundred yards. From where they stood, they could see that the street ended at the spectacularly defined border of the Great Salt Lick, which served as legislative chambers in the Voluntary State. At the center of the lick stood the Parthenon, and while no normal citizens walked the salt just then, there was plenty of motion and color.

Two bears were laying face down in the Lick, bobbing their heads as they took in sustenance from the ground. A dozen or more Legislators slowly unambulated, their great slimy bodies leaving trails of gold or silver depending on their party affiliation. One was engulfing one of the many salt-white statues that dotted the grounds, gaining a few feet of height to warble its slogan songs from. And, unmoving at the corners of the rectangular palace in the center of it all, four Commodores stood.

They were tangled giants of rust, alike in their towering height and in the oily bathyspheres encasing the scant meat of them deep in their torsos, but otherwise each a different silhouette of sensor suites and blades, each with a different complement of articulated limbs or wings or wheels.

"Can you tell which ones they are?" Japheth asked the blue-eyed boy, who had begun murmuring to himself under his breath, eyes darting from Commodore to Commodore.

"Ruby-eyed Sutcliffe, stomper, smasher,
Tempting Nguyen, whispering, lying,
Burroughs burrows, up from the underground..."

The boy hesitated, shaking his head. "Northeast corner looks kind of like Praxis Dale, but she's supposed to be away West, fighting the Federals. Saint Sandalwood's physical presence had the same profile as Dale's, but we believe he's gone, consumed by Athena after their last sortie against the containment field cost her so much."

"I'll never understand why she plays at politics with her subordinates when she *is* her subordinates," said Japheth.

The Owl said, "That's not as true with the Commodores as with a lot of the... inhabitants. I think it *is* Saint Sandalwood; she must have reconstituted him, or part of him. And remember his mnemonic?"

"Sandalwood staring," sang the blue-eyed boy.

"Inside and outside," finished Japheth, looking the Owl in the eye. "Time then?"

"Once we're on the Lick I'd do anything she told me, even empty as I am," said the Owl. "Bind me."

Then the blue-eyed boy took Soma by the arm, kept encouraging him to take in the sights of the Parthenon, turning his head away from where the Crows were wrapping the Owl in grapevines. They took the Owl's helmet from a rucksack and seated it, cinching the cork seals at the neck maybe tighter than Soma would have thought was comfortable.

Two of the Crows hoisted the Owl between them, his feet stumbling some. Soma saw that the eyeholes of the mask had been blocked with highly reflective tape.

Japheth spoke to the others. "The bears won't be in this; they'll take too long to stand up from their meal. Avoid the Legislators, even their trails. The THP will be on the ground, but won't give you any trouble. You boys know why you're here."

The two Crows holding the Owl led him over to Japheth, who took him by the hand. The blue-eyed boy said, "We know why we're here, Japheth. We know why we were born."

And suddenly as that, the four younger Crows were gone, fleeing in every direction except back up Church Street.

"Soma Painter," said Japheth. "Will you help me lead this man on?"

Soma was taken aback. While he knew of no regulation specifically prohibiting it, traditionally no one actually trod the Lick except during Campaign.

"We're going into the Salt Lick?" Soma asked.

"We're going into the Parthenon," Japheth answered.

As they crossed Church Street from the south, the car suddenly stopped.

"Now what, car?" said Jenny. Church Street was her least favorite thoroughfare in the capital.

The car snuffled around on the ground for a moment, then, without warning, took a hard left and accelerated, siren screeching. Tourists and sunset gazers scattered to either side as the car and Jenny roared toward the glowing white horizon.

The Owl only managed a few yards under his own power. He slowed, then stumbled, and then the Crow and the painter were carrying him.

"What's wrong with him?" asked Soma.

They crossed the verge onto the salt. They'd left the bravest sightseers a half-block back.

"He's gone inside himself," said Japheth.

"Why?" asked Soma.

Japheth half laughed. "You'd know better than me, friend."

It was then that the Commodore closest to them took a single step forward with its right foot, dragged the left a dozen yards in the same direction, and then, twisting, fell to the ground with a thunderous crash.

"Whoo!" shouted Japheth. "The harder they fall! We'd better start running now, Soma!"

Soma was disappointed, but unsurprised, to see that Japheth did not mean run *away*.

There was only one bear near the slightly curved route that Japheth picked for them through the harsh glare. Even light as he was, purged of his math, the Owl was still a burden and Soma couldn't take much time to marvel at the swirling colors in the bear's plastic hide.

"Keep up, Soma!" shouted the Crow. Ahead of them, two of the Commodores had suddenly turned on one another and were landing terrible blows. Soma saw a tiny figure clinging to one of the giants' shoulders, saw it lose its grip, fall, and disappear beneath an ironshod boot the size of a bundle bug.

Then Soma slipped and fell himself, sending all three of them to the glowing ground and sending a cloud of the biting crystal salt into the air. One of his sandaled feet, he saw, was coated in gold slime. They'd been trying to outflank one Legislator only to stumble on the trail of another.

Japheth picked up the Owl, now limp as a rag doll, and with a grunt heaved the man across his shoulders. "Soma, you should come on. We might make it." *It's not a hard decision to make at all. How can you not make it? At first he'd needed convincing, but then he'd been one of those who'd gone out into the world to convince others. It's not just history; it's after history.*

"Soma!"

Japheth ran directly at the unmoving painter, the deadweight of the Owl across his shoulders slowing him. He barreled into Soma, knocking him to the ground again, all of them just missing the unknowing Legislator as it slid slowly past.

"Up, up!" said Japheth. "Stay behind it, so long as it's moving in the right direction. I think my boys missed a Commodore." His voice was very sad.

The Legislator stopped and let out a bellowing noise. Fetid steam began rising from it. Japheth took Soma by the hand and pulled him along, through chaos. One of the Commodores, the first to fall, was motionless on the ground, two or three Legislators making their way along its length. The two who'd fought lay locked in one another's grasp, barely moving and glowing hotter and hotter. The only standing Commodore, eyes like red suns, seemed to be staring just behind them.

As it began to sweep its gaze closer, Soma heard Japheth say, "We got closer than I would have bet."

Then Soma's car, mysteriously covered with red crosses and wailing at the top of its voice, came to a sliding, crunching stop in the salt in front of them.

Soma didn't hesitate, but threw open the closest rear door and pulled Japheth in behind him. When the three of them—painter, Crow, Owl—were stuffed into the rear door, Soma shouted, "Up those stairs, car!"

In the front seat, there was a woman whose eyes seemed as large as saucers.

commodores faulting headless people in the lick protocols compel reeling in, strengthening, temporarily abandoning telepresence locate an asset with a head asset with a head located

Jenny-With-Grease-Beneath-Her-Fingernails was trying not to go crazy. Something was pounding at her head, even though she hadn't tried to open it herself. Yesterday, she had been working a remote repair job on the beach, fixing a smashed window. Tonight, she was hurtling across the Great Salt Lick, Legislators and bears and *Commodores* acting in ways she'd never seen or heard of.

Jenny herself acting in ways she'd never heard of. Why didn't she just pull the emergency brake, roll out of the car, wait for the THP? Why did she just hold on tighter and pull down the sunscreen so she could use the mirror to look into the backseat?

It *was* three men. She hadn't been sure at first. One appeared to be unconscious and was dressed in some strange getup, a helmet of some kind completely encasing his head. She didn't know the man in the capacitor jacket, who was craning his head out the window, trying to see something above them. The other one though, she recognized.

"Soma Painter," she said. "Your car is much better, though it has missed you terribly."

The owner just looked at her glaze-eyed. The other one pulled himself back in through the window, a wild glee on his face. He rapped the helmet of the prone man and shouted, "Did you hear that? The unpredictable you prophesied! And it fell in our favor!"

Soma worried about his car's suspension, not to mention the tires, when it slalomed through the legs of the last standing Commodore and bounced up the steeply cut steps of the Parthenon. *He hadn't had a direct hand in the subsystems design—by the time he'd begun to develop the cars, Athena was already beginning to take over a lot of the details. Not all of them, though; he couldn't blame her for the guilt he felt over twisting his animal subjects into something like onboard components.*

But the car made it onto the platform inside the outer set of columns, seemingly no worse for wear. The man next to him—Japheth, his name was Japheth and he was from Kentucky—jumped out of the car and ran to the vast, closed counterweighted bronze doors.

"It's because of the crosses. We're in an emergency

vehicle according to their protocols." That was the mechanic, Jenny, sitting in the front seat and trying to staunch a nosebleed with a greasy rag. "I can hear the Governor," she said.

Soma could hear Japheth raging and cursing. He stretched the Owl out along the back seat and climbed out of the car. Japheth was pounding on the doors in futility, beating his fists bloody, spinning, spitting. He caught sight of Soma.

"*These* weren't here before!" he said, pointing to two silver columns that angled up from the platform's floor, ending in flanges on the doors themselves. "The doors aren't locked, they're just sealed by these fucking cylinders!" Japheth was shaking. "Caw!" he cried. "Caw!"

"What's he trying to do?" asked the woman in the car.

Soma brushed his fingers against his temple, trying to remember.

"I think he's trying to remake Tennessee," he said.

The weight of a thousand cars on her skull, the hoofbeats of a thousand horses throbbing inside her eyes, Jenny was incapable of making any rational decision. So, irrationally, she left the car. She stumbled over to the base of one of the silver columns. When she tried to catch herself on it, her hand slid off.

"Oil," she said. "These are just hydraulic cylinders." She looked around the metal sheeting where the cylinder disappeared into the platform, saw the access plate. She pulled a screwdriver from her belt and used it to removed the plate.

The owner was whispering to his car, but the crazy man had come over to her. "What are you doing?" he asked.

"I don't know," she said, but she meant it only in the largest sense. Immediately, she was thrusting her wrists into the access plate, playing the licenses and government bonds at her wrists under a spray of light, murmuring a quick apology to the machinery. Then she opened a long vertical cut down as much of the length of the hydraulic hose as she could with her utility blade.

Fluid exploded out of the hole, coating Jenny in the slick, dirty green stuff. The cylinders collapsed.

The man next to Jenny looked at her. He turned and looked at Soma-With-The-Paintbox-In-Printer's Alley and at Soma's car.

"We must have had a pretty bad plan," he said, then rushed over to pull the helmeted figure from the backseat.

breached come home all you commodores come home cancel emergency designation on identified vehicle and downcycle now jump in jump in jump in

Jenny could not help Soma and his friend drag their burden through the doors of the temple, but she staggered through the doors. She had only seen Athena in tiny parts, in the mannequin shrines that contained tiny fractions of the Governor.

Here was the true and awesome thing, here was the forty-foot-tall sculpture—armed and armored—attended by the broken remains of her frozen marble enemies. Jenny managed to lift her head and look past sandaled feet, up cold golden raiment, past tart painted cheeks to the lapis lazuli eyes.

Athena looked back at her. Athena leapt.

Inside Jenny's head, inside so small an architecture, there was no more room for Jenny-With-Grease-Beneath-Her-Fingernails. Jenny fled.

Soma saw the mechanic, the woman who'd been so kind to his car, fall to her knees, blood gushing from her nose and ears. He saw Japheth laying out the Owl like a sacrifice before the Governor. *He'd been among the detractors, scoffing at the idea of housing the main armature in such a symbol-potent place.*

Behind him, his car beeped. The noise was barely audible above the screaming metal sounds out in the Lick. The standing Commodore was swiveling its torso, turning its upper half toward the Parthenon. Superheated salt melted in a line slowly tracking toward the steps.

Soma trotted back to his car. He leaned in and *remembered the back door, the Easter egg he hadn't documented.* A twist on the ignition housing, then press in, and the key sank into the column. The car shivered.

"Run home as fast you can, car. Back to the ranch with your kin. Be fast, car, be clever."

The car woke up. It shook off Soma's ownership and closed its little head. It let out a surprised beep and then fled with blazing speed, leaping down the steps, over the molten salt, and through the storm, bubblewinged bicycles descending all around. The Commodore began another slow turn, trying to track it.

Soma turned back to the relative calm inside the Parthenon. Athena's gaze was baleful, but he couldn't feel it. The Owl had ripped the ability from him. The Owl lying before Japheth, defenseless against the knife Japheth held high.

"Why?" shouted Soma.

But Japheth didn't answer him, instead diving over the Owl in a somersault roll, narrowly avoiding the flurry of kicks and roundhouse blows being thrown by Jenny. Her eyes bugged and bled. More blood flowed from her ears and nostrils, but still she attacked Japheth with relentless fury.

Japheth came up in a crouch. The answer to Soma's question came in a slurred voice from Jenny. Not Jenny, though. Soma knew the voice, remembered it from somewhere, and it wasn't Jenny's.

"there is a bomb in that meat soma-friend a knife a threat an eraser"

Japheth shouted at Soma. "You get to decide again! Cut the truth out of him!" He gestured at the Owl with his knife.

Soma took in a shuddery breath. "So free with lives. One of the reasons we climbed up."

Jenny's body lurched at Japheth, but the Crow dropped onto the polished floor. Jenny's body slipped when it landed, the soles of its shoes coated with the same oil as its jumpsuit.

"My Owl cousin died of asphyxiation at least ten minutes ago, Soma," said Japheth. "Died imperfect and uncontrolled." Then, dancing backward before the scratching thing in front of him, Japheth tossed the blade in a gentle underhanded arc. It clattered to the floor at Soma's feet.

All of the same arguments.

All of the same arguments.

Soma picked up the knife and looked down at the Owl. The fight before him, between a dead woman versus a man certain to die soon, spun on. Japheth said no more, only looked at Soma with pleading eyes.

Jenny's body's eyes followed the gaze, saw the knife in Soma's hand.

"you are due upgrade soma-friend swell the ranks of commodores you were 96th percentile now 99th soma-with-the-paintbox-in-printer's-alley the voluntary state of tennessee applauds your citizenship"

But it wasn't the early slight, the denial of entry to the circle of highest minds. Memories of before *and* after, decisions made by him and for him, sentiences and upgrades decided by fewer and fewer and then one; one who'd been a *product,* not a builder.

Soma plunged the knife into the Owl's unmoving chest and sawed downward through the belly with what strength he could muster. The skin and fat fell away along a seam straighter than he could ever cut. The bomb—the knife, the eraser, the threat—looked like a tiny white balloon. He pierced it with the killing tip of the Kentuckian's blade.

A nova erupted at the center of the space where math and Detectives live. A wave of scouring numbers washed outward, spreading all across Nashville, all across the Voluntary State to fill all the space within the containment field.

The 144 Detectives evaporated. The King of the Rock Monkeys, nothing but twisted light, fell into shadow. The Commodores fell immobile, the ruined biology seated in their chests went blind, then deaf, then died.

And singing Nashville fell quiet. Ten thousand thousand heads slammed shut and ten thousand thousand souls fell insensate, unsupported, in need of revival.

North of the Girding Wall, alarms began to sound.

At the Parthenon, Japheth Sapp gently placed the tips of his index and ring fingers on Jenny's eyelids and pulled them closed.

Then the ragged Crow pushed past Soma and hurried out into the night. The Great Salt Lick glowed no more, and even the lights of the city were dimmed, so Soma quickly lost sight of the man. But then the cawing voice rang out once more. "We only hurt the car because we had to."

Soma thought for a moment, then said, "So did I."

But the Crow was gone, and then Soma had nothing to do but wait. He had made the only decision he had left in him. He idly watched as burning bears floated down into the sea. A striking image, but he had somewhere misplaced his paints.

The Lost Pilgrim

Gene Wolfe

Gene Wolfe came to prominence as a writer in the late '60s with a sequence of short stories—including "The Hero as Werewolf," "Seven American Nights," and "The Island of Doctor Death and Other Stories"—in Damon Knight's Orbit *anthologies. His early major novels were* The Fifth Head of Cerberus *and* Peace, *but he established his reputation with a sequence of three long multi-volume novels—*The Book of the New Sun *(4 vols),* The Book of the Long Sun *(4 vols),* The Book of the Short Sun *(3 vols)—and pendant volume,* The Urth of the New Sun. *Wolfe has published a number of short story collections, including* The Island of Doctor Death and Other Stories *and* Other Stories, Endangered Species, *and* Strange Travelers. *He has won the Nebula Award and World Fantasy Award twice, the Locus Award four times, the John W. Campbell Memorial Award, the British Fantasy Award, the British SF Award, and is the recipient of the World Fantasy Award for Lifetime Achievement. Wolfe's most recent books are collection* Innocents Aboard *and major new fantasy novel* The Wizard Knight. *Upcoming is a new collection of science fiction stories.*

In the story that follows a modern day chrononaut unexpectedly finds himself off-target, out of step, and in the company of argonauts.

Before leaving my own period, I resolved to keep a diary; and indeed I told several others I would, and promised to let them see it upon my return. Yesterday I arrived, captured no Pukz, and compiled no text. No more inauspicious beginning could be imagined.

I will not touch my emergency rations. I am hungry, and there is nothing to eat; but how absurd it would be to begin in such a fashion! No. Absolutely not. Let me finish this, and I will go off in search of breakfast.

To begin. I find myself upon a beach, very beautiful and very empty, but rather too hot and much too shadeless to be pleasant. "Very empty," I said, but how can I convey just how empty it really is? (Pukz 1-3)

As you see, there is sun and there is water, the former remarkably hot and bright, the latter remarkably blue and clean. There is no shade, and no one who—

A sail! Some kind of sailboat is headed straight for this beach. It seems too small, but this could be it. (Puk 4)

I cannot possibly describe everything that happened today. There was far, far too much. I can only give a rough outline. But first I should say that I am no longer sure why I am here, if I ever was. On the beach last night, just after I arrived, I felt no doubts. Either

I knew why I had come, or I did not think about it. There was that time when they were going to send me out to join the whateveritwas expedition—the little man with the glasses. But I do not think this is that; this is something else.

Not the man getting nailed up, either.

It will come to me. I am sure it will. In such a process of regression there cannot help but be metal confusion. Do I mean metal? The women's armor was gold or brass. Something like that. They marched out onto the beach, a long line of them, all in the gold armor. I did not know they were women.

I hid behind rocks and took Pukz. (See Pukz 5-9) The reflected glare made it difficult, but I got some good shots just the same.

They banged their spears on their shields and made a terrible noise, but when the boat came close enough for us to see the men on it (Pukz 10 and 11) they marched back up onto the hill behind me and stood on the crest. It was then that I realized they were women; I made a search for "women in armor" and found more than a thousand references, but all those I examined were to Joan of Arc or similar figures. This was not one woman but several hundreds.

I do not believe there should be women in armor, anyway. Or men in armor, like those who got off the boat. Swords, perhaps. Swords might be all right. And the name of the boat should be two words, I think.

The men who got off this boat are young and tough-looking. There is a book of prayers in my pack, and I am quite certain it was to be a talisman. "O God, save me by thy name and defend my cause by thy might." But I cannot imagine these men being impressed by any prayers.

Some of these men were in armor and some were not. One who had no armor and no weapons left the rest and started up the slope. He has an intelligent face, and though his staff seemed sinister, I decided to risk everything. To tell the truth I thought he had seen me and was coming to ask what I wanted. I was wrong, but he would surely have seen me as soon as he took a few more steps. At any rate, I switched on my translator and stood up. He was surprised, I believe, at my black clothes and the buckles on my shoes; but he is a very smooth man, always exceedingly polite. His name is Ekkiawn. Or something like that. (Puk 12) Ekkiawn is as near as I can get to the pronunciation.

I asked where he and the others were going, and when he told me, suggested that I might go with them, mentioning that I could talk to the Native Americans. He said it was impossible, that they had sworn to accept no further volunteers, that he could speak the language of Kolkkis himself, and that the upper classes of Kolkkis all spoke English.

I, of course, then asked him to say something in English and switched off my translator. I could not understand a word of it.

At this point he began to walk again, marking each stride with his beautiful staff, a staff of polished hardwood on which a carved snake writhes. I followed him, switched my translator back on, and complimented him on his staff.

He smiled and stroked the snake. "My father permits me to use it," he said. "The serpent on his own is real, of course. Our tongues are like our emblems, I'm afraid. He can persuade anyone of anything. Compared to him, my own tongue is mere wood."

I said, "I assume you will seek to persuade those women that you come in peace. When you do, will they teach you to plant corn?"

He stopped and stared at me. "Are they women? Don't toy with me."

I said I had observed them closely, and I was quite sure they were.

"How interesting! Come with me."

As we approached the women, several of them began striking their shields with their spears, as before. (Puk 13) Ekkiawn raised his staff. "My dear young ladies, cease! Enchanting maidens, desist! You suppose us pirates. You could not be more mistaken. We are the aristocracy of the Minyans. Nowhere will you find young men so handsome, so muscular, so wealthy, so well bred, or so well connected. I myself am a son of Hodios. We sail upon a most holy errand, for we would return the sacred ramskin to Mount Laphystios."

The women had fallen silent, looking at one another and particularly at an unusually tall and comely woman who stood in the center of their line.

"Let there be peace between us," Ekkiawn continued. "We seek only fresh water and a few days' rest, for we have had hard rowing. We will pay for any supplies we receive from you, and generously. You will have no singing arrows nor blood-drinking spears from us. Do you fear sighs? Languishing looks? Gifts of flowers and jewelry? Say so if you do, and we will depart in peace."

A woman with gray hair straggling from under her helmet tugged at the sleeve of the tall woman. (Puk

14) Nodding, the tall woman stepped forward. "Stranger, I am Hupsipule, Queen of Lahmnos. If indeed you come in peace—"

"We do," Ekkiawn assured her.

"You will not object to my conferring with my advisors."

"Certainly not."

While the queen huddled with four other women, Ekkiawn whispered, "Go to the ship like a good fellow, and find Eeasawn, our captain. Tell him these are women and describe the queen. Name her."

Thinking that this might well be the boat I was supposed to board after all and that this offered as good a chance to ingratiate myself with its commander as I was ever likely to get, I hurried away. I found Eea-sawn without much trouble, assured him that the armed figures on the hilltop were in fact women in armor ("both Ekkiawn and I saw that quite clearly") and told him that the tallest, good-looking, black-haired, and proud, was Queen Hupsipule,

He thanked me. "And you are...?"

"A humble pilgrim seeking the sacred ramskin, where I hope to lay my heartfelt praise at the feet of God."

"Well spoken, but I cannot let you sail with us, Pilgrim. This ship is already as full of men as an egg is of meat. But should—"

Several members of the crew were pointing and shouting. The women on the hilltop were removing their armor and so revealing their gender, most being dressed in simple frocks without sleeves, collars, or buttons. (Puk 15) There was a general rush from the ship.

Let me pause here to comment upon the men's

clothing, of which there is remarkably little, many being completely naked. Some wear armor, a helmet and a breastplate, or a helmet alone. A few more wear loose short-sleeved shirts that cover them to mid-thigh. The most remarkable is certainly the captain, who goes naked except for a single sandal. (Pukz 16 and 17)

For a moment or two, I stood watching the men from the ship talking to the women. After conversations too brief to have consisted of much more than introductions, each man left with three or more women, though our captain departed with the queen alone (Puk 18), and Ekkiawn with five. I had started to turn away when the largest and strongest hand I have ever felt closed upon my shoulder.

"Look 'round here, Pilgrim. Do you really want to go to Kolkkis with us?"

The speaker was a man of immense size, bull-necked and pig-eyed (Puk 19); I felt certain that it would be dangerous to reply in the negative.

"Good! I promised to guard the ship, you see, the first time it needed guarding."

"I am not going to steal anything," I assured him.

"I didn't think so. But if you change your mind, I'm going to hunt you down and break your neck. Now, then, 1 heard you and Eeasawn. You watch for me, hear? While I go into whatever town those split tailed soldiers came out of and get us some company. Two enough for you?"

Not knowing what else to do, I nodded.

"Me?" He shrugged shoulders that would have been more than creditable on a bull gorilla. "I knocked up fifty girls in one night once. Not that I couldn't have done it just about any other night, too, only that was the only time I've had a crack at fifty. So a couple for you and as many as I can round up for me. And if your two have anything left when you're done up, send 'em over. Here." He handed me a spear. "You're our guard 'til I get back."

I am waiting his return; I have removed some clothing because of the heat and in the hope of ingratiating myself with any women who may return with him. Hahraklahs is his name.

Hours have passed since I recorded the account you just read. No one has come, neither to molest our boat nor for any other reason. I have been staring at the stars and examining my spear. It has a smooth hardwood shaft and a leaf-shaped blade of copper or brass. I would not have thought such a blade could be sharpened, but it is actually very sharp.

It is also wrong. I keep thinking of spears with flared mouths like trumpets. And yet I must admit that my spear is a sensible weapon, while the spears with trumpet mouths would be senseless as well as useless.

These are the most beautiful stars in the world. I am beginning to doubt that I have come at the right period, and to tell the truth I cannot remember what the right period was. It does not matter, since no one can possibly use the same system. But this period in which I find myself has the most beautiful stars, bar none. And the closest.

There are voices in the distance. I am prepared to fight, if I must.

We are at sea. I have been rowing; my hands are raw

and blistered. We are too many to row all at once, so we take turns. Mine lasted most of the morning. I pray for a wind.

I should have brought prophylactics. It is possible I have contracted some disease, though I doubt it. The women (Apama and Klays, Pukz 20-25, infrared) were interesting, both very eager to believe that I was the son of some king or other and very determined to become pregnant. Apama has killed her husband for an insult, stabbing him in his sleep.

Long after we had finished and washed ourselves in this strange tideless sea, Hahraklahs was still engaged with his fifteen or twenty. (They came and went in a fashion that made it almost impossible to judge the exact number.) When the last had gone, we sat and talked. He has had a hard life in many ways, for he is a sort of slave to one Eurustheus who refuses to speak to him or even look at him. He has been a stableman and so forth. He says he strangled the lion whose skin he wears, and he is certainly very strong. I can hardly lift his brass-bound club, which he flourishes like a stick.

If it were not for him, I would not be on this boat. He has taken a liking to me because I did not want to stay at Lahmnos. He had to kidnap about half the crew to get us out to sea again, and two could not be found. Kaeneus (Puk 26) says the crew wanted to depose Captain Eeasawn and make Hahraklahs captain, but he remained loyal to Eeasawn and would not agree. Kaeneus also confided that he himself underwent a sex-change operation some years ago. Ekkiawn warned me that Kaeneus is the most dangerous fighter on the boat; I suppose he was afraid I would ridicule him. He is a chief, Ekkiawn says, of the Lapiths; this seems to be a Native American tribe.

I am certainly on the wrong vessel. There are two points I am positive of. The first is the name of the captain. It was Jones. Captain Jones. This cannot be Eeasawn, whose name does not even begin with J. The second is that there was to be someone named Brewster on board, and that I was to help this Brewster (or perhaps Bradford) talk with the Lapiths. There is no one named Bradford among my present companions—I have introduced myself to all of them and learned their names. No Brewsters. Thus this boat cannot be the one I was to board.

On the positive side, I am on a friendly footing now with the Lapith chief. That seems sure to be of value when I find the correct ship and reach Atlantis.

I have discussed this with Argos. Argos (Puk 27) is the digitized personality of the boat. (I wonder if the women who lay with him realized that?) He points out—wisely, I would say—that the way to locate a vessel is to visit a variety of ports, making inquiries at each. In order to do that, one should be on another vessel, one making a long voyage with many ports of call. That is my situation, which might be far worse.

We have sighted two other boats, both smaller than our own.

Our helmsman, said to be an infallible weather prophet, has announced that we will have a stiff west wind by early afternoon. Our course is northeast for Samothrakah, which I take to be another island. We are forty-nine men and one woman.

She is Atalantah of Kaludon (Pukz 28-30), tall, slender, muscular, and quite beautiful. Ekkiawn introduced me to her, warning me that she would certainly kill me if I tried to force her. I assured her, and him, that I would never do such a thing. In all honesty I cannot say I have talked with her, but I listened to her for some while. Hunting is the only thing she cares about. She has hunted every large animal in her part of the world and joined Eeasawn's expedition in hope of hunting grups, a fierce bird never seen west of our destination. They can be baited to a blind to feed upon the bodies of horses or cattle, she says. From that I take them to be some type of vulture. Her knowledge of lions, stags, wild swine, and the dogs employed to hunt all three is simply immense.

At sea again, course southeast and the wind dead astern. Now that I have leisure to bring this account up to date, I sit looking out at the choppy waves pursuing us and wonder whether you will believe even a fraction of what I have to relate.

In Samothrakah we were to be initiated into the Cult of Persefonay, a powerful goddess. I joined in the preparations eagerly, not only because it would furnish insight into the religious beliefs of these amoral but very superstitious men, but also because I hoped— as I still do—that the favor of the goddess would bring me to the rock whose name I hare forgotten, the rock that is my proper destination.

We fasted for three days, drinking water mixed with wine but eating no solid food. On the evening of the third day we stripped and daubed each other with a thin white mixture which I suspect was little more than chalk dispersed in water. That done, we shared a ritual supper of boiled beans and raw onions. (Pukz 31 and 32)

Our procession reached the cave of Persefassa, as she is also called, about midnight. We extinguished our torches in an underground pool and received new ones, smaller torches that burned with a clear, almost white flame and gave off a sweet scent. Singing, we marched another mile underground.

My companions appeared undaunted. I was frightened, and kept my teeth from chattering only by an effort of will. After a time I was able to exchange places with Erginos and so walk behind Hahraklahs, that tower of strength. If that stratagem had not succeeded, I think I might hare turned and run.

The throne room of the goddess (Pukz 33-35) is a vast underground chamber of spectacular natural columns where icy water drips secretly and, as it were, stealthily. The effect is of gentle, unending rain, of mourning protracted until the sun burns out. The priestesses passed among us, telling each of us in turn, "All things fail. All decays, and passes away."

Ghosts filled the cavern. Our torches rendered them invisible, but I could see them in the darkest places, always at the edge of my field of Their whispers were like a hundred winds in a forest, and whenever one came near me I felt a cold that struck to the bone.

Deep-voiced horns, melodious and tragic, announced the goddess. She was preceded by the Kabeiri, stately women and men somewhat taller than Hahraklahs who appeared to have no feet. Their forms were solid to the knees, where they became translucent and quickly faded to nothing. They made an aisle for Persefonay, a lovely young woman far taller than they.

She was robed in crimson, and black gems bound her fair hair. (Pukz 36 and 37) Her features are quite beautiful; her expression I can only call resigned. (She may revisit the upper world only as long as the pomegranate is in bloom—so we were taught during our fast. For the rest of the year she remains her husband's prisoner underground.) She took her seat upon a rock that accommodated itself to her as she sat, and indicated by a gesture that we were to approach her.

We did, and her Kabeiri closed about us as if we were children shepherded by older children, approaching a teacher. That and Puk 38 will give you the picture; but I was acutely conscious, as I think we all were, that she and her servants were beings of an order remote from biological evolution. You will be familiar with such beings in our own period, I feel sure. I do not recall them, true. I do recall that knowledge accumulates. The people of the period in which I find myself could not have sent someone, as I have been sent, to join in the famous voyage whose name I have forgotten.

Captain Eeasawn stepped forward to speak to Persefonay. (Pukz 39 and 40) He explained that we were bound for Aea, urged upon our mission by the Pythoness and accompanied by sons of Poseidon and other gods. Much of what he said contradicted what I had been told earlier, and there was much that I failed to understand.

When he had finished, Persefonay introduced the Kabeiri, the earliest gods of Samothrakah. One or more, she said, would accompany us on our voyage, would see that our boat was never wrecked, and would rescue us if it were. Eeasawn thanked her in an elaborate speech, and we bowed.

At once every torch burned out, leaving us in utter darkness. (Pukz 39a and 40a infrared) Instructed by the priestesses, we joined hands, I with Hahraklahs and Atalantah, and so were led out of the cave. There our old torches were restored to us and rekindled. (Puk 41) Carrying them and singing, we returned to our ship, serenaded by wolves.

We have passed Ilion! Everyone agrees that was the most dangerous part of our voyage. Its inhabitants control the strait and permit no ships other than their own to enter or leave. We remained well out of sight of the city until night.

Night came, and a west wind with it. We put up the mast and hoisted our sail, and Periklumenos dove from the prow and took the form of a dolphin (Puk 42 infrared) to guide us though the strait. As we drew near Ilion, we rowed, too, rowing for all we were worth for what seemed half the night. A patrol boat spotted us and moved to intercept us, but Phaleros shot its helmsman. It sheered off—and we passed! That shot was five hundred meters if it was one, and was made by a man standing unsupported on a bench aboard a heeling, pitching boat urged forward by a bellying sail and forty rowers pulling for all they were worth. The arrow's flight was as straight as any string. I could not see where the helmsman was hit, but Atalantah says the throat. Knowing that she prides herself on her shooting, I asked whether she could have made that shot. She shrugged and said, "Once, perhaps, with a quiver-full of arrows."

We are docked now at a place called Bear Island.
We fear no bears here, nor much of anything else.
The king is the son of an old friend of Hahraklahs's.
He has invited us to his wedding, and all is wine and
garlands, music, dancing, and gaiety. (Pukz 43-48)
Eeasawn asked for volunteers to guard the boat. I
volunteered, and Atalantah offered to stay with me.
Everyone agreed that Eeasawn and Hahraklahs would
have to be present the whole time, so they were
excused; the rest drew lots to relieve us. Polydeukahs
the Clone and Kaeneus lost and were then subjected
to much good-natured raillery. They promise to relieve
us as soon as the moon comes up.

Meanwhile I have been leaning on my spear and
talking with Atalantah. Leaning on my spear, I said,
but that was only at first. Some kind people came
down from the town (Puk 49) to talk with us, and
left us a skin of wine. After that we sat side by side
on one of the benches and passed the tart wine back
and forth. I do not think that I will ever taste dry red
wine again without being reminded of this evening.

Atalantah has had a wretched life. One sees a tall,
athletic, good-looking young, woman. One is told
that she is royal, the daughter of a king. One assumes
quite naturally that hers has been a life of ease and
privilege. It has been nothing of the sort. She was
exposed as an infant—left in the forest to die. She was
found by hunters, one of whom had a captive bear
with a cub. He washed her in the bear's urine, after
which the bear permitted her to nurse. No one can
marry her who cannot best her in a foot-race, and no
one can. As if that were not enough, she is compelled
to kill the suitors she outruns. And she has, murdering

half a dozen fine young men and mourning them afterward.

I tried to explain to her that she could still have male friends, men other than suitors who like her and enjoy her company. I pointed out that I could never make a suitable mate for a beautiful young woman of royal blood but that I would be proud to call myself her friend. I would make no demands, and assist her in any way I could. We kissed and became intimate.

Have I gone mad? Persefonay smiled at me as we left. I shall never forget that. I cannot. Now this!

No, I am not mad. I have been wracking my brain, sifting my memory for a future that does not yet exist. There is a double helix of gold. It gives us the power to make monsters, and if it exists in that age it must exist in this. Look! (Pukz 50-58) I have paced off their height, and find it to be four and a half meters or a little more.

Six arms! All of them have six arms. (Pukz 54-57 show this very clearly.) They came at us like great white spiders, then rose to throw stones, and would have brained us with their clubs.

God above have mercy on us! I have been reading my little book by firelight. It says that a wise warrior is mightier than a strong warrior. Doubtless that is true, but I know that I am neither. We killed three. I killed one myself. Good Heavens!

Let me go at this logically, although every power in this mad universe must know that I feel anything but logical.

I have reread what I recorded here before the giants came. The moon rose, and not long after—say, three quarters of an hour—our relief arrived. They were somewhat drunk, but so were we.

Kastawr came with his clone Polydeukahs, not wanting to enjoy himself without him. Kaeneus came as promised. Thus we had five fighters when the giants came down off the mountain. Atalantah's bow served us best, I think, but they rushed her. Kaeneus killed one as it ran. That was simply amazing. He crouched under his shield and sprang up as the giant dashed past, severing an artery in the giant's leg with his sword. The giant took a few more steps and fell. Polydeukahs and Kastawr attacked another as it grappled Atalantah. I actually heard a rib break under the blows of Polydeukahs's fists. They pounded the giant's side like hammers.

People who heard our war cries, the roars of the giants, and Atalantah's screams came pouring down from the town with torches, spears, and swords; but they were too late. We had killed four, and the rest were running from us. None of the townspeople I talked to had been aware of such creatures on their island. They regarded the bodies with superstitious awe. Furthermore, they now regard us with superstitious awe—our boat and our whole crew, and particularly Atalantah, Kastawr, Polydeukahs, Kaeneus, and me. (Puk 59)

About midnight Atalantah and I went up to the palace to see if there was any food left. As soon as we were alone, she embraced me. "Oh, Pilgrim! Can you…Could anyone ever love such a coward?"

"I don't ask for your love, Atalantah, only that you

like me. I know very well that everyone on our boat is braver than I am, but—"

"Me! Me! You were—you were a wild bull. I was terrified. It was crushing me. I had dropped my bow, and I couldn't get to my knife. It was about to bite my head off, and you were coming! Augah! Oh, Pilgrim! I saw fear in the monster's eyes, before your spear! It was the finest thing that has ever happened to me, but when the giant dropped me I was trembling like a doe with an arrow in her heart."

I tried to explain that it had been nothing, that Kastawr and his clone had already engaged the giant, and that her own struggles were occupying its attention. I said, "I could never have done it if it hadn't had its hands full."

"It had its hands full?" She stared, and burst into laughter. In another minute I was laughing too, the two of us laughing so hard we had to hold onto each other. It was a wonderful moment, but her laughter soon turned to tears, and for the better part of an hour I had to comfort a sobbing girl, a princess small, lonely, and motherless, who stayed alive as best she could in a forest hut with three rough men.

Before I go on to speak of the extraordinary events at the palace, I must say one thing more. My companions shouted their war cries as they battled the giants; and I, when I rushed at the one who held Atalantah, yelled, "Mayflower! Mayflower!" I know that was not what I should have said. I know I should have said mayday, but I do not know what "mayday" means, or why I should have said it. I cannot offer even a hint as to why I found myself shouting mayflower instead. Yet I feel that the great question has been answered. It was what I am doing here. The answer, surely, is that I was sent in order that Atalantah might be spared.

The whole palace was in an uproar. (Pukz 60-62) On the day before his wedding festivities began, King Kuzikos had killed a huge lion on the slopes of Mount Dindumon. It had been skinned and its skin displayed on the stoa, no one in his country having seen one of such size before.

After Kaeneus, Polydeukahs, and Kastawr left the banquet, this lion (we were told) was restored to life, someone filling the empty skin with new lion, so to speak. (Clearly that is impossible; another lion, black-maned like the first and of similar size, was presumably substituted for the skin.) What mattered was that the new or restored lion was loose in the palace. It had killed two persons before we arrived and had mauled three others.

Amphiareaws was in a trance. King Kuzikos had freed his hounds, piebald dogs the size of Great Danes that were nearly as dangerous as any lion. (Pukz 63 and 64) Eeasawn and most of our crew were hunting the lion with the king. Hahraklahs had gone off alone in search of it but had left word with Ekkiawn that I was to join him. Atalantah and I hurried away, knowing no more than that he had intended to search the east wing of the palace and the gardens. We found a body, apparently that of some worthy of the town but had no way of knowing whether it was one of those whose deaths had already been reported or a fresh kill. It had been partly devoured, perhaps by the dogs.

We found Hahraklahs in the garden, looking very much like a lion on its hind legs himself with his lion skin and huge club. He greeted us cordially and seemed not at all sorry that Atalantah had come with me.

"Now let me tell you," he said, "the best way to kill a lion—the best way for me, anyhow. If I can get behind that lion and get my hands on its neck, we can go back to our wine. If I tried to club it, you see, it would hear the club coming down and jerk away. They've got sharp ears, and they're very fast. I'd still hit it—they're not as fast as all that—but not where I wanted, and as soon as I hit it, I'd have it in my lap. Let me get a grip on its neck, though, and we've won."

Atalantah said, "I agree. How can we help?"

"It will be simple, but it won't be easy. When we find it, I'll front it. I'm big enough and mean enough that it won't go straight for me. It'll try to scare me into running, or dodge around and look for an opening. What I need is for somebody to distract it, just for a wink. When I killed this one I'm wearing, Hylas did it for me, throwing stones. But he's not here."

I said I could do that if I could find the stones, and Atalantah remarked that an arrow or two would make any animal turn around to look. We had begun to tell Hahraklahs about the giants when Kalais swooped low and called, "It's coming! Path to your left! Quick!"

I turned my head in time to see its final bound, and it was like seeing a saddle horse clear a broad ditch. Three sparrows could not have scattered faster than we. The lion must have leaped again, coming down on Hahraklahs and knocking him flat. I turned just in time to see him throw it off. It spun through the air, landed on its feet, and charged him with a roar I will never forget.

I ran at it, I suppose with the thought of spearing

it, if I had any plan at all. One of Atalantah's arrows whistled past and buried itself in the lion's mane. Hahraklahs was still down, and I tried to pull the lion off him. His club, breaking the lion's skull, sounded like a lab explosion.

And it was over. Blood ran from Hahraklahs's immense arms and trickled from his fingers, and more ran down his face and soaked his beard. The lion lay dead between us, bigger than any horse I have ever seen. Kalais landed on its side as he might have landed on a table, his great white wings fanning the hot night air.

Atalantah embraced me, and we kissed and kissed again. I think that we were both overjoyed that we were still alive. I know that I had already begun to shake. It had happened much too fast for me to be afraid while it was happening, but when it was over, I was terrified. My heart pounded and my knees shook. My mouth was dry. But oh how sweet it was to hold Atalantah and kiss her at that moment, and have her kiss me!

By the time we separated, Hahraklahs and Kalais were gone. I took a few Pukz of the dead lion. (Pukz 65-67) After that, we returned to the wedding banquet and found a lot of guests still there, with Eea-sawn and most of our crew. As we came in, Hahraklahs called out, "Did you ever see a man that would take a lion by the tail? Here he is! Look at him!"

That was a moment!

We held a meeting today, just our crew. Eeasawn called it, of course. He talked briefly about Amphiareaws of Argolis, his high reputation as a seer, famous prophecies of his that had been fulfilled, and so on. I had already heard most of it from Kaeneus, and I believe most of our crew is thoroughly familiar with Amphiareaws's abilities.

Amphiareaws himself stepped forward. He is surprisingly young, and quite handsome, but I find it hard to meet his eyes; there is poetry in them, if you will, and sometimes there is madness. There may be something else as well, a quality rarer than either, to which I can put no name. I say there may be, although I cannot be sure.

He spoke very quietly. "We had portents last night. When we were told the lion had been resurrected, I tried to find out what god had done it, and why. At that time, I knew nothing about the six-armed giants. I'll come to them presently.

"Hrea is one of the oldest gods, and one of the most important. She's the mother of Father Zeus. She's also the daughter of Earth, something we forget when we shouldn't. Lions are her sacred animals. She doesn't like it when they are driven away. She likes it even less when they are killed. She's old, as I said, and has a great deal of patience, as old women generally do. Still, patience doesn't last forever. One of us killed one of her favorite lions some time ago."

Everyone looked at Hahraklahs when Amphiareaws said this; I confess I did as well.

"That lion was nursed by Hrea's daughter Hahra at her request, and it was set in the heavens by Hahra when it died—again at her mother's request. The man who killed it changed his name to 'Hahra's Glory' to avert her wrath, as most of us know. She spared him, and her mother Hrea let the matter go, at least for the present."

Amphiareaws fell silent, studying us. His eyes lingered on Hahraklahs, as was to be expected, but lingered on me even longer. (Puk 68) I am not ashamed to say they made me acutely uncomfortable.

"King Kuzikos offended Hrea anew, hunting down and killing another of her finest animals. We arrived, and she determined to avenge herself. She called upon the giants of Hopladamus, the ancient allies who had protected her and her children from her husband." By a gesture, Amphiareaws indicated the six-armed giants we had killed.

"Their plan was to destroy the *Argo*, and with most of us gone, they anticipated little difficulty. I have no wish to offend any of you. But had only Kaeneus and Polydeukahs been present, or only Atalantah and Pilgrim, I believe they would have succeeded without much difficulty. Other gods favored us, however. Polydeukahs and Kastawr are sons of Zeus. Kaeneus is of course favored by the Sea God, as are ships generally. Who can doubt that Augah favors Atalantah? Time is Pilgrim's foe—something I saw plainly as I began to speak. But if Time detests him, other gods, including Father Zeus, may well favor him.

"Whether that is so or otherwise, our vessel was saved by the skill in arms of those five, and by their courage, too. We must not think, however, that we have won. We must make what peace we can with Hrea, and so must King Kuzikos. If we fail, we must expect disaster after disaster. Perscfonay favors our cause. This we know. Father Zeus favors it as well. But Persefonay could not oppose Hrea even if she dared, and though Father Zeus may oppose his mother in some things, there will surely be a limit to his friendship.

"Let us sacrifice and offer prayers and praise to Hrea. Let us urge the king to do likewise. If our sacrifices are fitting and our praise and prayers sincere, she may excuse our offenses."

We have sacrificed cattle and sheep in conjunction with the king. Pukz 69-74 show the entire ceremony.

I have been hoping to speak privately with Amphiareaws about Time's enmity. I know that I will not be born for many years. I know also that I have traveled the wrong way through those many years to join our crew. Was that in violation of Time's ordinances? If so, it would explain his displeasure; but if not, I must look elsewhere.

Is it lawful to forget? For I know that I have forgotten. My understanding of the matter is that knowledge carried from the future into the past is clearly out of place, and so exists only precariously and transitorily. (I cannot remember who taught me this.) My offense may lie in the things I remember, and not in the far greater number of things I have forgotten.

I remember that I was a student or a scholar.

I remember that I was to join the crew of a boat (was it this one?) upon a great voyage.

I remember that I was to talk with the Lapiths.

I remember that there is some device among my implants that takes Pukz, another implant that enables me to keep this record, and a third implant that will let me rush ahead to my own period once we have brought the ramskin back to Mount Laphysios.

Perhaps I should endeavor to forget those things. Perhaps Time would forgive me if I did.

I hope so.

We will put to sea again tomorrow morning. The past two days have been spent making ready. (Pukz 75-81) The voyage to Kolkkis should take a week or ten days. The capital, Aea, is some distance from the coast on a navigable river. Nauplios says the river will add another two days to our trip, and they will be days of hard rowing. We do not care. Call the whole time two weeks. Say we spend two more in Aea persuading the king to let us return the ramskin. The ghost of Phreexos is eager to be home, Amphiareaws says. It will board us freely. In a month we may be homeward bound, our mission a success. We are overjoyed, all of us.

Atalantah says she will ask the king's permission to hunt in his territory. If he grants it, she will go out at once. I have promised to help her.

This king is Aeeahtahs, a stern ruler and a great warrior in his youth. His queen is dead, but he has a daughter, the beautiful and learned Mahdaya. Atalantah and I agree that in a kingdom without queen or prince, this princess is certain to wield great influence, the more so in that she is reported to be a woman of ability. Atalantah will appeal to her. She will certainly be interested in the particulars of our voyage, as reported by the only woman on board. Atalantah will take every opportunity to point out that her hunt will bring credit to women everywhere, and particularly to the women of Kolkkis, of whom Mahdaya is the natural leader. Should her hunt fail, however, there will be little discredit if any—everyone acknowledges that the grups is a terribly difficult quarry. I will testify to Atalantah's prowess as a huntress. Hahraklahs offers his testimony as well;

before our expedition set out they went boar hunting together.

We are loaded—heavily loaded, in fact—with food, water, and wine, It will be hard rowing, but no one is complaining so early, and we may hope for a wind once we clear the harbor. There is talk of a rowing contest between Eeasawn and Hahraklahs.

Is it possible to be too tired to sleep? I doubt it, but I cannot sleep yet. My hands burn like fire. I splashed a little wine on them when no one was looking. They could hurt no worse, and it may prevent infection. Every muscle in my body aches.

I am splashing wine in me, as well—wine mixed with water, Half and half, which is very strong.

It I had to move to write this, it would not be written.

We put out in fair weather, but the storm came very fast. We took down the sail and unshipped the mast. It was as dark as the inside of a tomb, and the boat rolled and shipped water, and rolled again. We rowed and we bailed. Hour after hour after hour. I bailed until someone grabbed my shoulder and sat me down on the rowing bench. It was so good to sit!

I never want to touch the loom of an oar again. Never!

More wine. If I drink it so fast, will I get sick? It might be a relief, but I could not stand, much less wade out to spew. More wine.

No one knows where we are. We were cast ashore by the storm. On sand, for which we thank every god on the mountain. If it had been rocks, we would have died. The storm howled like a wolf deprived of its prey as we hauled the boat higher up. Hahraklahs broke two ropes. I know that I, and a hundred more like me, could not have broken one. (Pukz 82 and 83, infrared) Men on either side of me—I do not know who. It does not matter. Nothing does. I have to sleep.

The battle is over. We were exhausted before they came, and we are exhausted now; but we were not exhausted when we fought. (Pukz 84, infrared, and 85-88) I should write here of how miraculously these heroes revived, but the fact is that I myself revived in just the same way. I was sound asleep and too fatigued to move when Lugkeos began shouting that we were being attacked. 1 sat up, blearily angry at being awakened and in the gray dawnlight saw the ragged line of men with spears and shields charging us from the hills above the beach.

All in an instant, I was wide awake and fighting mad. I had no armor, no shield, nothing but my spear, but early in the battle I stepped on somebody's sword. I have no idea how I knew what it was, but I did, and I snatched it up and fought with my spear in my right hand and the sword in my left. My technique, if I can be said to have had one, was to attack furiously anyone who was fighting Atalantah. It was easy since she frequently took on two or three at a time. During the fighting I was much too busy to think about it, but now I wonder what those men thought when they were confronted with a breastplate having actual breasts, and glimpsed the face of a beautiful woman under her helmet.

Most have not lived to tell anyone.

What else?

Well, Eeasawn and Askalafos son of Arahs were our leaders, and good ones, too, holding everybody together and going to help wherever the fighting was hottest. Which meant that I saw very little of them; Kaeneus fought on Atalantah's left, and his swordsmanship was simply amazing. Confronted by a man with armor and a shield, he would feint so quickly that the gesture could scarcely be seen. The shield would come down, perhaps only by five centimeters. Instantly Kaeneus's point would be in his opponent's throat, and the fight would be over. He was not so much fighting men as butchering them, one after another after another.

Hahraklahs fought on my right. Spears thrust at us were caught in his left hand and snapped like so many twigs. His club smashed every shield in reach, and broke the arm that held it. We four advanced, walking upon corpses.

Oh, Zeus! Father, how could you! I have been looking at my Pukz of the battle (84-88). King Kuzikos led our attackers. I recognized him at once, and he appears in 86 and 87. Why should he welcome us as friends, then attack us when we were returned to his kingdom by the storm? The world is mad!

I will not tell Eeasawn or Hahraklahs. We have agreed not to loot the bodies until the rain stops. If the king is among the dead, someone is sure to recognize him. If he is not, let us be on our way. A protracted quarrel with these people is the last thing we require.

I hope he is still alive. I hope that very much indeed.

The king's funeral games began today. Foot races, spear-throwing, all sorts of contests. I know I cannot win, but Atalantah says I must enter several to preserve my honor, so I have. Many will enter and all but one will lose, so losing will be no disgrace.

Eeasawn is buying a chariot and a team so that he can enter the chariot race. He will sacrifice both if he wins.

Hahraklahs will throw the stone. Atalantah has entered the foot races. She has had no chance to run for weeks, and worries over it. I tried to keep up with her, but it was hopeless. She runs like the wind. Today she ran in armor to build up her legs. (Puk 89)

Kastawr has acquired a fine black stallion. Its owner declared it could not be ridden by any man alive. Kastawr bet that he could ride it, laying his place on our boat against the horse. When its owner accepted the bet, Kastawr whistled, and the horse broke its tether to come to him. We were all amazed. He whispered in its ear, and it extended its forelegs so that he could mount more easily. He rode away bareback, jumped some walls, and rode back laughing. (Pukz 90-92)

"This horse was never wild," he told its previous owner. "You merely wanted to say that you nearly had a place on the *Argo*."

The owner shook his head. "I couldn't ride him, and neither could anyone else. You've won. I concede that. But can I try him just once more, now that you've ridden him?"

Polydeukahs got angry. "You'll gallop away, and my brother will never see you again. I won't permit it."

"Well, I will," Kastawr declared. "I trust him—and I think I know a way of fetching him back."

So the previous owner mounted; the black stallion threw him at once, breaking his neck. Kastawr will enter the stallion in the horse race. He is helping Eeasawn train his chariot horses as well.

The games began with choral singing. We entered as a group, our entire crew. I was our only tenor, but I did the best I could, and our director singled me out for special praise. Atalantah gave us a mezzo-soprano, and Hahraklahs supplied a thundering bass. The judges chose another group, but we were the popular favorites. These people realize, or at any rate most of them seem to, that it was King Kuzikos's error (he mistook us for pirates) that caused his death, a death we regret as much as they do.

As music opened the games today, so music will close them. Orfius of Thrakah, who directed our chorus, will play and sing for us. All of us believe he will win.

The one stade race was run today. Atalantah won, the only woman who dared run against men. She is celebrated everywhere. I finished last. But wait—

My performance was by no means contemptible. There were three who were no more than a step or two ahead of me. That is the first thing. I paced myself poorly, I know, running too fast at first and waiting until too late to put on a final burst of speed. The others made a final effort, too, and I had not counted on that. I will know better tomorrow.

Second, I had not known the customs of these people. One is that every contestant wins a prize of some kind—armor, clothing, jewelry, or whatever. The other is that the runner who comes in last gets the best prize, provided he accepts his defeat with good humor. I got a very fine dagger of the hard, yellowish metal all armor and weapons are made of here. There is a scabbard of the same metal, and both display extraordinary workmanship. (Pukz 93-95)

Would I rather have won? Certainly. But I got the best prize as well as the jokes, and I can honestly say that I did not mind the jokes. I laughed and made jokes of my own about myself. Some of them were pretty feeble, but everybody laughed with me.

I wanted another lesson from Kaeneus, and while searching for him I came upon Idmon, looking very despondent. He tells me that when the funeral games are over, a member of our crew will be chosen by lot to be interred with King Kuzikos. Idmon knows, he says, that the fatal lot will fall upon him. He is a son of Apollawn and because he is, a seer like Amphiareaws; long before our voyage began, he learned that he would go and that he would not return alive. (Apollawn is another of their gods.) I promised Idmon that if he was in fact buried alive I would do my utmost to rescue him. He thanked me but seemed as despondent as ever when I left him. (Puk 96)

The two-stade race was run this morning, and there was wrestling this afternoon. Both were enormously exciting. The spectators were beside themselves, and who can blame them?

In the two-stade race, Atalantah remained at the starting line until the rest of us had rounded the first turn. When she began to run, the rest of us might as well have been walking.

No, we were running. Our legs pumped, we gasped for breath, and we streamed with sweat. Atalantah was riding a turbocycle. She ran effortlessly, her legs and arms mere blurs of motion. She finished first and was already accepting her prize when the second-place finisher crossed the line.

Kastawr wrestled. Wrestlers cannot strike, kick, gouge or bite, but everything else seems to be permitted. To win, one must throw one's opponent to the ground while remaining on one's feet. When both fall together, as often happens, they separate, rise, and engage again. Kastawr threw each opponent he faced, never needing more than a minute or two. (Pukz 97-100) No one threw him, nor did he fall with his opponent in any match. He won, and won as easily, I thought, as Atalantah had won the two-stade race.

I asked Hahraklahs why he had not entered. He said he used to enter these things, but he generally killed or crippled someone. He told me how he had wrestled a giant who grew stronger each time he was thrown. Eventually Hahraklahs was forced to kill him, holding him over his head and strangling him. If I had not seen the six-armed giants here, I would not have believed the story, but why not? Giants clearly exist. I have seen and fought them myself. Why is there this wish to deny them? Idmon believes he will die, and that nothing can save him. I would deny giants, and the very gods, if I were not surrounded by so many of their sons.

Atalantah says she is of purely human descent. Why did her father order her exposed to die? Surely it must have been because he knew he was not her father save in name. I asked about Augah, to whom Atalantah is so often compared. Her father was Zeus, her mother a Teetan. May not Father Zeus (as he is rightly called) have fathered another, similar, daughter by a human being? A half sister?

When I congratulated Kastawr on his win, he challenged me to a friendly fencing match, saying he wanted to see how much swordcraft I had picked up from Kaeneus. I explained that Kaeneus and I have spent most of our time on the spear.

Kastawr and I fenced with sticks and pledged ourselves not to strike the face. He won, but praised my speed and resource. Afterward he gave me a lesson and taught me a new trick, though like Kaeneus he repeated again and again that tricks are of no value to a warrior who has not mastered his art, and of small value even to him.

He made me fence left-handed, urging that my right arm might someday be wounded and useless; it has given me an idea.

Stone-throwing this morning; we will have boxing this afternoon. The stadium is a hollow surrounded by hills, as my Pukz (101-103) show. There are rings of stone seats all around the oval track on which we raced, nine tiers of them in most places. Stone-throwing, boxing, and the like take place in the grassy area surrounded by the track.

Hahraklahs was the only member of our crew to enter the stone-throwing, and it is the only event he has entered. I thought that they would measure the throws, but they do not. Two throw together, and the one who makes the shorter throw is eliminated. When all the pairs have thrown, new pairs are chosen by lot, as before. As luck would have it, Hahraklahs was in the final pair of the first pairings. He went to the farther end of the stadium and warned the spectators that his stone might fall among them, urging them to leave a clear space for it. They would not take him seriously, so he picked up one of the stones and warned them again, tossing it into the air and catching it with one hand as he spoke. They cleared a space as he had asked, though I could tell that he thought it too small. (Puk 104)

He went back to the line at the other end of the field, picking up the second stone on his way. In his huge hands they seemed scarcely larger than cheeses. When he threw, his stone sailed high into the air and fell among the spectators like a thunderbolt, smashing two limestone slabs in the ninth row. It had landed in the cleared space, but several people were cut by flying shards even so.

After seeing the boxing, I wonder whether I should have entered the spear-dueling after all. The boxers' hands are bound with leather strips. They strike mostly at the face. A bout is decided when one contestant is knocked down; but I saw men fighting still when they were half blinded by their own blood. (Pukz 105-110) Polydeukahs won easily.

Since I am to take part in the spear-dueling, I had

better describe the rules. I have not yet seen a contest, but Kaeneus has explained everything. A shield and a helmet are allowed, but no other armor. Neither the spears nor anything else (stones for example) may be thrown. First blood ends the contest, and in that way it is more humane than boxing. A contestant who kills his opponent is banished at once—he must leave the city, never to return. In general a contestant tries to fend off his opponent's spear with his shield, while trying to pink his opponent with his own spear. Wounds are almost always to the arms and legs, and are seldom deep or crippling. It is considered unsportsmanlike to strike at the feet, although it is not, strictly speaking, against the rules.

Reading over some of my earlier entries, I find I referred to a "turbocycle." Did I actually know what a turbocycle was when I wrote that? Whether I did or not, it is gone now. A cycle of turbulence? Kalais might ride turbulent winds, I suppose. No doubt he does. His father is the north wind. Or as I should say, his father is the god who governs it.

I am alone. Kleon was with me until a moment ago. He knelt before me and raised his head, and I cut his throat as he wished. He passed swiftly and with little pain. His spurting arteries drenched me in blood, but then I was already drenched with blood.

I cannot remember the name of the implant that will move me forward in time, but I hesitate to use it. (They are still shoveling dirt upon this tomb. The scrape of their shovels and the sounds of the dirt falling from them are faint, but I can hear them now

THE BEST OF 2004

that the others are dead.) Swiftly, then, before they finish and my rescuers arrive.

Eeasawn won the chariot race. (Pukz 111-114) I reached the semifinals in spear-dueling, fighting with the sword I picked up during the battle in my left hand. (Pukz 115-118)

Twice I severed a spear shaft, as Kastawr taught me. (Pukz 119 and 120) I was as surprised as my opponents. One must fight without effort, Kaeneus said, and Kaeneus was right. Forget the fear of death and the love of life. (I wish I could now.) Forget the desire to win and any hatred of the enemy. His eyes will tell you nothing if he has any skill at all. Watch his point, and not your own.

I was one of the final four contestants. (Pukz 121) Atalantah and I could not have been happier if I had won. (Pukz 122 and 123)

I have waited. I cannot say how long. Atalantah will surely come, I thought. Hahraklahs will surely come. I have eaten some of the funeral meats, and drunk some of the wine that was to cheer the king in Persefonay's shadowy realm. I hope he will forgive me.

We drew pebbles from a helmet. (Pukz 124 and 125) Mine was the black pebble (Pukz 126), the only one. No one would look at me after that.

The others (Pukz 127 and 128) were chosen by lot, too, I believe. From the king's family. From the queen's. From the city. From the palace servants. That was Kleon. He had been wine steward. Thank you, Kleon, for your good wine. They walled us in, alive.

"Hahraklahs will come for me," I told them. "Atalantah will come for me. If the tomb is guarded—"

They said it would be.

"It will not matter. They will come. Wait. You will see that I am right."

They would not wait. I had hidden the dagger I won and had brought it into the tomb with me. I showed it to them, and they asked me to kill them.

Which I did, in the end. I argued. I pleaded. But soon I consented, because they were going to take it from me. I cut their throats for them, one by one.

And now I have waited for Atalantah.

Now I have waited for Hahraklahs.

Neither has come. I slept, and sat brooding in the dark, slept, and sat brooding. And slept again, and sat brooding again. I have reread my diary, and reviewed my Pukz, seeing in some things that I had missed before. They have not come. I wonder if they tried?

How long? Is it possible to overshoot my own period? Surely not, since I could not go back to it. But I will be careful just the same. A hundred years—a mere century. Here I go!

Nothing. I have felt about for the bodies in the dark. They are bones and nothing more. The tomb remains sealed, so Atalantah never came. Nobody did. Five hundred years this time. Is that too daring? I am determined to try it.

Greece. Not that this place is called Greece, I do not think it is, but Eeasawn and the rest came from Greece. I know that. Even now the Greeks have laid siege to Ilion, the city we feared so much. Agamemnawn and Akkilleus are their leaders.

Rome rules the world, a rule of iron backed by weapons of iron. I wish I had some of their iron tools right now. The beehive of masonry that imprisons me must surely have decayed somewhat by this time, and I still have my emergency rations. I am going to try to pry loose some stones and dig my way out.

The *Mayflower* has set sail, but I am not aboard her. I was to make peace. I can remember it now—can remember it again. We imagined a cooperative society in which Englishmen and Indians might meet as friends, sharing knowledge and food. It will never happen now, unless they have sent someone else.

The tomb remains sealed. That is the chief thing and the terrible thing, for me. No antiquarian has unearthed it. King Kuzikos sleeps undisturbed. So does Kleon. Again…

This is the end. The Chronomiser has no more time to spend. This is my own period, and the tomb remains sealed; no archeologist has found it, no tomb robber. I cannot get out, and so must die. Someday someone will discover this. I hope they will be able to read it.

Good-bye. I wish that I had sailed with the Pilgrims and spoken with the Native Americans—the mission we planned for more than a year. Yet the end might have been much the same. Time is my enemy. Cronus. He would slay the gods if he could, they said, and in time he did.

Revere my bones. This hand clasped the hand of Hercules.

These bony lips kissed the daughter of a god. Do not pity me.

The bronze blade is still sharp. Still keen, after four thousand years. If I act quickly I can cut both my right wrist and my left. (Pukz 129 and 130, infrared)

Memento Mori
Joe Haldeman

Joe Haldeman is one of the most respected and best-loved writers in science fiction. Born in Oklahoma in 1943, he grew up in Puerto Rico, New Orleans, Washington DC and Alaska. He studied astronomy, mathematics and computer science at the University of Maryland, before dropping out to become a writer. Between 1967 and 1969 he served as a combat engineer with the U.S. Army in Vietnam, an experience that formed the basis for his best-known work, The Forever War. *Published in 1975 it was the first major work to be inspired by Vietnam and went on to win the Hugo, Nebula, Locus and Ditmar Awards.*

Haldeman has written a number of novels based on his experiences, including Forever Peace, Forever Free, *autobiographical novel* War Year, *and* 1968. *His other novels include* Mindbridge, *the "Worlds" trilogy (*Worlds, Worlds Apart, *and* Worlds Enough and Time), The Hemingway Hoax, The Coming, Guardian, *and* Sea Change. *Upcoming is new novel* Old Twentieth. *Haldeman's short fiction has won the Hugo Award three times, the Nebula Award twice, the World Fantasy Award once, and has been collected in* Infinite

Dreams, Dealing in Futures, and None So Blind. Joe Haldeman teaches writing at M.I.T. and lives in Florida and Massachusetts with his wife, Gay.

The story that follows is short, sharp and classic Haldeman.

She sat on the examination table, trying to hold the open back of the hospital robe closed. Everything was cold chrome and eggshell white and smelled of air conditioning and rubbing alcohol. And of her, slightly.

The man stepped in and quietly closed the door behind him. He had a stethoscope and a nametag but was wearing all black.

He spoke her name and took her cold hand. His hand was warm and dry.

He listened for a heart and then for breathing. He put the stethoscope away in a drawer and left it open.

"You have to trust me completely," he said.

"Will it hurt?"

"Not really," he said. He wasn't actually lying. The pain would not belong to her.

"But people have died from it."

"People have died *during* it. Not many," he said. "What would death be to you?"

"I don't know. John Donne said something about it."

"'Death, thou shalt die.'" He almost smiled. "Take off the robe."

She took it off and tried to fold it, then just dropped it.

He didn't react to her strange nakedness. "Lie down here." She did. "Hold still."

With his finger he traced a line from her navel to her breastbone. Her skin was gray and tight, room temperature and parchment smooth. He kept his finger pressed there, marking a place midway between her small breasts.

He painted something cold there.

"You will just barely feel this," he said. She looked away. He pressed a round fitting firmly into the bone, with a small snap.

He blotted for blood. There wasn't any. "That wasn't bad," he said. "Was it?"

She nodded, eyes tightly closed.

"How did you die?" he asked.

"I don't really know. I woke up like this."

He tapped the fitting a few times and wiggled it. "This must be your first time," he said.

"Yes; I'm only 110."

He bound her wrists and ankles to the table with metal clamps.

"Is that really necessary? I'm weak as a kitten."

"You never know," he said. "Sometimes there's a violent reaction, hysterical strength."

He put on a chain necklace with a heavy silver cross, with rubies at the stigmata points. She heard the metallic rattle and opened her eyes. "I'm not a Christian. Will it work?"

"You don't have to be a believer," he said. "And this is not an exorcism, except in some metaphorical way. Metaphorical, not metaphysical."

"Okay."

"Close your eyes again," he said. He reached into the open drawer and withdrew a black metal rod that tapered to a point. He gently inserted the point of the long black tool into the fitting in her chest. Then he moistened his fingertips with his tongue and touched her ears and then her eyes, whispering in Latin. *"Exorcizo te, omnis spiritus immunde, in nomine Dei...."*

"So why the Latin? If it's not an exorcism."

"It's a message to both our bodies," he said. "An incantation that initializes us as patient and healer."

"That sounds as bad as exorcism."

"It's science," he said. "The nanozooans that keep you immortal have gone into an emergency mode. Some imbalance has to be addressed. They can stay alive themselves, in aggregate, but they can't keep you alive, beyond oxygenating your brain.

"Together, they have the intelligence of a small child. But it's not easy to get them to do anything out of their routine. Like organic cells, most of them have a single function in terms of keeping your body going. But instead of dying when things go wrong, they go into shutdown mode, and await instruction.

"We chose the old Latin rite as an instruction code because no one will run into it accidentally. If it were some common phrase, you might overhear it accidentally, and your body would start deconstructing itself. That would be frightening."

"I don't think I understand. I'm not a technical person. What is that black thing?"

"It's like medicine in the old days," he said. "Helping your body help itself. Try to let the Latin put you to sleep."

"Okay." She closed her eyes again.

"....in nomine Domini nostri Jesu Christi eradicare, et effugare ab hoc plasmate Dei. Ipse tibi imperat, qui

te de supernis caelorum in inferiora terrae demergi praecepit. Ipse tibi imperat, qui mari, ventis, et tempestatibus imperavit..."

Her eyes snapped open, bright red, and she bucked against the restraints, howling. Lunging, she was almost able to bite him, with teeth suddenly long and sharp as fangs. He leaned into the short sword and pushed her back to the table. The door behind him banged open and two big attendants in green started in and hesitated.

"It's okay," he said. "Get the cleaning 'bot."

Her mouth overflowed with black foam and she shook her head violently, spraying the room. Yellow and gray worms came crawling out of her mouth and nose. Noxious gases rose out of her body and billowed into orange flame. Something like electricity crackled along her arms. Finally she fell limp.

He had studied her carefully through the whole seizure. Now he rotated the black tool patiently between his palms, like a man trying to start a fire, but more slowly. Green vapors rose out of her chest for a minute, and then stopped, and there was a little bright blood there. He put down the tool and found a cap in the open drawer, and closed off the fitting with it.

He undid the restraints. "Okay, guys," he said. "She's ready for clean-up." The two big men came in and carried her away, while the cleaning robot scuttled around after wriggling worms and various excreta.

She came slowly back to consciousness seated in a luke-warm shower. There was a kindly-looking matron in a candy-stripe uniform watching her. "Are you coming around?"

"Yes. Yes, I am." The dead gray skin sloughed off, and the skin underneath glowed bright healthy pink. "That didn't hurt at all."

The man in black appeared in the door. "Good thing. There'd be hell to pay."

PeriAndry's Quest

Stephen Baxter

*Stephen Baxter lives in Buckinghamshire in the British
Midlands and has been a full-time writer since 1995.
His first stories appeared in* Interzone *in the late '80s
and he has subsequently published twenty novels (two
in collaboration with Sir Arthur C. Clarke and five for
younger readers), three collections of short fiction, and
three non-fiction books. He has won the Philip K Dick,
John W. Campbell Memorial, British Science Fiction
Association, Kurd Lasswitz, Seiun, Locus, and Sidewise
awards. His latest novel,* Exultant, *moves his new
"Destiny's Children" series decisively into the far future
of his sprawling "Xeelee" future history. Upcoming is
final "Destiny's Children" novel,* Transcendent *and*
Sunstorm, *a new novel with Sir Arthur C. Clarke. His
story "Breeding Ground" was reprinted in* Science Fiction: Best of 2003.*

*The story that follows tells a tale of love distorted by
social expectation in a world where time itself is distorted.*

The funerary procession drew up in the courtyard of the great House. The blueshifted light of Old Earth's sky washed coldly down over the shuffling people, and through a screen of bubbling clouds Peri glimpsed stars sailing indifferently by.

Peri took his place at the side of his older brother, MacoFeri. His mother CuluAndry, supported by her two daughters, stood behind him. ButaFeri's hearse would be drawn by two tamed spindlings. Peri's father had been a big man in every sense, a fleshy, loud, corpulent man, and now his coffin was a great box whose weight made the axles of his hearse creak.

Despite his bulk, or perhaps because of it, Buta had always been an efficient man, and he had trained his wife, sons, and daughters in similar habits of mind. So it was that the family was ready at the head of the cortege long before the procession's untidy body, assembled from other leading citizens of Foro, had gathered in place. Their coughs and grumbles in the chill semi-dark were a counterpoint to the steady wash of the river Foo, from which the town had taken its name, as it passed through its channeled banks across the Shelf.

"It's that buffoon of a mayor who's holding everybody up," MacoFeri complained.

Culu's face closed up in distress. BoFeri, Peri's eldest sister, snapped, "Hold your tongue, Maco. It's not the time."

Maco snorted. "I have better things to do than stand around waiting for a fat oaf like that—even today." But he subsided.

As the family continued to wait in the chill, servants from the Attic moved silently among them, bearing trays of hot drinks and pastries. The servants were dressed in drab garments that seemed to blend into the muddy light, and they kept their faces averted; the servants tried to be invisible, as if their trays floated through the air by themselves.

The delay gave PeriAndry, seventeen years old, an unwelcome opportunity to sort through his confused emotions. This broad circular plaza was the courtyard of ButaFeri's grand town House. The lesser lights of the town were scattered before the cliff face beneath which Foro nestled, dissipating in the enigmatic ruins at the town's edge. In this setting the House glowed like a jewel—but ButaFeri had always counseled humility. Foro had been a much prouder place before the last Formidable Caress, he said. The "town" as it was presently constituted seemed to have been carved out of the remains of a palace, a single mighty building within a greater city. And once, ButaFeri would say, even this wide courtyard had been enclosed by a vast, vanished dome, and over this ancient floor, now crossed by the hooves of spindlings, the richer citizens of a more fortunate time had strolled in heated comfort. Buta had been a wise man, but he had shared such perspectives all too infrequently with his younger son.

Just at that moment, as PeriAndry's sense of loss was deepest, he first saw the girl.

Suddenly she was standing before him, offering him pastries baked in the shape of birds. This Attic girl was taller than most of her kind; that was the first thing that struck him. Though she wore as shapeless a garment as the others, where the cloth draped conveniently he made out the curve of her hips. She was slim; she must be no more than sixteen. Her face, turned respectfully away, was an oval, with prominent cheekbones under flawless skin. Her mouth was small, her lips full. Her coloring was dark, rather like his own family's—but this was a girl from the Attic, a place where time ran rapidly, and he wondered if her heart beat faster than his.

As his inspection continued, she looked up, uncertain. Her eyes were a complex gray-blue. When she met his gaze, she gasped, startled, and the dense hot warmth of her breath drew him helplessly.

BoFeri, his elder sister, hissed at him. "Lethe, Peri, take a pastry or let her go. You're making an exhibition of us all."

He came back to himself. BoFeri was right, of course; a funeral was no place to be ogling serving girls. Clumsily he grabbed at a pastry. The girl hurried away, back to the Elevator that would return her to her Attic above the House.

MacoFeri had seen all this, of course. Buta's eldest son sneered, "You really are a spindling's arse, Peri. She's an Attic girl. She'll burn out ten times as fast as you. She'll be an old woman before you've started shaving…"

Maco's taunting was particularly hard for Peri to take today. After the ceremony, MacoFeri and BoFeri, as eldest son and daughter, the co-heirs of ButaFeri's estate and the only recipients of his lineage name, would sit down and work out the disposition of Buta's wealth. While Bo had shown no great interest in this responsibility, Maco had made the most of his position. "You love to lord it over me, don't you?" Peri said bitterly. "Well, it won't last forever, Maco, and then we'll see."

Maco blew air through his finely chiseled nostrils. "Your pastry's going cold." He turned away.

Peri broke open the little confection. A living bird, encased in the pastry, was released. As it fluttered up into faster time the beating of its wings became a blur, and it shot out of sight. Peri tried to eat a little of the pastry, but he wasn't hungry, and he was forced to cram the remnants of it into his pocket, to more glares from his siblings.

At last the cortege was ready. Even the Mayor of Foro, a wheezing man as large as ButaFeri, was in his place. Maco and Bo shouted out their father's name and began to pace out of the courtyard. The procession followed in rough order. The spindlings, goaded by their drivers, dipped their long necks and submitted to the labor of hauling the hearse; each animal's six iron-shod hooves clattered on the worn tiles.

The road they took traced the managed banks of the river Foo. Rutted and worn, it ran for no more than half a mile from the little township at the base of the cliff and across the Shelf, and even at a respectfully funereal pace the walk would take less than half an hour. As they proceeded the roar of falling water slowly gathered.

The Shelf was a plateau, narrow here but in places miles wide, that stretched into the mist to left and right as far as Peri could see. Behind the Shelf the land rose in cliffs and banks, up towards mistier heights lost in a blueshifted glare; and before it the ground fell away towards the Lowland. Foro was just one of a number of towns scattered along the Shelf, whose rich soil, irrigated by ancient canals, was dense with farms. Peri knew that representatives of towns several days' ride away had come to see off Buta today.

At last the hearse was drawn up to the very edge of the Shelf. The family took their places beside the carriage. Peri's mother had always had a fear of falling, and her daughters clustered around her to reassure her. There was another delay as the priest tried to light her ceremonial torch in the damp air.

The edge was a sheer drop where, with a shuddering roar, the river erupted into a waterfall. Reddening as it fell, the water spread out into a great fan that dissipated into crimson mist long before it reached the remote plain far below. The Lowland itself, stretching to a redshifted horizon, was a mass of deep red, deeper than blood, the light of slow time. But here and there Peri saw flashes of a greater brilliance, a pooling of daylight. There was no sun in the sky of Old Earth; it was the glow of these evanescent ponds of pink-white light, each miles wide, reflecting from high, fast-moving clouds, which gave people day and night, and inspired their crops to grow.

Standing here amid this tremendous spectacle of water and light, and with the stars wheeling through their three-minute days above his head, Peri was rather exhilarated. He felt as if he was cupped in the palm of mighty but benevolent forces—forces that made his life and concerns seem trivial, and yet which cherished him even so. This perspective eased the pain of his father's loss.

At last the priest had her torch alight. With a murmuring of respectful words, she touched her fire to the faggots piled in the carriage around the coffin. Soon flame nuzzled at the box which confined ButaFeri.

Among the faggots were samples of Buta's papers—diaries, correspondence, other records—the bulk of which was being torched simultaneously at Buta's home. This erasure was the custom, and a comfort. When the next Formidable Caress came and civilization fell once more, everything would be lost anyhow—all painfully accumulated learning dissipated, all buildings reduced to ruin—and it was thought better to destroy these hard-won monuments now rather than leave them to the relentless workings of fate.

For long minutes, family, priest, and crowd watched the fire hopefully. They were waiting for an Effigy to appear, a glimpse of a miracle. The spindlings grazed, indifferent to human sentiment.

And in that difficult moment Peri saw the Attic girl again. Once more she moved through the crowd bearing a tray of steaming drinks, restoratives after the march from Foro. Now she was wearing a dress of some black material that clung languidly to her curves, and her dark hair was tied up so that the sweep of her neck was revealed. Peri couldn't take his eyes off her.

Maco nudged him. "She's changed, hasn't she? It's—what, an hour?—since you last saw her. But in that time she's been to the Attic and back; perhaps half a day has passed for her. And perhaps it's not just her clothes she's changed." He grinned and licked his lips. "At that age these colts can grow rapidly, their little bodies flowing like hot metal. I should

125

know. There was a girl I had, oh, three years ago—an old crone by now, no doubt—but—"

"Leave me alone, Maco."

"I happen to know her name," Maco whispered. "Not that it's any concern of yours—not while our father burns in his box."

Peri couldn't help but give him his petty victory. "Tell me."

"Lora. Much good it will do you." Maco laughed and turned away.

There was a gasp from the crowd. A cloud of pale mist burst soundlessly from the burning coffin. It hovered, tendrils and billows pulsing—and then, just for a heartbeat, it gathered itself into a form that was recognizably human, a misty shell with arms and legs, torso and head. It was ButaFeri, no doubt about that; his bulk, reproduced faithfully, was enough to confirm it.

Buta's widow was crying. "He's smiling. Can you see? Oh, how wonderful..." It was a marvelous moment. Only perhaps one in ten were granted the visitation of an Effigy at death, and nobody doubted that ButaFeri was worthy of such an envoi.

The sketch of Buta lengthened, his neck stretching like a spindling's, becoming impossibly long. Then the distorted Effigy shot up into the blueshifted sky and arced down over the edge of the cliff, hurling itself after the misty water into the flickering crimson of the plain below. It was seeking its final lodging deep in the slow-beating heart of Old Earth, where, so it was believed, something of Buta would survive even the Formidable Caresses.

The watching dignitaries broke into applause, and, the tension released, the party began to break up. Peri did his best within the bounds of propriety to search for the girl Lora, but he didn't glimpse her again that day.

MacoFeri and BoFeri, brother and sister armed with the name of their dead father, went into conclave for two days. They emerged smiling, clearly having decided the fates of their siblings, their mother and the cast of servants in the House and its Attic. But they stayed silent, to PeriAndry's fury; they would take their own sweet time about revealing their decisions to those grateful recipients. Though his uncertainty was thereby prolonged, there was nothing Peri could do about it.

Maco's first independent decision was to organize a wild spindling hunt. He proclaimed the hunt would be a final celebration of his father's life. Despite his own turmoil, Peri could hardly refuse to take part.

A party of a dozen formed up on laden spindlings and galloped off along the Shelf. It was a young group; Maco, at twenty-three, was the oldest of them. He carried a bundle of goodwill letters to hand to the mayors of the towns they passed. And he prevailed upon his youngest sister KelaAndry to keep a chart of their travels; the world wasn't yet so well known that there wasn't more to be mapped.

As they rode, the roar of the Foo diminished behind them, and Foro was soon lost in the mist. It would likely take them many days before they even glimpsed their first wild spindling. After the Formidable Caress, it was said, the spindlings had come to graze in the very ruins of the ancient, abandoned towns, and to kill or capture them had been easy; but as the settle-

127

ments at the foot of the cliff had grown again, the wild spindling herds were harder to find. But the journey itself was pleasant. The party settled into a comfortable monotony of riding, making camp, cooking, sleeping.

Of the dozen who traveled, seven were women, and there was a good deal of badinage and flirting. As early as the second night three couples had formed.

Peri had always been a vigorous, athletic type, and he had hoped that the hunt would take his mind off his own troubles. But he kept himself to himself, by day and by night.

It was not that he was inexperienced. Since the age of fifteen, his father had programmed for him a series of liaisons with local girls. The first had been pretty, compliant, and experienced, Buta's intention being to tutor his son and to build his confidence and prowess. After that had come brighter, tough-minded girls, and subtler pleasures followed as Peri learned to explore relationships with women who were his peers. Though he had formed some lasting friendships, nothing permanent had yet coalesced for him. That was only a matter of time, of course.

The trouble was that now it would not be his father selecting potential mates for him: no, from now on it would be his brother Maco, with perhaps a little advice from Bo. Perhaps the women on this very trip had been invited with that in mind—although Peri was sure Maco would sample the wares before allowing his inferior brother anywhere near them.

All this, and the lingering uncertainty over his destiny, was hard to bear. He seemed to lose confidence. He had no desire to mix with the others, had nothing to add to their bantering conversations. And as he lay in his skin sleeping bag, with the warm presence of his favorite spindling close by, Peri found his thoughts returning to Lora, the girl he had glimpsed on the day of his father's funeral.

He hadn't forgotten the surge of helpless longing he had felt as he studied her demure face, her carelessly glimpsed figure. She hadn't said a word to him, or he to her—and yet, though she was just a servant, he sensed there had been something between them, as elusive yet as real as an Effigy, there to be explored if only he had the chance. And how he longed for that chance!

In his obsessive imagining, Peri constructed a fantasy future in which he would seek out the girl. He would show her his life, perhaps fill in the inevitable gaps in her learning— though not too quickly; he rather liked the idea of impressing her with his worldliness. They would grow together, but not through any seduction or displays of wealth: their Effigies would call to each other, as the saying had it. At last they would cement their love, and much of his detailed imagining centered on *that*.

After that, well, he would present their liaison to his family as an accomplished fact. He would ride out their predictable objections, claim his inheritance, and begin his life with Lora… At that point things got a bit vague.

It was all impossible, of course. There were few hard and fast laws in Foro; the community was too young for that, but it went against all custom for a Shelf man to consort with an Attic servant, save for pure pleasure. But for Peri, a romance with Lora would bring none of the complication of his liaisons with women from the town, none of the unwelcome overlay of inheritance and familial alliance—and none of his brother's gleeful manipulation, for this would be Peri's own choice.

Elaborating this comforting fantasy made the days and nights of the hunt easier to bear. Or at least that was so before Maco, with almost preternatural acuity, figured out what he was thinking.

It was a bright morning, a couple of weeks after the hunters had set off. They were running down a small herd of wild spindlings, perhaps a score of the animals including foals. Here the Shelf was heavily water-carved, riddled with gullies and banks, and the southern cliffs were broken into round-shouldered hills. The party was galloping at top speed, their spare mounts galumphing after them, and they raised a curtain of dust that stretched across the Shelf.

The spindlings' six-legged running looked clumsy, but was surprisingly effective, a mixture of a loping run with leaps forward powered by the back pair of legs. The spindlings' six-limbed body plan was unlike those of most of Old Earth's land animals, including humans. But then, so it was said, the spindlings' ancestors had not come from Earth. Unladen, the wild spindlings were naturally faster than their hunters' mounts, but, panicking, they would soon run themselves out.

Maco rode alongside Peri. He yelled across, "So how's my little brother this morning?"

"What do you want, Maco?"

Maco was very like his father when young—dark, handsome, forceful—but already he showed traces of Buta's corpulence in his fleshy jowls. "We've been talking about you. You're keeping yourself to yourself, aren't you? Head full of dreams as usual—not that there's room in there for much else. The thing is, I think I know what you've been dreaming about. That serving girl at the funeral. *Lora.* Your tongue has been hanging out ever since..." He clenched his fist and made obscene pumping motions. "Is she keeping you warm in your sack?"

"You're disgusting," Peri said.

"Oh, don't be a hypocrite. You know, you're a good hunter, PeriAndry, but you've a lot to learn. I think you will learn, though. You're certainly going to have plenty of opportunity."

Peri hauled on his reins to bring his spindling to a clattering halt. Maco, startled, rode on a few yards before pulling up and trotting back. Their two panting beasts dipped their long dusty heads and nuzzled each other.

Peri, furious now, said, "If you're talking of my inheritance, then tell me straight. I'm tired of your games."

Maco laughed. "You're not a very good sport, little brother."

Peri clenched his fists. "I'll drag you off that nag and show you what a good sport I am."

Maco held up his hands. "All right, all right. Your inheritance, then: in fact, it's one reason I organized this hunt—to show you what I'm giving you."

"What do you mean?"

Maco swept his arm wide. "All the land you see here, across the width of the Shelf—all this belonged to Buta. Our father bought the land as a speculation from a landowner in Puul, the last town, half a day back. Right now it's got nothing much to offer but wild spindlings and scrub grass..."

"And this will be mine," Peri said slowly.

"It's a good opportunity," Maco said earnestly. "There's plenty of water in the area. Some of these gullies may actually be irrigation channels, silted up and abandoned. Good farming land—perhaps not for our generation, but certainly our children. You could establish a House, set up an Attic in those hills. You could make your mark here, Peri."

"This is a dismal place. My life will be hauling rocks and breaking dirt. And we're fourteen days' ride from home."

"*This* will be your home," Maco said. As he spoke of Peri's inheritance, Maco had seemed to grow into his role, sounding masterful, even wise. But now a brother's taunts returned, sly, digging under Peri's skin. "Perhaps you could bring your little serving girl. She can make you pastries all day and let you hump her all night..."

Peri blurted out, "It is only custom which keeps me from her."

Maco let his jaw drop. "Hey—you aren't serious about this foal, are you?"

"Why should I not be?"

Maco said harshly, "Kid, she lives in the Attic. Up there, for every day that passes for you, ten or twelve pass for her. Already months have gone by for her... I know from experience: those Attic girls are sweet, but they turn to dust in your hands, until you can't bear to look at them. Already your Lora must be ageing, that firm body sagging..."

If it had gone on a minute longer Peri might have lost control, even struck his brother, and the consequences would have been grave. But there were cries from across the plain. Peri saw that the party had backed the family of spindlings into a dry gully. Grateful for an excuse to get away, Peri spurred his mount into motion.

The spindlings, cornered, clustered together. There were more than a dozen adults, perhaps half as many colts. They seemed helpless as the hunters closed their circle.

But then four of the adults craned their necks high in the air, and their heads, three yards above their bodies, turned rapidly. With a whinny the four broke together, clattering up the gully's dusty wall. The movement was so sudden and coordinated they cut through the hunters' line and escaped.

The spindlings' long necks were an evolutionary response. On Old Earth, time passed more rapidly the higher you went, a few percent for each yard. The spindlings were not native to Earth, but they had been here more than a million years, long enough for natural selection to work. That selection had favored tall animals: with their heads held high, the longer-necked were able to think just a little faster and, over time, that margin of a few percent offered a survival advantage. Now these accelerated adults had abandoned the young, the old and feeble, but they would live to breed again.

The young hunters didn't care about evolutionary strategies. The aged adults made easy meat, and the captured youngsters could be broken and tamed. The hunters closed in, stabbing spears and ropes at the ready. Already they sang of the feast they would enjoy tonight.

But PeriAndry did not sing. He had made up his

mind. Before the night came, he would leave the party. Perhaps this desolate stretch of remote scrubland was his destiny, but he was determined to explore his dreams first—and to achieve that he had to return home.

It took Peri just ten days to ride back to Foro. Each day he drove on as long as he could, until exhaustion overtook him or his mounts.

When he got home, he spoke to his mother briefly, only to reassure her of the safety of the rest of the hunting party, then retired to his room for the night.

His sister BoFeri insisted on seeing him, though, and she briskly extracted the truth of what he intended.

"Listen to me," she said. "We're different stock, we folk of the Shelf, from the brutes of the Attic, and similar lofty slums. Time moves at a stately pace here—and that means it has had less opportunity to work on us." She prodded his chest. "*We* are the ones who are truest to our past—we are the closest to the original stock of Old Earth. The Attic folk have been warped, mutated by too much time. Think about it—those rattling hearts, the flickering of their purposeless generations! The Attic folk aren't human as we are. Not even the pretty ones like Lora. Good for tupping, yes, but nothing more..."

"I don't care what you say, Bo, or Maco."

Her face was a mixture of his mother's kindness with Maco's hard mockery. "It is adolescent to have crushes on Attic serving girls. You are evading your responsibilities, Peri; you are escaping into fantasy. You are so immature!"

"Then let me grow up in my own way."

"You don't know what you will find up there," she said, more enigmatically. "I'm afraid you will be hurt."

But he turned away, and would not respond further.

He longed to sleep, but could not. He didn't know what the next day would bring. None of his family, to his knowledge, had ever climbed the cliff before, but that was what he must do. He spent the night in a fever of anticipation, clutching at shards of the elaborate fantasy he had inflated, which Maco had so easily seen and punctured.

In the morning, with the first light, he set out in search of Lora—if not yet his lover, then the recipient of his dreams.

There were two ways up the cliff: the Elevator, and the carved stairways. The Elevator was a wooden box suspended from a mighty arrangement of ropes and pulleys, hauled up a near-vertical groove in the cliff face by a wheel system at the top. This mechanism was used to bring down the servants and the food, clean clothes and everything else the Attic folk prepared for the people of the House; and it carried up the dole of bread and meat that kept the Attic folk alive.

The servants who handled the Elevator were stocky, powerful men, their faces greasy with the animal fat they applied to their wooden pulleys and their rope. When they realized what Peri intended, they were startled and hostile. This dismayed Peri; though he had anticipated resistance from his family, somehow he hadn't considered the reaction of the Attic folk, though he had heard that among them there was a taboo about folk from the House visiting their aerial village—not that anybody had ever wanted to before.

But anyhow he had already decided to take the stairs. He imagined the simple exertion would calm him. Ignoring the handlers, without hesitation he placed his foot on the first step and began to climb, counting as he went. "One, two, three..."

These linked staircases, zigzagging off into the blue-tinged mist over his head, had been carved out of the face of the cliff itself; they were themselves a monumental piece of stonework. But the steps were very ancient and worn hollow by the passage of countless feet. The first change of direction came at fifty steps, as the staircase ducked beneath a protruding granite bluff. "Fifty-four, fifty-five, fifty-six..." The staircase was not excessively steep, but each step was tall. By the time he had reached a hundred and fifty steps, he was out of breath, and he paused.

He had climbed high above Foro. The little town, unfamiliar from this angle, was tinged by a pinkish redshift mist. He could see people coming and going, a team of spindlings hauling a cart across the courtyard before his House. He imagined he could already see the world below moving subtly slower, as if people and animals swam through some heavy, gelatinous fluid. Perhaps it wasn't the simple physical effort of these steps that tired him out, he mused, but the labor of hauling himself from slow time to fast, up into a new realm where his heart clattered like a bird's.

But he could see much more than the town. The Shelf on which he had spent his whole life seemed thin and shallow, a mere ledge on a greater terraced wall that stretched up from the Lowland to far above his head. And on the Lowland plain, those pools of daylight, miles wide, came and went. The light seemed to leap from one transient pool to another, so that clusters and strings of them would flare and glow together. It was like watching lightning spark between storm clouds. There were rhythms to the sparkings, though they were unfathomable to Peri's casual glance, compound waves of bright and dark that chased like dreams across the cortex of a planetary mind. These waves gave Old Earth a sequence of day and night, and even a kind of seasonality.

He continued his climb. "One hundred and twenty-one, one hundred and twenty-two…"

He imagined what he would say to Lora. Gasping a little, he even rehearsed little snippets of speech. "Once—or so it is said—all of Old Earth enjoyed the same flow of time, no matter how high you climbed. Some disaster has disordered things. Or perhaps our stratified time was given to us long ago for a purpose. What do you think?" Of course his quest was foolish. He didn't even know this girl. Even if he found her, could he really love her? And would his family ever allow him to attain even a fragment of his dreams? But if he didn't try he could only imagine her, up here in the Attic, ageing so terribly fast, until after just a few years he could be sure she would be dead, and lost forever. "Ah, but the origin of things hardly matters. Isn't it wonderful to know that the slow rivers of the Lowlands will still flow sluggishly long after we are dead, and that in the wheeling sky above stars explode with every breath you take?" And so on.

At the Shelf's lip, where his father's pyre still smoldered, he saw the Foo waterfall tumble into space, spreading into a crimson fan as it fell. Buta had once tried to explain to him *why* the water should spread out instead of simply falling straight down. The water, trying to force its way into the plain's glutinous deep time, was pushed out of the way by the continual tumble from behind, and so the fan formed. It was the way of things, Buta had said. The stratification of time was the key to everything on Old Earth, from the simple fall of water to the breaking of human hearts.

At last the staircase gave onto a rocky ledge. He rested, bent forward, hands on his knees, panting hard. He had counted nine hundred steps; he had surely climbed more than two hundred yards up from the Shelf. He straightened up and inspected his surroundings.

There was a kind of village here, a jumble of crude buildings of piled stone or wood. So narrow was the available strip of land that some of these dwellings or storerooms or manufactories had been built in convenient crevices in the cliff itself, connected by ladders and short staircases. This was the Attic, then, the unregarded home and workplace of the generations of servants who served the House of Feri.

He walked along the Attic's single muddy street. It was a grim, silent place. There were a few people about— some adults trudging wearily between the rough shanties, a couple of kids who watched him wide-eyed, fingers picking at noses or navels. Everybody else was at work, it seemed. If the children were at least curious, the adults were no friendlier than the Elevator workers. But there was something lacking in their stares, he thought: they were sullen rather than defiant. At the head of the Elevator the pale necks of tethered spindlings rose like flowers above weeds. They were here to turn the wheel that hauled the Elevator cage up and down. One weary animal eyed him; none of its time-enhanced smartness was any use to it here.

Near some of the huts cooking smells assailed him. Though it was only morning yet, the servants must be working on courses for that evening's dinner. The hour that separated two courses on the ground corresponded to no less than ten hours here, time enough to produce dishes of almost magical perfection, regardless of the unpromising conditions of these kitchens.

A woman emerged from a doorway, wiping a cauldron with a filthy rag. She glared at Peri. She was short, squat, with arms and hands made powerful by a lifetime's labor, and her tunic was a colorless rag. He had no idea how old she was: at least fifty, judging from the leathery crumples of her face. But her eyes were a startling blue-blue—startling for they were beautiful despite their setting, and startling for their familiarity.

He stood before her, hands open. He said, "Please—"

"You don't belong in blueshift."

"I have to find somebody."

"Go back to the red, you fool."

"Lora," he said. He drew himself up and tried to inject some command into his voice. "A girl, about sixteen. Do you know her?" He fumbled in his pocket for money. "Look, I'll make it worth your while."

The woman considered his handful of coins. She pinched one nostril and blew a gout of snot into the mud at his feet. But, ignoring the coins, wiping her hands on her filthy smock, she turned and led him further into the little settlement.

They came to the doorway of one more unremarkable shack. He heard singing, a high, soft lilt. The song seemed familiar. His breath caught in his throat at its beauty, and, unbidden, fragments of his elaborate fantasy came back to him.

He stepped to the doorway and paused, letting his eyes adapt to the gloom. The hut's single room contained a couple of sleeping pallets, a hole in the ground for a privy, and a surface for preparing food. The place was hot; a fire burned in a stone-lined grate.

A woman stood in one shadowed corner. She was ironing a shirt, he saw, wrestling at tough creases with a flat-iron; more irons were suspended over the fire. The work was obviously hard, physical. The woman stopped singing when he came in, but she kept laboring at the iron. Her eyes, when they met his, were unmistakable, unforgettable: a subtle blue-blue.

For a moment, watching her, he couldn't speak, so complex and intense were his emotions.

That could be my shirt she's ironing: that was his first thought. All his life he had been used to having his soiled clothes taken and returned as soon as he wanted, washed and folded, ironed and scented. But here was the cost, he saw now, a woman laboring for ten hours for every hour lived out by the slow-moving aristocrats below, burning up her life for his comfort. And if he lived as long as his father, he might see out *ten generations* of such ephemeral servants before he died, he realized with a shock: perhaps even more, for he could not believe that people lived terribly long here.

But she was still beautiful, he saw with relief. A year had passed for her in the month since he had seen her last, and that year showed in her; the clean profile of a woman was emerging from the softness of youth. But her face retained that quality of sculpted calm he had so prized on first glimpsing it. Now, though, there was none of the delicious startle he had seen when he had first caught her eye; in her expression he saw nothing but suspicion.

He stepped into the hut. "Lora—I know your name, but you don't know mine... Do you remember me? I saw you at my father's funeral—you served me pastries—I thought then, though we didn't speak, that something deeper than words passed between us... Ah, I babble." So he did, all his carefully prepared speeches having flown from his head. He stammered, "Please—I've come to find you."

Something stirred on one of the beds: a rustling of blankets, a sleepy gurgle. It was a baby, he realized dimly, as if his brain was working at the sluggish pace of the ground. Lora carefully set down her iron, walked to the bed and picked up the child. No wonder her song had seemed familiar: it was a lullaby.

She had a baby. Already his dreams of her purity were shattered. The child was only a few months old. In the year of her life that he had already lost, she must have conceived, come to term, delivered her child. But the conception must have happened soon after the funeral...

Or at the funeral itself.

She held out the child to him. "Your brother's," she said. They were the first words she had said to him.

He recoiled. Without thinking about it, he stumbled out of the hut. For a moment he was disoriented, uncertain which way he had come. The dreadful facts slowly worked into his awareness. *Maco*: had he really wanted her—or had he taken her simply because he could, because he could steal her from his romantic fool of a younger brother?

The old woman was here, the woman with Lora's eyes—her mother, he realized suddenly. "You mustn't be here," she growled. "You'll bring harm."

In his befuddled state, this was difficult to decode. "Look, I'm a human being as you are. You've no reason to be frightened of me... This is just superstition." But perhaps that superstition was useful for the House folk to maintain, if it kept these laboring servants trapped in their Attic. And this mother's anger was surely motivated by more than a mere taboo. He didn't understand anything, he thought with dismay.

The woman grabbed his arm and began to drag him away. Still dazed, his emotions wracked, he allowed himself to be led through the mud. There seemed to be more people about now. They all glared at him. He had the odd idea that the only thing that kept them from harming him was that it hadn't occurred to them.

He reached the Elevator. The boxy cage was laden with cereals, fruit, platters of cold meat, pressed tablecloths. It was the stuff of a breakfast, he thought dully; no matter how much time had elapsed up here, on the ground the House had yet to wake up. He took his place in the cage and waited for the descent to begin, with as much dignity as he could muster.

"... And you can go too, you with your red-tinged bastard!"

He turned. The scowling woman had dragged Lora out of her hut and had hauled her by main force to

142

the Elevator. For a second Lora resisted; holding her child, she met Peri's eyes. Perhaps if he had acted then, perhaps if he had found the right words, he could have saved her from this dreadful rejection. But there was nothing inside him, nothing left of the foolish dream he had constructed around this stranger. Shamed, he looked away. With a final shove the hard-faced woman deposited Lora inside the cage.

As they waited for the captive spindlings to start marching in their pen, Peri and Lora avoided each other's gaze, as if the other didn't even exist.

The Elevator descended. Peri imagined slow time flowing through him once more, dulling his wits. His mood became sour, claustrophobic, resentful. But even as he cowered within himself, he reflected how wrong BoFeri had been. These Attic folk couldn't be so different from the people of the Shelf after all, not if a son of the House could sire a baby by an Attic woman.

At last the Elevator cage thumped hard against the ground. The heaps of cold meat and tablecloths slumped and shifted.

Peri threw open the gate—but it was Lora who pushed out of the cage first. She ran from the Elevator, away from the House, and made for the cobbled road that led to Buta's pyre by the edge of the Shelf. Peri, moved by shame, wanted nothing more to do with her. But he followed.

At the edge of the Shelf he came on his eldest sister BoFeri. She was feeding more papers into the smoldering heap of the pyre. For all the time he had spent in the Attic, here on the Shelf it was still early morning.

The girl Lora was only a few yards away. Clutching

her baby she stood right on the edge of the Shelf and peered down at the waterfall as it poured into the red mist below. The wind pushed back her hair, and her beautiful face glistened with spray.

Bo eyed Peri. "So you went up into the Attic." She had to shout over the roar of the Foo. "And I suppose that's the girl Maco tupped so brazenly at Buta's funeral."

Peri felt as if his world was spinning off its axis. "You knew about that? Was I the only one who didn't see?"

Bo laughed, not unkindly. "Perhaps you were the one who least wanted to see. I said you would be hurt if you went up there."

"Do you think she's going to jump?"

"Of course." Bo seemed quite unconcerned.

"It's my fault she's standing there. If I hadn't gone up, they might have let her be. I have to stop her."

"No." Bo held his arm. "She has no place in the Attic now. But what will she do here, with her half-breed runt? No, it's best for all of us that it ends here. And besides, she believes she has hope."

It was a lot to take in. "Best for all of us? How? And—hope? Hope of what?"

"*Look down,* Peri. The Lowland is deep beneath us here, for the waterfall has worn a great pit. Lora believes that if she hurls herself down, she and her baby will sink deeper and deeper into slow time. She won't even reach the bottom of the pit. Her heart will stop beating, and she and her baby will be preserved like flies in amber. There have been jumpers before, you know. No doubt they are there still, arms flung out, their last despairing thoughts frozen into their brains, trapped in space and time—as dead as if they had slit their throats. Let her join that absurd flock."

Lora still hesitated at the edge, and Peri wondered if she was listening to this conversation. "And how is her death supposed to benefit us?"

BoFeri sighed. "You have to think in the long term, Peri. Maco and I enjoyed long conversations with Buta; our father was a deep thinker, you know… Have you never thought how vulnerable we are? The Attic folk live ten times as fast as we do. If they got it into their heads to defy us, they could surround us, manufacture weapons, bombard us with rocks—destroy us before we even knew what was happening. And yet that obvious revolution fails to occur. Why? Because, generation by generation, we siphon off the rebels, the defiant ones, the leaders. We allow them to destroy themselves on the points of our swords, on our guillotines or scaffolds—or simply by hurling themselves into oblivion."

Again Peri had the sense that Lora was listening to all this. "So each generation we cull the smart ones. We are selectively breeding our servants."

"It's simple husbandry," Bo said. "Remember, ten of their generations pass for each one of ours…" She studied him, her face, a broader feminine version of his own, filled with an exasperated kindness. "You're thinking this is inhuman. But it isn't—not if you look at it from the correct point of view. While the Attic folk waste their fluttering lives above, they buy us the leisure we need to think, to develop, to invent—and to make the world a better place for those who will follow us, who will build a greater civilization than we can imagine, before the next Caress comes to erase it all again.

"My poor baby brother, you have too much romance in your soul for this world! You'll learn, as I've had to. One day things will change for the better. But not yet, not yet."

Lora was watching the two of them. Deliberately she stepped back from the edge of the Shelf and approached them. "You think blueshift folk are fools."

Bo seemed shocked to silence by Lora's boldness. Even now, Peri was entranced by the blaze of light in the girl's face, the liquid quality of her voice.

"Addled by taboo, that's what you think. But *you* can't see what's in front of your nose. Look at me. Look at my coloring, my hair, my height." Her pale eyes blazed. "Three of your seasons ago, my mother was as I am now. MacoFeri took what he wanted from her. He left her to grow old, while he stayed young—but he left her *me.*"

For Peri the world seemed to swivel about her suddenly familiar face. "You're Maco's daughter? *You're my niece?*"

"And," she went on doggedly, "despite our shared blood, now MacoFeri has taken what he wanted of me in turn."

Peri clenched his fists. "His own daughter—I will kill him."

Bo murmured, "It's only the Attic. It doesn't matter what we do up there. Perhaps it's better Maco has such an outlet for his strange lusts…"

Lora clutched her baby. "You think we are too stupid to hate. But we do. Perhaps things will change sooner than you think."

She wiped the mist from her baby's face, and walked away from the cliff. Around her, the flickering light of day strengthened.

Three Days in a Border Town

Jeff VanderMeer

Jeff VanderMeer was born in Pennsylvania and grew up in New York, Florida, and the Fiji Islands. He attended the University of Florida where he studied journalism, English and history. VanderMeer founded The Ministry of Whimsy Press in 1984, began publishing stories in 1985, and attended Clarion in 1992. He is perhaps best known for his "Ambergris" series of stories (including Sturgeon Memorial Award finalist "Dradin, in Love" and World Fantasy Award winner "The Transformation of Martin Lake"), which have been collected in City of Saints and Madmen: The Book of Ambergris. *His most recent novel,* Veniss Underground, *is a World Fantasy Award nominee. Other recent books include major retrospective collection* Secret Life, *and non-fiction collection* Why Should I Cut Your Throat? *VanderMeer is also a respected editor and anthologist. His "Leviathan" series of anthologies have won the World Fantasy Award, while* The Thackery T. Lambshead Pocket Guide to Eccentric & Discredited Diseases *has been nominated for both the Hugo and World Fantasy Awards. Vander-Meer is currently working on a new novel and a new "Leviathan" anthology.*

The story that follows, set in the same far-far future as his novel Veniss Underground, *tells of one person's quest to find a moving city that few have ever seen.*

You remember the way he moved across the bedroom in the mornings, with a slow, stumbling stride. His black hair ruffled and matted. The sharp line down the middle of his back, the muscles arching out from it. The taut curve of his ass. The musky smell of him that kissed the sheets. The stutter-step as he put on his pants, the look back at you to see if you'd noticed his clumsiness. The way he stared at you sometimes before he left for work.

Day One

When you come out of the desert into the border town, you feel like a wisp of smoke rising into the cloudless sky. You're two eyes and a dry tongue. But you can't burn up; you've already passed through flame on your way to ash. Even the sweat between your breasts is ethereal, otherworldly. Not all the blue in the sky could moisten you.

The border town, as many of them did, manifested itself to you at the end of your second week in the desert. It began as a trickle of silver light off imagined metal, a suggestion of a curved sheen. You could have ignored it as false. You could have taken it for another of the desert's many tricks.

But *The Book of the City* corrected you, with an entry under "Other Towns":

> Often, you will find that these border towns, in unconscious echo of the City, are centered around a metal dome. This dome may be visible long before the rest of the town. These domes often prove to be the tops of ancient buildings long since buried beneath the sand.

Drifting closer, the blur of dome comes into focus. It is wide and high and damaged. It reflects the old building style, conforming to the realities of a lost religion, the workmanship of its metal predating the arrival of the desert.

Around the dome hunch the sand-and-rock-built houses and other structures of the typical border town. The buildings are nondescript, yellow-brown, rarely higher than three stories. Here and there, a solitary gaunt horse, some chickens, a rooting creature that resembles a pig. Above fly the sea gulls that have no sea to return to.

Every border town has given you something: information, a wound, a talisman, a trinket. At one, you bought the blank book you now call *The Book of the City*. At another, you discovered much of what is written in that book. The third took a gout of flesh from your left thigh. The fourth put a pulsing stone inside your head. When the City is near, the stone throbs and you feel the ache of a pain too distant to be of use.

It has been a long time since you felt that pain. You're beginning to think your quest is hopeless.

About the City, your book tells you this:

> There is but one City in all the world. Ever it travels across the face of the Earth, both as promise and as curse. None of us shall but glimpse It from the corner of one eye during our lifetimes. None of us shall ever fully see the Divine, in this life.
>
> It is said that border towns are ghosts of the City. If so, they are faint and tawdry ghosts, for those who have seen the City know that It has no Equal.

A preacher for a faith foreign to you quoted that from his own holy text, but you can't worship anything that has taken so much away from you.

He had green eyes and soft lips. He had calloused hands, a fiery red when he returned from work. His temper could be harsh and quick, but it never lasted. The moodiness in him he tried to keep from you. Most of the time he hid it well. The good humor, when he had it, he shared with you. It was a good life.

At the edge of town, you encounter the sentinel. He sits in his chair atop a tall tower, impassive and sand-worn, sun-soaked. An old man, wrinkled and white-bearded. You stand there and look up at him for a long time. Perhaps you recognize some part of yourself in him. Perhaps you trust him because of it.

The sentinel stares down at you, but you cannot tell if he recognizes you. There is about him an immutability, as if beneath the coursing red thirst of his flesh, the decaying arteries and veins, the heart that fights against its own inevitable stoppage, there is nothing but fissured stone. This quality comes out most vividly in the color of his eyes, which are like gray slate broken by flashes of the blue sky.

"Are you a ghost?" the sentinel asks. A half smile.

You laugh, shading your eyes against the sun. "A ghost?" There'd be more moisture in a ghost, and more hope. "I'm a traveler. Just passing through. I'm looking for the City."

You catch a hint of slippage in the sentinel's impassive features, a hint of disappointment at such an ordinary quest. Half the people of the world seek the City.

"You may enter," the sentinel says, and suddenly his gaze has shifted back to the horizon, and narrowed and deepened, no doubt due to some ancient binocular technology affixed to his eyes.

The town lies open to you. What will you make of it?

Your father didn't like him, and your mother didn't care. "He's shallow. He's not good enough for you," your father said, but you knew this wasn't true. He kept his own counsel. He got nervous in large groups. He didn't like small talk. These were all things that made him seem unapproachable at first. But, over time, they both grew to love him almost as much as you loved him.

Everyone eventually wanted to like him, even when he was unlikable. There was something about him—a presence that had nothing to do with words or mannerisms or the body. It followed him everywhere. Sometimes you think it must have been the presence of the City, the distant breath and heat of it.

In this border town, as the streets and the people on them come into focus, you realize the sentinel's question was not baseless: you are a ghost. As you reach the outskirts, the sand somehow finer and looser, you stop for a second, hands on your hips, like a runner who has reached the end of a race. Your solitude of two weeks has been broken. It's as if you have breached an invisible bubble. It's as if you have lunged through a portal into a different place. The desert is done with. You are no longer alone.

Although you might as well be. As you walk farther into the town, no one acknowledges you. These are short, dark-skinned people who wear brown or gray robes, some with a bracelet or necklace that reveals a sudden splash of color, some without. Their eyes are large and either brown or black. Small noses and thin lips, or wide noses and thick lips. Some of them have skin so black it almost looks blue. They speak to each other in the border town patois that has become the norm, but you catch a hint of other languages as well. A smell of spice encircles them. It prickles your nostrils, but not in the same way as a hint of lime. Lime would indicate the presence of the City.

For a moment, you think that perhaps your solitude has entered the town with you. That somehow you really have become a wisp of smoke. You are invisible and impervious, as unnoticeable as a speck of dust. You walk the streets watching others ignore you.

Soon, a procession dawdles down the street, slower then faster, to the beat of metal drums. As it approaches, you stand to one side. Twenty men and women, some with drums, some shouting, and in the middle four men holding a box that can only be a coffin. The coffin is as plain as the buildings in this place. The procession travels past you. Passersby do not acknowledge it. They keep walking. You cannot help feeling the oddness here. To ignore a stranger is one thing. To ignore twenty men and women banging on drums while shouting is another. Even the sea gulls rise at its approach, the chickens scattering to the side.

When the procession is thirty feet past you, an odd thing happens. The coffin opens and a man jumps out. He's naked, penis dangling like a shriveled pendulum, face painted white. He has a gray beard and wrinkled skin. He shouts once, then runs down the street, out of sight.

As he does so, the passersby stop and clap. Then they continue walking. The members of the procession recede into the side alleys. The empty coffin remains in the middle of the street.

What does it mean? Is it something you need to write down in your book? You ponder that for a moment, but decide this is not about the City. There is nothing about what you saw that involves the City.

Then dogs begin to gather at the coffin. This startles you. When they bark, you are alarmed. In *The Book of the City* it is written:

Dogs will not be fooled. They will not live silent in the presence of the City—they will bark, they will whine, they will be ill-at-ease. And the closer the City approaches, the more these symptoms will manifest themselves.

Is a piece of the City nearby? An inkling of it? Your heart beats faster. Not the source, but a tributary.

Otherwise, your head would be aching, trying to break apart.

But no: as they nose the coffin lid open, you see the red moistness of meat. There is raw meat inside the coffin for some reason. The dogs feast. You move on.

Above you, the silver dome seems even more enigmatic than before.

His name was Delorn. You were married in the summer, under the heat of the scorching sun, in front of your friends and family. You lived in a small town, centered around a true oasis and water hole. For this, your people needed a small army, to protect it against those marauders who might want to take it for themselves. You served in that army, while Delorn worked as a farmer, picking dates, planting vegetable seeds, fine-tuning the irrigation ditches.

You were in surveillance and sharpshooting. You could handle a gun as well as anyone in the town. After a time, they put you in charge of a small band of other sharpshooters. No one ever came to steal the land because the town was too well-prepared. Near the waterhole, your people had long ago found a stockpile of old weapons. Most of them worked. These weapons served as a deterrent.

Delorn and you had your own small home—three rooms that were part of his parents' compound at the edge of town. From your window, you could see the watch fires at night, along the perimeter. Some nights, you stared back at your house from that perimeter. On those nights, the air seemed especially cold as the desert receded further from the heat of the day.

When you came home, you would crawl into bed next to Delorn and bring yourself close to his body heat. He always ran hot; you could always use him as a hedge against the cold.

So you float like a ghost again. You let your footfalls be the barometer of your progress, and release the idea of solitude or no solitude.

As night approaches, you become convinced for a moment that the town is a mirage, and all the people in it. If so, you still have water in your backpack. You can make it another few days without a border town. But can you make it without company? The thirst for contact. The desiccation of only hearing your own voice.

Someone catches your eye—a messenger or courier, perhaps—weaving his way among the others like a sinuous snake, with a destination in mind. The movement is unique for a place so calm, so random.

You stand in front of him, force him to stop or run into you. He stops. You regard each other for a moment.

He is all tufts of black hair and dark skin and startling blue eyes. A pretty chin. A firm mouth. He could be thirty or forty-five. It's hard to tell. What does he think of you?

"You come out of the desert," he says in his patois, which you can just understand. "The sentinel told us. But he also said he thought you might be a ghost. You're not a ghost."

How has the sentinel told them already? But it doesn't matter...

"Could a ghost do this," you say, and pinch his cheek. You smile to reassure him.

People are staring.

He rubs his cheek. His hands are much paler than his face.

"Maybe," he says. "Ghosts from the desert can do many things."

You laugh. "Maybe you're right. Maybe I'm a ghost. But I'm a ghost who needs a room for the night. Where can I find one?"

He stares at you, appraises you. It's been a long time since anyone looked at you so intensely. You fight the urge to turn away.

Finally, he points down the street. "Walk that way two blocks. Turn left across from the bakery. Walk two more blocks. The tavern on the right has a room."

"Thank you." You touch his arm. You can't say why you do it, or why you ask him, "What do you know of the City?"

"The City?" he echoes. A wry, haunted smile. "The ghost of it passes by us, in the night." His eyes become wider, but you don't believe the thought frightens him. "Its ghost is so large it blocks the sky. It makes a sound. A sound no one can describe. Like...like sudden rain. Like..." As he searches for words, he is looking at the sky, as if imagining the City floating there, in front of him. "Like distant drum beats. Like weeping."

You're still holding his arm. Your grip is tight, but he doesn't notice.

"Thank you," you say, and release him.

As soon as you release him, it's as if the border town becomes real to you. The sounds of shoes on the street or pavement. The trickling tease of whispered conversations, loud and broad. It is a kind of illusion, of course: the border town comes alive at dusk, after the heat has left the air and before the cold creeps in.

What did the Book say about border towns?

Every border town is the same; in observing unspoken fealty to the City, it dare not replicate the City too closely. By necessity, every border town replicates its brothers and sisters. In speech. In habits. If every border town is most alive at dusk, then we may surmise that the City is most alive at dawn.

You find the tavern, pay the surly owner for a room, climb to the second floor, open the rickety wooden door, hurl your pack into a corner, and collapse on the bed with a sense of real relief. A bed, after so long in the desert, seems a ridiculous luxury, but also a necessity.

You lie there with your arms outstretched and stare at the ceiling.

What more do you know now? That the dogs in this place are uneasy. That a messenger-courier believes the ghost of the City haunts this border town. You have heard such rumors elsewhere, but never delivered with such conviction, hinting at such frequency. What does it mean?

What do you want it to mean?

You don't sleep well. You never do in enclosed spaces now, even though the desert harshness has expended your patience with open spaces, too. You keep seeing a ghost city superimposed over the border town. You see yourself flying invisible through the town, approaching ever closer to the phantom City, but becoming more and more corporeal, until by the time you reach its walls, you move right through them.

In your book, you have written down a joke that is not really a joke. A man in a bar told it to you right before he tried to grope you. It's the last thing you remember as you finally drift away.

Two men are fighting in the dust, in the sand, in the shadow of a mountain. One says the City exists. The other denies this truth. Neither has ever been there. They fight until they both die of exhaustion and thirst. Their bodies decay. Their bones reveal themselves. These bones fall in on each other. One day, the City rises over them like a new sun. But it is too late.

You loved Delorn. You loved his sly wit in the taverns, playing darts, joking with his friends. You loved the rough grace of his body. You loved the line of his jaw. You loved his hands on your breasts, between your legs. You loved the way he rubbed your back when you were sore from sentinel duty. You loved that he fought his impatience and his anger when he was with you, tried to turn them into something else. You loved him.

Day Two

On your second day in the border town, you wake from dreams of a nameless man to the sound of trumpets. Trumpets and... accordions? You sit up in bed. Your mouth feels sour. Your back is sore again.

You're ravenous. But: trumpets! The thought of any musical instrument in this place more optimistic than a drum astounds you.

You quickly dress and walk out to the main street.

The sides of the streets are crowded and noisy—where have all these people come from?—and they are no longer drab and dull. Now they wear clothing in bright greens, reds, and blues. Some of them clap. Some of them whistle. Others stomp their feet. From the edge of the crowd it is hard to see, so you push through to the front. A man claps you on the back, another nudges you. A woman actually hugs you. Are you, then, suddenly accepted?

When you reach the curbside, you encounter yet another odd funeral procession. Six men dressed in black robes carry a coffin slowly down the street. In front and back come jugglers and a few horses, decorated with thin colored paper—streamers of pale purple, green, yellow. There is a scent like oranges.

To the sides stand children with boxy holographic devices in their hands. They are using these toys to generate the ghosts of clowns, fire eaters, bearded ladies, and the like. Because the devices are very old, the holograms are patchy, ethereal, worn away at the edges. The oldest holograms, of a m'kat and a flesh-dog, are the most grainy and yet still make you shiver. Harbingers from the past. Ghosts with the very real ability to inflict harm.

But the most remarkable thing is that the man in the coffin is, again, not dead! He has been tied into the coffin this time, but is thrashing around.

"Put it back in my brain!" he screams, over and over again. "Put it back in my brain! Please. I'm begging you. Put it back!" His eyes are wide and moist, his scalp covered in a film of blood that looks like red sweat.

You stand there, stunned, and watch as the procession lurches by. Sometimes a person in the crowd will run out to the coffin, leap up, and hit the man in the head, after which he falls silent for a minute or two before resuming his agonized plea.

You watch the dogs. They growl at the man in the coffin. The coffin passes you, and you stare at the back of the man's neck as he tries to rise once again from "death." The large red circle you see there makes you forget to breathe for a moment.

You turn to the person on your left, a middle-aged man as thin as almost everyone else in town.

"What will happen to him?" you ask, hoping he will understand you.

The man leers at you. "Ghost, they will kill him and bury him out in the desert where he won't be found."

"What did he do?" you ask.

The man just stares at you for a moment, as if speaking to a child or an idiot, and then says, "He came from the outside—with a familiar."

Your body turns cold. A familiar. The taste of lime. The sudden chance. Perhaps this town does have something to add to the book. You have never seen a familiar, but an old woman gave you something her father had once written about familiars. You added it to the book:

The tube of flesh is quite prophetic. The tube of flesh, the umbilical, is inserted at the base of the neck, although sometimes inserted by mistake toward the top of the head, which can result in unexpected visions. The umbilical feeds into the central nervous system. The nerves of the familiar's umbilical wind around the nerves in the person's neck. Above the recipient, the manta ray, the familiar, rises and grows full with the knowledge of the host. It makes itself larger. It elongates. The subject goes into shock, convulses, and becomes limp. Motor control passes over to the familiar, creating a moving yet utilitarian symbiosis. The neck becomes numb. A tingling forms on the tongue, and taste of lime. There is no release from this. There should be no release from this. Broken out from their slumber, hundreds are initiated at a time, the tubes glistening and churling in the elision of the steam, the continual need. Thus fitted, all go forth in their splendid ranks. The eye of the City opens and continues to open, wider and wider, until the eye is the world.

So it says in the *Book of the City*, the elusive city, the city that is forever moving across the desert, powered by... what? The sun? The moon? The stars? The sand? What? Sometimes you despair at how thoroughly the city has eluded you.

You stand in the crowd for a long time. You let the crowd hide you, although what are you hiding from? A hurt and a longing rise in your throat. Why should that be? It's not connected to the man who will be dead soon. No, not him—another man altogether. For a long, suffocating moment you seem so far away from your goal, from what you seek, that you want to scream as the man screamed: Give me back the familiar!

In this filthy, run-down backwater border town with its insultingly enigmatic dome, where people believe in the ghost of the City and kill men for having familiars—aren't you as far from the City as you have ever been? And still, as you turn and survey your fate, does it matter? Would it have been any different walking through the desert for another week? Would you have been happier out in the Nothing, in the Nowhere, without human voices to remind you of what human voices sound like?

Once, maybe six months before, you can't remember, a man said to you: "In the desert there are many other people. You walk by them all the time. Most all of them are dead, their flesh flapping off of them like little flags." A bitterness creeps into the back of your throat.

You look up at the blue sky—a mockery of a sky that, cloudless, could never give anyone what they really need.

"We should harvest the sky," Delorn said to you once. You remember because the day was so cool. Even the sand and the dull buildings of your town looked beautiful in the light that danced its way from the sun. "We should harvest the sky," he said again, as you sat together outside of your house, drinking date wine. It was near the end of another long day. You'd had guard duty since dawn and Delorn had been harvesting the last of the summer squash. "We should take the blue right out of the sky and turn it into water. I'm sure they had ways to do that in the old days."

You laughed. "You need more than blue for that. You need water."

"Water's overrated. Just give me the blue. Bring the blue down here, and put the sand up there. At least it would be a change."

He was smiling as he said it. It was nonsense, but a comforting kind of nonsense.

He had half-turned from you as he said this, looking out at something across the desert. His face was in half-shadow. You could see only the outline of his features.

"What are you looking at?" you asked him.

"Sometimes," he said. "Sometimes I think I can see something, just on the edge, just at the lip of the horizon. A gleam. A hint of movement. A kind of... presence."

Delorn turned to you then, laughed. "It's probably just my eyes. My eyes are betraying me. They're used to summer squash and date trees and you."

"Ha!" you said, and punched him lightly on the shoulder. The warmth you felt then was not from the sun.

The rest of the day you spend searching for the familiar. It might already be dead, but even dead, it could tell you things. It could speak to you. Besides, you have never seen one. To see something is to begin to understand it. To read about something is not the same.

You try the tavern owner first, but he, with a fine grasp of how information can be dangerous, refuses to speak to you. As you leave, he mutters, "Smile. Smile sometimes."

You go back to the street where you found the courier. He isn't there. You leave. You come back. You have nothing else to do, nowhere else to go. You still have enough money left from looting desert corpses to buy supplies, to stay at the tavern for awhile if you need to. But there's nothing like rifling through the pockets of dead bodies to make you appreciate the value of money.

Besides, what is there to squander money on these days? Even the Great Sea, rumored to exist so far to the West that it is East, is little more than a lake, the rivulets that tiredly trickle down into it long since bereft of fish. It's all old, exhausted, with only the City as a rumor of better.

You come back to the same street again and again. Eventually, near dusk, you see the courier. You plant yourself in front of him again. You show him your money. He has no choice but to stop.

"There is something you did not tell me yesterday," you say.

The courier grins. He is older than you thought—now you can see the wrinkles on his face, at the sides of his eyes.

"There are many things I will not tell a ghost," he says. "And because you did not ask."

"What if I were to ask you about a familiar?"

The grin slips. He probably would have run away by now if you hadn't shown him your money.

"It's dangerous."

"I'm sure. But for me, not for you."

"For me, too."

"It's dangerous for you to be seen talking to me at all, considering," you say. "It's too late now—shouldn't you at least get paid for the risk?"

Some border towns worship the City because they fear it. Some border towns fear the City but do not worship it. You cannot read this border town. Perhaps it will be your turn for the coffin ride tomorrow. Perhaps not.

The courier says, "Come back here tomorrow morning. I might have something for you."

"Do you want money now?"

"No. I don't want to be seen taking money from you."

"Then I'll leave it in my room, 2E, at the tavern, and leave the door unlocked when I come to meet you."

He nods.

You pull aside your robe so he can see the gun in your holster.

"It doesn't use bullets," you say. "It uses something much worse."

The man blanches, melts into the crowd.

He wanted a child. You didn't. You didn't want a child because of your job and your duty.

"You just want a child because you're so used to growing things," you said, teasing him. "You just want to grow something inside of me."

He laughed, but he wasn't happy.

Nightfall. Night. Hours ticking by. You still can't sleep. Your head aches. It's such a faint ache that you can't tell if it's from the stone in your head. This time the sense of claustrophobia and danger is so great that you get dressed and walk through the empty streets until you have reached the desert. Standing there, between the town and the open spaces, it reminds you of your home.

There's a certain relief, the sweat drying on your skin although there is no wind. You welcome the chill. And the smell of sand, almost like a spice. Your headache is worse, but your surroundings are better.

You walk for a fair distance—this is what you've become most used to: walking—and then turn and look back toward the town. There is a half-moon in the sky, and so many stars you can't count them. Looking at the lights in the sky, the sporadic dotting of light from the town, you think, with a hint of sadness, that the old stories, even those told by a holographic ghost, must be wrong. *If humans had made it to the stars we would not have come to this. If we had gone there, our collapse could not have been so complete.*

You fall asleep, then, or so you believe. Perhaps your headache makes you pass out. When you wake, it is still night, but your head pounds, and the stars are moving. At least, that is your first thought: The stars are moving. Then you realize there are too many lights. Then, with a sharp intake of breath, you know that you are looking at the ghost of the City.

For you have seen the City before, if only once and not for long, and you know it like you know your home. This sudden apparition that slides between you and the stars, that seems to envelop the border town, looks both like and unlike the City.

There were underground caverns near where you grew up. These caves led to an underground aquifer. In those caves, you and your friends would sometimes find phosphorescent jellyfish in the saltish water. By their light you would sometimes find and catch fish.

They were like miniature lighted domes, their bodies translucent, so that you could see every detail of their organs, the lines of their boneless bodies.

This "City" you now see is much like that. You can see into and through it. You can examine every detail. Like a phantom. Like a wraith. Familiars and people transparent, gardens and walls, in so much detail it overwhelms you. The City-ghost rises over the border town ponderously but makes no sound. The edges of this vision, the edges of the City, crackle and spark, discharging energy. You can smell the overpowering scent of lime. You can taste it on your mouth, and your skull is filled with a hundred hammers as your headache spins out of control. You think you are screaming. You think you are throwing up.

The City sways back and forth, covering the same ground.

You start to run. You are running back toward the border town, toward this Apparition. And then, just as suddenly as it appeared, the City puts on speed—a great rush and flex of speed—and it either disappears into the distance or it disintegrates or…you cannot imagine what it might or might not have done.

Sometimes you argued because he was sick of being a farmer, because he was restless, because you were both human.

"I could do what you do," he said once. "I could join your team."

"No, you couldn't," you said. "You don't have the right kind of discipline."

He looked hurt.

"Just like I don't have the skills to do what you do," you said.

They seemed like little arguments at the time. They seemed like nothing.

When you reach the outskirts of the border town, you find no great commotion, no awe-struck hubbub. The streets are still empty. You spy a stray cat skulking around a corner. A nighthawk worships a lamppost.

You approach the sentinel's chair. He peers down at you from the raised platform. It's the same sentinel from the other day.

"Did you see it?" you ask him.

"See what?" he replies.

"The City! The phantom City."

"Yes. As usual."

"As usual?"

"Yes. Every two weeks, at the same time."

"What do you see? From inside the town."

He frowns. "See? A hologram, invading the streets. Just an old ghost. A molted skin—like the snakes out in the desert."

Your curiosity is aroused. You hardly know this man, but something about his dismissal of such a marvelous sight bothers you.

"Why aren't you excited?" you ask him.

A sad smile. "Should I be? It means nothing." He stands on his platform, looking down. "It doesn't bring me any closer to the City."

In his gaze, you see a hurt and a yearning that is mirrored in your own. You mistook his look when you first met him. He wasn't disappointed in you, but in himself.

Maybe all reasons are the same when examined closely.

You walk home through a border town so empty it might as well be a ghost town itself. No one to document the coming of the wraith-City. How had it manifested? For an instant, had the dome of the border town and the dome of the City been superimposed as one?

When people begin to ignore a miracle, does that mean it is no longer miraculous?

A man stands in your room. You put out your gun. It's the courier. He has a sad look on his face. Startled, you draw back, but he puts out a hand in a gesture of reassurance, and you're so tired you choose to believe it.

"It is not what you think," he says. "It's not what you think."

"What is it then?"

"I need a place. I need a place."

In his look you see a hundred reasons and explanations. But you don't need any of them. This is a man you will never know, that you will never come to know. It does not matter what his reasons are. Lonely, tired, lost. It's all the same.

"What's your name?" you ask.

"Benkaad," he tells you.

He sleeps on the bed with you, facing away from you. His skin is so dark, glinting black in the dim light from the street. His breathing is rapid and short. After a time, you put your arm around his chest. Sometime during the night, you reverse positions and he is curled at your back, his arm around your stomach.

It is innocent. It is different. It's not like before.

Once, you had to shoot a scavenger, a rogue—a man who would have killed someone in your community. He'd gone bad in the head. It was clear from his ranting. He had a gun. He came out of the desert like a curse or a blight. Had he been crazy before he went into the desert? You will never know. But he staggered toward the guard post, aiming his gun at you, and you had to shoot him. Because you let him get too close—you shouting at him to drop his weapon—you had to shoot to kill.

The man lay there, covered in sand and blood, arms crumpled underneath him. You stood there for several minutes as your team ran up to you. You stood there and looked out at the desert, wondering what else might come out of it.

They told Delorn, and he came to take you home, you dazed, staring but not seeing. Once inside, Delorn took off all of your clothes. He placed you in the tiny bathtub. He used precious water to calm you, massaging your skin. He rubbed your head. He cleaned the salt and sweat from your body. He toweled you dry. And then he laid you down on the bed and he made love to you.

You had been far away, watching the dead man in the sand. But Delorn's tongue on your skin brought you back to yourself. When you came, it was in a rush, like the water in the bath. It was a luxury he had given to you.

You remember looking at him as if he were unreal. He was selfless in that moment. He was a part of you.

Day Three

In the morning, Benkaad is gone, leaving just the imprint of his body on your bed. The money you promised him has been taken from what you left in your bag. You try to remember why you let him sleep next to you, but the thought behind the impulse has fled.

Out into the sun, past the tavern keeper, cursing at someone. The day is hot, almost oppressive. You can walk the desert for two weeks without faltering, but after two days of a bed, you've already lost some of your toughness. The sun finds you. It makes you uncomfortable.

Benkaad waits for you on the street. As soon as he sees you, he drops a piece of paper and walks away. His gaze lingers on you before he's lost around a corner, as if to remember you, for a time at least.

You pick up the paper. Unfold it. It is a map, showing where to find the familiar. A contact name and a password. Is it a trap? Perhaps, but you don't care. You have no choice.

You have woken refreshed for the first time in over a year, and somehow that makes you feel guilty as you follow the map's instructions—through a warren of streets you would not have believed could exist in so small a town, each one forgotten as soon as you leave it.

As you walk, a sense of calm settles over you. You're calm because everything you face is inevitable.

You have no choice. This is the missing piece of the Book. This replaces the Book. You're afraid, yes, but also past caring.

Sometimes there's only one chance.

Finally, an hour later, you're there. You knock on a metal door in a run-down section of town. The directions had been needlessly complex, unless Benkaad meant to delay you.

You've got one hand on your gun as the door opens. An old woman stands there. You give her the password. She opens the door a little wider and you slip inside.

"Do you have the money?" she asks.

"Money? I paid the one who led me here."

"You need more money to see it and connect to it."

A surge of adrenalin. It is here. A familiar.

Two men appear behind the woman. Both are armed with bullet-fed guns. Ancient.

You walk past them to the room that holds the familiar.

"Only half an hour," the one man says. "It's dying. Any more and it'll be too much for you, and for it."

You stare past him. Someone is just finishing up with the familiar. He has detached from its umbilical, but there is still a look of stupefied wonder on his face.

The umbilical is capped by an odd cylindrical devicc.

"What's that?" you ask the old woman.

"The filter. If that thing gets all the way into your mind, you'd never get free."

"Strip," one of the men says.

"Strip? Why?"

"Just strip. We need to search you," the man says, and raises his gun.

"Strip?" you say again.

The old woman looks away.

That's when you shoot the two men, the old woman, and the customer. For some reason, none of them seemed to expect it. They fall with the same look of startled surprise on their faces.

You don't know if they'll wake up; the gun is unpredictable. Hopefully they will, but you don't much care at the moment. It surprises you that you don't care.

Your head is throbbing.

You enter the room.

There, in front of you, lies the familiar, its wings fluttering on the bed. It seems to both press down into the bed and try to float above it. Its wings are ragged. Instead of being black, it is dead white. It looks as if it has been drifting, content to travel wherever the air might take it.

You take the umbilical and bring it around to the back of your head. The umbilical slides through the filter. You feel a weak pressure, a probing presence, then a firm, more assured grasp, a prickling—then a wet piercing. The taste of lime enters your mouth. A scratchiness at the back of your throat. You gasp, take two deep breaths, and then you hear a voice inside your head.

You are different.

"Maybe," you say. "Maybe I'm the same."

I don't think you are the same. I think you are different. I think that you know why.

"Because I've actually seen the City."

No. Because of why you want to find it.

"Can you take me there?"

Do you know what you are asking?

"I attached myself to you."

True. But there is a filter weakening our connection.

"Yes, but that might change."

You don't know how I came to be here, do you?

"No."

I was cast out. I was defective. You see my color. You see my wings. I was created this way. I was meant to die in the desert. I let a man I found attach himself so that would not happen. Eventually, it killed him.

"I'm stronger than that."

Maybe. Maybe not.

"Do you know your way back to the City?"

In a way. I can feel the City. I can feel it sometimes, out there, moving...

"I have a piece of the City in my head."

I know. I can sense it. But it may not help. And how do you plan to leave this place? Do you know that even with the filter, in a short time, it will be too late to unhook yourself from me. Is that what you want? Do you want true symbiosis?

Is it what you want? You don't know. It seems a form of madness, to want this, to reach for it, but there is a passage in the *Book of the City* that reads:

Take whatever the City gives you. If it gives you a cane, take it and use it. If it gives you dust, take the dust and make a house of it. If it gives you wisdom, take wisdom. The City does not give gifts lightly. It is not that kind of City.

You're crying now. You've been strong for so long you've forgotten the relief of being weak. What if it's the wrong choice? What if you never get him back even after all of this?

Are you sure? the familiar says inside your mind. *It is different than connecting for a short while. It is a surrender of self.*

You wipe the tears from your face. You remember the smell of Delorn, the feel of his body, his laugh. The smell of lime is crushing.

"Yes," *I'm sure,* you say, and you find that it is true, even as you disconnect the filter, even as you begin to feel the tendrils of unfamiliar thoughts intertwining with your own thoughts.

You have chosen.

The most secret part of the *Book of the City*, which you have never reread, is hidden on the back pages. It reads:

I lived in a border town called Haart, where I served as a border guard and my husband Delorn worked as a farmer at the oasis that sustained our people. We loved each other. I still love him. One night, he was taken from me, and that is why I keep this book. One night, I woke and he was not beside me. At first, I thought he had gotten up for a glass of water or to use the bathroom. But I soon discovered he was not in the house. I searched every room. Then I saw the light, through the kitchen window, saw the light, flooding the darkness, and heard the quiet breath of the City. I ran outside. There it lay, in all its awful glory, just to the west. And there were the imprints of my husband's boots, illumined by the City—heading toward it. The City was spinning and hovering and gliding back and forth across the desert. Then it was gone.

In the morning, we followed my husband's tracks out into the desert. At a certain point, they stopped. The boot prints were gone. Delorn was gone. The City was gone. It was just me, screaming and shrieking, and the last set of tracks, and the friends who had come out with me.

And every day since I have had a question buried in my head along with my love for my husband.

Did he choose the City over me? Did he go because he wanted to, or because It called to him and he had no choice?

At dusk, you escape, the familiar wrapped around your body, under the robes you've stolen from a dead man. Your collar is high to disguise the place where it entered you and you entered it. Out into the desert, where, when the border town is far distant, you can release him from beneath your robes and he, unfurling, can rise above you, your familiar, crippled wings beating, and together you can seek out the City.

It is a cool night, and a long night, and you will be miles away by dawn.

Elector

Charles Stross

Charles Stross has been one of the revelations of the new decade and is fast becoming one of the most important writers working in science fiction today. His first stories appeared in the early '90s and he attracted wider attention with the 2001 Theodore Sturgeon Memorial Award nominee "Antibodies" and novella "A Colder War." His major work to date has been the "Accelerando" sequence of stories, which detail the lives of three generations in a family making its way through a Vingean Singularity. Individually, the stories have been nominated for the Hugo, Nebula, British Science Fiction, and Theodore Sturgeon Memorial awards. A novel incorporating all nine "Accelerando" stories will appear later this year. Stross's first story collection Toast and Other Rusted Futures *was published in 2002, and first novel and Hugo nominee* Singularity Sky *appeared in 2003. Almost overwhelmingly prolific, Stross also published novels* The Atrocity Archives, Iron Sunrise *(a sequel to* Singularity Sky*) and* The Family Trade *in 2004. Upcoming are novels* The Hidden Family, The Clan Corporate, *and* Glasshouse. *His story "Flowers from Alice" (written with Cory*

Doctorow) was reprinted in Science Fiction: Best of 2003.

The story that follows is the penultimate tale in the "Accelerando" cycle. While a familiarity with the earlier stories helps, it's not essential to appreciate this extraordinary piece of science fiction.

Sirhan walks, shrouded in isolation, through the crowds gathered for the festival. The only people who see him are the chattering ghosts of dead politicians and writers, deported from the inner system by order of the Vile Offspring. The great terraforming project is nearly complete, the festival planet dressed for a jubilee that will last almost twenty of its years—four pre-singularity lifetimes—before the Demolition. The green and pleasant plain stretches toward a horizon a thousand kilometers away, beneath a lemon-yellow sky. The air smells faintly of ammonia and the big spaces are full of small ideas: for this is the last human planet in the solar system.

"Excuse me, are you real?" someone asks him in American-accented English.

It takes a moment or two for Sirhan to disengage from his introspection and realize that he's being spoken to. "What?" he asks, slightly puzzled. Wiry and pale, Sirhan wears the robes of a Berber goatherd on his body and the numinous halo of a utility fog-bank above his head: in his abstraction, he vaguely resembles a saintly shepherd in a post-singularity nativity play. "I say, what?" Outrage simmers at the back of his mind—*is nowhere private?*—but, as he turns, he sees that one of the ghost pods has split lengthwise across its white mushroom-like crown, spilling a trickle of left-over construction fluid and a completely hairless, slightly bemused-looking anglo male who wears an expression of profound surprise.

"I can't find my implants," the anglo male says, shaking his head. "But I'm really *here*, aren't I? Incarnate?" He glances round at the other pods. "This isn't a sim."

Sirhan sighs—*another exile*—and sends forth a daemon to interrogate the ghost pod's abstract interface. It doesn't tell him much—unlike most of the resurrectees, this one seems to be undocumented. "You've been dead. Now you're alive. I *suppose* that means you're now almost as real as I am. What else do you need to know?"

"When is—" The newcomer stops. "Can you direct me to the processing center?" He asks carefully. "I'm disoriented."

Sirhan is surprised—most immigrants take a lot longer to figure that out. "Did you die recently?" he asks.

"I'm not sure I died at all." The newcomer rubs his bald head, looking puzzled. "Hey, no jacks!" He shrugs, exasperated. "Look, the processing center…?"

"Over there." Sirhan gestures at the monumental mass of the Boston Museum of Science (shipped all the way from Earth a couple of decades ago to save it from the demolition of the inner system). "My mother runs it." He smiles thinly.

"Your mother—" the newly resurrected immigrant stares at him intensely, then blinks. "Holy shit." He takes a step toward Sirhan. "Wow, you're—"

Sirhan recoils and snaps his fingers. The thin trail of vaporous cloud that has been following him all this time, shielding his shaven pate from the diffuse red glow of the swarming shells of orbital nanocomputers that have replaced the inner planets, extrudes a staff of hazy blue mist that stretches down from the air and slams together in his hand like a quarterstaff spun from bubbles. "Are you threatening me, sir?" he asks, deceptively mildly.

"I—" the newcomer stops dead. Then he throws back his head and laughs. "You must be Sirhan. You take after your grandmother, kid."

"Kid?" Sirhan bristles. "Who do you think—" A horrible thought occurs to him. "Oh. Oh dear." A wash of adrenalin drenches him in warm sweat. "I do believe we've met, in a manner of speaking...." *Oh boy, this is going to upset* so *many applecarts*, he realizes, spinning off a ghost to think about the matter. If grandfather is back, the implications are enormous.

The naked newcomer nods, grinning at some private joke. "And now I'm human again." He runs his hands down his ribs, pauses, and glances at Sirhan owlishly. "Um. I didn't mean to frighten you. But I don't suppose you could find your aged grandfather something to wear?"

Sirhan sighs and points his staff straight up at the sky. The rings are edge-on, for the lillypad continent floats above an ocean of cold gas along Saturn's equator, and they glitter like a ruby laser beam slashed across the sky. "Let there be aerogel."

A cloud of whispy soap-bubble congeals in a cone shape above the newly resurrected ancient and drops over him, forming a kaftan. "Thanks," he says. He looks round, twisting his neck, then winces. "Damn, that *hurt*. Ouch. I need to get myself a set of implants."

"They can sort you out in the processing center. It's in the basement in the west wing. They'll give you something more permanent to wear, too." Sirhan peers at him. "Your face—" he pages through rarely used memories. Yes, it's Manfred Macx, as he looked in the early years of the last century. As he looked around the time mother-not was born. There's something positively indecent about meeting your own grandfather in the full flush of youth. "Are you sure you haven't been messing with your phenotype?" he asks suspiciously.

"No, this is what I used to look like. I think. Back in the naked ape again, after all these years as an emergent function of a flock of passenger pigeons." His grandfather smirks. "What's your mother going to say?"

"I really don't know—" Sirhan shakes his head. "Come on, let's get you to immigrant processing. You're sure you're not just a historical simulation?"

The place is already heaving with the re-simulated. Just why the Vile Offspring seem to feel it's necessary to apply valuable exaquops to the job of deriving accurate simulations of dead humans—outrageously accurate simulations of long-dead lives, annealed until their written corpus matches that inherited from the pre-singularity era in the form of chicken scratchings on mashed tree pulp—much less beaming them at the refugee camps on Saturn—is beyond Sirhan's ken: but he wishes they'd stop.

"Just a couple of days ago, I crapped on your lawn. Hope you don't mind." Manfred cocks his head to one side and stares at Sirhan with beady eyes. "Actually, I'm here because of the upcoming election. It's got the potential to turn into a major crisis point, and I figured Amber would need me around."

"Well you'd better come on in, then," Sirhan says resignedly as he climbs the steps, enters the foyer, and leads his turbulent grandfather into the foggy haze of utility nanomachines that fill the building.

He can't wait to see what his mother will do when she meets her father in the flesh, after all this time.

Welcome to Saturn, your new home world. This FAQ (Frequently Asked Questions) memeplex is designed to orient you and explain the following:

How you got here

Where "here" is

Things you should avoid doing

Things you might want to do as soon as possible

Where to go for more information

If you are remembering this presentation, you are probably *re-simulated*. This is not the same as being *resurrected*. You may remember dying. Do not worry: like all your other memories, it is a fabrication. In fact, this is the first time you have ever been alive. (Exception: if you died after the *singularity* you may be a genuine *resurrectee*. In which case, why are you reading this FAQ?)

How you got here: the center of the solar system—Mercury, Venus, Earth's Moon, Mars, the asteroid belt, and Jupiter—have been dismantled, or are being dismantled, by weakly godlike intelligences. [NB: monotheistic clergy and Europeans who remember living prior to 1600, see alternative

memeplex *"in the beginning."*] A weakly godlike
intelligence is not a supernatural agency, but the
product of a highly advanced society that learned how
to artificially create souls [late twentieth century:
software] and translate human minds into souls and
vice versa. [Core concepts: human beings all have
souls. Souls are software objects. Software is not
immortal.]

Some of the weakly godlike intelligences appear to
cultivate an interest in their human antecedents—for
whatever reason is not known. (Possibilities include
the study of history through horticulture, entertainment through live-action roleplaying, revenge, and
economic forgery.) While no definitive analysis is
possible, all the re-simulated persons to date exhibit
certain common characteristics: they are all based on
well-documented historical persons, their memories
show suspicious gaps [see: *smoke and mirrors*], and
they are ignorant of or predate the *singularity* [see:
Turing Oracle, Vinge Catastrophe].

It is believed that the weakly godlike agencies have
created you as a vehicle for the introspective study of
your historical antecedent by backward-chaining from
your corpus of documented works, and the back-
projected genome derived from your collateral descendants, to generate an abstract description of your
computational state vector. This technique is
extremely intensive [see: *expTime-complete algorithms,
Turing Oracle, time travel, industrial magic*] but mar-
ginally plausible in the absence of supernatural
explanations.

After experiencing your life, the weakly godlike
agencies have expelled you. For reasons unknown,

they chose to do this by transmitting your upload state and genome/proteome complex to receivers owned and operated by a consortium of charities based on Saturn. These charities have provided for your basic needs, including the body you now occupy.

In summary: you are a *reconstruction* of someone who lived and died a long time ago, not a *reincarnation*. You have no intrinsic moral right to the identity you believe to be your own, and an extensive body of case law states that you do not inherit your antecedent's possessions. Other than that, you are a free individual.

Note that *fictional re-simulation* is strictly forbidden. If you have reason to believe that you may be a fictional character, you must contact the City *immediately*. [See: *James Bond, Spider Jerusalem.*] Failure to comply is a *felony*.

Where are you? You are on Saturn. Saturn is a gas giant planet 120,500 kilometers in diameter, located 1.5 billion kilometers from Earth's sun. [NB: Europeans who remember living prior to 1580, see alternative memeplex *"the flat earth—not."*] Saturn has been partially terraformed by *posthuman* emigrants from Earth and Jupiter orbit: the ground beneath your feet is, in reality, the floor of a hydrogen balloon the size of a continent, floating in Saturn's upper atmosphere. [NB: Europeans who remember living prior to 1790, internalize the supplementary memeplex: *"the Brothers Mongolfier."*] The balloon is very safe, but mining activities and the use of ballistic weapons are strongly deprecated because the air outside is unbreathable and extremely cold.

The society you have been instantiated in is *extremely wealthy* within the scope of Economics 1.0, the value-transfer system developed by human beings during and after your own time. Money exists, and is used for the usual range of goods and services, but the basics—food, water, air, power, off-the-shelf clothing, housing, historical entertainment, and monster trucks—are *free*. An implicit social contract dictates that in return for access to these facilities, you obey certain laws.

If you wish to opt out of this social contract, be advised that other worlds may run *Economics 2.0* or subsequent releases. These value-transfer systems are more efficient—hence wealthier—than Economics 1.0, but true participation in Economics 2.0 is not possible without dehumanizing cognitive surgery. Thus, in *absolute* terms, although this society is richer than any you have ever heard of, it is also a poverty-stricken backwater compared to its neighbors.

Things you should avoid doing: Many activities that have been classified as crimes in other societies are legal here. These include but are not limited to: acts of worship, art, sex, violence, communication, or commerce between consenting competent sapients of any species, except where such acts transgress the list of prohibitions below. [See additional memeplex: *competence defined*.]

Some activities are prohibited here, but may have been legal in your previous experience. These include: willful deprivation of ability to consent [see: *slavery*], interference in the absence of consent [see: *minors, legal status of*], formation of limited-liability companies [see: *singularity*], and invasion of defended privacy [see: *The Slug, Cognitive Pyramid Schemes, Brain Hacking, Thompson Trust Exploit*].

Some activities unfamiliar to you are highly illegal and should be scrupulously avoided. These include: possession of nuclear weapons, possession of unlimited autonomous replicators [see: *gray goo*], coercive assimilationism [see: *borganism, aggressive*], coercive halting of Turing-equivalent personalities [see: *Basilisks*], and applied theological engineering [see: *God Bothering*].

Some activities superficially familiar to you are merely stupid and should be avoided for your safety, although they are not illegal as such. These include: giving your bank account details to the son of the Nigerian Minister of Finance, buying title to bridges, skyscrapers, spacecraft, planets, or other real assets, murder, selling your identity, and entering into financial contracts with entities running Economics 2.0 or higher.

Things you should do as soon as possible: Many material artifacts you may consider essential to life are freely available—just ask the city, and it will grow you clothes, a house, food, or other basic essentials. Note, however, that the library of public domain structure templates is of necessity restrictive, and does not contain items that are highly fashionable or that remain in copyright. Nor will the city provide you with replicators, weapons, sexual favors, slaves, or zombies.

You are advised to register as a citizen as soon as possible. If the individual you are a resimulation of can be confirmed dead, you may adopt their name but not—in law—any lien or claim on their property, contracts, or descendants. You register as a citizen by asking the city to register you; the process is painless and typically complete within four hours. Unless you are registered, your legal status as a sapient organism may be challenged. The ability to request citizenship rights is one of the legal tests for sapience, and failure to comply may place you in legal jeopardy. You can renounce your citizenship whenever you wish: this may be desirable if you emigrate to another polity.

While many things are free, it is highly likely that you posses no employable skills, and therefore no way of earning money with which to purchase unfree items. The pace of change in the past century has rendered almost all skills you may have learned obsolete [see: *singularity*]. However, due to the rapid pace of change, many cooperatives, trusts, and guilds offer on-the-job training or educational loans.

Your ability to learn depends on your ability to take information in the format in which it is offered. *Implants* are frequently used to provide a direct link between your brain and the intelligent machines that surround it. A basic core implant set is available on request from the city. [See: *implant security, firewall, wetware*.]

Your health is probably good if you have just been reinstantiated, and is likely to remain good for some time. Most diseases are curable, and, in event of an incurable ailment or injury a new body may be provided—for a fee. (In event of your murder, you will be furnished with a new body at the expense of your killer.) If you have any pre-existing medical conditions or handicaps, consult the city.

The city is an agoric-annealing participatory democracy with a limited-liability constitution. Its current executive agency is a weakly godlike intelligence that chooses to associate with human-equivalent intelligences: this agency is colloquially known as "Hello Kitty," "Beautiful Cat," or "Aineko," and may manifest itself in a variety of physical avatars if corporeal interaction is desired. (Prior to the arrival of "Hello Kitty," the city used a variety of human-designed expert systems that provided sub-optimal performance.)

The city's mission statement is to provide a mediatory environment for human-equivalent intelligences and to preserve same in the face of external aggression. Citizens are encouraged to participate in the ongoing political processes of determining such responses. Citizens also have a duty to serve on a jury if called (including senatorial service), and to defend the city.

Where to go for further information: Until you have registered as a citizen and obtained basic implants, all further questions should be directed to the city. Once you have learned to use your implants, you will not need to ask this question.

There's a market specializing in clothing and fashion accessories about fifty kilometers away from the transplanted museum where Sirhan's mother lives, at a transportation nexus between three lillypad habitats where tube trains intersect in a huge maglev cloverleaf. The market is crowded with strange and spectacular visuals, algorithms unfolding in faster-than-real time before the candy-striped awnings of tents. Domed yurts belch aromatic smoke from crude fire-places—what *is* it about hairless primates and their tendency toward pyromania?—around the feet of diamond-walled groundscrapers that pace carefully across the smart roads of the city. The crowds are variegated and wildly mixed, immigrants from every continent shopping and haggling, and, in a few cases, getting out of their skull on strange substances on the pavements in front of giant snail-shelled shibeens and squat bunkers made of thin layers of concrete sprayed over soap-bubble aerogel. There are no automobiles here, but a bewildering range of personal transport gadgets, from gyro-stabilized pogo sticks and segways to kettenkrads and spiderpalanquins, jostle for space with pedestrians and animals.

Two women stop outside what, in a previous century, might have been the store window of a fashion boutique: the younger one (blonde, with her hair bound up in elaborate cornrows, wearing black leggings and a long black leather jacket over a camouflage T) points to an elaborately retro dress. "Wouldn't my bum look big in that?" she asks, doubtfully.

"Ma cherie, you have but to try it—" The other woman (tall, wearing a pin-striped man's business suit from a previous century) flicks a thought at the window and the mannequin morphs, sprouting the younger woman's head, aping her posture and expression.

"I missed out on the authentic retail experience, you know? It still feels weird to be back somewhere with *shops*. 'S what comes of living off libraries of public domain designs for too long." Amber twists her hips,

190

experimenting. "You get out of the habit of *foraging*. I don't know about this retro thing at all. The Victorian vote isn't critical, is it…?" She trails off.

"You are a twenty-first century platform selling to electors re-simulated and incarnated from the Gilded Age. And yes, a bustle your derriere does enhance. But—" Annette looks thoughtful.

"Hmm." Amber frowns, and the shop window dummy turns and waggles its hips at her, sending tiers of skirts swishing across the floor. Her frown deepens. "If we're really going to go *through* with this election shit, it's not just the resimulant voters I need to convince, but the contemporaries, and that's a matter of substance, not image. They've lived through too much media warfare. They're immune to any semiotic payload short of an active cognitive attack. If I send out partials to canvass them that look as if I'm trying to push buttons—"

"—They will listen to your message and nothing you wear or say will sway them. Don't worry about them, ma cherie. The naive re-simulated are another matter, and perhaps might be swayed. This your first venture into democracy is, in how many years? Your privacy, she is an illusion now. The question is, *what* image will you project? People will listen to you only once you gain their attention. Also, the swing voters you must reach, they are future-shocked, timid. Your platform is radical, should you not project a comfortably conservative image?"

Amber pulls a face, an expression of mild distaste for the whole populist program. "Yes, I suppose I must, if necessary. But on second thoughts *that*—" Amber snaps her fingers and the mannequin turns around once more before morphing back into neutrality, aureolae perfect puckered disks above the top of its bodice—"is just too much."

She doesn't need to merge in the opinions of several different fractional personalities, fashion critics and psephologists both, to figure out that adopting Victorian/Cretan fusion fashion—a breast-and-ass fetishist's fantasy—isn't the way to sell herself as a serious politician to the nineteenth-century post-singularity fringe. "I'm not running for election as the mother of the nation, I'm running because I figure we've got about a billion seconds, at most, to get out of this rattrap of a gravity well before the Vile Offspring get seriously medieval on our CPU cycles, and if we don't convince everyone to come with us, they're doomed. Let's look for something more practical that we can overload with the right signifiers."

"Like your coronation robe?"

Amber winces. "Touché." The Ring Imperium is dead, along with whatever was left over from its early orbital legal framework, and Amber is lucky to be alive as a private citizen in this cold new age at the edge of the halo. "But that was just scenery-setting. I didn't fully understand what I was doing, back then."

"Welcome to maturity and experience." Annette smiles distantly at some faint. "You don't *feel* older, you just know what you're doing this time. I wonder, sometimes, what Manny would make of it if he were here."

"That bird-brain!" Amber says dismissively, stung by the idea that her father might have something to contribute. She follows Annette past a gaggle of mendicant street evangelists preaching some new religion and in through the door of a real department store, one with actual human sales staff and fitting rooms to cut the clothing to shape. "If I'm sending out fractional me's tailored for different demographics, isn't it a bit self-defeating to go for a single image? I mean, we could drill down and tailor a partial for each individual elector—"

"Per-haps." The door re-forms behind them. "But you need a core identity." Annette looks around, hunting for eye contact with the sales consultant. "To start with a core design, a style, then to work outward, tailoring you for your audience. And besides, there is tonight's—ah, bonjour!"

"Hello. How can we help you?" The two female and one male shop assistants who appear from around the displays—cycling through a history of the couture industry, catwalk models mixing and matching centuries of fashion—are clearly chips off a common primary personality, instances united by their enhanced sartorial obsession. If they're not actually a fashion borganism they're not far from it, dressed head-to-foot in the highest quality Chanel and Armani replicas, making a classical twentieth-century statement. This isn't simply a shop, it's a temple to a very peculiar art form, its staff trained as guardians of the esoteric secrets of good taste.

"Mais oui. We are looking for a wardrobe for my niece here." Annette reaches through the manifold of fashion ideas mapped within the shop's location cache and flips a requirement spec one of her ghosts has just completed at the lead assistant. "She is into politics going, and the question of her image is important."

"We would be *delighted* to help you," purrs the proprietor, taking a delicate step forward: "perhaps you could tell us what you've got in mind?"

"Oh. Well." Amber takes a deep breath, glances sidelong at Annette: Annette stares back, unblinking. *It's your head,* she sends. "I'm involved in the accelerationista administrative program. Are you familiar with it?"

The head coutureborg frowns slightly, twin furrows rippling her brow between perfectly symmetrical eyebrows, plucked to match her classic New Look suit. "I have heard reference to it, but a lady of fashion like myself does not concern herself with politics," she says, a touch self-deprecatingly. "Especially the politics of her clients. Your, ah, aunt said it was a question of image?"

"Yes." Amber shrugs, momentarily self-conscious about her casual rags. "She's my election agent. My problem, as she says, is there's a certain voter demographic that mistakes image for substance and is afraid of the unknown, and I need to acquire a wardrobe that triggers associations of probity, of respect and deliberation. One suitable for a representative with a radical political agenda but a strong track record. I'm afraid I'm in a hurry to start with—I've got a big fund-raising party tonight. I know it's short notice, but I need something off the shelf for it."

"What exactly is it you're hoping to achieve?" asks the male couturier, his voice hoarse and his r's rolling with some half-shed Mediterranean accent. He sounds fascinated. "If you think it might influence your choice of wardrobe…?"

"I'm running for the assembly," Amber says bluntly. "On a platform calling for a state of emergency and an immediate total effort to assemble a starship. This solar system isn't going to be habitable for much longer, and we need to emigrate. All of us, you included, before the Vile Offspring decide to reprocess us into computronium. I'm going to be doorstepping the entire electorate in parallel, and the experience needs to be personalized." She manages to smile. "That means, I think, perhaps eight outfits and four different independent variables for each, accessories, and two or three hats—enough that each is seen by no more than a few thousand voters. Both physical fabric and virtual. In addition, I'll want to see your range of historical formalwear, but that's of secondary interest for now." She grins. "Do you have any facilities for response-testing the combinations against different personality types from different periods? If we could run up some models, that would be useful."

"I think we can do better than that." The manager nods approvingly, perhaps contemplating her gold-backed deposit account. "Hansel, please divert any further visitors until we have dealt with madam…?"

"Macx. Amber Macx."

"—Macx's requirements." The manager shows no sign of familiarity with the name. Amber winces slightly; it's a sign of how hugely fractured the children of Saturn have become, and of how vast the population of the halo, that only a generation has passed and already barely anyone remembers the Queen of the Ring Imperium. "If you'd come this way, please, we can begin to research an eigenstyle combination that matches your requirements—"

Welcome to decade the eighth, singularity plus one gigasecond (or maybe more—nobody's quite sure when, or indeed *if*, a singularity has been created). The human population of the solar system is either six billion, or sixty billion, depending on whether you class forked state vectors of posthumans and the simulations of dead phenotypes running in the Vile Offspring's Schrödinger boxes as people. Most of the physically incarnate still live on Earth, but the lillypads floating beneath content-sized hot hydrogen balloons in Saturn's upper atmosphere already house a few million, and the writing is on the wall for the rocky inner planets. All the remaining human-equivalent intelligences with half a clue to rub together are trying to emigrate before the Vile Offspring decide to recycle Earth to fill in a gap in the concentric shells of nano-computers they're running on, a nested Matrioshka doll of Dyson spheres that darkens the skies of Earth and has caused a massive crash in the planets photo-synthetic biomass, as plants starve for short-wavelength light.

Since decade the seventh, the computational density of the solar system has soared. Within the asteroid belt, more than half the available planetary mass has been turned into nanoprocessors, quantum-entangled states tying them together into a web so dense that each gram of matter can simulate all the possible life-experiences of an individual human being in a scant handful of minutes. Economics 2.0 is itself obsolescent, forced to mutate in a furious survivalist arms race by the arrival of the Slug, an extraterrestrial parasite that preys on new posthuman intelligences by subverting their value systems. Only the name remains, as a vague shorthand for merely human-equivalent intelligences to use when describing inter-actions they don't understand.

The latest generation of posthuman entities is less overtly hostile to humans, but much more alien than the generations of the forties and sixties. Among their less-comprehensible activities, the Vile Offspring are engaged in exploring the phase space of all possible human experiences from the inside out. Perhaps they caught a dose of the Tiplerite heresy along the way, for now a steady stream of resimulant uploads is pouring through the downsystem relays in Titan orbit. The Rapture of the Nerds has been followed by the Resurrection of the Extremely Confused, except that they're not *really* resurrectees—they're simulations based off their originals' recorded histories, blocky and missing chunks of their memories, as bewildered as baby ducks herded into the wood-chipper of the future.

Sirhan al-Khurasani despises them with the abstract contempt of an antiquarian for a cunning but ultimately transparent forgery. But Sirhan is young, and he's got more contempt than he knows what to do with: it's a handy outlet for his frustration. He has a lot to be frustrated at, starting with his intermittently dysfunctional family, the elders among whose globular cluster his planet caroms helplessly, in chaotic traject-ories of enthusiasm and distaste.

Sirhan fancies himself a philosopher-historian of the singular age, a chronicler of the incomprehensible, which would be a fine thing to be except that his greatest insights are all derived from the family's antique robot cat. He alternately fawns over and rages against his mother—Amber Macx, one-time queen of the Ring Imperium and now a leading light in the refugee community—and honors (when not attempt-ing to evade the will of) his father—Sadeq al Khuras-ani, sometime Islamic scholar, theist heretic, and lately a rising philosophical patriarch within the Conserva-

197

tionist faction. He's secretly in awe (not to mention slightly resentful of) of his famous grandfather, Manfred Macx, who usually manifests in the shape of a flock of passenger pigeons, a rain of snails, or something equally unconventional. In fact, Manfred's abrupt reincarnation in the flesh has quite disconcerted Sirhan. And he sometimes listens to his stepgrandmother Annette, who has reincarnated in more or less her original twenty-twenties body after spending some years as a great ape, and who seems to view him as some sort of personal project.

Only right now, Annette isn't being very helpful, his mother is campaigning on an electoral platform calling for a vote to blow up the world, his grandfather is trying to convince him to entrust everything he holds dear to a rogue lobster, and the cat isn't talking.

And you thought you had problems?

They've transplanted imperial Brussels to Saturn in its entirety, mapped tens of megatons of buildings right down to nanoscale and beamed them into the outer darkness to be reinstantiated down-well on the lillypad colonies that dot the stratosphere of the gas giant. (Eventually, the entire surface of the Earth will follow—after which the Vile Offspring will core the planet like an apple, and dismantle it into a cloud of newly formed quantum nanocomputers to add to their burgeoning Matrioshka brain.) Due to a resource contention problem in the Festival committee's planning algorithm—or maybe it's simply an elaborate joke—Brussels now begins just on the other side of a diamond bubble-wall from the Boston Museum of Science, less than a kilometer away as the passenger pigeon flies. Which is why, when it's time to celebrate a birthday or nameday—meaningless though those concepts are, out on Saturn's synthetic surface—Amber tends to drag people over to the bright lights in the big city.

This time, she's throwing a rather special party. At Annette's canny prompting, she's borrowed the Atomium and invited a horde of guests to a big celebration. It's not a family bash—although Annette's promised her a surprise—so much as a business meeting, testing the water as a preliminary to declaring her candidacy. It's a media event, an attempt to engineer Amber's re-entry into the mainstream politics of the human system.

Sirhan doesn't really want to be here. He's got far more important things to do, like cataloging Aineko's memories of the voyage of the *Field Circus*. He's also collating a series of interviews with re-simulated logical positivists from Oxford, England (the ones who haven't retreated into gibbering near-catatonia upon realizing that their state vectors are all members of the set of all sets that do not contain themselves), when he isn't attempting to establish a sound rational case for his belief that extraterrestrial intelligence is an oxymoron and that the vast network of quantum-entangled Routers that orbit the brown dwarfs of the Milky Way galaxy is just an accident, one of evolution's little pranks.

But Tante Annette twisted his arm, and promised he was in on the surprise if he came to the party. And despite everything, he wouldn't miss being a fly on the wall during the coming meeting between Manfred and Amber for all the tea in China.

Sirhan walks up to the gleaming stainless steel dome

that contains the entrance to the Atomium, and waits for the lift. He's in line behind a gaggle of young-looking women, skinny and soigne in cocktail gowns and tiaras lifted from 1920's silent movies. (Annette declared an Age of Elegance theme for the party, knowing full-well that it would force Amber to focus on her public appearance.) Sirhan's attention is, however, elsewhere. The various fragments of his mind are conducting three simultaneous interviews with philosophers ("whereof that we cannot speak we cannot know" in spades), controlling two bots that are overhauling the museum plumbing and air-recycling system, and he's busy discussing observations of the alien artifact orbiting the brown dwarf Hyundai +4904/-56 with Aineko. What's left of him exhibits about as much social presence as a pickled cabbage.

The elevator arrives and accepts a load of passengers. Sirhan is crowded into one corner by a bubble of high-society laughter and an aromatic puff of smoke from an improbable ivory cigarette holder as the elevator surges, racing up the sixty-meter shaft toward the observation deck at the top of the Atomium. It's another ten meter diameter metal globe, spiral staircases and escalators connecting it to the seven spheres at the corners of an octahedron that make up the former centerpiece of the 1950 World Fair. Unlike most of the rest of Brussels, it's the original bits and atoms, bent alloy structures from before the space age shipped out to Saturn at enormous expense. The lift arrives with a slight jerk. "Excuse *me,*" squeaks one of the good-time girls as she lurches backward, elbowing Sirhan.

He blinks, barely noticing her black bob of hair, chromatophore-tinted shadows artfully tuned around her eyes. "Nothing to excuse." In the background, Aineko is droning on sarcastically about the lack of interest the crew of the *Field Circus* exhibited in the cat's effort to decompile their hitch-hiker, the Slug (an alien entity, or financial instrument, or parasitic pyramid scheme, or something) who had returned to the solar system with them, in return for helping them break free from the feral economic fragments that had captured them in the demilitarized zone on the far side of the Router. It's distracting as hell, but Sirhan feels a desperate urge to understand what happened out there. It's the key to understanding his not-mother's obsessions and weaknesses—which, he senses, will be important in the times to come.

He evades the gaggle of overdressed good-time girls and steps out onto the lower of the two stainless steel decks that bisect the sphere. Accepting a fruit cocktail from a discreetly humanoform waitron, he strolls toward a row of triangular windows that gaze out across the arena toward the American Pavilion and the World Village. The metal walls are braced with turquoise-painted girders, and the perspex transparencies are fogged with age. He can barely see the one-tenth scale model of an atomic powered ocean liner leaving the pier below, or the eight-engined giant seaplane beside it. "They never once asked me if the Slug had attempted to map itself into the human-compatible spaces aboard the ship," Aineko bitches at him. "I wasn't expecting them to, but really! Your mother's too trusting, boy."

"I suppose you took precautions?" Sirhan's ghost murmurs to the cat. That sets the irascible metafeline off again on a long discursive tail-washing rant about the unreliability of Economics 2.0-compliant financial instruments. Economics 2.0 apparently replaces the single-indirection layer of conventional money, and the multiple-indirection mappings of options trades, with some kind of insanely baroque object-relational framework based on the parameterized desires and subjective experiential values of the players, and as far as the cat is concerned, this makes all such transactions intrinsically untrustworthy.

Which is why you're stuck here with us apes, Sirhan-prime cynically notes as he spawns an Eliza ghost to carry on nodding its head politely at the cat while he experiences the party.

It's uncomfortably warm in the Atomium sphere—not surprising, there must be thirty people milling around up here, not counting the waitrons—and several local multicast channels are playing a variety of styles of music to synchronize the mood swings of the revelers to hardcore techno, waltz, raga....

"Having a good time, are we?" Sirhan breaks away from integrating one of his timid philosophers and realizes that his glass is empty and his mother is grinning alarmingly at him over the rim of a cocktail glass containing something that glows in the dark. She's wearing spike-heeled boots and a black velvet cat suit that hugs her contours like a second skin, and she's already getting drunk. In wall-clock years, she is younger than Sirhan; it's like having a bizarrely knowing younger sister mysteriously injected into his life to replace the eigenmother who stayed home and died with the Ring Imperium decades ago. "Look at you, hiding in a corner at my party! Hey, your glass is empty. Want to try this capirinha? There's someone you've got to meet over here—"

It's at moments like this that Sirhan really wonders what in Jupiter's orbit his father ever saw in this woman. (But then again, in the world-line this instance of her has returned from, he *didn't*. So what does *that* signify?) "As long as there's no fermented grape juice in it," he says resignedly, allowing himself to be led past a gaggle of conversations and a mournful-looking gorilla slurping a long drink through a straw. "More of your *accelerationista* allies?"

"Maybe not." It's the girl-gang he avoided noticing in the lift, their eyes sparkling, really getting into this early twen-cen drag party thing, waving their cigarette holders and cocktail glasses around with wild abandon. "Rita, I'd like you to meet Sirhan, my other fork's son. Sirhan, this is Rita. She's a historian too. Why don't you —"

—Dark eyes, emphasized not by powder or paint but by chromatophores inside her skin cells: black hair, chain of enormous pearls, slim black dress sweeping the floor, a look of mild embarrassment on her heart-shaped face: she could be a dark-haired Audrey Hepburn in any other century—"Didn't I just meet you in the elevator?" The embarrassment shifts to her cheeks, visible now.

Sirhan flushes, unsure how to reply. Just then, an interloper arrives on the scene, pushing in between them. "Are you the curator who reorganized the Precambrian gallery along teleology lines? I've got some things to say about *that!*" The interloper's tall, assertive, and blonde. Sirhan hates her from the first sight of her wagging finger.

"Oh shut up, Marissa, this is a party, you've been being a pain all evening." To his surprise, Rita-the-historian rounds on the interloper angrily.

"It's not a problem," he manages to say. In the back of his mind, something makes the Rogerian puppet-him that's listening to the cat sit up and dump-merge a whole lump of fresh memories into his mind—something important, something about the Vile Offspring sending a starship to bring something back from the Router—but the people around him are soaking up so much attention that he has to file it for later.

"Yes it *is* a problem," Rita declares. She points at the interloper, who is saying something about the invalidity of teleological interpretations, trying to justify herself, and says, *"Plonk.* Phew. Where were we?"

Sirhan blinks. Suddenly everyone but him seems to be ignoring that annoying Marissa person. "What just happened?" he asks cautiously.

"I killfiled her. Don't tell me, you aren't running Superplonk yet, are you?" Rita flicks a location-cached idea at him and he takes it cautiously, spawning a couple of specialized Turing oracles to check it for halting states. It seems to be some kind of optic-lobe hack that accesses a collaborative database of eigen-faces, with some sort of side-interface to Broca's region. "Share and enjoy, confrontation-free parties."

"I've never seen—" Sirhan trails off as he loads the module distractedly. (The cat is rambling on about god modules and metastatic entanglement and the difficulty of arranging to have personalities custom-grown to order somewhere in the back of his head, while his fractional-self nods wisely whenever it pauses.) Something like an inner eyelid descends. He looks round: there's a vague blob at one side of the room, making an annoying buzzing sound. His mother seems to be having an animated conversation with it. "That's rather interesting."

"Yes, it helps no end at this sort of event." Rita startles him by taking his left arm in hand—her cigarette holder shrivels and condenses until it's no more than a slight thickening around the wrist of her opera glove—and steers him toward a waitron. "I'm sorry about your foot, earlier, I was a bit overloaded. Is Amber Macx really your mother?"

"Not exactly, she's my eigenmother," he mumbles. "The reincarnated download of the version who went out to Hyundai +4904/-56 aboard the *Field Circus*. She married a French-Algerian confidence-trick analyst instead of my father, but I think they divorced a couple of years ago. My *real* mother married an imam, but they died in the aftermath of Economics 2.0." She seems to be steering him in the direction of the window bay Amber dragged him away from earlier. "Why do you ask?"

"Because you're not very good at making smalltalk," Rita says quietly, "and you don't seem very good in crowds. Is that right? Was it you who performed that amazing dissection of Wittgenstein's cognitive map? The one with the pre-verbal Godel string in it?"

"It was—" he clears his throat. "You thought it was amazing?" Suddenly, on impulse, he detaches a ghost to identify this Rita person and find out who she is, what she wants. It's not normally worth the effort to get to know someone more closely than casual smalltalk, but she seems to have been digging into his background and he wants to know why. Along with the him that's chatting to Aineko that makes about three instances pulling in near-realtime resources. He'll be running up an existential debt soon if he keeps forking ghosts like this.

"I thought so," she says. There's a bench in front of the wall and somehow he finds himself sitting on it next to her. *There's no danger, we're not in private or anything,* he tells himself stiffly. She's smiling at him, face tilted slightly to one side and lips parted, and for a moment a dizzy sense of possibility washes over him: *what if she's about to throw all propriety aside? How undignified!* Sirhan believes in self-restraint and dignity. "I was really interested in this—" She passes him another dynamically loadable blob, encompassing a detailed critique of his analysis of Wittgenstein's matriophobia in the context of gendered language constructs and nineteenth-century Viennese society, along with a hypothesis that leaves Sirhan gasping with mild indignation at the very idea that *he* of all people might share Wittgenstein's skewed outlook—"what do you think?" She asks, grinning impishly at him.

"Nnngk." Sirhan tries to unswallow his tongue. Rita crosses her legs, her gown hissing. "I, ah, that is to say—" At which moment his partials re-integrate, dumping a slew of positively pornographic images into his memories. *It's a trap!* they shriek, her breasts and hips and pubes—clean-shaven, he can't help noticing—thrusting at him in hotly passionate abandon, *mother's trying to make you loose like her!* and he remembers what it *would* be like to wake up in bed next to this woman who he barely knows after being married to her for a year, because one of his cognitive ghosts has just spent several seconds of network time (or several subjective months) getting hot and sweaty with a ghost of her own, and she *does* have interesting research ideas, even if she's a pushy over-westernized woman who thinks she can run his life for him—"what *is* this?" he splutters, his ears growing hot and his garments constricting.

"Just speculating about possibilities. We could get a lot done together." She snakes an arm round his shoulders and pulls him toward her, gently. "Don't you want to find out if we could work out?"

"But, but—" Sirhan is steaming. *Is she offering casual sex?* he wonders, profoundly embarrassed by his own inability to read her signals. "What do you *want?*" he asks.

"You *do* know that you can do more with super-plonk than just killfile annoying idiots?" She whispers in his ear. "We can be invisible right now, if you like. It's great for confidential meetings—other things, too. We can work beautifully together, our ghosts annealed really well…."

Sirhan jumps up, his face stinging, and turns away. "No thank you!" he snaps, angry at himself. "Good-bye!" His other instances, distracted by his broadcast emotional overload, are distracted from their tasks and sputtering with indignation. Her hurt expression is too much for him: the killfile snaps down, blurring her into an indistinct black blob on the wall, veiled by his own brain as he turns and walks away, seething with anger at his mother for being so unfair as to make him behold his own face in the throes of fleshy passion.

Meanwhile, in one of the lower spheres, padded with silvery-blue insulating pillows bound together with duct tape, the movers and shakers of the accelerationista faction are discussing their bid for world power at fractional-C velocities.

"We can't outrun a collapse of the false vacuum," insists Manfred, slightly uncoordinated and slurring his vowels under the influence of the first glass of fruit punch he's experienced in nigh-on twenty realtime years. His body is young and still relatively featureless, hair still growing out, and he's abandoned his old no-implants fetish at last to adopt an array of internal interfaces that let him internalize all the exocortex processes that formerly he ran on an array of dumb Turing machines outside his body. He's standing on his own sense of style and is the only person in the room who isn't wearing some variation of dinner jacket or classical evening dress. "Entangled exchange via Routers is still slower-than-light in absolute terms—any phase change will catch up eventually, the network must have an end. And then where will we be, Sameena?"

"I'm not disputing that." The woman he's talking to, wearing a green-and-gold sari and a medieval maharajah's ransom in gold and natural diamonds, nods thoughtfully. "But it hasn't happened yet, and we've got evidence that superhuman intelligences have been loose in this universe for gigayears, so there's a fair bet that the worst-catastrophe scenarios are unlikely. And looking closer to home, we don't know what the Routers are for, or who made them. Until then...." She shrugs. "Look what happened last time somebody tried to probe them. No offense intended."

"It's already happened. If what I hear is correct, the Vile Offspring aren't nearly as negative about the idea of using the Routers as we old-fashioned metahumans might like to believe." Manfred frowns, trying to recall some hazy anecdote—he's experimenting with a new memory compression algorithm, necessitated by his pack-rat mnemonic habits when younger, and sometimes the whole universe feels as if it's nearly on the tip of his tongue. "So, we seem to be in violent agreement about the need to *know more* about what's going on, and to find out what they're doing out there. We've got cosmic background anisotropies caused by the waste heat from computing processes millions of light years across—it takes a big interstellar civilization to do that, and they don't seem to have fallen into the same rat-trap as the local Matrioshka brain civilizations. And we've got worrying rumors about the Vile Offspring messing around with the structure of spacetime in order to find a way around the Bekenstein bound. If the VO are trying that, then the folks out near the supercluster already know the answers. The best way to find out what's happening is to go and talk to whoever's responsible. Can we at least agree on that?"

"Probably not." Her eyes glitter with amusement. "It all depends on whether one believes in these civilizations in the first place. I *know* your people point to deep-field camera images going all the way back to some wonky hubble-bubble scrying mirror from the late twentieth, but we've got no evidence except some theories about the Casimir effect and pair production and spinning beakers of helium-3—much *less* proof that a whole bunch of alien galactic civilizations are trying to collapse the false vacuum and destroy the universe!" Her voice drops a notch. "At least, not enough proof to convince most people, Manny dear. I know this comes as a shock to you, but not *everyone* is a neophiliac posthuman body-surfer whose idea of a sabbatical is to spend twenty years as a flock of tightly networked seagulls in order to try and to prove the Turing oracle thesis—"

"—Not everyone is concerned with the deep future," Manfred interrupts. "It's important! If we live or die, that doesn't matter—that's not the big picture. The big question is whether information originating in our light cone is preserved, or whether we're stuck in a lossy medium where our very existence counts for nothing. It's downright *embarrassing,* to be a member of a species with such a profound lack of curiosity about its own future, especially when it affects us all personally! I mean, if there's going to come a time when there's nobody or nothing to remember us, then what does—"

"Manfred?"

He stops in mid-sentence, his mouth open, staring dumbly.

It's Amber, poised in black cat-suit with cocktail glass. Her expression is open and confused, appallingly vulnerable. Blue liquid slops, almost spilling out of her glass—the rim barely extends itself in time to catch the drops. Behind her stands Annette, a deeply self-satisfied smile on her face.

"You." Amber pauses, her cheek twitching as bits of her mind page in and out of her skull, polling external information sources. "You really *are*—"

A hasty cloud materializes under her hand as her fingers relax, dropping the glass.

"Uh." Manfred stares, at a complete loss for words. "I'd, uh." After a moment, he looks past her. "Why don't you explain?" he asks.

"We thought you could use the good advice,"

Annette speaks into the awkward silence. "And a family reunion. It was meant to be a surprise."

"A *surprise.*" Amber looks perplexed. "You could say that."

"You're taller than I was expecting," Manfred says unexpectedly.

"Yeah?" She looks at him, and he turns his head slightly, facing her. It's a historic moment, and Annette is getting it all on memory diamond, from every angle. The family's dirty little secret is that Amber and her father have *never met*, not face-to-face in sweaty physical meat-machine proximity. She was born more than a year after Manfred and Pamela separated, decanted pre-fertilized from a tank of liquid nitrogen to play a pawn's role in a bitter game of divorcee chess—promoted to queen by her own initiative in high orbit around Jupiter, extricated from her mother's stifling grip by a legal instrument Manfred smuggled to her inside his cat's brain, but this is the first time either of them have actually seen the other's face without electronic intermediation. And while they've said everything that needed to be said on a businesslike level, anthropoid family politics is still very much a matter of body language and pheromones. "How long have you been out and about?" she asks, trying to disguise her confusion.

"About six hours." Manfred manages a rueful chuckle, trying to take the sight of her in all at once. "Let's get you another drink and put our heads together?"

"Okay." Amber takes a deep breath and glares at Annette. "You set this up, *you* get to clean up the mess."

Annette just stands there smiling at the confusion of her accomplishment.

The cold light of dawn finds Sirhan angry, sober, and ready to pick a fight with the first person who comes through the door of his office. The room is about ten meters across, with a floor of polished marble and skylights in the intricately plastered ceiling. The walkthrough of his current project sprouts in the middle of the floor like a ghostly abstract cauliflower, fractal branches dwindling down to in-folded nodes tagged with compressed identifiers. The branches expand and shrink as Sirhan paces around it, zooming to readability in response to his eyeball dynamics. But he isn't paying it much attention. He's too disturbed, uncertain, trying to work out who to blame. Which is why when the door bangs open his first response is to whirl angrily and open his mouth—then stop. "What do *you* want?" he demands.

"A word, if you please?" Annette looks around distractedly. "This is your project?"

"Yes," he says icily, and banishes the walkthrough with a wave of one hand. "What do you want?"

"I'm not sure." Annette pauses. For a moment, she looks weary, tired beyond mortal words, and Sirhan momentarily wonders if perhaps he's spreading the blame too far. This eighty-something Frenchwoman who is no blood relative, just the love of his scatterbrained grandfather's life, seems like the least likely person to be trying to manipulate him, at least in such an unwelcome and intimate manner. But there's no telling. Families are strange things, and even though the current instantiations of his father and mother aren't the ones who ran his pre-adolescent brain through a couple of dozen alternative lifelines before he was ten, he can't be sure that they wouldn't enlist Tante Annette's assistance in fucking with his mind. "We need to talk about your mother," she continues.

"We do? Do we?" Sirhan turns around and sees the vacancy of the room for what it is, a socket, like a pulled tooth, informed as much by what is absent as by what is present. He snaps his fingers and an intricate bench of translucent bluish utility fog congeals out of the air behind him. He sits; Annette can do what she wants.

"Oui." She thrusts her hands deep into the pocket of the peasant smock she's wearing—a major departure from her normal style—and leans against the wall. Physically, she looks young enough to have spent her entire life blitzing around the galaxy at three nines of lightspeed, but her posture is world-weary and ancient. History is a foreign country and the old are unwilling emigrants, tired out by the constant travel. "Your mother, she has taken on a huge job, but it's one that needs doing. *You* agreed it needed doing, years ago, with the archive store. *She* is now trying to get it moving, that is what the campaign is about, to place before the electors a choice of how best to move an entire civilization. So I ask, why do you obstruct her?"

Sirhan works his jaw: he feels like spitting. *"Why?"* he snaps.

"Yes. Why?" Annette gives in and magics up a chair from the swirling fogbank beneath the ceiling. She crouches in it, staring at him. "It is a question."

"I have nothing against her political machinations,"

Sirhan says tensely. "But her uninvited interference in my personal life—"

"What interference?"

He stares. "Is that a question?" He's silent for a moment. Then: "throwing that wanton at me last night—"

Annette stares at him. "Who? What are you talking about?"

"That, that loose woman!" Sirhan is reduced to spluttering. "False pretenses! If this is one of father's matchmaking ideas, it is so *very* wrong that—"

Annette is shaking her head. "Are you crazy? Your mother simply wanted you to meet her campaign team, to join in planning the policy. Your father is not on this planet! But you stormed out, you *really* upset Rita, did you know that? Rita, she is the best belief-maintenance and story-construction operative I have! Yet you to tears try to reduce her. What is wrong with you?"

"I—" Sirhan swallows. "She's *what?*" he asks again, his mouth dry. "I thought..." he trails off. He doesn't want to say what he thought. The hussy, that brazen trollop, is part of his mother's campaign party? Not some plot to lure him into corruption? What if it was all a horrible misunderstanding?

"I think you to apologize to someone must," Annette says coolly, standing up. Sirhan's head is spinning between a dozen dialogs of actors and ghosts, a journal of the party replaying before his ghast-stricken inner gaze. Even the walls have begun to flicker, responding to his intense unease. Annette skewers him with a disgusted look. "When you can a woman behave toward as a person, not a threat, we can again talk. Until then." And she stands up and walks out of the room, leaving him to contemplate the shattered stump of his anger, so startled he can barely concentrate on his project, thinking, *is that really me? Is that what I look like to her?* as the cladistic graph slowly rotates before him, denuded branches spread wide, waiting to be filled with the nodes of the alien interstellar network just as soon as he can convince Aineko to stake him the price of the depth-first tour of darkness.

Manfred used to be a flock of pigeons—literally, his exocortex dispersed among a passel of bird-brains, pecking at brightly colored facts, shitting semi-digested conclusions. Being human again feels inexplicably odd. Not only does he get shooting pains in his neck whenever he tries to look over his left shoulder with his right eye, but he's lost the habit of spawning exocortical agents to go interrogate a database or bush robot or something then report back to him. Instead, he keeps trying to fly off in all directions at once, which usually leads to him falling over.

But right now, that's not a problem. He's sitting comfortably at a weathered wooden table in a beer garden behind a hall lifted from somewhere like Frankfurt, a liter glass of straw-colored liquid at his elbow and a comforting multiple whispering of knowledge streams tickling the back of his head. Most of his attention is focused on Annette, who frowns at him with mingled concern and affection.

"You are going to have to do something about that boy," she says. "He is close enough to upset Amber. And without Amber, there will be a problem."

"I'm going to have to do something about Amber,

215

too," Manfred retorts. "What was the idea, not warning her I was coming?"

"It was meant to be a surprise." Annette comes as close to pouting as Manfred's seen her recently. It brings back warm memories: he reaches out to hold her hand across the table.

"You know I can't handle the human niceties properly when I'm a flock." He strokes the back of her wrist. She doesn't pull back. "I expected you to manage all that stuff."

"That stuff." Annette shakes her head. "She's your daughter, you know? Did you have no curiosity left?"

"As a *bird?*" Manfred cocks his head to one side so abruptly that he hurts his neck and winces. "Nope. *Now* I do, but I think I pissed her off—"

"Which brings us back to point one."

"I'd send her an apology, but she'd think I was trying to manipulate her," Manfred takes a mouthful of beer. "And she'd be right."

"So? Don't brood." Annette pulls her hand back. "Something will sort itself out. Before the electoral problem becomes acute." When she's around him, the remains of her once-strong French accent almost vanish in a trans-Atlantic drawl, he realizes with a pang. He's been abhuman for too long—people who meant a lot to him have changed while he's been away.

"That's the trouble with this damned polity." Manfred takes another gulp of *hefeweisen*. "We've already got six million people living on this planet, and it's growing like the first generation Internet. Everyone who is anyone knows everyone, but there are so many incomers diluting the mix and not knowing that there *is* a small-world network here that everything is up for grabs again after only a couple of megaseconds. New networks form, and we don't even know they exist until they sprout a political agenda and surface under us. We're acting under time pressure. If we don't get things rolling now, we'll never be able to…" He shakes his head. "It wasn't like this for you in Brussels, was it?"

"No. Brussels was a mature system. And it will only get worse from here on in, I think."

"Democracy 2.0." He shudders briefly. "Do you think we can make this fly?"

"I don't see why not. If Amber's willing to play the People's Princess for us…" Annette picks up a slice of liverwurst and chews on it meditatively.

"I'm not sure it's workable, however we play it." Manfred looks thoughtful. "The whole democratic participation thing looks questionable to me under these circumstances. We're under direct threat, for all that it's a long-term one, and this whole culture is in danger of turning into a classical nation-state. Or worse, several of them layered on top of one another with complete geographical colocation but no social interpenetration. I'm not certain it's a good idea to try to steer something like that—pieces might break off, you'd get the most unpleasant side-effects. Although, on the other hand, if we can mobilize enough broad support to become the first visible planet-wide polity…"

"We need you to stay focused," Annette adds unexpectedly.

"Focused? *Me?*" He laughs, briefly. "I *used* to have an idea a second. Now it's maybe one a year."

"Yes, but you know the old saying? The fox has

many ideas—the hedgehog has only one, but it's a *big* idea."

"So tell me, what is my big idea?" Manfred leans forward, one elbow on the table, one eye focused on innerspace as a hot-burning thread of consciousness barks psephological performance metrics at him, analyzing the game ahead. "Where do you think I'm going?"

"I think—" Annette breaks off suddenly, staring past his shoulder. Privacy slips, and for a frozen moment Manfred glances round in mild horror and sees thirty or forty other guests in the crowded garden, elbows rubbing, voices raised above the background chatter. "Gianni!" She beams widely as she stands up. "What a surprise! When did you arrive?"

Manfred blinks. A slim young man, moving with adolescent grace but none of the awkward movements and sullen lack of poise—he's much older than he looks, chickenhawk genetics. *Gianni?* He thinks, and feels a huge surge of memories paging through his exocortex. He remembers ringing a doorbell in dusty, hot Rome: white toweling bathrobe, the economics of scarcity, autograph signed by the dead hand of Von Neumann—"Gianni?" he asks. "It's been a long time!"

The gilded youth, incarnated in the image of a metropolitan toy-boy from the noughties, grins widely and slides down onto the bench next to Annette, who he kisses with easy familiarity. "Manfred! So charmed!" He glances round curiously. "Ah, how very Bavarian." He snaps his fingers. "Mine will be a, what do you recommend? It's been too long since my last beer." His grin widens. "Not in this body."

"You're re-simulated?" Manfred asks, unable to stop himself.

Annette frowns at him disapprovingly. "No, silly! He came through the teleport gate—"

"Oh." Manfred shakes his head. "I'm sorry—"

"It's okay." Gianni Vittoria clearly doesn't mind being mistaken for a historical newbie, rather than someone who's traveled through the decades the hard way. *He must be over a hundred by now*, Manfred notes, not bothering to spawn a search thread to find out.

"It was time to move, and, well, the old body didn't want to move with me, so why not go gracefully and accept the inevitable?"

"I didn't take you for a dualist," Manfred says ruefully.

"Ah, I'm not—but neither am I reckless." Gianni drops his grin for a moment. The sometime minister for transhuman affairs, economic theoretician, and then retired tribal elder of the polycognitive liberals is serious. "I have never uploaded before, or switched bodies, or teleported. Even when my old one was seriously—tcha! Maybe I left it too long. But here I am, one planet is as good as another to be cloned and downloaded onto, don't you think?"

"You invited him?" Manfred asks Annette.

"Why wouldn't I?" There's a wicked gleam in her eye. "Did you expect me to live like a nun while you were a flock of pigeons? We may have campaigned against the legal death of the transubstantiated, Manfred, but there are limits."

Manfred looks between them then shrugs, embarrassed. "I'm still getting used to being human again," he admits. "Give me time to catch up? At an emotional level, at least." He focuses on Gianni. "I have a feeling I'm here for a purpose, and it isn't mine," he says slowly. "Why don't you tell me what you've got in mind?"

Gianni shrugs. "You have the big picture already. We are human, metahuman, and augmented human. But the *posthumans* are things that were never really human to begin with. Our mind children have reached their adolescence as a civilization in their own right, and the Vile Offspring want the place to themselves so they can throw a party. The writing is, as they say, on the wall: we frail mortals might wish to move to a neighborhood where the youth is less raucous and maybe less inclined to accidentally eat our planets and convert them into computronium. Don't you think?"

Manfred gives him a long stare. "The whole idea of running away in meatspace is fraught with peril," he says slowly. He picks up his mug of beer and swirls it around slowly. "Look. We know, now, that a singularity doesn't turn into a voracious predator that eats all the dumb matter in its path, triggering a phase change in the structure of space—at least, not unless they've done something very stupid to the structure of the false vacuum, somewhere outside our current light cone. Bandwidth limits the singularity, motivating the fast-thinkers to stay as close to the core of their civilization as they can. *Usually.* That's what we've seen in the local neighborhood.

"But if we run away, *we* are still going to be there. Sooner or later we'll have the same problem all over again; runaway intelligence augmentation, self-expression, engineered intelligences, whatever. Possibly that's what happened out past the Boötes void—not a galactic-scale civilization, but a race of pathological cowards fleeing their own exponential transcendence. We carry the seeds of a singularity with us wherever we go, and if we try to excise those seeds, we cease to be human, don't we? So... maybe you can tell me what you think we should do. Hmm?"

"It's a dilemma." A waitron inserts itself into their privacy-screened field of view. It plants a spun-diamond glass in front of Gianni, then pukes beer into it. Manfred declines a refill, waiting for Gianni to drink. "Ah, the simple pleasures of the flesh! I've been corresponding with your daughter, Manny. She loaned me her experiential digest of the journey to Hyundai +4904/-56. I found it quite alarming. Nobody's casting aspersions on her observations, not after that self-propelled stock market bubble or 419 scam or whatever it was got loose in the Economics 2.0 sphere, but the implications—the Vile Offspring will eat the solar system, Manny. Then they'll slow down. But where does that leave *us*, I ask you? What is there for orthohumans like us to do if what is essentially a non-human civilization of level II on the Kardashev scale—full control over the entire energy output of a star, full computational utilization of the resources of a solar system—decides it wants to recycle our mass?"

Manfred nods thoughtfully. "You've heard the argument between the accelerationistas and the time-binder faction, I assume?" he asks.

"Of course." Gianni takes a long pull on his beer. "What do *you* think of our options?"

"The accelerationistas want to upload everyone onto a fleet of starwhisps and charge off to colonize an uninhabited brown dwarf planetary system. Or maybe steal a Matrioshka brain that's succumbed to senile dementia and turn it back into planetary biomes with cores of diamond-phase computronium to fulfill some kind of demented pastoralist nostalgia trip. Rousseau's universal robots. I gather Amber thinks this is a good idea because she's done it before—at least, the charging off aboard a starwhisp part. 'To boldly go where no uploaded metahuman colony fleet has gone before' has a certain ring to it, doesn't it?" Manfred nods to himself. "Like I say, it wouldn't work. We'd be right back to iteration one of the waterfall model of singularity formation within a couple of gigaseconds of arriving. That's why I came back."

"So." Gianni prods, pretending to ignore the frowns that Annette is casting his way.

"And as for the time-binders." Manfred nods again. "They're like Sirhan. Deeply conservative, deeply suspicious. Holding out for staying here as long as possible, until the Vile Offspring come for Saturn—then moving out bit by bit, into the Kuiper belt. Colony habitats on snowballs half a light year from anywhere." He shudders. "Spam in a fucking can with a light-hour walk to the nearest civilized company if your fellow inmates decide to reinvent Stalinism or Objectivism. No thanks! I know they've been muttering about quantum teleportation and stealing toys from the Routers, but I'll believe it when I see it."

"Which leaves *what?*" Annette demands. "It is all very well, this dismissal of both the accelerationista and time-binder programs, Manny, but what can *you* propose in their place?" She looks distressed. "Fifty years ago, you would have had six new ideas before breakfast! *And* an erection."

Manfred leers at her unconvincingly. "Who says I can't have both?"

She glares. "Drop it!"

"Okay." Manfred chugs back a quarter of a liter of

beer, draining his glass, and puts it down on the table with a bang. "As it happens, I *do* have an alternative idea." He looks serious. "I've been discussing it with Aineko for some time, and Aineko has been seeding Sirhan with it—if it's to work optimally, we'll need to get a rump constituency of both the accelerationistas and the conservatives on board. Which is why I'm conditionally going along with this whole election nonsense. So. What's it worth to you for me to explain it?"

"So, who was the deadhead you were busy with today?" Asks Amber.

Rita shrugs. "Some boringly prolix pulp author from the early twentieth, with a body phobia of extropian proportions. I kept expecting him to start drooling and rolling his eyes if I crossed my legs. Funny thing is, he was also close to bolting from fear once I mentioned implants. We *really* need to nail down how to deal with these mind/body dualists, don't we?" She watches Amber with something approaching admiration; she's new to the inner circle of the accelerationista study faction, and Amber's social credit is sky-high. Rita's got a lot to learn from her, if she can get close enough. And right now, following her along a path through the landscaped garden behind the museum, seems like a golden moment of opportunity.

Amber smiles. "I'm glad I'm not processing immigrants these days, most of them are so stupid it drives you up the wall after a bit. Personally I blame the Flynn effect—in reverse. They come from a background of sensory deprivation. It's nothing that a course of neural growth enhancers can't fix in a year or two, but after the first few you skullfuck, they're all the same. So *dull*. Unless you're unlucky enough to get one of the documentees from a puritan religious period. I'm no fluffragette, but I swear if I get one more superstitious woman-hating clergyman, I'm going to consider prescribing forcible gender reassignment surgery. At least the Victorian English are mostly just open-minded lechers, when you get past their social reserve. And they like new technology."

Rita nods. *Woman-hating etcetera*...the echoes of patriarchy are still with them today, it seems, and not just in the form of re-simulated Ayatollahs and Archbishops from the dark ages. "My author sounds like the worst of both. Some guy called Howard, from Rhode Island. Kept looking at me as if he was afraid I was going to sprout bat-wings and tentacles or something." *Like your son,* she doesn't add. *Just what was he thinking, anyway?* she wonders. *To be that screwed up takes serious dedication....* "What are you working on, if you don't mind me asking?" She asks, trying to change the direction of her attention.

"Oh, pressing the flesh, I guess. Auntie 'Nette wanted me to meet some old political hack contact of hers who she figures can help with the program, but he was holed up with her and Dad all day." She pulls a face. "I had another fitting session with the image merchants, they're trying to turn me into a political catwalk clothes-horse. Then there's the program demographics again. We're getting about a thousand new immigrants a day, planet-wide, but it's accelerating rapidly and we should be up to eighty an hour by the time of the election. Which is going to be a huge problem, because if we start campaigning too early, a quarter of the electorate won't know what they're meant to be voting about."

"Maybe it's deliberate," Rita suggests. "The Vile Offspring are trying to rig the outcome by injecting voters." She *pings* a smiley emotion off Wednesday's open channel, raising a flickering grin in return. "The party of fuckwits will win, no question about it."

"Uh-huh." Amber snaps her fingers and pulls an impatient face as she waits for a passing cloud to solidify above her head and lower a glass of cranberry juice to her. "Dad said one thing that's spot-on, we're framing this entire debate in terms of what we should do to avoid conflict with the Offspring. The main bone of contention is how to run away and how far to go and which program to put resources into, not *whether* or *when* to run, let alone what else we could do. Maybe we should have given it some more thought. Are we being manipulated?"

Rita looks vacant for a moment. "Is that a question?" she asks. Amber nods, and she shakes her head. "Then I'd have to say that I don't know. The evidence is inconclusive, so far. But I'm not really happy. The Offspring won't tell us what they want, but there's no reason to believe they don't know what *we* want. I mean, they can think rings round us, can't they?"

Amber shrugs, then pauses to unlatch a hedge-gate that gives admission to a maze of sweet-smelling shrubs. "I really don't know. They may not care about us, or even remember we exist—the resimulants may be being generated by some autonomic mechanism, not really part of the higher consciousness of the Offspring. Or it may be some whacked-out post-Tiplerite meme that's gotten hold of more processing resources than the entire pre-singularity net, some kind of MetaMormon project directed at ensuring that everyone who can possibly ever have lived lives in the *right way* to fit some weird quasi-religious requirement we don't know about. Or it might be a message we're simply not smart enough to decode. That's the trouble. We don't know."

She vanishes around the curve of the maze. Rita hurries to catch up, sees her about to turn into another alleyway, and leaps after her. "What else?" She pants.

"Could be—" left turn— "*anything*, really." Six steps lead down into a shadowy tunnel: fork right, five meters forward, then six steps up lead back to the surface. "Question is, why don't they—" left turn—"just *tell* us what they want?"

"Speaking to tapeworms." Rita manages to nearly catch up with Amber, who is trotting through the maze as if she's memorized it perfectly. "That's how much the nascent Matrioshka brain can out-think us by, as humans to segmented worms. Would we do. What they told us?"

"Maybe." Amber stops dead, and Rita glances around. They're in an open cell near the heart of the maze, five meters square, hedged in on all sides. There are three entrances and a slate altar, waist high, lichen stained with age. "I think you know the answer to that question."

"I—" Rita stares at her.

Amber stares back, eyes dark and intense. "You're from one of the Ganymede orbitals by way of Titan. You knew my eigensister while I was out of the solar system flying a diamond the size of a coke can. That's what you told me. You've got a skill set that's a perfect match for the campaign research group, and you asked me to introduce you to Sirhan, then you pushed his buttons like a pro. Just what *are* you trying to pull? Why should I trust you?"

"I—" Rita's face crumples. "I *didn't* push his buttons! He *thought* I was trying to drag him into bed." She looks up defiantly. "I wasn't, I want to learn, what makes you—him—work." Huge dark structured information queries batter at her exocortex, triggering warnings. Someone is churning through distributed time-series databases all over the outer system, measuring her past with a micrometer. She stares at Amber, mortified and angry. It's the ultimate denial of trust, the need to check her statements against the public record for truth. "What are you doing?"

"I have a suspicion." Amber stands poised, as if ready to run—*run away from me?* Rita thinks, startled. "You said, what if the resimulants came from a subconscious function of the Offspring? And funnily enough, I've been discussing that possibility with Dad. He's still got the spark when you show him a problem, you know."

"I don't understand!"

"No, I don't think you do," says Amber, and Rita can feel vast stresses in the space around her: the whole ubicomp environment, dust-sized chips and utility fog and hazy clouds of diamond-bright optical processors in the soil and the air and her skin, is growing blotchy and sluggish, thrashing under the load of whatever Amber—with her management-grade ackles—is ordering it to do. For a moment, Rita can't feel half her mind, and she gets the panicky claustrophobic sense of being trapped inside her own head: then it stops.

"Tell me!" Rita insists. "What are you trying to

prove? It's some mistake—" And Amber is nodding, much to her surprise, looking weary and morose. "What do you think I've done?"

"Nothing. You're coherent. Sorry about that."

"Coherent?" Rita hears her voice rising with her indignation as she feels bits of herself, cut off from her for whole seconds, shivering with relief. "I'll give you coherent! Assaulting my exocortex—"

"Shut up." Amber rubs her face and simultaneously throws Rita one end of an encrypted channel.

"Why should I?" Rita demands, not accepting the handshake.

"Because." Amber glances round. *She's scared!* Rita suddenly realizes. "Just *do* it," she hisses.

Rita accepts the endpoint, and a huge lump of undigested expository data slides down it, structured and tagged with entrypoints and metainformation directories pointing to—

"Holy *shit,*" she whispers, as she realizes what it is.

"Yes." Amber grins humorlessly. She continues, over the open channel: *It looks like they're antibodies, generated by the devil's own semiotic immune system. That's what Sirhan is focusing on, how to avoid triggering them and bringing everything down at once. Forget the election, we're going to be in deep shit sooner rather than later and we're still trying to work out how to survive. Now are you sure you still want in?*

"Want in on *what?*" Rita asks, shakily.

The lifeboat Dad's trying to get us all into under cover of the accelerationista/conservationista split, before the Vile Offspring's immune system figures out how to lever us apart into factions and make us kill each other....

Welcome to the afterglow of the intelligence supernova, little tapeworm.

Tapeworms have on the order of a thousand neurons, pulsing furiously to keep their little bodies twitching. Human beings have on the order of a hundred billion neurons. What is happening in the inner solar system as the Vile Offspring churn and reconfigure the fast-thinking structured dust clouds that were once planets is as far beyond the ken of merely human consciousness as the thoughts of a Gödel are beyond the twitching tropisms of a worm. Personality modules bounded by the speed of light, sucking down billions of times the processing power of a human brain, form and reform in the halo of glowing nanoprocessors that shrouds the sun in a ruddy glowing cloud.

Mercury, Venus, Mars, Ceres, and the asteroids—all gone. Luna is a silvery iridescent sphere, planed smooth down to micrometer heights, luminous with diffraction patterns. Only Earth, the cradle of human civilization, remains untransformed: and Earth, too, will be dismantled soon enough, for already a trellis of space elevators webs the planet around its equator, lifting refugee dumb matter into orbit and flinging it at the wildlife reserves of the outer system.

The intelligence bloom that gnaws at Jupiter's moons with claws of molecular machinery won't stop until it runs out of dumb matter to convert into computronium. By the time it does, it will have as much brain power as you'd get if you placed a planet with a population of six billion future-shocked primates in orbit around every star in the Milky Way galaxy. But right now, it's still stupid, having converted barely a percentage point of the mass of the solar system—a mere Magellanic Cloud civilization, infantile and unsubtle and still perilously close to its carbon-chemistry roots.

It's hard for tapeworms living in warm intestinal mulch to wrap their thousand-neuron brains around whatever it is that the vastly more complex entities who host them are discussing, but one thing's sure—the owners have a lot of things going on, not all of them under conscious control. The churning of gastric secretions and the steady ventilation of lungs are incomprehensible to the simple brains of tapeworms, but they serve the purpose of keeping the humans alive and provide the environment the worms live in. And other more esoteric functions contribute to survival—the intricate dance of specialized cloned lymphocytes in their bone marrow and lymph nodes, the random permutations of antibodies constantly churning for possible matches to intruder molecules warning of the presence of pollution, it's all going on beneath the level of conscious control.

Autonomic defenses. Antibodies. Intelligence bloom gnawing at the edges of the outer system. And humans are not as unsophisticated as mulch wrigglers, they can see the writing on the wall. Is it any surprise that among the ones who look outward, the real debate is not over whether to run, but over how far and how *fast?*

There's a team meeting early the next morning. It's

still dark outside, and most of the attendees who're present in vivo have the faintly haggard look that comes from abusing melatonin antagonists. Rita stifles a yawn as she glances around the conference room—the walls expanded into huge virtual spaces to accommodate thirty or so exocortical ghosts from sleeping partners who will wake with memories of a particularly vivid lucid dream—and sees Amber talking to her famous father and a younger-looking man who one of her partials recognizes as a last-century EU politician. There seems to be some tension.

Now that Amber has granted Rita her conditional trust, a whole new tier of campaigning information has opened up to her inner eye—stuff steganographically concealed in a hidden layer of the project's collective memory space. There's stuff in here she hadn't suspected, frightening studies of resimulant demographics, surveys of emigration rates from the inner system, cladistic trees dissecting different forms of crude tampering that have been found skulking in the wetware of refugees. The *reason* why Amber and Manfred and—reluctantly—Sirhan are fighting for one radical faction in a planet-wide election, despite their various misgivings over the validity of the entire concept of democracy in this posthuman era. She blinks it aside, slightly bewildered, forking a couple of dozen personality subthreads to chew on it at the edges. "Need coffee," she mutters to the table as it offers her a chair.

"Everyone online?" asked Manfred. "Then I'll begin." He looks tired and worried, physically youthful but showing the full weight of his age. "We've got a crisis coming, folks. About a hundred kiloseconds ago, the bit rate on the re-simulation stream jumped. We're now fielding about one resimulated state vector a second, on top of the legitimate immigration we're dealing with. If it jumps again by the same factor, it's going to swamp our ability to check the immigrants for zimboes in vivo—we'd have to move to running them in secure storage or just resurrecting them blind, and if there *are* any jokers in the pack, that's about the riskiest thing we could do."

"Why do you not spool them to memory diamond?" asks the handsome young ex- politician to his left, looking almost amused—as if he already knows the answer.

"Politics." Manfred shrugs.

"It would blow a hole in our social contract," says Amber, looking as if she's just swallowed something unpleasant, and Rita feels a flicker of admiration for the way they're stage-managing the meeting. Amber's even talking to her father, as if she feels comfortable with him around, although he's a walking reminder of her own lack of success. Nobody else has gotten a word in yet. "If we don't instantiate them, the next logical step is to deny re-simulated minds the franchise. Which in turn puts us on the road to institutional inequality. And that's a very big step to take, even if you have misgivings about the idea of settling complex policy issues on the basis of a popular vote, because our whole polity is based on the idea that less competent intelligences—us—deserve consideration."

"Hrmph." Someone clears their throat. Rita glances round and freezes, because it's Amber's screwed-up eigenchild, and he's just about materialized in the chair next to her. *So he adopted superplonk after all?* she observes cynically. He doggedly avoids looking at her. "That was my analysis," he says reluctantly. "We need them alive. For the ark option, at least, and if not, even the accelerationista platform will need them on hand later."

Concentration camps, thinks Rita, trying to ignore Sirhan's presence near her, for it's a constant irritant, *where most of the inmates are confused, frightened human beings—and the ones who aren't* think *they are.* It's an eerie thought, and she spawns a couple of full ghosts to dream it through for her, gaming the possible angles.

"How are your negotiations over the lifeboat designs going?" Amber asks her father. "We need to get a portfolio of design schemata out before we go into the election—"

"Change of plan." Manfred hunches forward. "This doesn't need to go any further, but Sirhan and Aineko have come up with something interesting." He looks worried.

Sirhan is staring at his eigenmother with narrowed eyes, and Rita has to resist the urge to elbow him savagely in the ribs. She knows enough about him now to realize it wouldn't get his attention—at least, not the way she'd want it, not for the right reasons—and, in any case, he's more wrapped up in himself than her ghost ever saw him as likely to be. (How *anyone* could be party to such a detailed exchange of simulated lives and still reject the opportunity to do it in real life is beyond her: unless it's an artifact of his youth, when his parents pushed him through a dozen simulated childhoods in search of knowledge and ended up with a stubborn oyster-head of a son....) "We still need to look as if we're planning on using a lifeboat," he says aloud. "There's the small matter of the price they're asking in return for the alternative."

"What? What are you talking about?" Amber sounds confused. "I thought you were working on some kind of cladistic map. What's this about a price?"

Sirhan smiles coolly. "I *am* working on a cladistic map. In a manner of speaking. You wasted much of your opportunity when you journeyed to the Router, you know. I've been talking to Aineko."

"You—" Amber flushes. "What about?" She's visibly angry, Rita notices. Sirhan is needling his eigenmother. *Why?*

"About the topology of some rather interesting types of small-world network." Sirhan leans back in his chair, watching the cloud above her head. "And the Router. You went through it, then you came back with your tail between your legs as fast as you could, didn't you? Not even checking your passenger to see if it was a hostile parasite."

"I don't have to take this," Amber says tightly. "You weren't there and you have no idea what constraints we were working under."

"Really?" Sirhan raises an eyebrow. "Anyway, you missed an opportunity. We know that the Routers—for whatever reason—are self-replicating. They spread from brown dwarf to brown dwarf, hatch, tap the protostar for energy and material, and send a bunch of children out. Von Neumann machines, in other words. We also know that they provide high-bandwidth lightspeed communications to other Routers. When you went through the one at Hyundai +4904/-56, you ended up in an unmaintained DMZ attached to an alien Matrioshka brain that had degenerated, somehow. It follows that *someone* had collected a Router and carried it home, to link into the MB. So why didn't *you* bring one home with you?"

Amber glares at him. "Total payload on board the *Field Circus* was about ten grams. How large do you think a Router seed is?"

"So you brought the Slug home instead, occupying maybe half your storage capacity, and ready to wreak seven shades of havoc on—"

"Children!" They both look round automatically. It's Annette, Rita realizes, and she doesn't look amused. "Why do you not save this bickering for later?" She asks. "We have our own goals to be pursuing." Unamused is an understatement. Annette is fuming,

"This charming family reunion was *your* idea, I believe?" Manfred smiles at her, then nods coolly at the retread EU politician in the next seat.

"Please." It's Amber. "Dad, can you save this for later?" Rita sits up. For a moment, Amber looks ancient, far older than her subjective gigasecond of age. "She's right. She didn't mean to screw up. Let's leave the family history for some time when we can work it out in private. Okay?"

Manfred looks abashed. He blinks rapidly. "Alright." He takes a breath. "Amber, I brought some old acquaintances into the loop. If we win the election, then to get out of here as fast as possible, we'll have to use a combination of the two main ideas we've been discussing: spool as many people as possible into high density storage until we get somewhere with space and mass and energy to reincarnate them, and get our hands on a Router. The entire planetary polity can't afford to pay the energy budget of a relativistic starship big enough to hold everyone, even as uploads, and a sub-relativistic ship would be too damn vulnerable to the Vile Offspring. And it follows that instead of taking pot luck on the destination, we should learn about the network protocols the Routers use, figure out some kind of transferable currency we can use to pay for our reinstantiation with at the other end, and also how to make some kind of map so we know where we're going. The two hard parts are getting at or to a Router, and paying—that's going to mean traveling with someone who understands Economics 2.0 but doesn't want to hang around the Vile Offspring.

"As it happens, some old acquaintances of mine went out and fetched back a Router seed, for their own purposes. It's sitting about thirty light-hours away from here, out in the Kuiper belt. They're trying to hatch it right now. And I *think* Aineko might be willing to go with us and handle the trade negotiations." He raises the palm of his right hand and flips a bundle of tags into the shared spatial cache of the inner circles' memories.

Lobsters. Decades ago, back in the dim wastelands of the depression-ridden naughty oughties when Manfred was getting going as an agalmic entrepreneur, the uploaded lobsters had escaped onto the net and taken over a dodgy software users group in Moscow. Manfred brokered a deal whereby they'd get their very own cometary factory colony, in return for providing intelligent direction to a bunch of robot machine tools owned by the Franklin trust. Years later, Amber's expedition to the alien artifact known as the Router had run into eerie zombie lobsters, upload ghosts that had been taken over and reanimated by surprisingly stupid scavenger memes. But where the *real* lobsters had gotten to....

For a moment, Rita sees herself hovering in darkness and vacuum, the distant siren-song of a planetary gravity well far below. Off to her—left? north?—glows a hazy dim red cloud the size of the full moon as seen from Earth, a cloud that hums with a constant background noise, the waste heat of a galactic civilization thinking furious colorless thoughts to itself. Then she figures out how to slew her unblinking, eyeless viewpoint around, and secs the craft.

It's a starship in the shape of a crustacean three kilometers long. It's segmented and flattened, with legs projecting from the abdominal floor to stretch stiffly sideways and clutch fat balloons of cryogenic deuterium fuel. The blue metallic tail is a flattened fan wrapped around the delicate stinger of a fusion reactor. Near the head, things are different: no huge claws here, but the delicately branching fuzz of bush robots, nanoassemblers poised ready to repair damage in flight and spin the parachute of a ramscoop when the ship is ready to decelerate. The head is massively armored against the blitzkrieg onslaught of interstellar dust, its radar eyes a glint of hexagonal compound surfaces staring straight at her.

Behind and below the lobster-ship, a planetary ring looms vast and tenuous. The lobster is in orbit around Saturn, mere light seconds away. And as Rita stares at the ship in dumbstruck silence, it *winks* at her.

"They don't have names, at least not as individual identifiers," Manfred says apologetically, "so I asked if he'd mind being called something. He said Blue, because he is. So I give you the good lobster *Something Blue* ."

Sirhan interrupts, "You still need my cladistics project." He sounds somewhat smug. "To find your way through the network. Do you have a specific destination in mind?"

"Yeah, to both questions," Manfred admits. "We need to send duplicate ghosts out to each possible Router endpoint, wait for an echo, then iterate and repeat. Recursive depth-first traversal. The goal—that's harder." He points at the ceiling, which dissolves into a chaotic three-D spiderweb that Rita recognizes, after some hours of subjective head-down archive time, as a map of the dark matter distribution throughout a radius of a billion light years, galaxies glued like fluff to the nodes where strands of drying silk meet. "We've known for most of a century that there's something weird going on out there, out past the Bootes void—there are a couple of galactic superclusters around which there's something flaky about the cosmic background anisotropy. Most computational processes generate entropy as a by-product, and it looks like something is dumping waste heat into the area from all the galaxies in the region, very evenly spread in a way that mirrors the metal distribution in those galaxies, except at the very cores. And according to the lobsters, who have been indulging in some *very* long baseline interferometry, most of the stars in the nearest cluster are redder than expected, and metal-depleted. As if someone's been mining them."

"Ah." Sirhan stares at his grandfather. "Why should they be any different from the local nodes?"

"Look around you. Do you see any indications of large-scale cosmic engineering within a million light years of here?" Manfred shrugs. "Locally, nothing has quite reached... well. We can guess at the lifecycle of a post-spike civilization now, can't we? We've felt the elephant. We've seen the wreckage of collapsed Matrioshka minds. We know how unattractive exploration is to post-singularity intelligences, we've seen the bandwidth gap that keeps them at home." He points at the ceiling. "But over *there*, something *different* happened. They're making changes on the scale of an entire galactic supercluster, and they appear to be coordinated. They *did* get out and go places, and their descendants may still be out there. It looks like they're doing something purposeful and organized, something vast—a timing channel attack on the virtual machine that's running the universe, perhaps, or an embedded simulation of an entirely different universe. Up or down, is it turtles all the way, or is there something out there that's more real than we are? And don't you think it's worth trying to find out?"

"No." Sirhan crosses his arms. "Not particularly. I'm interested in saving people from the Vile Offspring, not taking a huge gamble on mystery transcendent aliens who may have built a galaxy-sized reality-hacking machine a billion years ago. I'll sell you my services, and even send a ghost along, but if you expect me to bet my entire future on it..."

It's too much for Rita. Diverting her attention away from the dizzying innerspace vista, she elbows Sirhan in the ribs. He looks round blankly for a moment, then with gathering anger as he lets his killfile filter slip. "Whereof one cannot speak, thereof one must be silent," she hisses. Then succumbing to a secondary impulse she knows she'll regret later, she drops a private channel into his public in-tray.

"Nobody's asking you to," Manfred is saying defensively, arms crossed. "I view this as a Manhattan project kind of thing, pursue all agendas in parallel, if we win the election we'll have the resources we need to do that. We should *all* go through the Router, and we will *all* leave backups aboard *Something Blue*. *Blue* is *slow*, tops out at about a tenth of cee, but what he can do is get a sufficient quantity of memory diamond the hell out of circumsolar space before the Vile Offspring's autonomic defenses activate whatever kind of trust exploit they're planning in the next few megaseconds—"

"What do you want?" Sirhan demands angrily over the channel. He's still not looking at her, and not just because he's focusing on the vision in blue that dominates the shared space of the team meeting.

"Stop lying to yourself," Rita sends back. *"You're lying about your own goals and motivations. You may not want to know the truth your own ghost worked out, but I do. And I'm not going to let you deny it happened."*

"So one of your agents seduced a personality image of me—"

"Bullshit—"

"—Do you mean to declare this platform openly?" asks the young-old guy near the platform, the europol. "Because if so, you're going to undermine Amber's campaign—"

"That's all right," Amber says tiredly, "I'm used to Dad "supporting" me in his own inimitable way."

"Is okay," says a new voice. "I are happy wait-state

grazing in ecliptic." It's the friendly lobster lifeboat, light-lagged by its trajectory outside the ring system.

"—*You're happy to hide behind a hypocritical sense of moral purity when it makes you feel you can look down on other people, but underneath it you're just like everyone else—*"

"—She *set you up to corrupt me, didn't she? You're just bait in her scheme—*"

"The idea was to store incremental backups in the paruliran's cargo cache in case a weakly godlike agency from the inner system attempts to activate the antibodies they've already disseminated throughout the festival culture," Annette explains, stepping in on Manfred's behalf.

Nobody else in the discussion space seems to notice that Rita and Sirhan are busy ripping the shit out of each other over a private channel, throwing emotional hand grenades back and forth like seasoned divorcees. "It's not a satisfactory solution to the evacuation question, but it ought to satisfy the conservatives' baseline requirement, and as insurance—"

"—*That's right, blame your eigenmother! Has it occurred to you that she doesn't care enough about you to try a stunt like that? I think you spent too much time with that crazy grandmother of yours. You didn't even integrate that ghost, did you? Too afraid of polluting yourself! I bet you never even bothered to check what it felt like from inside—*"

"—*I did—*" Sirhan freezes for a moment, personality modules paging in and out of his brain like a swarm of angry bees—"*make a fool of myself,*" he adds quietly, then slumps back in his seat. "*This is so embarrass-*

ing...." He covers his face with his hands. *"You're right."*

"I am?" Rita's puzzlement slowly gives way to understanding; Sirhan has finally integrated the memories from the partials they hybridized earlier. Stuck-up and proud, the cognitive dissonance must be enormous. *"No I'm not. You're just overly defensive."*

"I'm—" Embarrassed. Because Rita knows him, inside-out. Has the ghost-memories of six months in a simspace with him, playing with ideas, exchanging intimacies, later confidences. She holds ghost-memories of his embrace, a smoky affair that might have happened in realspace if his instant reaction to realizing that it *could* happen hadn't been to dump the splinter of his mind that was contaminated by impure thoughts to cold storage and to deny everything.

"We have no threat profile yet," Annette says, cutting right across their private conversation. "If there *is* a direct threat—and we don't even know that for sure, yet, the Vile Offspring might be enlightened enough to simply be leaving us alone—it'll probably be some kind of subtle attack aimed directed at the foundations of our identity. Look for a credit bubble, distributed trust metrics devaluing suddenly as people catch some kind of weird religion, something like that. Maybe a perverse election outcome. And it won't be sudden. They are not stupid, to start a headlong attack without slow corruption to soften the way."

"You've obviously been thinking about this for some time," Sameena says with dry emphasis. "What's in it for your friend, uh, Blue? Did you squirrel away enough credit to cover the price of renting a starship from the Economics 2.0 metabubble? Or is there something you aren't telling us?"

"Um." Manfred looks like a small boy with his hand caught in the sweet jar. "Well, as a matter of fact—"

"Yes, Dad, why don't you tell us just what this is going to cost?" Amber asks.

"Ah, well." He looks embarrassed. "It's the lobsters, not Aineko. They want, some payment."

Rita reaches out and grabs Sirhan's hand: he doesn't resist. *"Do you know about this?"* Rita queries him.

"All new to me...." A confused partial thread follows his reply down the pipe, and for a while, she joins him in introspective reverie, trying to work out the implications of knowing what they know about the possibility of a mutual relationship—"

"They want a written conceptual map. A map of all the accessible meme-spaces hanging off the Router network, compiled by a single human mind who they can use as a baseline, they say. It's quite simple—just fork a copy of the author to each Router we probe and have him return a finished draft before broadcasting himself to all the nodes linked to that particular Router."

"Do they have a particular author in mind?" Amber sniffs.

"Yes," says Manfred. "I'm used to being a multiplicity." He pauses, unhappily. "Right after I finally got myself together again...."

The pre-election campaign takes approximately three minutes and consumes more bandwidth than the sum of all terrestrial communications channels from pre-history to 2008. Approximately six million ghosts of Amber, individually tailored to fit the jib of the targeted audience, fork across the dark fiber meshwork underpinning all of the lillypad colonies, then out through ultrawideband mesh networks, instantiated in implants and floating dust motes to buttonhole the voters. Many of them fail to reach their audience, and many more hold fruitless discussions; about six actually decide they've diverged so far from their original that they constitute separate people and register for independent citizenship, two defect to the other side, and one elopes with a swarm of highly empathic modified African honeybees.

Ambers are not the only ghosts competing for attention in the public zeitgeist. In fact, they're in a minority. Most of the autonomous electoral agents are campaigning for a variety of platforms that range from introducing a progressive income tax—nobody is quite sure *why*, but it seems to be traditional—to a motion calling for the entire planet to be paved, which quite ignores the realities of element abundance in the upper atmosphere of a metal-poor gas giant, not to mention playing hell with the weather. The Faceless are campaigning for everyone to be assigned a new set of facial muscles every six months, the Livid Pranksters are demanding equal rights for sub-sentient entities, and a host of single-issue pressure groups are yammering about the usual lost causes.

Just how the election process anneals is a black mystery—at least, to those people who aren't party to the workings of the Festival Committee, the group who first had the idea of paving Saturn with hot-hydrogen balloons—but over the course of a complete diurn, almost forty thousand seconds, a pattern begins to emerge. This pattern will systematize the bias of the communications networks that traffic in reputation points across the planetary polity for a long time—possibly as much as fifty million seconds, getting on for a whole Martian year (if Mars still existed). It will create a parliament—a merged group-mind borganism that speaks as one supermind built from the beliefs of the victors. And the news isn't great, as the party gathered in the upper sphere of the Atomium (which Manfred insisted Amber rent for the dead dog party) is slowly realizing. Amber isn't there, presumably drowning her sorrows or engaging in post-election schemes of a different nature somewhere else. But other members of her team are about.

"It could be worse," Rita rationalizes, late in the evening. She's sitting in a corner of the seventh floor deck, in a 1950's wireframe chair, clutching a glass of synthetic single malt and watching the shadows. "We could be in an old-style contested election with seven shades of shit flying. At least this way we can be decently anonymous."

One of the blind spots detaches from her peripheral vision and approaches. It segues into view, suddenly congealing into Sirhan. He looks morose.

"What's *your* problem?" She demands. "Your faction are winning on the count."

"Maybe so." He sits down beside her, carefully avoiding her gaze. "Maybe this is a good thing. And maybe not."

"So when are you going to join the syncitium?" she asks.

"Me? Join that?" He looks alarmed. "You think I

want to become part of a parliamentary borg? What do you take me for?"

"Oh." She shakes her head. "I assumed you were avoiding me because—"

"No." He holds out his hand and a passing waitron deposits a glass in it. He takes a deep breath. "I owe you an apology."

About time, she thinks, uncharitably. But he's like that. Stiff-necked and proud, slow to acknowledge a mistake, but unlikely to apologize unless he really means it. "What for?" she asks.

"For not giving you the benefit of the doubt," he says slowly, rolling the glass between his palms. "I should have listened to myself earlier instead of locking him out of me."

The self he's talking about seems self-evident to her. "You're not an easy man to get close to," she says quietly. "Maybe that's part of your problem."

"Part of it?" He chuckles bitterly. "My mother—" He bites back whatever he originally meant to say. "Do you know I'm older than she is? Than this version, I mean. She gets up my nose with her assumptions about me...."

"They run both ways." Rita reaches out and takes his hand—and he grips her right back, no rejection this time. "Listen, it looks as if she's not going to make it into the parliament of lies. There's a straight conservative sweep, these folks are in solid denial. About 80 percent of the population are resimulants or old-timers from Earth, and that's not going to change before the Vile Offspring turn on us. What are we going to do?"

He shrugs. "I suspect everyone who thinks we're really under threat will move on. You know this is going to destroy the accelerationists' trust in democracy? They've still got a viable plan—Manfred's friendly lobster will work without the need for an entire planet's energy budget—but the rejection is going to hurt. I can't help thinking that maybe the real goal of the Vile Offspring was to simply gerrymander us into not diverting resources away from them. It's blunt, it's unsubtle, so we assumed that wasn't the point. But maybe there's a time for them to be blunt."

She shrugs. "Democracy is a bad fit for lifeboats." But she's still uncomfortable with the idea. "And think of all the people we'll be leaving behind."

"Well." He smiles tightly. "If you can think of any way to encourage the masses to join us…"

"A good start would be to stop thinking of them as masses to be manipulated." Rita stares at him. "Your family appears to have been developing a hereditary elitist streak, and it's not attractive."

Sirhan looks uncomfortable. "If you think *I'm* bad, you should talk to Aineko about it," he says, self-deprecatingly. "Sometimes I wonder about that cat."

"Maybe I will." She pauses. "And you? What are you going to do with yourself?"

"I—" He looks sideways at her. "I can see myself sending an eigenbrother," he says quietly. "I'm not going to gamble my entire future on a bid to reach the far side of the observable universe by wormhole, though. I'll stash a copy of myself with the lobsters. What about you?"

"You'll go all three ways?" she asks.

"Yes. I think so. What about you?"

She shrugs. "One to stay behind, one to wait in the

icy depths, and one to go exploring." She leans against him.

Then she says, "Me too."

Opal Ball

Robert Reed

Robert Reed graduated from Nebraska Wesleyan University in 1978 and worked as a laboratory technician before becoming a full-time writer in 1987, the same year his story "Mudpuppies" won the L. Ron Hubbard Writers of the Future Contest. Starting with The Leeshore *and* The Hormone Jungle *in 1987, he has published ten novels, most notably the far future science fiction novel* Marrow, *but is probably best known for his short fiction. An extraordinarily prolific writer, Reed has published over a hundred short stories, mostly in the pages of* The Magazine of Fantasy and Science Fiction *and* Asimov's, *which have been nominated for the Hugo, James Tiptree Jr, Memorial, Locus, Nebula, Seiun, Theodore Sturgeon Memorial, and World Fantasy awards, and have been collected in* The Dragons of Springplace *and* Chrysalide *(published in French). His most recent books are the story-suite* Sister Alice *and chapbook* Mere. *Upcoming is the novel* The Well of Stars, *a sequel to* Marrow, *and a new collection,* The Cuckoo's Boys. *Possibly Nebraska's only science fiction writer, he lives in Omaha with his wife and daughter.*

The moving story that follows asks whether we would really want to know the future if we possibly could.

She is a player, like Cliff.

Like him, she is in her early thirties, healthy and single. And like the best in their profession, she is financially secure.

They meet entirely by chance, share a lazy dinner on a whim, and like any two players left to themselves, talk endlessly about the future. Who wins the next presidential race, and assuming her, will she win reelection? When will the next alien transmission arrive, and what treasures, if any, will it hold? (The GrokTrok signal still sits raw on everyone's mind.) Will the world's stock markets continue their steady ascent, or will their gains accelerate? "Accelerate," Cliff decides. But the graph is trimodal, she reminds him; a persistent gloom-and-doom wager is riding on the prolonged plateau. Cliff asks what the Chinese will do about Tibet. She asks what the U.S. will do with Free Alaska. They wonder if the Europa mission will find life, and will the United Council fund the Alpha Centauri mission, and when will the Sun finally extinguish its nuclear fuel. Then with a wink and a sly little grin, Cliff predicts who is going to win the next World Series.

That brings a hearty laugh from his new friend. Athletics have adapted to the new circumstances: Players and teams are rigorously balanced, while the fields of play have been made wildly chaotic. Each ball has its own weight and distinct shape. Winds are generated on site, gusting and swirling in random directions, while the grass grows and shrivels according to its own whims, and the soil folds into little lumps in all the worst places. With every modern sport, rules reward competitors with enormous scores, and they punish with fat penalties, and predicting the outcome of any game, much less the season, is impossible—which is the only reason people still are willing to cheer for the home team.

Dinner is a joy, and it doesn't take any unique vision to see what happens next. Hours later, lying beneath the perfumed sheets of his new lover's home, Cliff relates his own history as a player: Teachers and his own ego told him that he enjoyed a certain talent with science, so he began there. But he predicted a rapid solution to the telemeres problem with life expansion, and there is none. He wagered heavily on a quantum theory of gravity that subsequently proved to be flawed. And he made a fool of himself in deep-space astronomy, predicting no observable supernova in the Milky Way for the next thirty years. Which seemed perfectly reasonable, he points out, since stars explode infrequently and the last blast was seen just six years before. But wiser souls—real scientists, devoted hobbyists, and a multitude of crafty AIs—correctly assessed both the historic record and the stellar actuarial tables. The recent supernova had been decades behind schedule, and the next one could happen any time. Eighteen months, to be exact. Suddenly money that Cliff had set on a thirty-year shelf was yanked down and divided among wiser players. Which wasn't awful news, of course. It wasn't all that much money, he pretends. But Cliff's greatest failure—a genuine disaster—was his bold prediction that the next alien transmission would come within the newborn year, and it would prove as beneficial as the Sag Prime signal of '37. Both wagers proved to be spectacular mistakes. The sky was silent for the entire year, and then two days too late, the GrokTrok signal finally arrived, bringing the good people of Earth nothing but a gloriously colorful, highly detailed image of an alien's flower-like hind end, brazenly displayed to the camera and to the universe at large.

That's how Cliff got into human prediction, at last. Here was a realm with importance as well as important money, and no damned AIs to compete against. ("If machines ever master human dynamics, I'm sunk.") And better still, the young man had a genuine talent for seeing the obvious. "Which of these ten houses would make me happiest? What new activity or sport or hobby should I attempt? Which classic novel fits my soul best? And what sort of man, or woman, should I marry? If I marry anyone, of course." He read the questions on the public boards, and if any tickled his interest, he examined the attached data tail. Biographies begged to be studied, including images and deep glances into these not-so-private lives. Certain questions interested him; who can say why? By various means, he looked past the tail, investigating these distant lives by every legal means. Then he looked again at the person asking for guidance, listening to the play of the voice, observing the tilt of the head and the nervous flicker of an arching eyebrow. That final gaze meant everything. Did he know this soul well enough to offer help? And if so, how much did he want to help? Five dollars' worth, or fifty? Or maybe a fat hundred?

"Prince Randolph was my crowning success," Cliff mentions.

"Truly?" his lover purrs, ignoring the graceless pun.

Being a thoroughly modern man, Randolph had asked the world, "Which girl should I marry?" And the world responded with fascination and fantastic sums of money. Half a dozen candidates were put on public display. The prince's brief life was sliced open and examined in clinical detail. Questions were posted on his public board, and he answered them for everyone to see. Of course old lovers were sought out. A pleasant mother and surly father offered a range of conflicting hopes and opinions. Then Cliff, along with another billion others—a shared intellect scattered across six continents, ten orbital cities, and the Moon—made their final wagers.

"I was one of those billion," his lover admits.

No small coincidence, that

Then she continues, mentioning, "'None of these girls are worth marrying,' I told the prince."

Which was what Cliff had decided, too. "But I made this substantial side wager," he boasts. "Randolph would settle for happiness and a certain woman twenty years his senior." And sure enough, six months later the heir to the British throne married his one-time nanny, and Cliff was one of the six hundred and two players who had seen the future the clearest.

In reward, he received a substantial share from a small ocean of earnings.

"And guess what," his lover purrs. "So did I."

"No," he blurts. "Truly?"

"Truly," she says. Then from the darkness, she asks, "What do you think it means, darling? Two great players coming together like this?"

The future has always been an opaque crystal. Shamans and popes have always seen the obvious, predicting the seasons as well as the inevitabilities of life and death. Then came science and computers, creating experts trained in every narrow field, and the future was a little less opaque. But even the most expert mind, armed with the finest tools, is limited. Is hamstrung. Every mind is finite; bias kills the most gifted visionary; and wishful thinking can do nothing but distort and then blind. It wasn't until humans and their smartest machines began to place wagers, risking money against tomorrow, that the future became a little more knowable, and workable, and for the serious player, a source of financial blood.

Without question, this is a Golden Age. With a multitude of eyes peering into the great Opal Ball, the future is being revealed as never before. And the world has never been as efficient or happy or half as flexible. Which only stands to reason: Unbiased observers have a better chance of predicting wars and economic downturns than do government officials and stock market mavens. No matter how brilliant, the individual is always dim next to the multitude. And no expert of souls and society can give the same shrewd personal advice that is delivered by just a few hundred busybodies looking at your little life.

Cliff is a stellar example:

He was an avid cyclist until strangers did an analysis of his body and muscles, predicting that he'd prefer sculling across open water. It is an obscure sport, and he had no previous interest. But sure enough, he quickly became one of the top thousand scullers in the country, and winning in any sport makes it into a thorough pleasure.

He believed that he adored Bach. But rock-and-roll from the last century is his new favorite, thanks to a few hundred invited suggestions.

He always wore blue, but black and white are his natural colors, and changing his wardrobe and the color of his hair has done wonders.

And now, purely by chance, the player-woman has come into his perfect life.

Spent and happy, he drags himself home in the morning. But before he finally sleeps, he turns to the public board, asking the entire world, "Is this the woman meant for me?"

A twenty-four-hour window feels right.

Seed money can spark interest, which is why he places a thousand of his own dollars on YES.

Then Cliff collapses in bed, sleeping hard till evening. And after a quick shower and a stimulant stew, he dresses in black and white before meeting his new love at what has already become their favorite restaurant.

Cliff's honest intention is to listen to the world. To hear its advice and absorb it, acting on its shared wisdom. But he is also in love—utterly, selfishly in love—and through the next night and into the morning hours, he assumes that of course the world will answer with a resounding, "YES."

Yet the world votes, "NO," with a ninety-two percent surety. "She is not and will never be right for you."

Cliff is sitting at home that next morning, exhausted again and this time feeling outraged. What to do, what to do? Finally, he decides to hide the results, at least for the time being. But she is a player—a believer by every measure—and of course she has already asked about Cliff and his worthiness. And the Opal Ball has come to the same unbiased and distinctly negative conclusion.

Her response is a quick and impulsive rage. She flings the stupid results into his face, and she curses a thousand strangers, and in the next breath, she declares, "Let's show them. Let's get married. And I mean right now."

The ceremony seems quicker than the ninety seconds that it takes.

The consequences are instantly apparent, ugly and sad and inescapable. Their first fight lasts an entire day, incandescent words leaving wounds not easily healed. And their last battle never ends. Even after the divorce, she and Cliff trade blows and furious looks, and sometimes he finds himself awake in the night, plotting the awful things that he could do to this monster-woman who stole four months out of his otherwise wondrous life.

Cliff vows: Never again will he doubt the advice of distant voices.

With the help of those voices, he remakes his wardrobe and appearance. He lets them select a new larger home to serve his maturing needs. Against every past interest, he takes up topiary gardening and holopainting. And of course both hobbies are wonderful successes. Then he asks the world, "Where should I go on a long vacation?" And a week later, he and his new ocean-ready scull set off on a voyage down the Chilean coast.

While Cliff is busy fighting the stiff ocean currents, his ex-wife dies.

A phone call delivers the news. Later, he learns the ugly particulars. Depressed and drunk, the woman posted her genetics and life history, and then asked the world about her own future. The Opal Ball responded instantly, showing her nothing that seemed overtly appealing. Small victories in the game, brief relationships that always end badly, and a growing tendency for black moods. So with pills and a length of razored rope, she managed to save herself from years of obscurity and disappointment, and the half a hundred players who had predicted suicide quietly pocketed their winnings.

Cliff feels embarrassingly happy for the first moment or two.

Then the sadness bears down, and he spends a full night sobbing wildly, ashamed of his actions and his glaring failures.

In the morning, an AI attorney contacts him. Was Cliff aware that a three-month-old fetus currently sits in cold storage, and that he and the dead woman are the parents?

The news is an enormous, numbing surprise.

"She conceived during your marriage," the machine explains. "The abortion was apparently kept secret from you."

"What happens to it now?" Cliff blurts out.

The AI hands him a tiny freezer.

"Why did she do this?" he sputters.

"I'm no expert in human emotions, sir," the machine replies. "Thank goodness."

She is born six months later.

Cliff's first act has become a tradition: He places a picture of his daughter and the usual genetic information on the public boards, and then he prepares to ask the world, "What is this child's future?"

But at the last moment, his hand hesitates.

His will fails him.

Or it exceeds what he believed possible, perhaps.

Before the damage is done, he wipes the question off the board. Then he returns to the new crib and peers into his child's eyes. Clearer than opals, they are. Transparent as crystal, and lovely, and when he peers inside them, every future seems real and assured, and lovely, and hers, hers, hers.

My Mother Dancing

Nancy Kress

Nancy Kress is the author of twenty-one books: thirteen novels of science fiction or fantasy, one YA novel, two thrillers, three story collections, and two books on writing. Although she started as a fantasy writer with first novel The Prince of Bells *in 1981, Kress is primarily a science fiction writer and is best known for the "Beggars" trilogy (Beggars in Spain, Beggars and Choosers, and Beggars Ride). Her other major novels include* Oaths and Miracles, Maximum Light, *and the "Probability" trilogy (Probability Moon, Probability Sun and Probability Space). Her most recent novels are* Crossfire *and* Nothing Human.

Kress is also an acclaimed short fiction writer. A three-time Nebula Award-winner, Kress has also received the Hugo, Campbell Memorial and Sturgeon Awards. Her award-winning fiction includes "Out of All Them Bright Stars," "Beggars In Spain," and "The Flowers of Aulit Prison," and has been collected in Trinity and Other Stories, The Aliens of Earth, *and* Beaker's Dozen.

The touching story that follows, originally published in the Robert Silverberg & Jacques Chambon-edited

French anthology Destination 3001 *in 2000, appeared in English for the first time this year.*

Fermi's Paradox, California, 1950: Since planet formation appears to be common, and since the processes that lead to the development of life are a continuation of those that develop planets, and since the development of life leads to intelligence and intelligence to technology—then why hasn't a single alien civilization contacted Earth?
Where is everybody?

They had agreed, laughing, on a form of the millennium contact, what Micah called "human standard," although Kabil had insisted on keeping hirs konfol and Deb had not dissolved hirs crest, which waved three inches about hirs and hummed. But, then, Deb! Ling had designed floating baktor for the entire ship, red and yellow mostly, that combined and recombined in kaleidoscopic loveliness that only Ling could have programmed. The viewport was set to magnify, the air mixture just slightly intoxicating, the tinglies carefully balanced by Cal, that master. Ling had wanted "natural" sleep cycles, but Cal's arguments had been more persuasive, and the tinglics massaged the limbic so pleasantly. Even the child had some. It was a party.

The ship slipped into orbit around the planet, a massive subJovian far from its sun, streaked with muted color. "Lovely," breathed Deb, who lived for beauty.

Cal, the biologist, was more practical: "I ran the

equations; by now there should be around two hundred thousand of them in the rift, if the replication rate stayed constant."

"Why wouldn't it?" said Ling, the challenger, and the others laughed. The tinglies really were a good idea.

The child, Harrah, pressed hirs face to the window. "When can we land?"

The adults smiled at each other. They were so proud of Harrah, and so careful. Hirs was the first gene-donate of all of them except Micah, and probably the only one for the rest of them except Cal, who was a certified intellect donor. Kabil knelt beside Harrah, bringing hirs face close to the child's height.

"Little love, we can't land. Not here. We must see the creations in holo."

"Oh," Harrah said, with the universal acceptance of childhood. It had not changed in five thousand years, Ling was fond of remarking, that child idea that whatever it lived was the norm. But, then... Ling.

"Access the data," Cal said, and Harrah obeyed, reciting it aloud as hirs parents had all taught hirs. Ling smiled to see that Harrah still closed hirs eyes to access, but opened them to recite.

"The creations were dropped on this planet E-years ago. They were the one-hundred-fortieth drop in the Great Holy Mission that gives us our life. The creations were left in a closed-system rift... what does that mean?"

"The air in the creations' valley doesn't get out to the rest of the planet, because the valley is so deep and the gravity so great. They have their own air."

"Oh. The creations are cyborged replicators, programmed for self-awareness. They are also programmed to expect human contact at the millennium. They…"

"Enough," said Kabil, still kneeling beside Harrah. He stroked hirs hair, black today. "The important thing, Harrah, is that you remember that these creations are beings, different from us but with the same life force, the only life force. They must be respected, just as people are even if they look odd to you."

"Or if they don't know as much as you," said Cal. "They won't, you know."

"I know," Harrah said. They made hirs an accommodator, with strong genes for bonding. They already had Ling for challenge. Harrah added, "praise Fermi and Kwang and Arlbeni for the emptiness of the universe."

Ling frowned. Hirs had opposed teaching Harrah the simpler, older folklore of the Great Mission. Ling would have preferred the child receive only truth, not religion. But Deb had insisted. Feed that imagination first, hirs had said, and later Harrah can separate science from prophecy. But the tinglies felt sweet, and the air mixture was set for a party, and hirs own baktors floated in such graceful pattern that Ling, not even Ling, could not quarrel.

"I wonder," Deb said dreamily, "what they have learned in 273 year."

"When will they holo?" Harrah said. "Are we there yet?"

Our mother is coming.

Tow hours more and they will come, from beyond the top of the world. When they come, there will be much dancing. Much rejoicing. All of us will dance and rejoice, even those who have detached and let the air carry them away. Those ones will receive our transmissions and dance with us.

Or maybe our mother will also transmit to where those of us now sit. Maybe they will transmit to all, even those colonies out of our transmission range. Why not? Our mother, who made us, can do whatever is necessary.

First, the dancing. Then, the most necessary thing of all. Our mother will solve program flaw. Completely, so that none of us will die. Our mother doesn't die. We are not supposed to die, either. Our mother will transmit the program to correct this.

Then the dancing there will be!

Kinney's Revolution, Bohr Station, 2662: Since the development of the Quantum Transport, humanity has visited nearly a thousand planets in our galaxy and surveyed many more. Not one of them has developed any life of any kind, no matter how simple. Not one.

No aliens have contacted Earth because there is nobody else out there.

Harrah laughed in delight. Hirs long black hair swung through a drift of yellow baktors. "The creations look like oysters!"

The holocube showed uneven rocky ground through thick, murky air. A short distance away rose the abrupt steep walls of the rift, thousands of feet high. Attached to the ground by thin, flexible mineral-conducting tubes were hundreds of uniform, metal-alloy double shells. The shells held self-replicating nanomachinery, including the rudimentary AI, and living eukaryotes sealed into selectively permeable membranes. The machinery ran on the feeble sunlight and on energy produced by anaerobic bacteria, carefully engineered for the thick atmospheric stew of methane, hydrogen, helium, ammonia, and carbon dioxide.

The child knew none of this. Hirs saw the "oysters" jumping up in time on their filaments, jumping and falling, flapping their shells open and closed, twisting and flapping and bobbing. Dancing.

Kabil laughed, too. "Nowhere in the original programming! They learned it!"

"But what could the stimulus have been?" Ling said. "How lovely to find out!"

"Sssshhh, we're going to transmit," Micha said. Hirs eyes glowed. Micah was the oldest of them all; hirs had been on the original drop. "Seeding 140, are you there?"

"We are here! We are seeding 140! Welcome, our mother!"

Harrah jabbed hirs finger at the holocube. "We're not your mother!"

Instantly, Deb closed the transmission. Micah said harshly, "Harrah! Your manners!"

The child looked scared, Deb said, "Harrah, we talked about this. The creations are not like us, but their ideas are as true as ours, on their own world. Don't laugh at them."

From Kabil, "Don't you remember, Harrah? Access the learning session!"

"I... remember," Harrah faltered.

"Then show some respect!" Micah said. "This is the Great Mission!"

Harrah's eyes teared. Kabil, the tenderhearted, put

hirs hand on Harrah's shoulder. "Small heart, the Great mission gives meaning to our lives."

"I... know...."

Micah said, "You don't want to be like those people who just use up all their centuries in mere pleasure, with no structure to their wanderings around the galaxy, no purpose beyond seeing what the nanos can produce that they haven't produced before, no difference between today and tomorrow, no—"

"That's sufficient," Ling says. Harrah understands, and regrets. Don't give an Arlbeni Day speech, Micah."

Micah said stiffly, "It matters, Ling."

"Of course it matters. But so do the creations and they're waiting. Deb, open the transmission again. Seeding 140, thank you for your welcome! We return!"

Arlbeni's Vision, Planet Cadrys, 2678: We have been fools.

Humanity is in despair. Nano has given us everything and nothing. Endless pleasures empty of effort, endless tomorrows empty of purpose, endless experiences empty of meaning. From evolution to sentience, sentience to nano, nano to the decay of sentience.

But the fault is ours. We have overlooked the greatest gift ever given humanity: the illogical emptiness of the universe. It is against evolution, it as against known physical processes. Therefore, how can it exist? And why?

It can exist only by the intent of something greater

than the physical processes of the universe. A conscious Intent.

The reason can only be to give humanity, the universe's sole inheritor, knowledge of this Intent. The emptiness of the universe—anomalous, unexplainable, impossible—has been left for us to discover, as the only convincing proof of God.

Our mother has come! We dance on the seabed. We transmit the news to the ones who have detached and floated away. We rejoice together, and consult the original program.

"You are above the planetary atmosphere," we say, new words until just this moment, but now understood. All will be understood now, all corrected. "You are in a ship, as we are in our shells."

"Yes," says our mother. "You know we cannot land."

"Yes," we say, and there is momentary dysfunction. How cant hey help us if they cannot land? But only momentary. This is our mother. And they landed us here once, didn't they? They can do whatever is necessary.

Our mother says, "How many are you now, Seeding 140?"

"We are 79,432," we say. Sadness comes. We endure it, as we must.

Our mother's voice changes in wavelength, in frequency. "Seventy-nine thousand? Are you... we had calculated more. Is this replication data correct?"

A packet of data arrives. We scan it quickly; it matches our programming.

"The data is correct, but..." We stop. It feels like another dying ceremony, suddenly, and it is not yet time for a dying ceremony. We will wait another few minutes. We will tell out mother in another few minutes. Instead, we ask, "What is your state of replication, our mother?"

Another change in wavelength and frequency. We scan and match data, and it is in our databanks: laughter, a form of rejoicing. Our mother rejoices.

"You aren't equipped for visuals, or I would show you our replicant," our mother says. "But the rate is much, much lower than yours. We have one new replicant with us on the ship."

"Welcome new replicant!" we say, and there is more rejoicing. There, and here.

"I've restricted transmission... there's the t-field's visual," Micah said.

A hazy cloud appeared to one side of the holocube, large enough to hold two people comfortably, three close together. Only words spoken in the filed would now transmit. Baktors scuttled clear of the ionized haze. Deb stepped inside the field, with Harrah; Cal moved out of it. Hirs frowned at Micah.

"They can't be only seventy-nine thousand-plus if the rate of replication held steady. Check the resource data, Micah."

"Scanning.... No change in available raw materials.... No change in sunlight per square unit."

"Scan their counting program."

"I already did. Fully functional."

"Then run an historical scan of replicants created."

"That will take time... there, it's started. What about attrition?"

Cal said, "of course. I should have thought of that.

Do a seismic survey and match it with the original data. A huge quake could easily have destroyed two-thirds of them, poor seedings...."

Ling said, "You could ask them"

Kabil said, "If it's not a cultural taboo. Remember, they have had time to evolve a culture, we left them that ability."

"Only in response to environmental stimuli. Would a quake or a mudslide create enough stimulus pressure to evolve death taboos?"

They looked at each other. Something new in the universe, something humanity had not created... this was why they were here! Their eyes shone, their breaths came faster. Yet they were uncomfortable, too, at the mention of death. How long since any of them... oh, yes. Ling's clone in that computer malfunction, but so many decades ago.... Discomfort, excitement, compassion for Seeding 140, yes compassion most of all, how terrible if the poor creations had actually lost so many in a quake.... All of them felt it, and meant it, the emotion was genuine. And in their minds the finger of God touched them for a moment, with the holiness of the tiny human struggle against the emptiness of the universe.

"Praise Fermi and Kwang and Arlbeni..." one of them murmured, and no one was sure who, in the general embarrassment that took them a moment later. They were not children.

Arlbeni's Vision, Planet Cadrys, 2678: In the proof of God lies its corollary. The Great Intent ahs left the universe empty, but for us. It is our mission to fill it.

Look around you, look at what we've become. At the

pointless destruction, the aimless boredom, the spiritual despair. The human race cannot exist without purpose, without vision, without faith. Filling the emptiness of the universe will rescue us from our own.

Our mother says, "Do you play games?"

We examine the data carefully. There is no match.

Our mother speaks again. "That was our new replicant speaking, Seeding 140. Hirs is only half-created as yet, and hirs program language is not fully functional. Hirs means, of the new programs you have created for yourselves since the original seeding, which ones are in response to the environment are expressions of rejoicing? Like dancing?"

"Yes!" we say. "We dance in rejoicing. And we also throw pebbles in rejoicing and catch pebbles in rejoicing. But not for many years since."

"Do it now!" our mother says.

This is our mother. We are not rejoicing. But this is our mother. We pick up some pebbles.

"No," our mother says quickly, "you don't need to throw pebbles. That was the new replicant again. Hirs does not yet understand that seedings do as they wish. Your... your mother does not command you. Anything you do, anything you have learned, is as necessary as what we do."

"I'm sorry again," our mother says, and there is physical movement registered in the field of transmission.

We do not understand. But our mother has spoken of new programs, of programs created since the seeding, in response to the environment. This we understand, and now it is time to tell our mother of our need. Our mother has asked. Sorrow floods us, rejoicing disappears, but now is the time to tell what is necessary.

Our mother will make all functional once more.

"Don't scold hirs like that, hirs is just a child," Kabil said. "Harrah, stop crying, we know you didn't mean to impute to them any inferiority."

Micah, hirs back turned to the tiny parental drama, said to Cal, "Seismic survey complete. No quakes, only the most minor geologic disturbances... really, the local history shows remarkable stability."

"Then what accounts for the difference between their count of themselves and the replication rate?"

"It can't be a real difference."

"But... oh! Listen. Did they just say—"

Hirs turned slowly toward the holocube.

Harrah said at the same moment, through hirs tears, "They stopped dancing."

Cal said, "repeat that," remembered hirself, and moved into the transmission field, replacing Harrah. "Repeat that, please, Seeding 140. Repeat your last transmission."

The motionless metal oysters said, "We have created a new program in response to the Others in this environment. The Others who destroy us."

Cal said, very pleasantly, "'Others'? What Others?"

"The new ones. The mindless ones. The destroyers."

"There are no others in your environment," Micah said. "What are you trying to say?"

Ling, across the deck in a cloud of pink bakterons, said, "Oh, oh... no... they must have divided into factions. Invented warfare amongst themselves! Oh...."

Harrah stopped sobbing and stood, wide-eyed, on hirs sturdy short legs.

Cal said, still very pleasant, "Seeding 140, show us these Others. Transmit visuals."

"But if we get close enough tot he Others to do that, we will be destroyed!"

Ling said sadly, "It is warfare."

Deb compressed hirs beautiful lips. Kabil turned away, to gaze out at the stars. Micah said, "Seeding... do you have any historical transmissions of the Others, in your databanks? Send those."

"Scanning... sending."

Ling said softly, "We always knew warfare was a possibility for any creations. After all, they have our unrefined DNA, and for millennia..." Hirs fell silent.

"The data is only partial," Seeding 140 said. "We were nearly destroyed when it was sent to us. But there is one data packet until the last few minutes of life."

The cheerful, dancing oysters had vanished from the holocube. In their place were the fronds of a tall, thin plant, waning slightly in the thick air. It was stark, unadorned, elemental. A multicellular organism rooted in the rocky ground, doing nothing.

No one on the ship spoke.

The holocube changed perspective, to a wide scan. Now there were whole stands of fronds, acres of them, filling huge sections of the rift. Plant after plant, drab olive green, blowing in the unseen wind.

After the long silence, Seeding 140 said, "Our mother? The Others were not there for ninety-two years, Then they replicate much faster than we do, and we die. Our mother, can you do what is necessary?"

Still no one spoke, until Harrah, frightened, said, "What is it?"

Micah answered, hirs voice clipped and precise. "According to the data packet, it is an aerobic organism, using a process analogous to the photosynthesis to create energy, giving off oxygen as a byproduct. The data includes a specimen analysis, broken off very abruptly as if the AI failed. The specimen is non-carbon-based, non-DNA. The energy sources sealed in Seeding 140 are anaerobic."

Ling said sharply, "present oxygen content of the rift atmosphere?"

Cal said, "Seven point six two percent." Hirs paused. "The oxygen created by these... these 'Others' is poisoning the seeding."

"But," Deb said, bewildered, "why did the original drop include such a thing?"

"It didn't," Micah said. "There is no match for this structure in the gene banks. It is not from Earth."

"Our mother?" Seeding 140 said, over the motionless fronds in the holocube. "Are you still there?"

Disciple Arlbeni, Grid 743.9, 2999: As we approach this millennium marker, rejoice that humanity has passed both beyond superstition and spiritual denial. We have a faith built on physical truth, on living genetics, on human need. We have, at long last, given our souls not to a formless Deity, but to the science of life itself. We are safe, and we are blessed.

Micah said suddenly, "It's a trick."

The other adults stared at hirs. Harrah has been hastily reconfigured for sleep. Someone—Ling, most likely, had dissolved the floating baktons and blanked the wall displays, and only the empty transmission field added color to the room. That, and the cold stars beyond.

"Yes," Micah continued, "a trick. Not malicious, of course. But we programmed them to learn, and they did. They had some seismic event, or some interwarfare, and it made them wary of anything unusual. They learned that the unusual can be deadly. And the most unusual thing they know if is us, set to return at 3,000. So they created a transmission program designed to repel us. Xenophobia, in a stimulus-response learning environment. You said it yourself, Ling, the learning components are built on human genes. And we have xenophobia as an evolved survival response!"

Cal jack-knifed across the room. Tension turned hirs ungraceful. "No. That sounds appealing, but nothing we gave Seeding 140 would let them evolve defenses that sophisticated. And there was no seismic event for the internal stimulus."

Micah said eagerly, "We're the stimulus! Our anticipated return! Don't you see . . . we're the 'Others!'"

Kabil said, "But they call us 'mother....' They were thrilled to see us. They're no xenophobic to us."

Deb spoke so softly the others could barely hear, "Then it's a computer malfunction. Cosmic bombardment of their sensory equipment. Or at least, of the unit that was 'dying'. Malfunctioning before the end, All that sensory data about oxygen poisoning is compromised."

"Of course!" Ling said. But hirs was always honest.

"At least… no, compromised data isn't that coherent, the pieces don't fit together so well biochemically…."

"And non-terrestrially," Cal said, and at the jagged edge in his voice, Micah exploded.

"California, these are not native life! There is no native life in the galaxy except on Earth!"

"I know that, Micah," Cal said, with dignity. "But I also know this data does not match anything in the d-bees."

"Then the d-bees are incomplete!"

"Possibly."

"Ling put hirs hands together, They were long, slender hands with very long nails, created just yesterday. I want to grab the new millennium with both hands, Ling had laughed before the party, and hold it firm. "Spores, Panspermia."

"I won't listen to this!" Micah said.

"An old theory," Ling went on, gasping a little. "Seeding 140 said the Others weren't there for their first hundred years. But if the spores blew in from space on the solar wind and the environment was right for them to germinate—"

Deb said quickly, "Spores aren't really life. Wherever they came from, they're not alive."

"Yes, they are," said Kabil. "Don't quibble. They're alive."

Micah said loudly. "I've given my entire life to the Great Mission. I was on the original drop for this very planet."

"They're alive," Ling said, "and they're not ours."

"My entire life!" Micah said. Hirs looked at each of them in turn, hirs face stony, and something terrible glinted behind the beautiful deep-green eyes.

Our mother does not answer. Has our mother gone away?

Our mother would not go away. It must be that they still are dancing.

We can wait.

"The main thing is Harrah, after all," Kabil said. Hirs sat slumped on the floor. They had been talking so long.

"A child needs secure knowledge. Purpose. Faith." Cal said.

Ling said wearily, "A child needs truth."

"Harrah," Deb crooned softly. "Harrah, made of all of us, future of our genes, small heart Harrah...."

"Stop it, Debaron," Cal said. "Please."

Micah said, "Those things down there are not real. Test it, Micah. I've said so already. Test it. Send down a probe, try to bring back samples. There's nothing there."

"You don't know that, Micah."

"I know!" Micah said, suddenly revitalized. Hirs sprang up. "Test it!"

Ling said, "A probe isn't necessary. We have the transmitted data and—"

"Not reliable!" Micah said.

"—and the rising oxygen content. Data from our own sensors."

"Outgassing!"

"Micah, that's ridiculous. And a probe—"

"A probe might come back contaminated," Cal said.

"Don't risk contamination," Kabil said suddenly. " Not with Harrah here."

"Harrah, made of us all...." Deb had turned hirs

back on the rest now, and lay almost curled into a ball, lost in hirs powerful imagination. Deb!

Kabil said, almost pleadingly, to Ling, "Harrah's safety must come first."

"Harrah's safety lies in facing the truth," Ling said. But hirs was not strong enough to sustain it alone. They were all so close, so knotted together, a family. Knotted by Harrah and by the Great Mission, to which Ling, no less than all the others, had given his life.

"Harrah, small heart," sang Deb.

Kabil said, "It isn't as if we have proof about these 'Others.' Not real proof. We don't actually know."

"I know," Micah said.

Cal looked bleakly at Kabil. "No. And it is wrong to sacrifice a child to a supposition, to a packet of compromised data, to a… a superstition of creations so much less than we are. You know that's true, even though we none of us ever admit it. But I'm a biologist. The creations are limited DNA, with no ability to self-modify. Also strictly regulated nano, and AI only within careful parameters. Yes, of course they're life forms deserving respect on their own terms, of course of course I would never deny that—"

"None of us would," Kabil said.

"—but they're not us. Not ever us."

A long silence broken only by Deb's singing.

"Leave orbit, Micah," Cal finally said, "before Harrah wakes up."

Disciple Arlbeni, Grid 743.9, 2999: We are not gods, never gods, no matter what the powers evolution and technology have given us, and we do not delude ourselves that we are gods, as other cultures have done at other millennia. We are human. Our salvation is that we know it, and do not pretend otherwise.

Our mother? Are you there? We need you to save us from the Others, to do what is necessary. Are you there?

Are you still dancing?

The People of Sand and Slag

Paolo Bacigalupi

Paolo Bacigalupi is a freelance writer who lives and works in Colorado. He has written about his travels in China for Salon, *and is the online editor/webmaster for* High Country News. *His first story, "A Pocketful of Dharma," appeared in* The Magazine of Fantasy & Science Fiction *in 1999 and his second, "The Fluted Girl," was reprinted in* Science Fiction: Best of 2003.

In the story that follows, Bacigalupi looks at a devastated industrial landscape where man is prepared to find pretty much anything except his best friend.

"Hostile movement! Well inside the perimeter! Well inside!"

I stripped off my Immersive Response goggles as adrenaline surged through me. The virtual cityscape I'd been about to raze disappeared, replaced by our monitoring room's many views of SesCo's mining operations. On one screen, the red phosphorescent tracery of an intruder skated across a terrain map, a hot blip like blood spattering its way toward Pit 8.

Jaak was already out of the monitoring room. I ran for my gear.

I caught up with Jaak in the equipment room as he grabbed a TS-101 and slashbangs and dragged his impact exoskeleton over his tattooed body. He draped bandoleers of surgepacks over his massive shoulders and ran for the outer locks. I strapped on my own exoskeleton, pulled my 101 from its rack, checked its charge, and followed.

Lisa was already in the HEV, its turbofans screaming like banshees when the hatch dilated. Sentry centaurs leveled their 101's at me, then relaxed as friend/foe data spilled into their heads-up displays. I bolted across the tarmac, my skin pricking under blasts of icy Montana wind and the jet wash of Hentasa Mark V engines. Overhead, the clouds glowed orange with light from SesCo's mining bots.

"Come on, Chen! Move! Move! Move!"

I dove into the hunter. The ship leaped into the sky. It banked, throwing me against a bulkhead, then the Hentasas cycled wide and the hunter punched forward. The HEV's hatch slid shut. The wind howl muted.

I struggled forward to the flight cocoon and peered over Jaak's and Lisa's shoulders to the landscape beyond.

"Have a good game?" Lisa asked.

I scowled. "I was about to win. I made it to Paris."

We cut through the mists over the catchment lakes, skimming inches above the water, and then we hit the far shore. The hunter lurched as its anti-collision software jerked us away from the roughening terrain.

Lisa overrode the computers and forced the ship back down against the soil, driving us so low I could have reached out and dragged my hands through the broken scree as we screamed over it.

Alarms yowled. Jaak shut them off as Lisa pushed the hunter lower. Ahead, a tailings ridge loomed. We ripped up its face and dropped sickeningly into the next valley. The Hentasas shuddered as Lisa forced them to the edge of their design buffer. We hurtled up and over another ridge. Ahead, the ragged cutscape of mined mountains stretched to the horizon. We dipped again into mist and skimmed low over another catchment lake, leaving choppy wake in the thick golden waters.

Jaak studied the hunter's scanners. "I've got it." He grinned. "It's moving, but slow."

"Contact in one minute," Lisa said. "He hasn't launched any countermeasures."

I watched the intruder on the tracking screens as they displayed real-time data fed to us from SesCo's satellites. "It's not even a masked target. We could have dropped a mini on it from base if we'd known he wasn't going to play hide-and-seek."

"Could have finished your game," Lisa said.

"We could still nuke him." Jaak suggested.

I shook my head. "No, let's take a look. Vaporizing him won't leave us anything and Bunbaum will want to know what we used the hunter for."

"Thirty seconds."

"He wouldn't care if someone hadn't taken the hunter on a joyride to Cancun."

Lisa shrugged. "I wanted to swim. It was either that, or rip off your kneecaps."

The hunter lunged over another series of ridges.

Jaak studied his monitor. "Target's moving away. He's still slow. We'll get him."

"Fifteen seconds to drop," Lisa said. She unstrapped and switched the hunter to software. We all ran for the hatch as the HEV yanked itself skyward, its auto pilot desperate to tear away from the screaming hazard of the rocks beneath its belly.

We plunged out the hatch, one, two, three, falling like Icarus. We slammed into the ground at hundreds of kilometers per hour. Our exoskeletons shattered like glass, flinging leaves into the sky. The shards fluttered down around us, black metallic petals absorbing our enemy's radar and heat detection while we rolled to jarred vulnerable stops in muddy scree.

The hunter blew over the ridge, Hentasas shrieking, a blazing target. I dragged myself upright and ran for the ridge, my feet churning through yellow tailings mud and rags of jaundiced snow. Behind me, Jaak was down with smashed arms. The leaves of his exoskeleton marked his roll path, a long trail of black shimmering metal. Lisa lay a hundred yards away, her femur rammed through her thigh like a bright white exclamation mark.

I reached the top of the ridge and stared down into the valley.

Nothing.

I dialed up the magnification of my helmet. The monotonous slopes of more tailings rubble spread out below me. Boulders, some as large as our HEV, some cracked and shattered by high explosives, shared the slopes with the unstable yellow shale and fine grit of waste materials from SesCo's operations.

Jaak slipped up beside me, followed a moment later by Lisa, her flight suit's leg torn and bloodied. She wiped yellow mud off her face and ate it as she studied the valley below. "Anything?"

I shook my head. "Nothing yet. You okay?"

"Clean break."

Jaak pointed. "There!"

Down in the valley, something was running, flushed by the hunter. It slipped along a shallow creek, viscous with tailings acid. The ship herded it toward us. Nothing. No missile fire. No slag. Just the running creature. A mass of tangled hair. Quadrupedal. Splattered with mud.

"Some kind of bio-job?" I wondered.

"It doesn't have any hands," Lisa murmured.

"No equipment either."

Jaak muttered. "What kind of sick bastard makes a bio-job without hands?"

I searched the nearby ridgelines. "Decoy, maybe?"

Jaak checked his scanner data, piped in from the hunter's more aggressive instruments. "I don't think so. Can we put the hunter up higher? I want to look around."

At Lisa's command, the hunter rose, allowing its sensors a fuller reach. The howl of its turbofans became muted as it gained altitude.

Jaak waited as more data spat into his heads-up display. "Nope, nothing. And no new alerts from any of the perimeter stations, either. We're alone."

Lisa shook her head. "We should have just dropped a mini on it from base."

Down in the valley, the bio-job's headlong run slowed to a trot. It seemed unaware of us. Closer now, we could make out its shape: A shaggy quadruped with a tail. Dreadlocked hair dangled from its shanks like ornaments, tagged with tailings mud clods.

It was stained around its legs from the acids of the catchment ponds, as though it had forded streams of urine.

"That's one ugly bio-job," I said.

Lisa shouldered her 101. "Bio-melt when I'm done with it."

"Wait!" Jaak said. "Don't slag it!"

Lisa glanced over at him, irritated. "What now?"

"That's not a bio-job at all." Jaak whispered. "That's a dog."

He stood suddenly and jumped over the hillside, running headlong down the scree toward the animal.

"Wait!" Lisa called, but Jaak was already fully exposed and blurring to his top speed.

The animal took one look at Jaak, whooping and hollering as he came roaring down the slope, then turned and ran. It was no match for Jaak. Half a minute later he overtook the animal.

Lisa and I exchanged glances. "Well," she said, "it's awfully slow if it's a bio-job. I've seen centaurs walk faster."

By the time we caught up with Jaak and the animal, Jaak had it cornered in a dull gully. The animal stood in the center of a trickling ditch of sludgy water, shaking and growling and baring its teeth at us as we surrounded it. It tried to break around us, but Jaak kept it corralled easily.

Up close, the animal seemed even more pathetic than from a distance, a good thirty kilos of snarling mange. Its paws were slashed and bloody and patches of fur were torn away, revealing festering chemical burns underneath.

"I'll be damned," I breathed, staring at the animal. "It really looks like a dog."

Jaak grinned. "It's like finding a goddamn dinosaur."

"How could it live out here?" Lisa's arm swept the horizon. "There's nothing to live on. It's got to be modified." She studied it closely, then glanced at Jaak. "Are you sure nothing's coming in on the perimeter? This isn't some kind of decoy?"

Jaak shook his head. "Nothing. Not even a peep."

I leaned in toward the creature. It bared its teeth in a rictus of hatred. "It's pretty beat up. Maybe it's the real thing."

Jaak said, "Oh yeah, it's the real thing all right. I saw a dog in a zoo once. I'm telling you, this is a dog."

Lisa shook her head. "It can't be. It would be dead, if it were a real dog."

Jaak just grinned and shook his head. "No way. Look at it." He reached out to push the hair out of the animal's face so that we could see its muzzle.

The animal lunged and its teeth sank into Jaak's arm. It shook his arm violently, growling as Jaak stared down at the creature latched onto his flesh. It yanked its head back and forth, trying to tear Jaak's arm off. Blood spurted around its muzzle as its teeth found Jaak's arteries.

Jaak laughed. His bleeding stopped. "Damn. Check that out." He lifted his arm until the animal dangled fully out of the stream, dripping. "I got me a pet."

The dog swung from the thick bough of Jaak's arm. It tried to shake his arm once again, but its movements were ineffectual now that it hung off the ground. Even Lisa smiled.

"Must be a bummer to wake up and find out you're at the end of your evolutionary curve."

The dog growled, determined to hang on.

Jaak laughed and drew his monomol knife. "Here you go, doggy." He sliced his arm off, leaving it in the bewildered animal's mouth.

Lisa cocked her head. "You think we could make some kind of money on it?"

Jaak watched as the dog devoured his severed arm. "I read somewhere that they used to eat dogs. I wonder what they taste like."

I checked the time in my heads-up display. We'd already killed an hour on an exercise that wasn't giving any bonuses. "Get your dog, Jaak, and get it on the hunter. We aren't going to eat it before we call Bunbaum."

"He'll probably call it company property," Jaak groused.

"Yeah, that's the way it always goes. But we still have to report. Might as well keep the evidence, since we didn't nuke it."

We ate sand for dinner. Outside the security bunker, the mining robots rumbled back and forth, ripping deeper into the earth, turning it into a mush of tailings and rock acid that they left in exposed ponds when they hit the water table, or piled into thousand-foot mountainscapes of waste soil. It was comforting to hear those machines cruising back and forth all day. Just you and the bots and the profits, and if nothing got bombed while you were on duty, there was always a nice bonus.

After dinner we sat around and sharpened Lisa's skin, implanting blades along her limbs so that she was like a razor from all directions. She'd considered monomol blades, but it was too easy to take a limb off accidentally, and we lost enough body parts as it was without adding to the mayhem. That kind of garbage was for people who didn't have to work: aesthetes from New York City and California.

Lisa had a DermDecora kit for the sharpening. She'd bought it last time we'd gone on vacation and spent extra to get it, instead of getting one of the cheap knock-offs that were cropping up. We worked on cutting her skin down to the bone and setting the blades. A friend of ours in L.A said that he just held DermDecora parties so everyone could do their modifications and help out with the hard-to-reach places.

Lisa had done my glowspine, a sweet tracery of lime landing lights that ran from my tailbone to the base of my skull, so I didn't mind helping her out, but Jaak, who did all of his modification with an old-time scar and tattoo shop in Hawaii, wasn't so pleased. It was a little frustrating because her flesh kept trying to close before we had the blades set, but eventually we got the hang of it, and an hour later, she started looking good.

Once we finished with Lisa's front settings, we sat around and fed her. I had a bowl of tailings mud that I drizzled into her mouth to speed her integration process. When we were weren't feeding her, we watched the dog. Jaak had shoved it into a makeshift cage in one corner of our common room. It lay there like it was dead.

Lisa said, "I ran its DNA. It really is a dog."

"Bunbaum believe you?"

She gave me a dirty look. "What do you think?"

I laughed. At SesCo, tactical defense responders were expected to be fast, flexible, and deadly, but the reality was our SOP was always the same: drop nukes on intruders, slag the leftovers to melt so they couldn't regrow, hit the beaches for vacation. We were independent and trusted as far as tactical decisions went, but there was no way SesCo was going to believe its slag soldiers had found a dog in their tailings mountains.

Lisa nodded. "He wanted to know how the hell a dog could live out here. Then he wanted to know why we didn't catch it sooner. Wanted to know what he pays us for." She pushed her short blond hair off her face and eyed the animal. "I should have slagged it."

"What's he want us to do?"

"It's not in the manual. He's calling back."

I studied the limp animal. "I want to know how it was surviving. Dogs are meat eaters, right?"

"Maybe some of the engineers were giving it meat. Like Jaak did."

Jaak shook his head. "I don't think so. The sucker threw up my arm almost right after he ate it." He wiggled his new stump where it was rapidly regrowing. "I don't think we're compatible for it."

I asked, "But we could eat it, right?"

Lisa laughed and took a spoonful of tailings. "We can eat anything. We're the top of the food chain."

"Weird how it can't eat us."

"You've probably got more mercury and lead running through your blood than any pre-weeviltech animal ever could have had."

"That's bad?"

"Used to be poison."

"Weird."

Jaak said, "I think I might have broken it when I put it in the cage." He studied it seriously. "It's not moving like it was before. And I heard something snap when I stuffed it in."

"So?"

Jaak shrugged. "I don't think it's healing."

The dog did look kind of beat up. It just lay there, its sides going up and down like a bellows. Its eyes were half-open, but didn't seem to be focused on any of us. When Jaak made a sudden movement, it twitched for a second, but it didn't get up. It didn't even growl.

Jaak said, "I never thought an animal could be so fragile."

"You're fragile, too. That's not such a big surprise."

"Yeah, but I only broke a couple bones on it, and now look at it. It just lies there and pants."

Lisa frowned thoughtfully. "It doesn't heal." She climbed awkwardly to her feet and went to peer into the cage. Her voice was excited. "It really is a dog. Just like we used to be. It could take weeks for it to heal. One broken bone, and it's done for."

She reached a razored hand into the cage and sliced a thin wound into its shank. Blood oozed out, and kept oozing. It took minutes for it to begin clotting. The dog lay still and panted, clearly wasted.

She laughed. "It's hard to believe we ever lived long enough to evolve out of that. If you chop off its legs, they won't regrow." She cocked her head, fascinated. "It's as delicate as rock. You break it, and it never comes back together." She reached out to stroke the matted fur of the animal. "It's as easy to kill as the hunter."

The comm buzzed. Jaak went to answer.

Lisa and I stared at the dog, our own little window into pre-history.

Jaak came back into the room. "Bunbaum's flying out a biologist to take a look at it."

"You mean a bio-engineer," I corrected him.

"Nope. Biologist. Bunbaum said they study animals."

Lisa sat down. I checked her blades to see if she'd knocked anything loose. "There's a dead-end job."

"I guess they grow them out of DNA. Study what they do. Behavior, shit like that."

"Who hires them?"

Jaak shrugged. "Pau Foundation has three of them on staff. Origin of life guys. That's who's sending out this one. Mushi-something. Didn't get his name."

"Origin of life?"

"Sure, you know, what makes us tick. What makes us alive. Stuff like that."

I poured a handful of tailings mud into Lisa's mouth. She gobbled it gratefully. "Mud makes us tick," I said.

Jaak nodded at the dog. "It doesn't make that dog tick."

We all looked at the dog. "It's hard to tell what makes it tick."

Lin Musharraf was a short guy with black hair and a hooked nose that dominated his face. He had carved his skin with swirling patterns of glow implants, so he stood out as cobalt spirals in the darkness as he jumped down from his chartered HEV.

The centaurs went wild about the unauthorized visitor and corralled him right up against his ship. They were all over him and his DNA kit, sniffing him, running their scanners over his case, pointing their 101's into his glowing face and snarling at him.

I let him sweat for a minute before calling them

away. The centaurs backed off, swearing and circling, but didn't slag him. Musharraf looked shaken. I couldn't blame him. They're scary monsters: bigger and faster than a man. Their behavior patches make them vicious, their sentience upgrades give them the intelligence to operate military equipment, and their basic fight/flight response is so impaired that they only know how to attack when they're threatened. I've seen a half-slagged centaur tear a man to pieces barehanded and then join an assault on enemy ridge fortifications, dragging its whole melted carcass forward with just its arms. They're great critters to have at your back when the slag starts flying.

I guided Musharraf out of the scrum. He had a whole pack of memory addendums blinking off the back of his skull: a fat pipe of data retrieval, channeled direct to the brain, and no smash protection. The centaurs could have shut him down with one hard tap to the back of the head. His cortex might have grown back, but he wouldn't have been the same. Looking at those blinking triple fins of intelligence draping down the back of his head, you could tell he was a typical lab rat. All brains, no survival instincts. I wouldn't have stuck mem-adds into my head even for a triple bonus.

"You've got a dog?" Musharraf asked when we were out of reach of the centaurs.

"We think so." I led him down into the bunker, past our weapons racks and weight rooms to the common room where we'd stored the dog. The dog looked up at us as we came in, the most movement it had made since Jaak put it in the cage.

Musharraf stopped short and stared. "Remarkable." He knelt in front of the animal's cage and unlocked the door. He held out a handful of pellets. The dog dragged itself upright. Musharraf backed away, giving it room, and the dog followed stiff and wary, snuffling after the pellets. It buried its muzzle in his brown hand, snorting and gobbling at the pellets.

Musharraf looked up. "And you found it in your tailings pits?"

"That's right."

"Remarkable."

The dog finished the pellets and snuffled his palm for more. Musharraf laughed and stood. "No more for you. Not right now." He opened his DNA kit, pulled out a sampler needle and stuck the dog. The sampler's chamber filled with blood.

Lisa watched. "You talk to it?"

Musharraf shrugged. "It's a habit."

"But it's not sentient."

"Well, no, but it likes to hear voices." The chamber finished filling. He withdrew the needle, disconnected the collection chamber and fitted it into the kit. The analysis software blinked alive and the blood disappeared into the heart of the kit with a soft vacuum hiss.

"How do you know?"

Musharraf shrugged. "It's a dog. Dogs are that way."

We all frowned. Musharraf started running tests on the blood, humming tunelessly to himself as he worked. His DNA kit peeped and squawked. Lisa watched him run his tests, clearly pissed off that SesCo had sent out a lab rat to retest what she had already done. It was easy to understand her irritation. A centaur could have run those DNA tests.

"I'm astounded that you found a dog in your pits," Musharraf muttered.

Lisa said, "We were going to slag it, but Bunbaum wouldn't let us."

Musharraf eyed her. "How restrained of you."

Lisa shrugged. "Orders."

"Still, I'm sure your thermal surge weapon presented a powerful temptation. How good of you not to slag a starving animal."

Lisa frowned suspiciously. I started to worry that she might take Musharraf apart. She was crazy enough without people talking down to her. The memory addendums on the back of his head were an awfully tempting target: one slap, down goes the lab rat. I wondered if we sank him in a catchment lake if anyone would notice him missing. A biologist, for Christ's sake.

Musharraf turned back to his DNA kit, apparently unaware of his hazard. "Did you know that in the past, people believed that we should have compassion for all things on Earth? Not just for ourselves, but for all living things?"

"So?"

"I would hope you will have compassion for one foolish scientist and not dismember me today."

Lisa laughed. I relaxed. Encouraged, Musharraf said, "It truly is remarkable that you found such a specimen amongst your mining operations. I haven't heard of a living specimen in ten or fifteen years."

"I saw one in a zoo, once," Jaak said.

"Yes, well, a zoo is the only place for them. And laboratories, of course. They still provide useful genetic data." He was studying the results of the tests, nodding to himself as information scrolled across the kit's screen.

Jaak grinned. "Who needs animals if you can eat stone?"

Musharraf began packing up his DNA kit. "Weeviltech. Precisely. We transcended the animal kingdom." He latched his kit closed and nodded to us all. "Well, it's been quite enlightening. Thank you for letting me see your specimen."

"You're not going to take it with you?"

Musharraf paused, surprised. "Oh no. I don't think so."

"It's not a dog, then?"

"Oh no, it's quite certainly a real dog. But what on Earth would I do with it?" He held up a vial of blood. "We have the DNA. A live one is hardly worth keeping around. Very expensive to maintain, you know. Manufacturing a basic organism's food is quite complex. Clean rooms, air filters, special lights. Recreating the web of life isn't easy. Far more simple to release oneself from it completely than to attempt to recreate it." He glanced at the dog. "Unfortunately, our furry friend over there would never survive weeviltech. The worms would eat him as quickly as they eat everything else. No, you would have to manufacture the animal from scratch. And really, what would be the point of that? A bio-job without hands?" He laughed and headed for his HEV.

We all looked at each other. I jogged after the doctor and caught up with him at the hatch to the tarmac. He had paused on the verge of opening it. "Your centaurs know me now?" he asked.

"Yeah, you're fine."

"Good." He dilated the hatch and strode out into the cold.

I trailed after him. "Wait! What are we supposed to do with it?"

"The dog?" The doctor climbed into the HEV and began strapping in. Wind whipped around us, carrying stinging grit from the tailings piles. "Turn it back to your pits. Or you could eat it, I suppose. I understand that it was a real delicacy. There are recipes for cooking animals. They take time, but they can give quite extraordinary results."

Musharraf's pilot started cycling up his turbofans.

"Are you kidding?"

Musharraf shrugged and shouted over the increasing scream of the engines. "You should try it! Just another part of our heritage that's atrophied since weeviltech!"

He yanked down the flight cocoon's door, sealing himself inside. The turbofans cycled higher and the pilot motioned me back from their wash as the HEV slowly lifted into the air.

Lisa and Jaakcouldn't agree on what we should do with the dog. We had protocols for working out conflict. As a tribe of killers, we needed them. Normally, consensus worked for us, but every once in a while, we just got tangled up and stuck to our positions, and after that, not much could get done without someone getting slaughtered. Lisa and Jaak dug in, and after a couple days of wrangling, with Lisa threatening to cook the thing in the middle of the night while Jaak wasn't watching, and Jaak threatening to cook her if she did, we finally went with a majority vote. I got to be the tie-breaker.

"I say we eat it," Lisa said.

We were sitting in the monitoring room, watching satellite shots of the tailings mountains and the infrared blobs of the mining bots while they ripped around in the earth. In one corner, the object of our discussion lay in its cage, dragged there by Jaak in an attempt to sway the result. He spun his observation chair, turning his attention away from the theater maps. "I think we should keep it. It's cool. Old-timey, you know? I mean, who the hell do you know who has a real dog?"

"Who the hell wants the hassle?" Lisa responded. "I say we try real meat." She cut a line in her forearm with her razors. She ran her finger along the resulting blood beads and tasted them as the wound sealed.

They both looked at me. I looked at the ceiling. "Are you sure you can't decide this without me?"

Lisa grinned. "Come on, Chen, you decide. It was a group find. Jaak won't pout, will you?"

Jaak gave her a dirty look.

I looked at Jaak. "I don't want its food costs to come out of group bonuses. We agreed we'd use part of it for the new Immersive Response. I'm sick of the old one."

Jaak shrugged. "Fine with me. I can pay for it out of my own. I just won't get any more tats."

I leaned back in my chair, surprised, then looked at Lisa. "Well, if Jaak wants to pay for it, I think we should keep it."

Lisa stared at me, incredulous. "But we could cook it!"

I glanced at the dog where it lay panting in its cage. "It's like having a zoo of our own. I kind of like it."

Musharraf and the Pau Foundation hooked us up

with a supply of food pellets for the dog and Jaak looked up an old database on how to splint its busted bones. He bought water filtration so that it could drink.

I thought I'd made a good decision, putting the costs on Jaak, but I didn't really foresee the complications that came with having an unmodified organism in the bunker. The thing shit all over the floor, and sometimes it wouldn't eat, and it would get sick for no reason, and it was slow to heal so we all ended up playing nursemaid to the thing while it lay in its cage. I kept expecting Lisa to break its neck in the middle of the night, but even though she grumbled, she didn't assassinate it.

Jaak tried to act like Musharraf. He talked to the dog. He logged onto the libraries and read all about old-time dogs. How they ran in packs. How people used to breed them.

We tried to figure out what kind of dog it was, but we couldn't narrow it down much, and then Jaak discovered that all the dogs could interbreed, so all you could do was guess that it was some kind of big sheep dog, with maybe a head from a Rottweiler, along with maybe some other kind of dog, like a wolf or coyote or something.

Jaak thought it had coyote in it because they were supposed to have been big adapters, and whatever our dog was, it must have been a big adapter to hang out in the tailings pits. It didn't have the boosters we had, and it had still lived in the rock acids. Even Lisa was impressed by that.

I was carpet bombing Antarctic Recessionists, swooping low, driving the suckers further and further along the ice floe. If I got lucky, I'd drive the whole

village out onto a vestigial shelf and sink them all
before they knew what was happening. I dove again,
strafing and then spinning away from their return
slag.

It was fun, but mostly just a way to kill time
between real bombing runs. The new IR was supposed to be as good as the arcades, full immersion
and feedback, and portable to boot. People got so
lost they had to take intravenous feedings or they
withered away while they were inside.

I was about to sink a whole load of refugees when
Jaak shouted. "Get out here! You've got to see this!"

I stripped off my goggles and ran for the monitoring
room, adrenaline amping up. When I got there, Jaak
was just standing in the center of the room with the
dog, grinning.

Lisa came tearing in a second later. "What? What
is it?" Her eyes scanned the theater maps, ready for
bloodshed.

Jaak grinned. "Look at this." He turned to the dog
and held out his hand. "Shake."

The dog sat back on its haunches and gravely
offered him its paw. Jaak grinned and shook the paw,
then tossed it a food pellet. He turned to us and
bowed.

Lisa frowned. "Do it again."

Jaak shrugged and went through the performance
a second time.

"It thinks?" she asked.

Jaak shrugged. "Got me. You can get it to do things.
The libraries are full of stuff on them. They're train-
able. Not like a centaur or anything, but you can make
them do little tricks, and if they're certain breeds, they
can learn special stuff, too."

"Like what?"

"Some of them were trained to attack. Or to find explosives."

Lisa looked impressed. "Like nukes and stuff?"

Jaak shrugged. "I guess."

"Can I try?" I asked.

Jaak nodded. "Go for it."

I went over to the dog and stuck out my hand. "Shake."

It stuck out its paw. My hackles went up. It was like sending signals to aliens. I mean, you expect a bio-job or a robot to do what you want it to. Centaur, go get blown up. Find the op-force. Call reinforcements. The HEV was like that, too. It would do anything. But it was designed.

"Feed it," Jaak said, handing me a food pellet. "You have to feed it when it does it right."

I held out the food pellet. The dog's long pink tongue swabbed my palm.

I held out my hand again. "Shake." I said. It held out its paw. We shook hands. Its amber eyes stared up at me, solemn.

"That's some weird shit," Lisa said. I shivered, nodding and backed away. The dog watched me go.

That night in my bunk, I lay awake, reading. I'd turned out the lights and only the book's surface glowcd, illuminating the bunkroom in a soft green aura. Some of Lisa's art buys glimmered dimly from the walls: a bronze hanging of a phoenix breaking into flight, stylized flames glowing around it; a Japanese woodblock print of Mount Fuji and another of a village weighed down under thick snows; a photo of the three of us in Siberia after the Peninsula campaign, grinning and alive amongst the slag.

Lisa came into the room. Her razors glinted in my book's dim light, flashes of green sparks that outlined her limbs as she moved.

"What are you reading?" She stripped and squeezed into bed with me.

I held up the book and read out loud.

Cut me I won't bleed. Gas me I won't breathe.
Stab me, shoot me, slash me, smash me
I have swallowed science
I am God.
Alone.

I closed the book and its glow died. In the darkness, Lisa rustled under the covers.

My eyes adjusted. She was staring at me. "'Dead Man,' right?"

"Because of the dog," I said.

"Dark reading." She touched my shoulder, her hand warm, the blades embedded, biting lightly into my skin.

"We used to be like that dog," I said.

"Pathetic."

"Scary."

We were quiet for a little while. Finally I asked, "Do you ever wonder what would happen to us if we didn't have our science? If we didn't have our big brains and our weeviltech and our cellstims and—"

"And everything that makes our life good?" She laughed. "No." She rubbed my stomach. "I like all those little worms that live in your belly." She started to tickle me.

Wormy, squirmy in your belly,
wormy squirmy feeds you Nelly.
Microweevils eat the bad,

and give you something good instead.

I fought her off, laughing. "That's no Yearly."

"Third Grade. Basic bio-logic. Mrs. Alvarez. She was really big on weeviltech."

She tried to tickle me again but I fought her off. "Yeah, well Yearly only wrote about immortality. He wouldn't take it."

Lisa gave up on the tickling and flopped down beside me again. "Blah, blah, blah. He wouldn't take any gene modifications. No c-cell inhibitors. He was dying of cancer and he wouldn't take the drugs that would have saved him. Our last mortal poet. Cry me a river. So what?"

"You ever think about why he wouldn't?"

"Yeah. He wanted to be famous. Suicide's good for attention."

"Seriously, though. He thought being human meant having animals. The whole web of life thing. I've been reading about him. It's weird shit. He didn't want to live without them."

"Mrs. Alvarez hated him. She had some rhymes about him, too. Anyway, what were we supposed to do? Work out weeviltech and DNA patches for every stupid species? Do you know what that would have cost?" She nuzzled close to me. "If you want animals around you, go to a zoo. Or get some building blocks and make something, if it makes you happy. Something with hands, for god's sake, not like that dog." She stared at the underside of the bunk above. "I'd cook that dog in a second."

I shook my head. "I don't know. That dog's different from a bio-job. It looks at us, and there's something there, and it's not us. I mean, take any bio-job out there, and it's basically us, poured into another shape, but not that dog...." I trailed off, thinking.

Lisa laughed. "It shook hands with you, Chen. You don't worry about a centaur when it salutes." She climbed on top of me. "Forget the dog. Concentrate on something that matters." Her smile and her razor blades glinted in the dimness.

I woke up to something licking my face. At first I thought it was Lisa, but she'd climbed into her own bunk. I opened my eyes and found the dog.

It was a funny thing to have this animal licking me, like it wanted to talk, or say hello or something. It licked me again, and I thought that it had come a long way from when it had tried to take off Jaak's arm. It put its paws up on my bed, and then in a single heavy movement, it was up on the bunk with me, its bulk curled against me.

It slept there all night. It was weird having something other than Lisa lying next to me, but it was warm and there was something friendly about it. I couldn't help smiling as I drifted back to sleep.

We flew to Hawaii for a swimming vacation and we brought the dog with us. It was good to get out of the northern cold and into the gentle Pacific. Good to stand on the beach, and look out to a limitless horizon. Good to walk along the beach holding hands while black waves crashed on the sand.

Lisa was a good swimmer. She flashed through the ocean's metallic sheen like an eel out of history and when she surfaced, her naked body glistened with hundreds of iridescent petroleum jewels.

When the Sun started to set, Jaak lit the ocean on

fire with his 101. We all sat and watched as the Sun's great red ball sank through veils of smoke, its light shading deeper crimson with every minute. Waves rushed flaming onto the beach. Jaak got out his harmonica and played while Lisa and I made love on the sand.

We'd intended to amputate her for the weekend, to let her try what she had done to me the vacation before. It was a new thing in L.A., an experiment in vulnerability.

She was beautiful, lying there on the beach, slick and excited with all of our play in the water. I licked oil opals off her skin as I sliced off her limbs, leaving her more dependent than a baby. Jaak played his harmonica and watched the Sun set, and watched as I rendered Lisa down to her core.

After our sex, we lay on the sand. The last of the Sun was dropping below the water. Its rays glinted redly across the smoldering waves. The sky, thick with particulates and smoke, shaded darker.

Lisa sighed contentedly. "We should vacation here more often."

I tugged on a length of barbed-wire buried in the sand. It tore free and I wrapped it around my upper arm, a tight band that bit into my skin. I showed it to Lisa. "I used to do this all the time when I was a kid." I smiled. "I thought I was so bad-ass."

Lisa smiled. "You are."

"Thanks to science." I glanced over at the dog. It was lying on the sand a short distance away. It seemed sullen and unsure in its new environment, torn away from the safety of the acid pits and tailings mountains of its homeland. Jaak sat beside the dog and played. Its ears twitched to the music. He was a good player. The mournful sound of the harmonica carried easily over the beach to where we lay.

Lisa turned her head, trying to see the dog. "Roll me."

I did what she asked. Already, her limbs were regrowing. Small stumps, which would build into larger limbs. By morning, she would be whole, and ravenous. She studied the dog. "This is as close as I'll ever get to it," she said.

"Sorry?"

"It's vulnerable to everything. It can't swim in the ocean. It can't eat anything. We have to fly its food to it. We have to scrub its water. Dead end of an evolutionary chain. Without science, we'd be as vulnerable as it." She looked up at me. "As vulnerable as I am now." She grinned. "This is as close to death as I've ever been. At least, not in combat."

"Wild, isn't it?"

"For a day. I liked it better when I did it to you. I'm already starving."

I fed her a handful of oily sand and watched the dog, standing uncertainly on the beach, sniffing suspiciously at some rusting scrap iron that stuck out of the beach like a giant memory fin. It pawed up a chunk of red plastic rubbed shiny by the ocean and chewed on it briefly, before dropping it. It started licking around its mouth. I wondered if it had poisoned itself again.

"It sure can make you think," I muttered. I fed Lisa another handful of sand. "If someone came from the past, to meet us here and now, what do you think they'd say about us? Would they even call us human?"

Lisa looked at me seriously. "No, they'd call us gods."

Jaak got up and wandered into the surf, standing knee-deep in the black smoldering waters. The dog, driven by some unknown instinct, followed him, gingerly picking its way across the sand and rubble.

The dog got tangled in a cluster of wire our last day on the beach. Really ripped the hell out of it: slashes through its fur, broken legs, practically strangled. It had gnawed one of its own paws half off trying to get free. By the time we found it, it was a bloody mess of ragged fur and exposed meat.

Lisa stared down at the dog. "Christ, Jaak, you were supposed to be watching it."

"I went swimming. You can't keep an eye on the thing all the time."

"It's going to take forever to fix this," she fumed.

"We should warm up the hunter," I said. "It'll be easier to work on it back home." Lisa and I knelt down to start cutting the dog free. It whimpered and its tail wagged feebly as we started to work.

Jaak was silent.

Lisa slapped him on his leg. "Come on, Jaak, get down here. It'll bleed out if you don't hurry up. You know how fragile it is."

Jaak said, "I think we should eat it."

Lisa glanced up, surprised. "You do?"

He shrugged. "Sure."

I looked up from where I was tearing away tangled wires from around the dog's torso. "I thought you wanted it to be your pet. Like in the zoo."

Jaak shook his head. "Those food pellets are expensive. I'm spending half my salary on food and water filtration, and now this bullshit." He waved his hand at the tangled dog. "You have to watch the sucker all the time. It's not worth it."

"But still, it's your friend. It shook hands with you."

Jaak laughed. "You're my friend." He looked down at the dog, his face wrinkled with thought. "It's, it's…an animal."

Even though we had all idly discussed what it would be like to eat the dog, it was a surprise to hear him so determined to kill it. "Maybe you should sleep on it." I said. "We can get it back to the bunker, fix it up, and then you can decide when you aren't so pissed off about it."

"No." He pulled out his harmonica and played a few notes, a quick jazzy scale. He took the harmonica out of his mouth. "If you want to put up the money for his feed, I'll keep it, I guess, but otherwise…" He shrugged.

"I don't think you should cook it."

"You don't?" Lisa glanced at me. "We could roast it, right here, on the beach."

I looked down at the dog, a mass of panting, trusting animal. "I still don't think we should do it."

Jaak looked at me seriously. "You want to pay for the feed?"

I sighed. "I'm saving for the new Immersive Response."

"Yeah, well, I've got things I want to buy too, you know." He flexed his muscles, showing off his tattoos. "I mean, what the fuck good does it do?"

"It makes you smile."

"Immersive Response makes you smile. And you don't have to clean up after its crap. Come on, Chen. Admit it. You don't want to take care of it either. It's a pain in the ass."

We all looked at each other, then down at the dog.

Lisa roasted the dog on a spit, over burning plastics and petroleum skimmed from the ocean. It tasted okay, but in the end it was hard to understand the big deal. I've eaten slagged centaur that tasted better.

Afterward, we walked along the shoreline. Opalescent waves crashed and roared up the sand, leaving jewel slicks as they receded and the Sun sank red in the distance.

Without the dog, we could really enjoy the beach. We didn't have to worry about whether it was going to step in acid, or tangle in barb-wire half-buried in the sand, or eat something that would keep it up vomiting half the night.

Still, I remember when the dog licked my face and hauled its shaggy bulk onto my bed, and I remember its warm breathing beside me, and sometimes, I miss it.

Tourists

M. John Harrison

*M. John Harrison was born in 1945 in England. His
first short story, "Marina," appeared in* Science Fantasy
in 1966. He worked on New Worlds *as editor and
reviewer in the late '60s when the magazine was under
the editorship of Michael Moorcock. Harrison's first
novel,* The Committed Men, *appeared in 1971, as
did* The Pastel City, *first in his "Viriconium" series
which continued with* A Storm of Wings, *and collections* In Viriconium *(shortlisted for the Guardian Fiction Prize),* Viriconium Nights, *and* Viriconium. *Harrison's other novels include space opera* The Centauri
Device, *which has been credited as the first major work
of the "new space opera,"* Signs of Life, Climbers
(winner of the Boardman Tasker Award), and The
Course of the Heart. *His short fiction has been collected in* The Machine in Shaft Ten and Other Stories,
The Ice Monkey and Other Stories, Travel Arrange-
ments, *and* Things That Never Happen.*

Harrison's most recent novel, the highly acclaimed
Light, *won the James Tiptree Award and provides the
backdrop for the story which follows.*

Jack Serotonin sat in a bar on Strait Street, just inside the aureole of the Raintown event, in conversation with a fat man from another planet who called himself Antoyne. They had been playing dice all night. It was just before dawn, and a brown light, polished but dim at the same time, crept out the streetlights to fill the place.

"I was never in there," the fat man admitted, meaning the event zone, "but what I think—"

"If this is going to be bullshit, Antoyne," Serotonin advised him, "don't even start."

The fat man looked hurt.

"Have another drink," Jack said.

The bar was about halfway down Strait, a cluttered, narrowish street of two-storey buildings, along which two out of three had their windows boarded up. Like all the streets in that part of Raintown, Strait was full of cats, especially at dawn and dusk, when they went in and out of the event site. As if in acknowledgment, the bar was called Black Cat White Cat. It featured a zinc counter slightly too high for comfort. A row of bottles which contained liquids of unlikely colours. A few tables. The long window steamed up easily, no one but Antoyne cared. In the morning the bar smelled of last night's garlic. Some mornings it smelled of mould too, as if something had crept out of the event aurcole in the dark and, after a few attempts to breathe the air in the bar, died underneath a corner table. Shadow operators hung high up in the join between the walls and the ceiling, like cobwebs. There wasn't much for them to do.

Jack was in the bar most days. He ate there. He ran his business out of it. He used it as a mail drop, and as a place to check out his clients: but really it was what they called a jump-off joint, positioned well, not too far back from the event site, not so close as to suffer effects. Another advantage it had: Jack was on good terms with the owner, a woman called Liv Hula who never put in a manager but ran it herself day and night. People thought she was the barkeep, that suited her. She wasn't known to complain. She was one of those women who draw in on themselves after their fortieth year, short, thin, with brush-cut grey hair, a couple of smart tattoos on her muscular forearms, an expression as if she was always thinking of something else. She had music in the bar. Her taste ran to the outcaste beats and saltwater dub you heard a few years back. That aged her as far as Jack Serotonin was concerned. Which is to say they'd been round a time or two.

"Hey," she told Jack now, "leave the fat man alone. Everyone's entitled to an opinion."

Serotonin stared at her. "I won't even answer that."

"Bad night, Jack?"

"You should know. You were there."

She poured him a shot of Black Heart rum, along with whatever the fat man was having. "I would say you were out there on your own, Jack," she said. "Much of the time." They both laughed. Then she looked over his shoulder at the open door of the bar and said—

"Maybe you got a customer here."

The woman who stood there was a little too tall to

wear the high heels in fashion then. She had long thin hands, and that way of looking both anxious and tranquil a lot of those tourist women have. There was a tentativeness about her. She was elegant and awkward at the same time. If she knew how to wear clothes, perhaps that was a learned thing, or perhaps it was a talent she had never fully brought out in herself. You thought instantly she had lost her way. When she came into the bar that morning, she was wearing a black two-piece with a little fitted jacket and calf-length kick-pleat skirt, under a long, honey-coloured fur coat. She stood there uncertainly in the doorway, with the cold morning light from Strait Street behind her, and the unflattering light from the window falling across one side of her face, and the first words anyone heard her say were, "Excuse me, I—"

At the sound of her voice, the shadow operators unfolded themselves and streamed towards her from every corner of the room, to whirl about her head like ghosts, bats, scrap paper, smoke, or old women clasping antique lockets of hair. They recognised privilege when they saw it.

"My dear," they whispered. "What beautiful hands."

"Is there anything we can do—

"—Can we do anything, dear ?"

"What lovely, lovely hands!"

Liv Hula looked amused. "They never did that for me," she admitted to the woman in the fur coat. Then she had a sudden vision of her own life as hard-won, dug out raw from nothing much even the few times it seemed to swoop or soar.

"You came for Jack, he's over there," she said.

She always pointed him out. After that she washed

her hands of whatever happened next. This time Jack was waiting. He was low on work, it was a slow year though you wouldn't guess that from the number of ships clustered in the tourist port. Jack accounted himself intelligent and determined; women, on the other hand, saw him as weak, conflicted, attractive, reading this as a failed attempt to feminise himself. He had been caning it for weeks with fat Antoyne and Liv Hula, but he still looked younger than his age. He stood there with his hands in his pockets, and the woman leaned towards him as if he was the only way she could get her bearings in the room. The closer she approached him the more uncertain she seemed. Like most of them, she wasn't sure how to broach things.

"I want you to take me in there," she said eventually.

Jack laid his finger on his lips. He could have wished for some statement less bald. "Not so loud," he suggested.

"I'm sorry."

He shrugged and said, "No problem."

"We're all friends here," Liv Hula said.

Jack gave Liv a look, which he then turned into a smile.

The woman smiled too. "Into the event site," she said, as if there might be any doubt about it. Her face was smooth and tight across longings Jack didn't quite understand. She looked away from him as she spoke. He should have thought more about that. Instead he ushered her to a table, where they talked for five minutes in low voices. Nothing was easier, he told her, than what she wanted. Though the risk had to be understood, and you underrated at your peril the seriousness of things in there. He would be a fool not to make that clear. He would be irresponsible, he said. Money changed hands. After a time they got up and left the bar.

"Just another sucker on the vine," Liv Hula said, loud enough to pause him in the doorway.

Antoyne claimed to have flown dipships with Ed Chianese. He passed the days with his elbows on the bar staring out through the window at the contrails of descending K-ships in the sky above the houses on the other side of Strait Street. To most people it seemed unlikely he flew with anyone, but he could take a message and keep his mouth shut. The only other thing he ever said about himself was:

"No one gives shit about a fat man called Antoyne."

"You got that right," Liv Hula often told him.

When Jack had gone, there was a silence in the bar. The shadow operators calmed down and packed themselves back into the ceiling corners so the corners looked familiar again—that is, as if they had never been cleaned. Antoyne stared at the table in front of him then across at Liv Hula. It seemed as if they'd speak about Jack or the woman but in the end neither of them could think of anything to say. The fat man was angry that Liv Hula had defended him to Jack Serotonin. He drove his chair back suddenly, it made a kind of complaining sound against the wooden floor. He got up and went over to the window, where he wiped the condensation off with the palm of his hand.

"Still dark," he said.

Liv Hula had to admit that was true.

"Hey," he said. "Here's Joe Leone."

Over the street from Black Cat White Cat it was the usual frontages, busted and askew, buildings which had lost confidence in their structural integrity and which now housed shoestring tailor operations specialising in cosmetics or one-shot cultivars. You couldn't call them "parlours". The work they did was too cheap for that. They got a trickle of stuff from the Uncle Zip and Nueva Cut franchises dowtown; also they took work from the Shadow Boys, work like Joe Leone. Just now Joe was pulling himself down Strait using the fences and walls to hold himself up. His energy ebbed and flowed. He would fall down, wait for a minute, then struggle up again. It looked like hard work You could see he was holding something in down there with one hand while he leaned on the fence with the other. The closer he got the more puzzled he looked.

Antoyne made a tube out of his two damp fists and said through it in the voice of a sports commentator at Radio Retro:

"...and will he make it this time ?"

"Be sure to let us know when you join the human race, Antoyne," Liv Hula said. The fat man shrugged and turned away from the window. "It's no bet," he said in his normal voice. "He never failed yet."

Joe kept dragging himself down Strait. As he approached you could see the tailors had done something to his face so it had a crude lion-like cast. It was white and sweated up, but it didn't move properly. They had given it a one-piece look as if it was sculpture, even the long hair swept back and out from his big forehead and cheekbones. Eventually he fell down outside one of the chopshops and stopped moving, and after a couple of minutes two men almost as big as him came out to drag him inside.

Joe started to fight when he was seven.

"Never strike out at the other, son," his father would explain in a patient way. "Because the other is your self."

Joe Leone didn't follow that, even at seven years old which everyone agreed was his most intelligent time. He liked to fight. By twelve it was his trade, nothing more or less. He had signed with the Shadow Boys. From that time on he lived in one-shot cultivars. He liked the tusks, the sentient tattoos, and the side-lace trousers. Joe had no body of his own. It cost him so much to run those cultivars he would never save up enough to buy himself back. Every day he was in the ring, doing that same old thing. He was getting pretty well messed up. "I lost count the times I seen my own insides. Hey, what's that? Lose your insides ain't so hard. Losing a fight, that's hard." And he would laugh and buy you another drink.

Every day they dragged the fucked-up cultivar out the ring, and the next day Joe Leone had been to the tailor on Strait and come out fresh and new and ready to do it all again. It was a tiring life but it was the life he loved. Liv Hula never charged him for a drink. She had a soft spot for him, it was widely acknowledged.

"Those fights they're cruel and stupid," she told the fat man now.

He was too smart to contradict that. After a moment, looking for something else to quarrel over, he said: "You ever do anything before you kept bar?"

She brought out a lifeless smile for him to consider.

"One or two things," she said.

"Then how come I never heard about them?"

"Got me there, Antoyne."

She waited for him to respond, but now something new on Strait had caught his attention. He wiped the window glass again. He pressed his face up against it. "Irene's a little late today," he said.

Liv Hula busied herself suddenly behind the bar.

"Oh yes?"

"A minute or two," he said.

"What's a minute or two to Irene?"

The fights were a dumb career, that was Liv Hula's opinion. They were a dumb life. Joe Leone's whole ambition was as dumb as his self-presentation until he met Irene: then it got worse. Irene was a Mona who had a good track record working the noncorporate spaceport. She was what you call petite, five three in transparent urethane heels and full of appeal with her flossy blonde hair. Like all those Uncle Zip products she had something organic about her, something real. She watched Joe Leone at the fights and after she smelled his blood she couldn't leave him alone. Every morning when he came home to the tailor's, Irene was there too. Between them they summed up New Venusport, the sex industry and the fight industry. When Joe and Irene were together you couldn't be sure which industry was which. They were a new form of entertainment in themselves.

Irene commenced to hammer at the chopshop door.

"How long you think they'll let her shout before they open up?" fat Antoyne asked. Liv Hula had found a map-shaped stain on the zinc bartop, which she stared at with interest.

"I don't know why you're asking me," she said.

"She's got feelings for him," said Antoyne, to press

his advantage. "That's undeniable. No one questions that... Jesus," he added to himself, "look at those tits."

He tried to imagine Joe Leone, dead and liquefied while his bones and organs reassembled themselves and Irene gave him the Mona side of her mouth. The joke was, Irene's opinion was no different than Liv Hula's. Every morning she made them fetch her an old wooden chair and put it at the head of Joe's tank, with his faded publicity slogan on it, Hold the painkillers. There she sat, ignoring the pink flashing LEDs, which were for show anyway, while the tank proteome slushed around like warm spit, cascades of autocatalysis through a substrate of forty thousand molecular species, flushing every twenty minutes to take off what unwanted product the chemistry couldn't eliminate. She hated the sucking noises it made.

One day you won't get back, she would tell the Lion. One more fight and you're fucked with me. But Joe was an algorithm by now, somewhere off in operator space. He was choosing new tusks from the catalogue, he was getting tuning to his glycolytic systems. He couldn't hear a word.

Oh Joe, I really mean it, she'd say. One more fight.

Liv Hula sometimes watched the rockets too.

Near dawn, you got her and the fat man standing by the window together as two tubby brass-looking freighters lifted from the corporate yard. Then a K-ship exited the military pits on the hard white line from its fRAM engine. In the backwash of light a warmer expression came on her face than you would expect. By then the Kefahuchi Tract had begun to fade from the sky, which was tilted like a lid to show one thin eastern arc of pale green, false dawn. Off-shore winds would come up soon and, forced along the narrow pipe of Strait Street, churn the low-lying fogs of the event site. That would be the signal for all sorts of people to start the day. Live Hula and Antoyne the fat man watched the K-ship cut the sky like scissors.

"You ever fly one of those, Antoyne ?" she remarked.

He blinked and turned his head away. "There's no need for that," he said. "There's no need for sarcasm like that."

Just then, Jack Serotonin came back in the bar, walking quickly and looking behind him. He had the air of someone whose morning was already off its proper track. His face was white, with a graze on one cheek leaking beads of blood. He had waded through oily water not long ago it seemed; and his zip-up gabardine jacket had one sleeve half off at the shoulder—as if someone had held on to it while they fell, Liv Hula thought immediately, although she did not know why.

"Jesus, Jack," she said.

"Get me a drink," Jack Serotonin said.

He walked halfway across the room as if he was going to drink it at the counter, then changed his mind and sat down suddenly at the nearest table. Once there he didn't seem to know what to do. A few shadow operators detached themselves from the ceiling to examine him; he stared through them. "Shit," he kept saying in a quiet, surprised way. After a while his breathing calmed down.

The fat man forgot his hurt feelings as soon as Jack came in. He pulled up a chair and began to tell Jack some story, leaning into it in his enthusiasm so his soft body enveloped the table-edge. His voice was quiet and urgent, but you could hear the odd word, "entradista," "hard X rays." "Ed Chianese." Jack stared through him too, then said, "Shut up or I'll shoot you where you sit." The fat man looked hopelessly away. He said all he wanted in this bar was a chance, Jack should give him a chance. He was trying not to cry. "I'm sorry," Jack said, but he was already thinking about something else, and when Liv Hula brought him his drink, and sat down and said, "Black Heart, Jack, just the way you like it," he barely seemed to recognise her.

"Shit," he said again.

"Where's the woman, Jack?"

"I don't know," he said.

"Only I don't want to hear you left her there."

"She cracked and ran. She's in the aureole somewhere. Antoyne, go to the door, tell me if anyone's in the street."

"All I want is a chance to fit in," the fat man said.

"For fuck's sake Antoyne."

Antoyne said, "No one understands that."

Serotonin opened his mouth to say more, then he seemed to forget Antoyne altogether. "I never saw panic like it," he said. He shook his head. "You couldn't even say we'd got inside. It's bad this morning, but it's not that bad." He finished his drink and held out the glass. Instead of taking it, Liv Hula caught his wrist.

"So how bad is it?" she said. She wouldn't let go until he told her.

"Things are moving about," he admitted. "I've seen worse, but usually further in."

"Where is she, Jack?"

He laughed. It was a laugh he had practised too often. "I told you," he said tiredly, "she's somewhere in the aureole. We never got any further. She runs off between the buildings, I see silk stockings and that fucking fur coat, then I see nothing. She was still calling from somewhere when I gave up," he said. "Get me another drink, Liv, or I don't know what I'll do."

Liv Hula said: "You didn't go after her, Jack."

He stared.

"You stayed where it was safe, and shouted a couple times, and then you came home."

"Jack would never do that," the fat man said in a blustering way. No one was going to say Jack would do that. "Hey, Jack. Tell her. You would never do that!" He got up out of his chair. "I'm going in the street and keep an eye open now, just the way you wanted. You got a wrong idea about Jack Serotonin," he said to Liv Hula, "if you think he'd do that." As soon as he had gone, she went to the bar and poured Jack another Black Heart rum, while Jack rubbed his face with his hands like someone who was very tired and couldn't see his way through life any more. His face had an older look than it had when he left. It was sullen and heavy, and his blue eyes took on a temporary pleading quality which one day would be permanent.

"You don't know what it's like in there," he told her.

"Of course I don't," she said. "Only Jack Serotonin knows that."

"Streets transposed on one another, everything laid down out of sync one minute to the next. Geography

that doesn't work. There isn't a single piece of
dependable architecture in the shit of it. You leave
the route you know, you're finished. Lost dogs bark-
ing day and night. Everything struggling to keep
afloat."

She wasn't disposed to let him get away with that.

"You're the professional, Jack," she reminded him.
"They're the customers. Here's your other drink if you
want it." She leaned her elbows on the bar. "You're
the one has to hold himself together."

This seemed to amuse him. He took the rum down
in one swallow, the colour came back into his face,
and they looked at one another in a more friendly
way. He wasn't finished with her though. "Hey Liv,"
he said softly after a moment or two, "what's the difference between what you've seen and what you are?
You want to know what it's like in there? The fact is,
you spend all those years trying to make something
of it. Then guess what, it starts making something of
you."

He got up and went to the door.

"What are you fucking about at, Antoyne?" he
called. "I said 'look.' I said 'take a look.'"

The fat man, who had trotted up Strait a little into
the predawn wind to clear his head, also to see if he
could get a glimpse of Irene the Mona through a chink
in the boarded windows of the chopshop, came in
grinning and shivering with the cold. "Antoyne here
can tell us all about it," Jack Serotonin said.
"Everything he knows."

"Leave Antoyne alone."

"You ever been in there when everything fell apart,
Antoyne?"

"I was never in there, Jack," Antoyne said hastily. "I never claimed I was."

"Everything was just taken away. and you had no idea what established itself in exchange? The air's like uncooked pastry. It's not a smell in there, it's a substrate. In every corner there's a broken telephone nailed to the wall. They're all labelled Speak but there's no line out. They ring but no one's ever there."

Liv Hula gave him a look, then shrugged. To the fat man she explained, "Jack just so hates to lose a client."

"Fuck you," Jack Serotonin said. "Fuck the two of you."

He pushed his glass across the counter and walked out.

After Jack Serotonin left silence returned to the bar. It crowded in on itself, so that Liv Hula and the fat man, though they wanted to speak, were hemmed in with their own thoughts. The onshore wind decreased; while the light increased until they could no longer deny it was dawn. The woman washed and dried the glass Jack Serotonin had used, then put it carefully in its place behind the bar. Then she went upstairs to the room above, where she thought about changing her clothes but in the end only stared in a kind of mounting panic at the disordered bed, the blanket chest and the bare white walls.

I ought to move on, she thought. I ought to leave here now.

When she came down again, Antoyne had resumed his place by the window and with his hands on the sill stood watching the payloads lift one after another from the corporate port. He half-turned as if to speak but, receiving no encouragement, turned back again.

Across the street someone opened the chopshop door.

After a brief quiet struggle, Irene the Mona stumbled out. She took an uncertain step or two forward, peering blindly up and down Strait like a drunk assessing heavy traffic, then sat down suddenly on the edge of the sidewalk. The door slammed shut behind her. Her skirt rode up. Antoyne pressed his face closer to the glass. "Hey," he whispered to himself. Irene, meanwhile, set her little shiny red urethane vanity case down beside her and began to claw through its contents with one hand. She was still sitting there two or three minutes later, showing all she had, sniffing and wiping her eyes, when the cats came out of the Raintown event site in an alert silent rush.

Who knew how many of those cats there were? Another thing, you never found so much as a tabby among them, every one was either black or white. When they poured out of the zone it was like a model of some chaotic mixing flow in which, though every condition is determined, the outcome can never be predicted. Soon they filled Strait in both directions, bringing with them the warmth of their bodies, also a close, dusty but not unpleasant smell. Irene struggled upright, but the cats took no more notice than if she had been one of the street lamps.

Irene was born on a planet called Perkin's Rent. She left there tall and bony, with an awkward walk and big feet. When she smiled her gums showed, and she did her hair in lacquered copper waves so tight and complex they could receive the mains hum, the basic transmissions of the universe. She had a sweet way of laughing. When she boarded the rocket to leave, she was seventeen. Her suitcase contained a yellow cotton dress with a kind of faux-Deco feel, tampons, and four pairs of high heel shoes. "I love shoes," she would explain to you when she was drunk. "I love shoes." You got the best of her in those days. She would follow you anywhere for two weeks then follow someone else. She loved a rocket jockey.

Now she stood with tears streaming down her face, watching the Raintown cats flow around her, until Liv Hula waded fastidiously into the stream and fetched her back to the bar, where she sat her down and said:

"What can I get you, honey ?"

"He's dead this time," Irene said in a rush.

"I can't believe that," Liv Hula said. Immediately she was tidying up inside, planning to stay back inside herself away from the fact of it. But Irene kept repeating in her disorganised way, "He's dead this time, that's all," which made it hard to dissociate. Irene took Liv Hula's hand and pressed it to her cheek. It was her opinion, she said, that something makes men unfit for most of life; to which Liv Hula replied, "I always thought so too." Then Irene broke into snuffling again and had to fetch out her vanity mirror. "Especially the best parts," she said indistinctly.

Later, when Antoyne came and tried to make conversation with her, she gave him the full benefit of her looks. He bought her a drink which settled out the same colours as her skirt, pink and yellow, and which he said they drank on some dumb planet he knew fifty lights down the line.

"I been there, Fat Antoyne," she told him with a sad smile.

That original Irene, she thought, wasn't good at being on her own. She would sit on the bed one place or another, listening to the rain and trying to hold herself together. On the other hand, she never lacked ambition. The stars of the Halo were like one big neon sign to her. The sign said: All the shoes you can eat. When she bought the Mona package, the tailor promised her hair would always smell of peppermint shampoo. She had gone through the catalogues, and that was what she wanted, and the tailor designed it in. On the Raintown streets it was her big selling point.

"I been there," she told Antoyne, letting him get the peppermint smell, "and just now I'm glad to meet someone else who's been there too."

Antoyne was as encouraged by this as any man. He sat on after she finished the drink, trying to engage her with stories of the places he had seen back when he rode the rockets. But Irene had been to all those places too—and more, Liv Hula thought—and fat Antoyne had all he was going to get for one cheap cocktail drink. Liv watched them from a distance, her own thoughts so churned she didn't care how it ended. Eventually even Antoyne could see the way things were. He scraped his chair back and retreated to his place by the window. What time was it? How had the things happened that ended him up here? He looked out on to Strait. "It's day," he said. "Hey," he grumbled, "I actually respected the guy. You know?" Meanwhile the stream of cats flowed on like a problem in statistical mechanics, without any apparent slackening or falling away of numbers, until suddenly it turned itself off and Strait was empty again. Across the road at the tailor's they were flushing Joe Leone's proteins down the drain.

At the civilian port, the cruise ships, half-hidden in

the mist, towered above the buildings; while along the tall narrow streets a traffic of rickshaw girls and tattoo boys had begun, ferrying the tourists from the New Cafe Al Aktar to Moneytown, from the Church on the Rock to the Rock Church, while around them their shreds and veils of shadow operators whispered, "A sight everyone will be sure to see, a discourse of oppositions." Fur coats were all over Raintown by eight, dyed the colour of honey or horse chestnut, cut to flow like some much lighter fabric. What sort of money was this? Where did it come from? It was off-planet money. It was corporate money. However cruel the trade that produced them, you could hardly deny the beauty of those coats and their luxurious surfaces.

Shortly after the last cat had vanished into the city, Jack's client returned to the bar.

Where Jack had come back filthy, she came back clean. You wouldn't notice anything new about her, except her shoulders were a little hunched and her face was still. Her hands she thrust into the pockets of her coat. Nothing had been taken away from her: but she held her head more carefully than before, always looking forward as if her neck hurt, or as if she was trying not to notice something happening in the side of her eye. It was hard to read body language like that. She placed herself with care at a table near the window, crossed one leg over the other and asked in a low voice for a drink. After a little while she said, "I wonder if someone could give that other man the rest of his fee."

Antoyne sat forward eagerly.

"I can do that," he offered.

"No you can't," Liv Hula warned him. To the

woman in the fur coat she said: "Jack's cheap, he left you for dead. You owe him nothing."

"Still," the woman said. "I feel he should have the rest of his money. It's here. And I was fine, really." She stared ahead of herself. "A little puzzled, I suppose, at how unpleasant it is."

Liv Hula threw up her hands.

"Why do they come here?" she asked fat Antoyne in a loud voice. Before he could say anything, she added: "They leave the nice safe tour and they end up in this bar here. They always find our Jack."

"Hey, Jack's OK," the fat man said.

"Jack's a joke, Antoyne, and so are you."

Antoyne struggled to his feet and looked as if he was going to challenge that, but in the end he only shrugged. Jack's client gave him a faint, encouraging smile, but then seemed to look past him. Silence drew out a moment or two; then a chair scraped back and Irene the Mona came over to the table where these events were happening. Her little urethane shoes clattered on the wooden floor. She had wiped her tears and done her lipstick. She was over Joe the Lion now. What had she been on, to invest her considerable life-energy that way? Irene had a future in front of her, everyone agreed, and it was good, light-hearted one. She had her plans, and they were good ones too. Though it was true she would keep Joe in her heart pocket many years because that was the kind of girl she knew herself to be.

"That sure is a beautiful coat," she said. She held out her hand.

For a moment, the woman looked nonplussed. Then she shook Irene's hand and said, "Thank you. It is, isn't it ?"

"Very beautiful, and I admire it so," Irene agreed. She gave a little bob, seemed about to add something, then suddenly went and sat down again and toyed with her glass. "Don't be hard on him, honey," she called across to Liv Hula. "He's nothing but a man after all." It was hard to tell which man she meant.

"I feel he should have his money," appealed the woman in the fur coat. When no one answered she set the cash on the table in front of her, in high denomination notes. "Anyway, it's here for him," she said.

"Jesus," was Liv Hula's comment. "Antoyne," she said, "you want another drink?"

But the fat man had lost patience with the way they treated him in there. He was just a man trying to fit in, someone who had seen as much as anyone else, more than some. It made him angry they didn't listen. He thought about when he rode the dynaflow ships, and all the planets he saw then, and the things he saw on them. Gay Lung, Ambo Danse and Fourth Part, Waitrose Two and the Thousand Suns: he had scattered himself like money across the Beach stars and down into Radio Bay. He had gone deep in those days. Surfed the Alcubiere warp with Ed Chianese. Owned a rocket, he called her the Kino Chicken. Failed at being solitary. On Santa Muerte inhaled something that deviated both his septum and his sense of where things were. That was it for being a sky pilot.

What the hell, he thought. Nothing's ever yours to keep.

At least he was out of that place now, into the morning somewhere he could breathe, heading for Moneytown and the strip mall wonderland running south of Strait, down past the spaceports to the sea.

He was narrowing his eyes in the strong light glittering up off the distant water. He was going to look for work. He was going to look for people who meant it when they smiled.

After he had gone Liv Hula's bar was silent. One by one, the shadow operators detached themselves furtively from the ceiling and went to the woman in the fur coat, who acknowledged them absently. Smells crept out of the kitchen and out of the pipes. The three women appeared preoccupied with their own thoughts. Every so often one or the other of them would go to the door and peer up Strait Street towards the event zone, wreathed—silent, heaving and questionable—in its daytime chemical fogs; while the others watched her expectantly.

All of Us Can Almost...

Carol Emshwiller

Carol Emshwiller was born in Ann Arbor, Michigan in 1921 and grew up in Michigan and France. A MacDowell Colony Fellow, she has received a National Endowment for the Arts grant, a New York State Creative Artists Public Service grant, a New York State Foundation for the Arts grant, and has won the World Fantasy, Nebula, Philip K. Dick, Gallun, and Icon awards.

Her short fiction has appeared in The Magazine of Fantasy & Science Fiction, Century, Scifiction, Lady Churchill's Rosebud Wristlet, New Directions, Orbit, The Voice Literary Supplement, Omni, SciFiction, *and many other anthologies and magazines. It has been collected in World Fantasy Award winner* The Start of the End of it All, Verging on the Pertinent, Joy in Our Cause, *and* Report to the Men's Club and Other Stories. *She is also the author of four novels,* Carmen Dog, Ledoyt, Leaping Man Hill, *and Philip K Dick Award winner* The Mount. *Upcoming is a new short story collection,* I Live with You and You Don't Know It, *and a new young adult novel,* Mr Boots. *Emshwiller lives in New York City in the winter where*

329

she teaches at New York University School of Continuing Education. She spends her summers in a shack in the Sierras in California.

Her story here, set in the same universe as several other recent stories deals with, among other things, the desire to fly, a frequently recurring motif in her work.

...fly, that is. Of course lots of creatures can *almost* fly. But all of us are able to match any others of us, wing span to wing span. Also to any other fliers. But though we match each other wing to wing we can't get more than inches off the ground. If that. But we're impressive. Our beaks look vicious. We could pose for statues for the birds representing an empire. We could represent an army or a president. And, actually, we are the empire. We may not be able to fly, but we rule the skies. And most everything else, too.

Creatures come to us for advice on flying. They see us kick up dust and flap and stretch and are awed.

We croak out what we have to say in quacks. We tell them, "The sky is a highway. The sky is of our time and recent. The sky is flat. It's blue because it's happy." They thank us with donations. That's how we live.

The sound of our clacking beaks carries across the valley. It adds to our reputation as powerful—though what good is it really? It's just noise.

Nothing said of us is true, but must we live by truths? Why not keep on living by our lies?

Soaring! Think of it! The stillness of it. Not even the sound of flapping. They say we once did that. Perhaps we still can and just forgot how to begin.

How make that first jump? How get the lift? But we grew too large. We began to eat the things that fell and lots of things fall.

I could leap off a cliff. Test myself. But I might become one of those things tumbling down. Even my own kind would tear me apart.

Loosely...very loosely speaking, I do fly. My sleep is full of nothing but that. The joy of it.

But where's the joy in *almost* doing it. Flapping in circles. Making a great wind for nothing but a jump or two. We don't even look good to ourselves.

I don't know what we're made for. It's neither sky nor water nor... especially not...the waddle of the land. We can't sing. Actually we can't do anything. Except look fierce.

Pigeons circle overhead. Meadowlarks sing. Geese and ducks, in Vs, do their seasonal things. We stay. We *have* to. Winter storms come and we're still here. We puff up as much as we can and wrap our wings around ourselves. Perhaps that's what our wings were for in the first place. We're designed merely to shelter ourselves. Even our dreams of flying are yet more lies.

But none others are as strong as we are... at least none *seem* to be. We win with looks alone and a big voice. We stand, assured and sure.

When creatures ask me for a ride I say, "I'd take you up any time you want—hop and skip and up we go—except you're too heavy. Next time measure wings, mine against some other of us. You'll need a few inches more on each side. Tell a bigger one I said to take you up."

"Take to the air along with us," I say. "Follow me up and up." I'm shameless. But I suspect it's only the young that really believe. The older ones pretend to because of our beaks, because of the wind we can stir up—our clouds of dust.

Still, I go on, "Check out my wing span. Check out my evil eye. Listen. *My* voice."

They jump at my squawk.

They bring me food just to watch me tear at it. At least I'm good at that. I put on a good show. Every creature backs away.

One of the young ones keeps wanting me to take him up. He won't stop asking. I say, "A sparrow could do better." That's true, but he takes it as a joke. I say, "Why not at least ask a male."

"Males scare me."

Finally, just to shut him up, I say, "Yes, but not until the next section of time."

He runs off yelling, "Whee! Whee! Whee! She's taking me up!"

Now how will I get out of it? I only have from one moon to the other. But who knows? One of the big males may have eaten him by that time. They don't care where their food comes from. He was right to be scared.

Who knows how we lost our ability to fly? Maybe we're just lazy. Maybe we just don't exercise our flying muscles. How could we fly, sitting around eating dead things all the time? If anyone can fly, it seems to me more likely one of us smaller females could than a big male.

That little one keeps coming back and saying, *"Really? Are you really going to take me up?"*

And I keep saying, "I said I would didn't I? When

have any of us ever lied?" (Actually, when have we ever told the truth?)

He keeps yelling back and forth to all who'll listen. The way he keeps on with it, I could eat him myself.

But we have to be careful. Sometimes those ground dwellers get together and decide not to feed us. Whoever they don't feed always dies. They waddle around trying to get someone of us to share, but we don't. We're not a sharing kind.

I *should* like these ground dwellers because of the food they bring, but I don't. I pretend to, just like they pretend to believe us. They call us Emperor, Leader, Master, but why are they doing this? It could be a conspiracy to keep us fat and lazy so we won't be lords of the sky anymore. So we're tamed and docile. Maybe they started this whole thing, stuffing us with their leftovers. Maybe they're the real emperors of the sky. Master of the sky though never in it anymore than we are. At least they can climb trees.

I wonder what they want us for? Or maybe it's the best way to know where we are and what we're doing.

Feed your enemies. Tame them.

I ask some of us, "Where is that cliff they say we used to soar out from?"

"Was there a cliff? Did there used to be a cliff?"

I'm sure there must have been one. How could birds the size of us get started without one—a high one? Maybe that's our problem, we've lost our cliff. We forgot where it is.

Evenings when all are in their burrows, and my own kind, wrapped in their wings, are clustered under the lean-tos set out for us by lesser beings, I stretch and flap. Reach. Jump. Only the nightingale sees me flop. It's a joy to be up to hear her and to be flipping and flopping.

I'll take that pesky little one all the way to wherever that cliff of ours is. Wouldn't that be something? See the sights? Be up in what we always call "Our element."

But there's a male, has his eye on me. Has had for quite some time. That's another good reason to take off. I'd like to get out of here before the time is ripe.

Or perhaps he's heard the little one yelling, "Whee, Whee," and likes the idea of me with one of those little ones on my back. Easy pickin's, *both* of us. Little one for one purpose and me for another. I can just see it, me distracted, defending the little, and the big taking care of both things while I struggle, front *and* back.

He may be the biggest, but I don't want him. Maybe that's how we got too big to fly, we kept mating with the biggest. It's our own fault we got so big. I'm not going to do that. Well, also the big ones are the strongest. This biggest could slap down all the other males.

If not for the fact that we hardly speak to each other, we females could get together and stop it. Go for the small and the nice. If there are any nice. Not a single one of us is noted for being nice.

I hate to think what mating will be like with one so huge. I'd ask other females if we were the kind who asked things of each other.

He keeps following me around. I don't know how

I'm going to avoid him if he's determined. I won't get any help from any of the others. They'll just come and watch. Probably even squawk him onward. I've done it myself.

I'm thinking of ways to avoid that male, so when that little one comes to ask, yet again, "Why wait for next moon?" I say, "You're right. We'll do it now but I have to find our platform."

"Why?"

"Have you ever seen any of us take off from down here? Of course you haven't. I need a place to soar from."

"Can't we start flying from right here so everybody can see me?"

"No. I have to have a place to take off from. Get on my back. I'll take you there."

"I can walk faster than this all by myself."

"I know, but bear with me."

"My name is Hobie. What's yours?"

"We don't have names. We don't need them."

The big one comes waddling after us. A few of us follow him, wanting to see what's going to happen. I don't think the big realizes how far I'm going. Nobody does.

When we get to the end of the nesting places, Hobie says, "I've never been this far. Is this all right to do?"

"It's all right."

"Your waddling is making me sick."

"We'll rest in a few minutes."

I don't dare stop now, so near the nests. Everybody will waddle out to us. We have to get out of sight.

Out there I could eat Hobbie myself if need be. I don't suppose anybody will be feeding us way out here.

I don't stop soon enough. Hobie throws up on my back. It smells of dirt dweller's food. And we're still not out of sight.

"Hang on. I'll stop at that green patch just ahead."

I waddle a little faster but that just makes him fall off. I'm thinking, Oh well, go on back and let the big male do what he needs wants to do. It can't last more than a couple of minutes. If he breaks my legs it might be better than what I'm going through now.

But I wait for Hobie to get back on. I say, "Not much farther." He climbs on slowly. I wonder if he suspects I might eat him.

That big is coming along behind us but he's slower even that I am. Who'd have thought I was worth so much trouble.

In the green patch there's water—a stream. We both drink and I start washing my back. Hobie keeps saying, "I couldn't help it."

"I know that. Now stop talking so I can think."

I leave foot prints. Maybe best if I go along the stream for a while. Then we can drink any time we want. I turn towards the high side, where the stream comes down from. If there really is a take off platform it's got to be high.

"Whcre are we going?"

"There's a place in the sky that'll give mc a good lift.

"What kind of a place?"

"A cliff."

"How far is it?"

"Oh for the sky's sake keep quiet."

"Why does your kind always say, for the sky's sake?"

"Because we're sky creatures. Not like you. Now let me think about walking."

Even in this little stream there's fish. Wouldn't it be nice if I could catch one by myself?

"Hang on!"

I dive. But I forgot about the water changing the angle of view. I miss. I say, "Next time."

Hobie says, "I can."

I let him off to stand on the bank and dive and he does it. Gives the fish to me even though I'll bet he's getting hungry, too.

"Thank you, Hobie. Now get one for yourself."

At dusk we find a nice place to nest in among the trees along the stream— soft with leaves. Hobie curls up right beside my beak. Practically under it. I'm more afraid of my bite than he is. I hope I don't snap him up in my sleep.

Towards morning we hear something coming... lumbering along. Sounding tired for sure. We both know who. Hobie doesn't like big males any more than I do. He scrambles up on my back and says, "Shouldn't we go?"

Because I'm so much smaller than any male, I waddle a lot faster. It gets steeper but I'm still doing pretty well. It's so steep I have hopes of finding our cliff. I turn around and look back down and here comes the big, but a long ways off. Staggering, stumbling. Am I really worth all this effort?

"Are we far enough ahead? Are we getting some place? How long now?"

"Do you ever say anything that isn't a question?"
"You do it. That's a question."

I'm not used to waddling all day long, especially not uphill. It's the hardest thing I've ever done. But the big…. He's still coming. It's getting steeper. I hope one as large as he is can't get up here. This is just what I wanted. The launching platform has got to be here. How did it ever come to be that we got stuck down in the flat places?

And finally here it is, *the* flat place at the top of the cliff. I look over the edge. I'm so scared just looking I start to feel sick. I'm not sure I can even pretend to jump.

"Why are you shaking so much? It's going to make me sick again."

Should I eat Hobie now before he tells everybody I not only can't fly, I can't even get close to the edge without trembling and feeling sick?

But it's been nice having company. I've gotten used to his paws tangled in my feathers, making a mess of them. I'd miss his questions.

I move back and look over the other side. It's steep on that side, too, though not so much. This platform is a promontory going off into nothing on all sides but one. It must have been perfect for fliers.

I look around to see if I can see any signs that it was used as a launching place, but there's nothing. I suppose, up here so high, the weather would have worn away any signs of that. I wonder if that big male knows anything more about it than I do.

It's breezy up here. I flap my wings to test myself, but I do it well away from the edges.

Hobie says, "Go, go, go."

Maybe I should just get closer and closer to edge…get used to it little by little… until I don't feel quite so scared.

I look over the side again though from a few feet away. I see the big male is still coming. I see him turn around and look down at exactly the same spot where we did. Then he looks up. Right at us. He spreads his wings at us so I'll see his wingspan. Then he turns side view. That's so I'll get a good look at his profile… the big hooked beak, the white ruff…. Then he starts up again.

I look over the more sloping side again. I think I might be able to slide down there though it's a steep slide. At the bottom there's a lot of trees and brush. That would break our fall.

That big one is getting so close I can hear him shuffling and sliding just like I did. I sit over by the less steep side and wait.

Pretty soon I see the fierce head looking up at us, the beady eye, and then the whole body. He has an even harder time than I had lifting himself on to the launching platform.

Hobie says, "I'm scared of males," and I say, "I am, too."

As soon as the big catches his breath he says, "You're beautiful."

I say, "That's neither here nor there."

He says, "I love you." As if any of us knew what that word meant.

I say, "Love is what you feel for a nice piece of carrion."

He looks a mess. I must, too. Dusty, feathers every which way. Hobie and I filled up on fish back at the stream, but I don't think he did. He looks at Hobie like the next meal. I back up a little closer to the slide. I say, "This one's mine." *That*, he'll understand.

He's inching closer. He thinks I don't notice. If he grabs me there's no way I can escape. I back up even more.

And then.... I didn't mean to. Off we go. Skidding, sliding, but like flying. Almost! Almost!

Hobie is yelling, "Whee. Whee. Whee." At least he's happy.

When we get down as far as the trees and bushes, I grab at them with my beak to slow us. And then I hear the big coming behind us. I never thought he...such a big one...would dare follow.

There's a great swish of gravel sliding with us. Even more as the big comes down behind us. Here he is, landed beside us, but, thank goodness, not exactly on.

Hobie and I are more or less fine. Scratched and bruised and dusty, but the big is moaning.

We're in a sort of ditch full of lots of brush and trees. It looks to be up hill on all sides. I wonder if either of us... the big and I could waddle out of it. Hobie could.

Hobie and I dust off.

Hobie says. "That was great. I wish the others could have seen me."

He can't, can he? Can't *possibly* think that was flying?

Then I see that the big one's legs slant out at odd angles. His weight was his undoing. My lightness saved me.

The big says, "Help me." But why should I? I say, "It's all your fault in the first place."

He's in pain. I brush him off. I even dare to preen him a bit. I don't think he'll hurt me or try to mate. He couldn't with those broken legs, anyway. He needs me. He has to be nice. That'll be a change.

These big males are definitely bigger than they need to be. He's twice my size. Where will all this bigness lead? Just to less and less, ever again, the possibility of flight, that's where.

Hobie doesn't even need to be asked. "I'm hungry. Can I go get us some food?"

"Of course you can."

"After you flew me I owe you lots."

Off he goes into the brush. I take a look at the big one's legs and wonder what to do. Can I make splints? And what to use to bind them with? Though there's always lots of stringy things in our carrion if Hobie finds us food.

"You're not only never going to fly, you may never waddle either."

He just groans again.

"I'll try to straighten these out." I give him a stick to bite on. And then I do it. After I look for sticks as splints.

In no time Hobie brings three creatures. I think one for each of us but he says he ate already. He's says this place is all meals. Nothing has been hunting here in a long time, maybe never. He says, "You could even hunt for yourself."

Now there's a thought. I think I will.

I leave the three creatures for the big male and start out but the big says, "Don't leave me." Just like a chick.

I say, "If you eat Hobie that's the last you'll ever see of me." And I go.

Hobie is right, all the little meals are easy to catch. I eat four and keep all the stringy things. I also look around at where we are and if we could ever get out. There's that little stream from below, cool and clear, bubbling along not far from where we fell. Beside it there's a nice place for a nest. I think about chicks. How I'd try to get them flapping right from the start. Even the baby males. And maybe, if we all were thinner and had to scramble for our food like I just had to do, and if all the food would get to know the danger and make us scramble harder and we'd get even thinner and stronger, and first thing you know we wouldn't have to climb out of here, we'd fly. All of us. Could that really come to be?

I throw away the stringy things I was going to make splints with. I have everything under control. I'll tell Hobie he can go on home if he wants to, though I'll tell him I do wish he'd stay, just for the company. And just in case we never do learn to fly again, we'd need his help when the food gets smarter and scarcer.

The Tang Dynasty
Underwater Pyramid

Walter Jon Williams

Walter Jon Williams' first science fiction novel,
Ambassador of Progress, *appeared in 1984 and was
followed by fifteen more, most notably* Hardwired,
Aristoi, Metropolitan *and sequel* City on Fire, *and the
first two volumes in his "Praxis" trilogy,* The Praxis
and The Sundering. *Upcoming is the final "Praxis"
novel,* The Orthodox War.

*A prolific short story writer, Williams' first short
story "Side Effects" appeared in 1985 and was followed
by a string of major stories that were regularly nominated for major awards, including "Dinosaurs," "Surfa-
cing," "Wall, Stone, Craft," "Lethe," and Nebula Award
winner "Daddy's World," a number of which were collected in* Facets *and* Frankensteins and Foreign Devils.
Williams lives and works in rural New Mexico.

*The story that follows is an amusing tale of fun,
intrigue and biology gone awry.*

What we might call the Tang Dynasty Underwater Pyramid Situation began in the Staré M sto on a windy spring day. We were clumped beneath the statue of Jan Hus and in the midst of our medley of South American Tunes Made Famous by North American Pop Singers. The segué from "Cielito Lindo" to "El Condor Pasa" required some complicated fingering, and when I glanced up from my *guitarra* I saw our contact standing in the crowd, smoking a cigaret and making a bad show of pretending he had nothing better to do but stand in Prague's Old Town and listen to a family of nine Aymara Indians deconstruct Simon and Garfunkel.

My uncle Iago had described the man who was planning to hire us, and this man matched the description: a youngish Taiwanese with a fashionable razor cut, stylish shades, a Burbury worn over a cashmere suit made by Pakistani tailors in Hong Kong, a silk tie, and glossy handmade Italian shoes.

He just didn't look like a folk music fan to me.

After the medley was over I called for a break, and my cousin Rosalinda passed the derby among the old hippies hanging around the statue while my other cousin Jorge tried to interest the crowd in buying our CDs. I ambled up to our contact and bummed a smoke and a light.

"You're Ernesto?" he asked in Oxford-accented English.

"Ernesto, that's me," I said.

"Your uncle Iago suggested I contact you," he said. "You can call me Jesse."

His name wasn't Jesse any more than mine was really Ernesto, this being the monicker the priest gave me when the family finally got around to having me baptised. I'd been born on an artificial reed island drifting around Lake Titicaca, a place where opportunities for mainstream religious ceremony were few.

My real name is Cari, just in case you wondered.

"Can we go somewhere a little more private?" Jesse asked.

"Yeah, sure. This way."

He ground out his cigaret beneath one of his wingtips, and followed me into the Church of St Nicholas while I wondered if there was any chance that we were really under surveillance, or whether Jesse was just being unreasonably paranoid.

Either way, I thought, it would affect my price.

The baroque glories of the church burst onto my retinas as I entered, marble statues and bravura frescos and improbable amounts of gold leaf. Strangely enough, the church belonged to the Hussites, who you don't normally associate with that sort of thing.

Booms and bleats echoed through the church. The organist was tuning for his concert later in the day, useful interference in the event anyone was actually pointing an audio pickup at us.

Jesse didn't spare a glance for the extravagant ornamentation that blazed all around him, just removed his shades as he glanced left and right to see if anyone was within listening distance.

"Did Iago tell you anything about me?" Jesse asked.

"Just that he'd worked for you before, and that you paid."

Iago and his branch of the family were in Sofia doing surveillance on a ex-Montenegrin secret policeman who was involved in selling Russian air-to-surface ATASM missiles from Transnistria through the Bosporus to the John the Baptist Liberation Army, Iraqi Mandaean separatists who operated out of Cyprus. Lord alone knew what the Mandaeans were going to do with the missiles, as they didn't have any aircraft to fire them *from*—or at we can only hope they don't. Probably they were just middlemen for the party who really wanted the missiles.

I'd been holding my group ready to fly to Cyprus if needed, but otherwise the Iraqi Mandaeans were none of my concern. Reflecting on this, I wondered if the world had always been this complicated, or if this was some kind of twenty-first century thing.

"We need you to do a retrieval," Jesse said.

"What are we retrieving?"

His mouth gave an impatient twitch. "You don't need to know that."

He was beginning to irritate me. "Is it bigger than a breadbox?" I asked. "I need to know if I'll need a crane or truck or…"

"A boat," Jesse said. "And diving gear."

The organist played a snatch of Bach—the D Minor, I thought, and too fast.

If you hang out in European churches, you hear the D Minor a lot. Over the years I had become a connoisseur in these matters.

"Diving gear," I said cautiously. "That's interesting."

"Three days ago," Jesse said, "the 5000-ton freighter *Goldfish Fairy* sank in a storm in the Pearl River Delta off Hong Kong. Our cargo was in the hold. After the Admiralty Court holds its investigation, salvage rights will go on offer. We need you to retrieve our cargo before salvage companies get to the scene."

I thought about this while organ pipes bleated above my head. "Five thousand tons," I said, "that's a little coaster, not a real ship at all. How do you know it didn't break up when it went down?"

"When the pumps stopped working the *Goldfish Fairy* filled and sank. The crew got away to the boats and saw it sink on an even keel."

"Do you know where?"

"The captain got a satellite fix."

"How deep did it sink?"

"Sixty meters."

I let out a slow breath. A depth of sixty meters required technical diving skills I didn't possess.

"The Pearl River Delta is one of the busiest sea lanes in the world," I said. "How are we going to conduct an unauthorized salvage operation without being noticed?"

There was a moment's hesitation, and then Jesse said, "That's your department."

I contemplated this bleak picture for a moment, then said, "How big is the your cargo again?"

"We were shipping several crates—mainly research equipment. But only one crate matters, and it's about two meters long by eighty centimeters wide. The captain said they were stored on top of the hold, so all you have to do is open the hold and raise the box.

"

That seemed to simplify matters. "Right," I said. "We'll take the job."

"For how much?"

I let the organist blat a few times while I considered, and then I named a sum. Jesse turned stern.

"That's a lot of money," he said.

"Firstly," I said, "I'm going to have to bribe some

people to get hernias, and that's never fun. Then I've got to subcontract part of the job, and the subcontractors are notoriously difficult."

He gave me a look. "Why don't I hire the subcontractors myself, then?"

"You can try. But they won't know who needs to get hernias, and besides, they can't do the *other* things my group can do. We can give you *worldwide coverage,* man!"

He brooded a bit behind his eyelids, then nodded. "Very well," he said.

I knew that he would concede in the end. If he was moving important cargo in a little Chinese coaster instead of by Federal Express, then that meant he was moving it illegally—smuggling, to use the term that would be employed by the Admiralty Court were Jesse ever caught. He had to get his job done quickly and discreetly, and for speed and discretion he had to pay.

I gave him the information about which bank account to wire the money to, and he wrote it down with a gold-plated pen. I began to wonder if I had undercharged him.

We left the church and made our way back to the square, where Jan Hus stood bleakly amid a sea of iron-grey martyrs to his cause. The band had begun playing without me, our Latin-Flavored Beatle Medley. "You'll want to check this out," I told Jesse. "My brother Sancho does an *amaaazing* solo on 'Twist and Shout' with his *malta*—that's the medium-sized pan pipe."

"Is pop tunes all you do?" Jesse asked, his expression petulant. "I thought you were an authentic folk band."

I must admit that Jesse's comment got under my

skin. Just because he'd bought our services didn't mean we'd *sold out*.

Besides, "El Condor Pasa" *was* an authentic folk tune.

"We play what the public will pay for," I said. "And there are relatively few Latin folk fans in Prague, believe it or not." I took off my fedora and held it out to him. "But I didn't realize you were an *aficianado*. If it's authentic folk music you want, then it's what you'll get."

Jesse gave an amused little grin, reached into his Burbury, and produced a wad of notes which he dropped into my hat.

"*Gracias*," I said, and put the hat on my head. I didn't realize till later that he'd stuck me with Bulgarian currency.

I returned to my chair and took my *guitarra* in hand. Jesse hung around on the fringes of the crowd and talked on his cell phone. When the medley was over I led the band into "Llaqui Runa," which is about as authentic folk music as you can get.

Jesse put away his cell phone, put on his shades, and sauntered away.

But that wasn't what put me in a bad mood.

What had me in bad temper was the fact that I'd have to deal with the water ballet guys.

Three beautifully manicured pairs of hands rose from the water, the fingers undulating in wavelike motions. The hands rose further, revealing arms, each pair arced to form an O. Blue and scarlet smoke billowed behind them. The owners of these arms then appeared above the wavetops and were revealed to be mermaids, scales glinting green and gold, each smiling with cupid's-bow lips.

The mermaids began to rotate as they rose, free of the water now, water streaming from their emerald hair, each supported by a pair of powerful male hands. As the figures continued to rise, the male hands were revealed to belong to three tanned, muscular Apollos with sun-bleached hair and brilliant white smiles.

The figures continues to rotate, and then the brilliant clouds behind billowed and parted as three more figures dived through the smoke, arrowing through the circles of the mermaids' arms to part the water with barely a splash.

The Apollos leaned mightily to one side, allowing the mermaids to slip from their embrace and fall into the water. Then the Apollos themselves poised their arms over their head and leaned back to drop beneath the waves.

For a moment the water was empty save for the curls of red and blue smoke that licked the tops of the waves, and then all nine figures rose as one, inverted, arms moving in unison, after which they lay on their sides, linked themselves with legs and arms, and formed an unmistakable Leaping Dolphin.

The Leaping Dolphin was followed by Triton in His Chariot, the Anemone, the Tiger Shark, the Water Sprite, the Sea Serpent, and a Salute to the Beach Boys, which featured the California Girl, the Deuce Coupe, and climaxed with Good Vibrations. The finale featured more smoke, each of the mermaids rising from the water wearing a crown of sparklers while the six men held aloft billowing, colorful flares.

"Magnificent!" I applauded. "I've never seen anything like it! You've outdone yourself!"

One of the Apollos swam to the edge of the pool and looked up at me, his brow furrowed with a modesty that was charming, boyish, and completely specious.

"You don't think the Deuce Coupe was a little murky?" he said.

"Not at all. I've never seen a Deuce Coupe in my life, and I recognized it at once!"

I was in California, while the rest of my band was on their way to Hong Kong, where they could expedite their visas to the mainland. I myself was traveling on a U.S. visa belonging to my cousin Pedrito, who was in Sofia and not using it, and who looked enough like me—at least to a U.S. Customs agent—for me to pass.

Laszlo deVign—he of Laszlo deVign's Outrageous Water Ballet of Malibu—vaulted gracefully from the pool and reached for a towel, making sure as he did so that I had a chance to appreciate the definition of his lats and the extension of arm and body. "So you have some kind of job for us?" he said.

"Recovery of a coffin-sized box from the hold of a sunken ship, lying on an even keel in sixty meters of water."

He straightened, sucked in his tummy just a little to better define the floating ribs, and narrowed his blue eyes. "Sixty meters? What's that in feet?"

I ran an algorithm through my head. "Just under two hundred, I think."

"Oh." He shrugged. "That should be easy enough."

I explained how the whole operation had to be conducted on the Q.T., with no one finding out.

351

He paused and looked thoughtful again.

"How do you plan to do that?"

I explained. Laszlo nodded. "Ingenious," he said.

"You've got to get over to Hong Kong right away," I said. "And bring your gear and cylinders of whatever exotic gasses you're going to need to stay at depth. The ship will give you air or Nitrox fills, but they're not going to have helium or whatever else you're going to need."

"Wait a minute," Laszlo said. He struck a pose of belligerence, and in so doing made certain I got a clear view of his profile. "We haven't talked about money."

"Here's what I'm offering," I said, and told him the terms.

He argued, but I held firm. I happened to know he'd blown his last gig in Vegas because of an argument with the stage manager over sound cues, and I knew he needed the cash.

"Plus," I pointed out, "they'll love you over there. They'll never have seen anything like what you do. You're going to hit popular taste smack between the eyes."

He looked firm. "There's one thing I'm going to insist on, though."

I sighed. We'd reached the moment I'd been dreading for the last two days.

"What's that?" I asked, knowing the answer.

He brandished a finger in the air, and his blue eyes glowed with an inner flame "I must," he said, "I absolutely *must* have *total artistic control!*"

Six days later we found ourselves in Shanghai,

boarding the *Tang Dynasty*. It had taken that long for me to bribe two key members of the Acrobat Troupe of Xi'an into having hernias, thus leaving the Long Peace Lounge without an opening act for the Bloodthirsty Hopping Vampire Show. Fortunately I'd been in a position to contact the ship's Entertainment Director—who was underpaid, as was most of the ship's crew—and I was able to solve both his problems, the absence of an opening act and his lack of a decent salary. That he could have a genuine California water ballet, complete with Deuce Coupe, for a token sum was just a fraction of the good luck I bestowed upon him.

The *Tang Dynasty* was a themed cruise ship that did the Shanghai-Hong Kong-Macau route twice a week. The bulbous hull was more or less hull-like, though it was entwined with fiberglass dragons; but the superstructure looked like a series of palaces from the Forbidden City, each with the upturned eaves common in China and with the ridgepoles ornamented with the "fish tail" standard in Tang Dynasty architecture—a protection against fire, I was told, as in the event of a blaze the tail was supposed to slap the water and drown the conflagration. The buildings were covered with ornament, slathered with gold and vermilion, crowned with phoenixes, twined with dragons, fronted with lions.

To say nothing of the audioanimatronic unicorns.

The interior carried on the theme. The staterooms, swathed with silks and embroidery, gave every impression of being rooms of state in a thousand-year-old palace. At any moment of the day, passengers could dine at the Peaches of Heaven Buffet, have a reading from any one of four fortune tellers (Taoist,

Buddhist, Animist, and an alcoholic Gypsy imported from Romania), get a pedicure at the Empress Wu Pavilion of Beauty, light incense at the Temple of Tin Hau, Goddess of the Sea, or defy the odds in the Lucky Boy Casino (international waters and Macau SAR only).

The crew were dressed in Tang Dynasty costumes, with the captain garbed as the Emperor, in yellow robes covered with the five-toed dragons reserved for the Son of Heaven. Those of us who played in the lounges were not required to dress as Chinese entertainers, except of course unless they *were* Chinese entertainers.

The water ballet guys favored Speedos whether they were in the water or not, and spent a lot of time in the ship's gym, pumping iron and admiring themselves in the mirrors. I and my band, when performing, abandoned the contemporary look we'd adopted in Europe and did so in our traditional alpaca-wool ponchos.

Our first performance, as the *Tang Dynasty* sped south through the night toward Hong Kong, was received fairly well, especially considering that we performed in a language that no one else on the ship actually spoke, and that the audience had come to see the hopping vampires anyway.

All but one. Right in the front row, where I could scarcely miss him, was a man in a red poncho and a derby hat. He spent the entire concert grinning from ear to ear and bobbing his head in time with my nephew Esteban's electric bass. I could have understood this behavior if the head under the derby had been from the Andean highlands, but the face that grinned at me so blindingly was plump and bespectacled and Asian.

The man in the poncho gave us a standing ovation and generated enough enthusiasm in the audience to enable us to perform a second encore. Afterwards, he approached.

"*Mucho fantastico!*" he said, in what was probably supposed to be Spanish. "*Muy bien!*"

"Thanks," I said.

"I'm a huge fan," he said, dropping into something like English. "That was a terrific rendition of 'Urupampa,' by the way."

"I noticed you were singing along."

I soon understood that he was a Japanese businessman named Tobe Oharu, and that he belonged to a club devoted to Andean folk music. He and a group of fellow enthusiasts met weekly at a bar dressed in ponchos and derbies, listened to recordings, and studied Spanish from books.

He was so enthusiastic that I never had the heart to tell him that in our culture it's the women who wear the derby hats, whereas the men wear knit caps, or in my case a fedora.

"I had no idea you were performing here till I looked on the *Tang Dynasty* web site the night before I left!" he said. "My friends are going to be so jealous!"

I tried this story on for size and decided that the odds were that it was too bizarre not to be true. Besides, I knew that Japanese hobbyists were very particular about wearing the right uniform, dressing up for instance as cowboys while listening to Country and Western.

"How did you happen to become a fan of Andean music?" I asked.

"Pure accident. I was on a business trip to Brussels, and I heard a group playing at the central station. I fell in love with the music at once! How could I help it, when it was Fernando Catacachi I heard on the *kena*."

Since Fernando happened to be my uncle, I agreed at once that he was the best, though personally I've always had a soft spot for the playing of another uncle of mine, Arturo.

Oharu's eyes glittered behind his spectacles. "And of course," he said, "Fidel Perugachi is supreme on the *secus*."

There I had to disagree. "His playing is full of showy moves and cheap audience-pleasing tricks," I said. "Compared to my brother Sancho, Perugachi is an alpaca herder."

Oharu seemed a little taken aback. "Do you think so?"

"Absolutely. It's a pity we're playing only traditional music, and you can't hear Sancho on 'Twist and Shout.'"

Oharu considered this. "Perhaps this could be an encore tune tomorrow night?"

I had to credit Oharu for being a man of sound ideas. "Good plan," I said.

He offered to stand us all a round of drinks, but I begged off, pleading jct lag. I had to meet with Jesse and with the water ballet guys between the first and second show and get involved in some serious plotting.

I did stick around for the opening of the Bloodthirsty Hopping Vampire Show, however. The title was irresistible, after all. I'd tried to chat with the performers during the interlude, but with no success.

Apparently the actors all spoke a Chinese dialect shared by no one else on the ship: they were just told the time they had to show up, and went on from there.

The massed vampires, with their slow, synchronous hops, achieved a genuine eerie quality, and the young hero and his girlfriend were clearly in jeopardy, and were rapidly depleting their considerable store of flashy kung fu moves when I had to drag myself away for the meeting with Laszlo.

Next morning, after breakfast, *Tang Dynasty*'s tourists swarmed from the ship for their encounters with the boutiques of Tsim Sha Tsui and the bustle of Stanley Market. From the other side of the ship, unobserved by the majority of the passengers, I and the entire Water Ballet of Malibu motored off on one of the ship's launches for our top-secret rendezvous with the *Goldfish Fairy*.

Laszlo had told everyone we were going, and he'd told everyone about the top-secret part, too—except he'd made out it was a top-secret rehearsal of new water ballet moves, moves that he wished to conceal from the eyes of jealous rivals. His supercilious character and his obsession with artistic control helped to make this story more plausible, but even so I'm not sure we would have been given a boat if we hadn't greased a few palms among the crew.

It hadn't taken me long to work out that there was no way to conceal the fact of our presence in the Pearl River Delta, and secret water ballet rehearsals was the best cover story I could work out on short notice. It was bizarre, I knew, but it was bizarre enough to be true, and Laszlo and his crew were going to make it truer by conducting some genuine training.

The day was warm and humid, with shifting mists at dawn that had burned off by mid–morning. We roared south out of Hong Kong's harbor, with bronzed Apollos striking poses on the gunwales like figureheads on the USS *Muscle Beach*. The posing wasn't entirely affected, as with all the diving gear stowed in the boat there was scant room for people; and the women of the troupe, with cigarettes in their sunscreen-slathered lips, draped themselves disdainfully on the bags that held the towels and the softer bits of scuba gear, and declined to speak to anyone.

About an hour after leaving port our satellite locators told us we had reached our destination, and we sent our anchor down, shortly followed by Laszlo, one of the Apollos, and my own highly reluctant person.

I had decided that, as the person in charge I should inspect the *Goldfish Fairy* myself. Though I had acquired diving skills for a task that involved retrieving documents from the cabin of a Tupolev aircraft that had made the mistake of crashing into the Black Sea, the Tupolev had been at a mere twenty-five meters, and the *Goldfish Fairy* was at sixty, well below the depth at which it was safe for sport divers such as myself to venture. But Laszlo and his crew—who by the way all had names like Deszmond and Szimon—had instructed me in the various skills required in staying alive at two hundred feet, and they would be on hand to look after me if I had a misadventure. I decided that the risk was worth taking.

I was carrying a ton of weight as I went over the side, not only the two cylinders on my back but another pair that would be clipped onto the anchor line at certain depths so that they could aid our decompression stops. Our of deference to me, I suspect, we were all breathing air, instead of the nitrogen-oxygen-helium mixture usually employed at depth—I had no experience with "Trimix," as it's known, and Laszlo had decided to save the exotic mixtures for time when the water ballet guys actually had to stay down for a while and work. This would be a fast reconnaissance, it was thought, fast down, and slowly but surely up again. There was no need to worry.

It was nevertheless one highly nervous Injun that flopped backward off the side of the boat into the Pearl River Delta, and descended with the others into the murky water in search of Jesse's lost cargo.

In the event I needn't have been so worried. From the forty-meter mark, I spent the entire dive in a state of complete hilarity.

I chortled. I laughed. I giggled. I found the fish in my vicinity a source of mirth, and tried to point out the more amusing aspects of their anatomy to my fellow divers. Eventually I became so helpless with laughter that Laszlo, wearing an expression of greater disgust even than was normal for him, grabbed me by one of the shoulder straps of my buoyancy compensator, or B.C., and simply hauled me around like a package.

I had become prey to nitrogen narcosis, more colorfully known as "rapture of the deep."

When we got within sight of the muddy bottom, it was clear that the *Goldfish Fairy* was not to be seen. The captain appeared to be a little off on his calculations. So, still a good fifteen or so meters off the bottom, Laszlo checked his compass and we began searching the bottom, so many kicks in one direction followed by a ninety-degree turn and so many kicks in the next, the whole creating a kind of squarish, outwardly-expanding spiral.

We found the *Goldfish Fairy* within moments, the bow section looming suddenly out the murk like that of the *Titanic* in, well, the film *Titanic*. Bibbling with laughter, I tried to point out this similarity to Laszlo, who simply jerked me in the direction of the sunken ship and yanked me over the bows to begin his inspection of the vessel.

The bow section was a little crumpled, having struck first, but the rest of the little ship was more or less intact. The hatches were still secure. These would present very little trouble, but the fly in the ointment was the ship's mast, which had fallen over both hatches and which presented a nasty tangle of wire designed as if on purpose to entangle divers.

Laszlo grimly dragged me over the ship as he made his survey, and I spat my air supply from my mouth and tried to explain to a school of nearby fish the finer points of playing the *charango*, which is the little ten-string guitar with its body made from the shell of an armadillo. Eventually Laszlo had to look at me *very* severely and wrote a message on the underwater slate he kept clipped to his B.C.

I think you should breathe now, I read, and I flashed him the okay sign and returned the regulator to my mouth.

Our survey complete, Laszlo tied a buoy to the stern rail of the ship so that we could find it again, inflated the buoy from his air supply, and then led us in stages to the surface, breathing during our decompression stops from the cylinders we'd attached to the anchor line. As soon as we passed the forty-meter mark I became cold sober. The transition was instantaneous, and I wanted to dive down a bit and see if I could trigger the narcosis once more—just as an experiment—but Laszlo wasn't about to permit this, so we continued to rise until we saw from below the remaining members of the water ballet practicing their moves. The women were wearing their mermaid tails, the better to convince any prying eyes that their reasons for being here had nothing to do with any hypothetical wrecks lying on the bottom sixty meters below, while the men swam in formation and flexed their muscles in synchrony.

"Just sit in the boat and *don't do anything*," Laszlo hissed to me after we were back in the launch and had got our gear off. "And don't *say* anything, either," he added as he saw me about to speak, even though I had only opened my mouth to apologize.

A pair of Apollos went down next, breathing the gas mixtures that would enable them to stay longer at depth. They were to enter the hold through one of the crew passages that led down through the deck, and in order to find their way back carried a reel with a long line on it, one end of which they attached to the launch, and the rest of which, like Theseus in the Labyrinth, they payed out behind them as they swam.

"That approach won't work, I'm afraid," Laszlo explained to Jesse later. "When the ship hit the bottom, it threw everything in the hold forward against the bulkhead. We can't shift it from down there, so we'll have to open the hold and go in that way.

"It should be an easy enough job." We were sipping drinks in Jesse's palatial Tang Dynasty lodgings. He had, of course, acquired a suite, complete with a little

Taoist shrine all in scarlet and gold. The Taoist god, with pendulous earlobes the size of fists, gazed as us with a benign smile from his niche as we plotted our retrieval.

"Clearing the wire is going to be the most dangerous part of it," Laszlo continued. "Afterwards we'll have to use jacks to get the mast off the cargo hatch. Actually opening the hatch and retrieving the target will be the easiest part of all."

"Do you have all the gear you need?" Jesse asked.

"We'll have it flown to Macau to meet us," Laszlo said. "It's just a matter of your giving us your credit card number."

"There isn't a cheaper or quicker way to do this?" Jesse asked.

"Total. Artistic. Control," said Laszlo, which settled it as far as he was concerned.

As for myself, I planted some sandalwood incense in Jesse's shrine and set it alight along with a prayer for success and safety. It seemed only sensible to try to get the local *numina* on my side.

Happy with a drink in my hand and my feet up on a cushion, I was inclined to loiter in Jesse's sumptuous suite as long as I could. The passengers lived in a Forbidden City of pleasures and delights, but the crew and entertainers were stuck in little bare cabins below the water line, with no natural light, precious little ventilation, and with adjacent compressors, generators, and maneuvering thrusters screaming out in the small hours of the night.

Eventually, though, Jesse grew weary of our company, and I wandered out to the Peaches of Heaven Buffet for a snack. I got some dumplings and a bottle of beer, and who should I encounter but folk music fan Tobe Oharu, fresh from bargain-hunting at the Stanley Market, who plunked down opposite me with some ox-tendon soup and a bottle of beer.

"I got some pashmina shawls for my mother," he said with great enthusiasm, "and some silk scarves and ties for presents, and some more ties and some cashmere sweaters for myself."

"Very nice," I said.

"How did you spend your day?"

"I went out for a swim," I said, "but I didn't have a good time." I was still embarrassed that I had so completely flaked out at the forty-meter mark.

"That's a shame," Oharu said. "Was the beach too crowded?"

"The company *did* leave something to be desired," I said, after which he opened what proved to be a highly informed discussion of Andean music.

The audiences for our shows that night were modest, because most of the passengers were still enjoying the fleshpots of Hong Kong, but Oharu was there, right in front as before, wearing his poncho and derby and leading the audience in applause. We tried "Twist and Shout" as an encore number, and it was a hit, getting us a second encore, which meant that the band took Oharu to the bar for several rounds of thank-you drinks.

After the second show I stuck around for the entire Hopping Vampire Show, and had a splendid time watching Chinese demons chomp ingenues while combating a Taoist magician, who repelled them with glutinous rice, and the hero and heroine, who employed spectacular kung fu, which enabled them to dodge attack long enough to control the vampires with yellow paper magic, in which a sutra or spell was written on yellow paper with vermilion ink, then stuck on the vampire's forehead like a spiritual Post-It note.

I made a note to remember this trick in case I ever encountered a Hopping Vampire myself.

The *Tang Dynasty* was getting under way for its short run to Macau, and I knew that I wouldn't be able to sleep with the maneuvering thrusters shrieking and the anchor chain clattering inboard, so I took a turn on deck. The ship lay in a pool of mist, an even cloud lightened only slightly by the distant moon. The ship was just getting under way, picking up speed as it swung onto a new heading… and then suddenly the air was full of the scent of sandalwood. It was as if we were no longer in fog, but in the smoke produced by an entire sandalwood grove going up in flames.

I had scant time to marvel at this when I heard, magnified by the fog, the sound of a *toyo*, the largest of the Andean pan pipes. The sound was loud and flamboyant and showy, featuring triple-stopping and double-tonguing slick as the pomade on Elvis's hair, and it was followed by a roar of applause.

"Damn it!" I shouted into the mist. "It's *Fidel Perugachi!*"

And then I ran for the nearest companionway.

While I was banging on Jesse's cabin door—and simultaneously trying to reach him on his cell phone—I was interrupted by my cousin Jorge and my brother Sancho, who were strolling down the corridor with their fan Oharu, who carried an umbrella drink in one hand, hade an inebriated smile on his face, and was still wearing his poncho and derby.

"What's up, bro?" Jorge asked.

I replied in Aymara. "The Ayancas have turned up. Get rid of our friend here as soon as you can and get back here." When I spoke to Oharu I switched back to English. "I'm trying to collect some gambling winnings."

"Ah," he nodded. "Good luck." He raised a pudgy fist. "You want me to bash him on the head?"

"Ah," I said, "I don't think that will be necessary."

Jesse opened the door and answered his cell phone simultaneously, blinking in the corridor light. "What's happening?"

"We need to talk," I said, and shoved my way into his room.

"The Ayancas are here!" I said while Jesse put on a dressing gown. "They're out in the fog, taunting us with flute music! We've got to *do* something!"

"Like what?" Jesse, still not exactly *compos*, groped on the lacquered side table for a cigarette.

"Get some machine guns! Mortars! Rocket launchers! Those guys are *evil!*"

Jesse lit his coffin nail and inhaled. "Perhaps you had better tell me who these Ayancas are, exactly."

It was difficult to condense the last thousand years of Andean history into a few minutes, but I did my best. It was only the last forty years that mattered anyway, because that's when my uncle Iago, returning from a trip to Europe (to buy a shipment of derby hats, believe it or not), saw his first James Bond movie and decided to form his own private intelligence service, and subsequently sent his young relatives (like me) to an elite Swiss prep school, while the rest formed into bands of street musicians who could wander the streets, not unobtrusive but at least unsuspected as they went about their secret work.

"Fidel Perugachi is a traitor and a copycat cheat!" I said. "He formed his own outfit and went into competition with us." I shook a fist. "Perugachi's nothing but llama spit!"

"So there are competing secret organizations of Andean street musicians?" Jesse said, slow apparently to wrap his mind around this concept.

"All the musicians belong to one group or the other," I said. "But the Ayancas lack our heritage. They're sort-of cousins to the Urinsaya moiety, but *we're* the Hanansaya moiety! *Our* ancestors were the Alasaa, and were buried in stone towers!"

Jesse blinked. "Good for them," he said. "But do you really think the Ayancas are here for the *Goldfish Fairy*?"

"Why else would they be in Hong Kong at this moment?" I demanded. "You were *right* in Prague when you worried that you were being shadowed. Your opposition found out you were hiring us, so they countered by hiring the Ayancas. Why else would Fidel Perugachi be off playing his *toyo* in the fog and the clouds of sandalwood smoke?"

"Sandalwood?" he said, puzzled.

"Like your incense," I said, and pointed to his little shrine. "There were great gusts of sandalwood smoke coming over the rail along with Perugachi's music."

Jesse puffed on his cigarette while considering this, and then he slammed his hand on the arm of his chair. "*Thunderbolt Sow!*" he said.

I looked at him. "Beg pardon?"

"The Thunderbolt Sow is a holy figure in Buddhism. But *Thunderbolt Sow* is also the name of another cruise ship—Buddhist-themed, with a huge temple to Buddha on the stern, and several very well-regarded vegetarian restaurants. I bet that temple pours out a lot of sandalwood incense."

"At this time of night?"

"Do you know about the smoke towers? Those coils of incense that hang from the roofs of the temples? They burn twenty-four hours per day—some of them are big enough to burn for weeks."

"So Perugachi wasn't taunting us," I said. "He got a job like ours, on a cruise ship, and he was finishing his second show as the ship came into harbor." I thought about this and snarled. "Copycat! What did I tell you!"

"The question is," Jesse said, "what kind of menace is this, and what are we going to do?"

So we had an early-morning conference, with the water ballet guys and Jesse and the members of my band. Jesse connected with the Internet through the cellular modem on his notebook, and we found that *Thunderbolt Sow* belonged to the same cruise line as *Tang Dynasty*, and followed the same schedule, only a day later.

"We'll be anchoring in Macau in an hour or so," Laszlo said, from beneath the avocado-green beauty mask he hadn't bothered to wash off. "But we won't be able to get our salvage gear till mid-morning at the earliest." He considered. "We'll spend tomorrow clearing off that tangle of cable, and maybe get a start on shifting the mast. The day following *Tang Dynasty* discharges most of its passengers, takes on a new ones, and heads for Shanghai to start the circuit all over again, so we won't be able to dive."

"But the Ayancas *can*," I pointed out. "They can take advantage of all the preparatory work you've done and lift the package while we're on our way to Shanghai and back."

"In that case," Jesse said, "don't do anything tomorrow. Just sit on the site to keep the Ayancas from pillaging it, and let *them* deal with the cable and the mast."

"We can spend the day rehearsing!" Laszlo said brightly, and the members of his troupe rolled their eyes.

I rubbed my chin and gave this some thought. Jesse's idea was well enough, but it lacked savor somehow. I felt it was insufficient in terms of dealing with the Ayancas. With Fidel Perugachi and his clique, I prefer instead to employ the more decisive element of diabolical vengeance.

"Instead," I suggested calmly, "why don't we mislead the Ayancas, and drive them mad?"

Jesse seemed a little taken aback by this suggestion. "How?" he asked.

"Let's give them the *Goldfish Fairy*, but give them a *Goldfish Fairy* that will drive them insane!"

"You mean sabotage the ship?" Jesse blinked. "So that they dive down there and get killed?"

"It's not that murdering the Ayancas wouldn't be satisfying," I said, "but practically speaking it would only motivate them toward reprisal. No, I mean simply give them a day of complete frustration, preferably one that will cause them in the end to realize that *we* were the cause of their difficulties."

I turned to Laszlo. "For example," I said, "this

morning you attached a buoy to the *Goldfish Fairy* that would make it easier to find. Suppose that tomorrow you move that buoy about five hundred meters into deeper water. They'll waste at least one dive, possibly more, finding the ship again."

Laszlo grinned, his white teeth a frightening contrast to his green mask.

"You can only dive that deep a certain number of times each day," Laszlo explained to Jesse. "If we waste their dives, we use up their available bottom time."

"And," I added, "suppose you clear the wire only from the *front* half of the ship. You use the jacks to move the mast partly off the fore hatch. This will suggest to them that their target is in the forward hold, not in the after hold."

Lazslo's grin broadened. He looked like a bloodthirsty idol contemplating an upcoming sacrifice.

"They'll spend all day getting into the forward hold, and find *nothing!*" he said. "Brilliant!" He nodded at me and gave his highest accolade.

"Ernesto," he said, "you're an *artist!*"

I spent the next day on the launch at the dive site, but I didn't so much as put a foot into the water. Instead I watched the horizon for signs of the Ayancas—and there *was* a boat that seemed to be lurking between us and Hong Kong—while the mermaids and the off-duty Apollos swam about the boat and practiced their moves. The mermaids were even more listless, if possible, than the day before, and Laszlo felt obliged to offer them several sharp reproofs.

When Laszlo and a colleague made their second

dive to the wreck, the others happily called a lunch break. Someone turned a radio to a station filled with bouncy Cantonese pop music. The Apollos sat in the stern slathering on sun oil, performing dynamic tension exercises, and quaffing drinks into which, to aid in building muscle, vast arrays of steaks and potatoes seem to have been scientifically crammed. Since no one else seemed inclined to pay attention to the ladies, I perched on the forward gunwales with the mermaids and helped them devour some excellent dim sum that we'd abstracted from the kitchens of the Grand Dynasty Restaurant that morning.

"So how do you find the water ballet business?" I asked one of the mermaids, a nymph from Colorado named Leila.

She took her time about lighting up a cigarette. "After Felicia and I came in sixth in the Olympics, we turned pro," she said. "I'm not sure what I expected, but it certainly wasn't this. *You* try cramming your lower half into one of those rubber fish tails for an hour a day."

"Yet here you are in the Pacific, on a beautiful sunny day, on a grand adventure and with the whole of Asia before you."

She flicked cigarette ash in the direction of the Apollos. *"That's* not what I'd call the whole of Asia."

"You're not fond of your co-workers?" I asked. For it was obvious that the mermaids kept very much to themselves, and I'd wondered why.

"Let's just say that they and I have a different idea of what constitutes an object of desire."

"Surely they can't *all* be gay," I said, misunderstanding.

"They aren't," Leila said. "But they *are* all narcissists. When I cuddle on a couch with a guy, I want him to be looking at *me*, not at his own reflection in a mirror."

"I take your point. Perhaps you ought to confine yourself to homely men."

She looked at me. *"You're* homely," she pointed out.

"As homely as they come," I agreed, and shifted a bit closer to her on the gunwale.

These pleasantries continued until Laszlo finished his dive and demanded more rehearsals. Since he had Total Artistic Control, there was little I could say on the matter.

By the time the water ballet guys had finished all the dives safety procedures would allow, they'd prepared *Goldfish Fairy* to a fare-thee-well. The wire tangle had been shifted aft and, according to Laszlo, looked awful but would be relatively easy to clear when the time came. The mast had been partially shifted off the forward hatch, with the marks of the jacks plain to see, but the jacks themselves had been removed—if the Ayancas didn't bring their own, they were out of luck.

In a final bit of mischief we shifted the buoy half a kilometer, then raced back to the *Tang Dynasty* just in time for our first show. Leila and I made plans to meet after the second show. Among other things, I wanted to hear her memories of the Olympics— I'd actually been to an Olympics once, but I'd been too busy dodging homicidal Gamsakhurdians to pay much attention to the games.

We'd barely got into the general wretchedness of the judging at synchronized swimming events when my cell played a bit of Mozart, and I answered to hear the strained tones of the ship's Entertainment Director.

"I thought you should know that there's a problem," he said, "a problem with your friend, the one in Emperor Class."

"What sort of problem?" I asked as my heart foundered. The tone of his voice was answer enough to my question..

"I'm afraid he's been killed."

"Where?"

"In his room."

"I'll meet you there."

I told Leila to go to Laszlo's room, and after she yelped in protest I told her that she had to contact everyone in the troupe, and insist that no one was to be alone for the rest of the trip. Apparently my words burned with conviction, because her eyes grew wide and she left the room fast.

I sprinted to Jesse's room and called Jorge, who was our forensics guy, and Sancho, who was the strongest, just in case we needed to rearrange something.

The entertainment director stood in front of Jesse's door, literally wringing his hands.

"The cabin steward brought him a bottle of cognac he'd ordered," he said, "and found him, ah…" His voice trailed away, along with his sanguinary complexion.

"I'll have to call the police soon," he said faintly. "Not to mention the captain. It's lucky I was on watch, and not someone else."

I was so utterly glad that I'd bribed the man. There's nothing you can trust like corruption and dishonesty, and I made a mental note to slip the entertainment director a few extra hundred at the end of the voyage.

"Where's the steward?"

"I told him to stay in my office."

Sancho and Jorge arrived—Jorge with a box of medical gloves that he shared with us—and our confidant opened the cabin door with his passkey.

"I won't go in again, if you don't mind," he said, swallowing hard, and stepped well away.

I put on gloves and pushed the door open. We entered and closed the door behind us.

"Well," Jorge said, "I can tell you right away that it's not a subtle Oriental poison."

Nor was it. Jesse lay on his back in the center of his suite, his throat laid open, his arms thrown out wide, and an expression of undiluted horror on his face. There was a huge splash of blood on the wall hangings and more under the body.

"Don't step in it," I said.

Jorge gingerly knelt by the body and examined the wound. "You're not going to like this," he said.

"I *already* don't like it," I said.

"You're going to like it less when I tell you that his throat appears to have been torn open by the fangs of an enormous beast."

There was a moment of silence.

"Maybe we should talk to the Hopping Vampires," Sancho said.

"Nobody *can* talk to them," I said. "They don't speak anybody's language."

"So they claim," Sancho said darkly.

"Never mind that now," I decided. "Search the room."

I found Jesse's wallet and card case, from which I

learned that his name was actually Jiu Lu, and that he was the head of the microbiology department at Pacific Century Corporation.

Well. Who knew?

I also found his cell phone, with all the numbers he'd set on speed dial.

"Where's his notebook computer?" I asked.

We couldn't find it, or the briefcase he'd carried it in, or any notes that may have been in the briefcase.

"Let's hope he kept everything on that machine encrypted," Jorge said.

We left the wallet where we found it, but took the cell phone and one of Jesse's business cards. When we slipped out of the room, the entertainment director almost fainted with relief.

"Go ahead and call the cops," I told him.

"Macanese police." His eyes were hollow with tragedy. "You have no idea."

With Sancho guarding my back, I went on the fantail and called every number that Jesse had set on his speed dial. For the most part I got answering machines of one sort or another, and any actual human beings answered in an irate brand of Mandarin that discouraged communication from the start. I tried to inquire about "Jiu Lu," but I must not have got any of the tones right, because no one understood me.

In the morning I would call again, with the entertainment director as interpreter.

Most of the ship's passengers disembarked that morning, all those who weren't making the round trip to Shanghai and who preferred to remain in the languid, mildly debauched atmosphere of Macau, or who were heading by hydrofoil ferry back to the hustle of Hong Kong.

Whatever the Macanese police were doing by way of investigation, they weren't interfering with the wheels of commerce as represented by the cruise ship company.

"There goes Jesse's killer," Jorge said glumly as, from the rail, we watched the boats fill with cheerful, sunburned tourists.

Rosalinda, who gloomed at my other elbow, flicked her cigar ash into the breeze. "This afternoon the boats will come back with his replacement."

"Unless the killer is a Hopping Vampire who's sleeping in his coffin at this very moment," Sancho added, from over my shoulder.

Most of those who came aboard that afternoon were people who had come to Macau on *Tang Dynasty*'s previous journey, and who were returning home by way of Shanghai. Only two actually made Macau their point of initial departure, and when we got ahold of a passenger manifest we made these the objects of particular scrutiny. One of them was an elderly man who trailed an oxygen bottle behind him on a cart. He went straight to the casino and began to bet heavily on roulette while lighting up one cigarette after another, which certainly explained the oxygen bottle. The other was his nurse.

Given that I hailed from a family of Aymara street musicians who also formed a private intelligence-gathering agency, at the moment operating in tandem with a water ballet company aboard a passenger ship disguised as a Tang Dynasty palace, I was not about to discount the less unlikely possibility that the old gambler and his nurse were a pair of assassins, so I slipped the entertainment director a few hundred Hong Kong dollars for the key to the old man's room, and gave it a most professional going-over.

No throat-ripping gear was discovered, or anything the least bit suspicious.

Sancho and a couple of cousins also tossed the Hopping Vampires' cabin, and they found throat-ripping gear aplenty, but nothing that couldn't be explained with reference to their profession.

The entertainment director had got through to the people on Jesse's speed dial who he believed were Jesse's employers, but he was Cantonese and his Mandarin was very shaky, and he wasn't certain.

Because of the smallish crowd on board, and consequent low demand, we were scheduled for only one show that night, and I confess that it wasn't one of our best. The band as a whole lacked spirit. Our dejection transmitted itself to our music. Even the presence of our mascot Oharu in his poncho and derby hat failed to put heart into us.

After the show, Jorge and Sancho carried Oharu off to the Western Paradise Bar while I visited the entertainment director and again borrowed his pass-key.

I found a yellow Post-It note and wrote a single word on it with a crimson pen.

And when Oharu stepped into his cabin with Jorge and Sancho behind him, I lunged from concealment and slapped the note on his forehead, just as the Taoist Sorcerer slapped his yellow paper magic on the foreheads of the Bloodthirsty Hopping Vampires in their stage show.

Oharu looked at me in dazed surprise.

"What's this about?" he asked.

"Read it," I said.

He peeled the note off his forehead and read the single scarlet word, "Confess."

"You should have got off at Macau," I told him. "You would have got clean away." I held up the bloodstained ninja gear I'd found in his room, the leather palm with the lethal steel hooks that could tear open a throat with a single slap.

At that point Oharu fought, of course, but his responses were disorganized by the alcohol that Sancho and Jorge had been pouring down his throat for the last hour, and of course Sancho was a burly slab of solid muscle and started the fight by socking Oharu in the kidney with a fist as hard as hickory. It wasn't very long before we had Oharu stretched out on his bed with his arms and legs duct-taped together, and I was booting up Jesse's computer, which I had found in Oharu's desk drawer.

"Our next stop," I told Oharu, "is Shanghai, and Shanghai's in the People's Republic, not a Special Administrative Region like Hong Kong or Macau. If we turn you in, you get shot in the back of the head, and your family gets a bill for the bullet."

Oharu spat out a blood clot and spoke through mashed lips. "I'll tell them all about *you*."

I shrugged. "So? Nothing *we're* doing is illegal. All we're doing is recovering an item on behalf of its legitimate owners."

"That's debatable. I could still make trouble for you."

I considered this. "If that's the case," I said. "Maybe we ought not to keep you around long enough to say *anything* to the authorities."

He glowered. "You wouldn't dare kill me."

Again I shrugged. "*We* won't kill you. It'll be the *ocean* that'll do that."

Sancho slapped a hand over Oharu's mouth just as he inhaled to scream. In short order we taped his mouth shut, hoisted him up, and thrust him through his cabin porthole. There he dangled, with Sancho hanging onto one ankle, and Jorge the other.

I took off his right shoe and sock.

"Clench your toes three times," I said, "when you want to talk. But make it quick, because you're overweight and Jorge is getting tired."

Jorge deliberately slackened his grip, and let Oharu drop a few centimeters. There was a muffled yelp and a thrash of feet.

The toe-clenching came a few seconds later. We hauled Oharu in and dropped him onto his chair.

"So tell us," I began, "who hired you."

A Mr. Lau, Oharu said, of Shining Spectrum Industries in the Guangzhong Economic Region. He went on to explain that Dr. Jiu Lu, or Jesse as we'd known him, had worked for Shining Spectrum before jumping suddenly to Pacific Century. Magnum had suspected Jesse of taking Shining Spectrum assets with him, in the form of a project he was developing, and made an effort to get it back.

"This got Jiu scared," Oharu said, "so he tried to smuggle the project out of Guangzhou to Taiwan, but his ship went down in a storm. You know everything else."

"Not quite," I said. "What *is* the project?"

"I wasn't told that," Oharu said. "All I know is that it's biotechnology, and that it's illegal, otherwise Jui wouldn't have had to smuggle it out."

A warning hummed in my nerves. "Some kind of weapon?"

Oharu hesitated. "I don't think so," he said. "This operation doesn't have that kind of vibe."

I took that under advisement while I paged through the directory on Jesse's computer. Everything was in Chinese, and I didn't have a clue. I tried opening some of the files, but the computer demanded a password.

"Where did you send the data?" I asked.

"I never sent it anywhere," Oharu said. "I was just going to turn it over to Mr. Lau when I got off the boat tomorrow."

"You have a meeting set?" I asked.

A wary look entered his eyes. "He was going to call."

"Uh-huh." I grinned. "Too bad for Mister Lau that you didn't get off in Macau and fly to Shanghai to meet him."

He looked disconsolate. "I really *am* an Andean folk music fan," he said. "That part I didn't make up. I wanted to catch your last show."

Somehow I failed to be touched.

I shut down the computer and looked through the papers that Oharu had got out of Jesse's briefcase. They were also in Chinese, and likewise incomprehensible. I put them aside and considered Oharu's situation.

He had murdered my employer, and besides that cut into my action with Leila, and I wasn't inclined to be merciful. On the other hand I wasn't an assassin, and cold-bloodedly shoving him out the porthole wasn't my style.

On the third hand, I could see that he was turned

over to the authorities once the ship reached Shanghai, and let justice take its course. Getting shot in the
neck by Chinese prison guards was too good for him.

But on the fourth hand, he *could* make trouble for
us. The knowledge that there was illegal biotechnology being shipped to Taiwan was enough to make
the Chinese authorities sit up and take notice.

"Right," I said, "this is what's going to happen." I
pointed to the ninja gear I'd laid out on the bed. "In
the morning, the cabin steward is going to find out
your murder implements laid out, and it will be
obvious that you killed our employer."

He glared at me. "I'll tell the police all about you,"
he said. "They're not going to appreciate Western
spies in their country."

"You're not going to get a chance to talk to the
police," I said. "Because by then you'll have gone out
the porthole."

He filled his lungs to scream again, but Sancho
stifled him with a pillow.

"However," I said, raising my voice a little to make
sure he was paying attention as he flopped around
on the bed, "we'll wait till we make Shanghai before
you go into the drink, and we'll untie you first."

Oharu calmed somewhat. Once I had his attention,
I continued. "You won't go to your Mr. Lau for help,
because once your employers realize you're a wanted
man, they'll cut your throat themselves."

He glared at me from over the top of the pillow. I
signaled Sancho to lift the pillow off his face.

"Where does that leave me?" he asked. "Stuck in
Shanghai in the early morning, having swum ashore
soaking wet?"

"You're the ninja," I said. "Deal with it."

The plan went off without complications, which did my morale some good. *Tang Dynasty* made Shanghai about four in the morning, and pulled into its pier. Oharu's porthole faced away from the pier, and out into the drink he went.

I suppose he made it to shore, though I won't mourn if it turned out otherwise. All I know is that I never saw him again.

The cabin steward went into the room about seven o'clock with Oharu's breakfast tea and was horrified to discover the murder gear lying in plain sight. The alarm was raised. I was asleep in my cabin by then, with Jesse's computer under my pillow.

Tang Dynasty discharged its passengers, then the crew spent the day scrubbing the ship from top to bottom. The entertainment had the day off, and the band took advantage to see a few of the sights of Shanghai, although we went in pairs, just in case enemy ninjas were lurking somewhere in the crowds. We wore our everyday clothes, not our traditional ponchos, and the locals probably thought we were Uighurs or something.

Laszlo and the guys went off to refill their helium cylinders. I don't think Leila and the mermaids left their cabin. I tried to tell her through the door that she was the least likely of any of us to be murdered, but I don't think I succeeded in reassuring her.

In the course of the night *Thunderbolt Sow* pulled into the next berth in a cloud of sandalwood incense. I kept an eye on the ship, and an ear too, but I neither saw nor heard the evil-eyed Perugachi or his minions.

That day Jesse's replacements turned up, a white-haired Doctor Pan and his assistant, a round-faced, bespectacled Doctor Chun, who radiated enough anxiety for both of them. Each of them had body-guards, slablike Westerners with identical ponytails—I won't swear to it, but I believe the language they used among themselves was Albanian.

"Another three dives," Laszlo said, "maybe four. The first to clear the wire away and get started on moving the mast. The second to finish with the mast, then another to open the hatch. If cargo's shifted on top of your box, we might need another dive to clear that away. But we should be finished tomorrow."

Doctor Pan gave a smooth smile and said that was good, then lit one of his little cigars. Doctor Chun didn't look any less anxious than he had at the start of the meeting.

That night our shows went off as per normal, if you consider scoping the audience for potential assassins to be normal, which for us it all too often was. We'd been over the passenger manifest, and the only last-minute additions had been Doctor Pan and his party, so I thought we were reasonably safe.

When we awakened next morning we were anchored off Hong Kong Island, and I joined the water ballet guys in their launch with a box of dim sum I'd nicked from the kitchens. To my disappointment, I found that the mermaids were not going along.

"It's so *unprofessional*," Laszlo complained. "They think someone's going to come along and rip their throats out."

"You could offer them hazardous duty pay," I suggested hopefully.

"But it's not hazardous!" he said. "Diving to seven atmospheres breathing exotic gasses is *hazardous*—but do I hold *you* up for extra money?"

I shrugged—he'd *tried*, after all—and resigned myself to a heavy lunch of dim sum.

In short order we were bobbing in the swell over the wreck, and Laszlo and one of the guys went down on the first dive of the day. As the dive plan called for Laszlo to stay under the water for over two hours, I was surprised to see him break the surface ninety minutes early.

"What's wrong?" I asked as I helped him over the gunwale.

His face was grim. "You've got to go down and look at it yourself."

"What is it? Did Perugachi get the cargo?"

"Maybe the cargo got *him*," he said, and he turned to one of the Apollos. "Sztephen," he said, "take Ernesto down to the wreck, show him around, and make sure he doesn't die."

Sztephen gave me a dubious look while he struck a pose that emphasized his triceps development. I gave him what was meant to be a reassuring grin and reached for my wet suit.

Because I'd been so thoroughly narked on my last trip, Laszlo insisted that I make this one on Trimix, which involved two extra-heavy cylinders on my back and a mixture that was fifty percent helium and fifteen percent oxygen. We also carried stage cylinders on our chests, for use in decompression, which we were to rig to our descent line as we went down.

It was all unfamiliar enough to have my nerves in a jangle by the time I splashed into the briny, and lamented the fact that while I breathed Trimix instead of air the consolations of nitrogen narcosis were beyond my reach. Still the descent went well enough, and the great stillness and silence and darkness helped to calm my throbbing heart.

Which was a pity, because my heart slammed into overdrive again once I saw *Goldfish Fairy*. The wreck lay with a black cavern just behind the bows, where the covers to the fore hatch had been thrown off. Much of the cargo had also been lifted from the hold and thrown over the side, where it lay in piles. Such of the cargo as I saw seemed to consist of t-shirts with the Pokari Sweat logo on them.

But Pokari Sweat was not long in my thoughts, because I observed something pale and geometric protruding from the after hatch, and when I kicked toward the object, I discovered that it was a brilliant white pyramid.

No, I corrected on further inspection, not a pyramid, a tetrahedron, a four-sided figure with each side making an equilateral triangle. It had broken out of the hatch, and its colorless tip had shoved aside the mast and was reaching for the surface, sixty meters above. The brilliant whiteness of the tetrahedron was so striking that it looked like a belated iceberg turned up too late for the sinking.

So fascinated was I by this object that I let myself drift toward it, only to be checked by Sztephen, who seized my arm and drew me back. There was an expression of horror on his face.

I decided that Sztephen had a point. Whatever this thing was, it wasn't in our dive plan, and it might be in some way hostile.

It occurred to me to wonder whether it was a surprise that Fidel Perugachi had left for us.

I made a careful circuit of the after hatch to judge the object's size—a proper estimate was difficult as the tetrahedron's base was in the darkness of the hold, but it seemed about eight or nine meters per side. Then my heart lurched as I saw another, smaller tetrahedron—about the size of my palm—on the deck near the rail. I drifted downward to get a look at it, and this time saw a number of even smaller pyramids on the ship's hull, leading down to a cluster of them on the muddy bottom, none of them larger than my fingernail.

I began to have a feeling that all of them would be Giza-sized, given time.

I made a circuit of *Goldfish Fairy* in order to see how far the pyramid plague had spread, and found a smaller number of the four-sided items on the other side of the large. I checked the forward hold, and there I saw the cause of it all. Fidel Perugachi's crew, when they realized that the forehold didn't have what they were looking for, and that they didn't have time to open the rear hold, had tried to break into the after hold through a hatch high in the bulkhead. But the hatch hadn't opened because the cargo in the aft hold had been thrown forward when the *Goldfish Fairy* hit the bottom, and Perugachi's raiders had tried to force it open with the jacks they'd brought to shift the fallen mast.

They'd ended up opening more than the hatch, I thought. Their attempt to shove the hatch open had broken whatever contained Jesse's biotech.

It wasn't Fidel Perugachi who had created these objects. These pyramids now growing silently beneath the sea were what we'd been hired to *prevent*.

I reckoned I'd seen enough, so I signaled to Sztephen that it was time to head for the surface, and he agreed with wide-eyed relief.

It took some time to rise, as we had to pause every three meters or so for a decompression stop, and at certain intervals we had to shift to a different gas mixture, first to Nitrox 36 and then to O_2, making use of the cylinders we'd tethered to our line. Sztephen assisted with the unfamiliar procedures, and I managed them without trouble.

By which I did mean to imply that there was no trouble at all. We were at a depth of twenty meters, hovering at our decompression stop while juggling a formidable number of depleted cylinders, when we heard the rumble of a boat approaching, and looked up to see the twin hulls of a catamaran cutting the water toward our launch.

My overtaxed nerves gave a sustained quaver as the jet-powered catamaran cut its impellers and drifted up to the launch. I could only imagine what was happening on the surface—Pearl River pirates slitting the throats of everyone aboard; water police from the People's Republic putting everyone under arrest for disturbing the wreck; Fidel Perugachi sneering as he brandished automatic weapons at the hapless Apollos of the water ballet; ninjas feathering everyone aboard with blowgun darts...

Whatever was happening, I wasn't going to be a part of it. I probably wouldn't actually *die* if I bolted to the surface from a depth of twenty meters, but ere long I'd be damned sick with a case of the bends, and hardly in a condition to aid my cause.

So Sztephen and I sat in the heavy silence, both our imaginations and our nerves running amok, while we made our regulation number of decompression stops, the last being at ten meters. A myriad of schemes whirled through my mind, all of them useless

386

until I actually knew what was going on above my head.

The last seconds of our decompression stop ticked away. While Sztephen watched with puzzled interest, I reached for one of the Nitrox cylinders and removed the first-stage regulator, the device through which a diver actually breathes the contents of the cylinder. I then turned the valve to crack open the cylinder slightly and produced a satisfying stream of bubbles that rose unbroken to the surface. Then I did the same to another cylinder.

Anyone on the surface, looking for divers, would be able to track us simply by observing our exhaust bubbles rising. I had now given them a false bubble trail to watch.

Gesturing for Sztephen to follow, I kicked off from our line, positioned myself beneath the catamaran, and at slow, deliberate speed rose to the surface, my head breaking water between the twin hulls. Once there, I dropped my weight belt to the ocean bottom, then climbed out of my scuba gear, leaving myself just the mask, flippers, and snorkel.

And my dive knife, which was strapped to my leg. Many divers—usually the beginners—buy knives the length of their forearm, formidable enough to fight the U.S. Marines singlehanded.

Unfortunately for my cause, I had developed a more realistic appraisal of the circumstances under which I might need a knife underwater, and my own blade was about the length of my little finger. It was unlikely to stop a sufficiently determined Pekingese, let alone the U.S. Marines. I whispered a query to Sztephen, and like a true professional he produced one no larger than my own.

I sighed inwardly, and explained my plan such as it was. Sztephen, who liked my plan no more than I did but couldn't think of a better, likewise climbed out of his gear. We then inflated the B.C.s just enough to float and tied them together with B.C. straps. It was unlikely we'd need the gear again, but it didn't seem right to sink it.

I listened carefully all the while, but all I heard was the rumble of the idling engines and the surge and slap of waves against the white fiberglass hull—no screams, no shots, no maniacal cackling from a sadistic enemy.

It was time to do it, whatever it was. Those bubbles rising from the decoy cylinders wouldn't last forever.

The catamaran's port hull was moored to our launch, so I swam to the starboard hull, took a breath, and swam beneath the hull to surface cautiously on the other side. No one seemed to be looking for me, and by this point I was hearing nothing but the throbbing of my own heart. The ocean chop lifted me most of the way up the hull, and with a strong kick with my flippers I managed to get a hand around a chrome stanchion used to support the double safety line that ran around the fore part of the boat. The stanchion was strong enough to support my weight, and I pulled myself up, crawled under the safety line, and lay on the deck for a moment gathering my wits and my breath.

I was lying against the pilothouse of what clearly was a dedicated dive boat. The wide platform between the two hulls was ideal for moving gear around, and divers could simply jump off the back when they wanted to enter the sea. Cylinders were set in racks aft of me, and when I blinked up against the bright sun I could see the silhouette of a crane intended to raise salvage from the depths.

I pulled my mask down around my neck and worked my flippers off my feet. At this point Sztephan's sunbleached head appeared above the deck, looking at me wide-eyed: I'd told him to wait a moment or two before following me, and wait to hear if there was gunfire. Apparently this warning had made an impression on him.

I helped him aboard, hoping he wouldn't make too much noise, and he was about as silent as the situation permitted. While he stripped off his flippers I rose to a crouch and chanced a look through the open door into the boat's pilothouse. No one was visible, so I crept inside, and then froze.

Two figures were visible, and though I hadn't met either one I recognized them from photographs that my uncle Iago had made me memorize. They were both members of Fidel Perugachi's band, the bass player and the *bombo* player to be exact. It appeared that Perugachi had brought his whole rhythm section. One crouched in a wet suit on the after deck, working with some cylinders and a B.C., readying the outfit for a dive. Every few seconds he'd glance aft, to make certain that bubbles were still rising from our decoy cylinder. The other Ayanca, in shorts, baseball cap, and a Pokari Sweat t-shirt he must have stolen from the wreck, stood forward of the pilothouse by the port rail, watching whatever was going on in the launch.

A pistol was stuck casually into his shorts at the small of his back, and I recognized the distinctive toggle of a German Luger. The century-old Luger had been the standard sidearm of the P.R.C. police until recently, and when it was replaced by another weapon the thrifty Chinese had sold tens of thousands of Lugers all at once. Perugachi must have picked up this one in the Hong Kong or Macau black market.

At least Fidel Perugachi hadn't been able to bring his own weaponry into China with him, and this gave me hope that his resources were fairly limited.

If I attacked the man with the Luger, it would be in full view of everyone on the launch; whereas the *bombo* player in the stern was crouched down out of sight. I gestured for Sztephen to be quiet, then slipped further into the cabin in search of a weapon. I suppose I could have slit the drummer's throat with my little knife, but that seemed drastic, and I hated to set that kind of precedent unless I needed to.

I was considering one of the five-pound lead divers' weights when I noticed that the drummer had his toolbox open. Two crouching steps took me to the box, where I found a large wrench laid out neatly in its own compartment. Another two steps took me to the *bombo* player, who I promptly whanged behind the ear.

I probably hit him much harder than I intended to, as he only began to wake a couple hours later. Blame an excess of adrenaline if you will.

After checking my victim to see if he was still alive, I slipped to the rear corner of the boat, where a line had been tied holding the catamaran to the launch. I slipped the line off the cleat, then moved forward again, back to the pilot house, where I had a quick whispered conversation with Sztephen about whether he felt he could steer the boat. He gave a quick scan of the instrument board and said that he could. The engines were idling, and all he had to do was put them in gear and shove the throttles forward.

As we hadn't heard any shouts or complaints that we were drifting away from the launch, I surmised that there was another mooring line, and that this one was forward, and under the supervision of the bass player..

I told Sztephen to shove the throttles forward when I yelled, then slipped out of the pilothouse on the port side, the side away from the launch. I intended to use the pilot house for cover on the approach, come up behind the bass player, then pull his own pistol and stick it in his back. If Perugachi's crew saw me at that point it wouldn't matter, as I'd have a ready-made hostage.

It didn't work out that way. I crept around the pilothouse and approached my target, using as cover a big galvanized storage compartment. I looked around the corner of the compartment and saw the bass player a few paces away. His back was to me and he was chatting in Aymara with a man in the launch.

My heart gave a sudden thud against my ribs as I realized that this second man was Fidel Perugachi himself, and then another great knock as I saw Perugachi's heavy-lidded, demonic eyes drop from his bass player to look straight at me. I suddenly realized how hot it was inside my wet suit, and how odd that was considering it was still full of seawater.

Before the loathsome offspring of the Ayanca moiety could cry a warning, I crossed the deck in three strides and kicked the bass player with both feet in the small of the back. This catapulted him over the safety line and—the most satisfying part—on top of Perugachi himself. Then, yelling demented abuse at the Ayancas in our native language, I sprawled forward on the deck to reach for the remaining mooring line.

"Allu!" I yelled. *"Umata urqu!"*

Taking my gibberish as his cue, Sztephen threw the catamaran into gear and shoved the throttles forward. Impellers screamed, jets boiled, and the craft lunged into the next wave, taking the launch with it.

This was fortunate, as it turns out, because the Ayancas were in the process of organizing a response just as the sudden acceleration jerked them off their feet. I untied the mooring line and let it fly through the chrome-plated cleat and off the boat.

Luger bullets flew wild as the launch, checked by its anchor, came to an abrupt halt astern, and everyone on the boat took another tumble.

I rose and shook a fist. *"Jallpiña chinqi,* you *lunthata llujchi!"* I shouted.

It was only then that I noticed the dive boat had another passenger. Leila was crouched in the shadow of the pilothouse where I hadn't been able to see her, and was looking in alarm at the Ayancas, all of whose arms were suddenly waving weapons.

I got to my feet and ran to the pilothouse, where Sztephen was crouched down in cover, steering the boat with a wild expression on his face.

"Good work," I said, and took the controls.

Fidel Perugachi still had the launch, which had a powerful motor and could quite possibly outspeed the heavily laden catamaran once they got the anchor up. I didn't want to risk being boarded by a clutch of angry Ayancas, and besides I wanted the water ballet guys back.

I swung the boat into a wide circle, aimed straight at the launch, and let the boat build speed. There was

a fusillade of shots from the Ayancas—I had to wonder what possible good they thought it would
do—and then the white splashes of five bronzed
Apollos making perfect entries into the water. The
Ayancas stared at the twin-hulled doom approaching
at flank speed, and then most of them followed the
Apollos.

Fidel Perugachi was made of sterner stuff. He stood
on the boat's thwart, arms folded in an attitude of
defiance, glaring at me with his ferocious eyes until
the catamaran thundered right over him.

Showy, flamboyant, and self-dramatizing. What
did I tell you? Just like his flute-playing.

I didn't want to cut the launch in half, so I struck
it a glancing blow with the left hull, which was strong
enough to roll the craft under. It came bobbing up
astern—it was a tough boat, stuffed with foam to
make it unsinkable and suitable for use as a lifeboat—but we lost most of our diving gear.

I slowed and began to circle. That provided me an
opportunity to step out of the pilot house and glare
at Leila, who was still crouched against the pilot
house, paralyzed with shock at the bullets her
erstwhile allies had been volleying in her direction.
She seemed otherwise unharmed.

"Young lady," I said, shaking a finger, "I'm *very*
disappointed in you."

She looked up at me. "Fidel met my price," she said.
"We needed money to start the Fabulous Femmes
Water Ballet of Zuma."

My indignation at her being on a first-name basis
with Perugachi only heightened my disapproval.
"You'll get nowhere through this kind of imitation,"
I said. "Look at where it got the Ayancas."

We picked up the Apollos first, and they sat wet and bedraggled on the stern deck—I believe it was the only time I in our acquaintance when at least some of them weren't posing—and then we brought aboard the Ayancas, one by one. They hadn't hung onto their weapons, but we patted them down just in case, and tied them on the afterdeck and put them under guard of the Apollos, who soon regained their swagger.

Fidel Perugachi came aboard last, having survived the collision intact save for a dramatic and bloody cut on his forehead. He glared at me as we tied him and dropped him like a sack on the deck, and I flashed him a grim smile.

"Serves you right for killing my employer," I said.

"That wasn't my idea," he said, "and I didn't do it. I advised against it, in fact. I knew it would only piss you off."

"So whose idea *was* it?" I asked. I didn't expect him to reply, and he didn't.

We took the waterlogged launch in tow and headed for the People's Republic, where we dropped the Ayancas on a deserted rocky shore after making them bail out the launch. We also took their clothing.

Stranding them naked in a deserted corner of China, with no papers for crossing back into Hong Kong and no way of communicating with their employers, seemed likely to keep the Ayancas out of our hair for a while.

We also stranded the Fabulous Femme of Zuma, though we left her a towel for modesty's sake.

Leila was sullen and tried to bum a cigaret, but Perugachi did not take it well. He waded into the sea after us and shook his fist, filling the air with colorful Aymara oaths.

"Allu!" he called. *"Jama!"*

"Don't mess with the Hanansaya moiety!" I shouted back at him. "Our ancestors were *kings!*"

Which in our democratic age may seem a bit of aristocratic pretension, but quite frankly I thought it was time that Fidel Perugachi was put in his place.

"A pyramid," murmured Doctor Pan. "A white pyramid."

"Tetrahedron," I corrected helpfully.

His assistant Chun ignored me and gave Pan a desperate, hollow-eyed look. "The culture wasn't supposed to be able to survive in nature," he said.

"Didn't test it in the nutrient-rich effluent of the Pearl River, now, did you?" I asked.

Again Chun ignored me. "I can't understand the part about the pyramids. That's not supposed to happen at all."

"Tetrahedrons," I said again, "and *what* culture?" I focused on him a glower that would do Fidel Perugachi proud. "I was exposed to it, after all. If I'm about to turn into a four-sided polygon, I have the right to know."

We were in Pan's luxurious suite aboard *Tang Dynasty*, all silk hangings and rich furniture inlaid with mother-of-pearl, and air thick with tobacco smoke from Chun's pipe and Pan's disgusting little cigars. Those of us who had returned from the *Goldfish Fairy*—minus Deszmond, who had been assigned to run the catamaran hard around in Aberdeen harbor and then take the bus back—had decided it was time to confront Doctor Pan and find out just what our little mission was all about.

Pan caved in without resistance. "Our colleague Doctor Jiu," he said, referring to Jesse, "was working with a type of diatom. These are small one-celled algae that live in colonies and create crystalline structures."

"Divers know about diatoms," Laszlo said.

Pan nodded. "What Doctor Jiu managed to create was a diatom modified to excrete polycarbon plastic instead of a silicate. Since our current lines of plastics are created from fossil fuels, our company was quick to see the economic advantages of a far cheaper plastic that was created from, well, nothing, and we acquired both Doctor Jiu and his, ah, creation."

"And now the sea's got it," I said.

"The plastic structure is itself organic," Chun said added hopefully. "Sooner or later, other microorganisms will eat it. And in the meantime it's a very nice sink for carbon dioxide."

I looked at them. "Is that before or after the white tetrahedron breaks surface in the shipping lanes?"

Sometimes it is necessary to be blunt in order to shock some of these more cerebral types back to reality. Both Pan and Chun winced.

Pan combed his distinguished white hair with his fingers and looked at Laszlo. "What is normally done to stop an underwater contamination?"

Laszlo stared at his right biceps while absent-mindedly flexing it "Well," he said, "in cases of sea-weed, like that *caulerpa taxifolia* that can infest whole ecosystems, you cover the infected area with plastic, then pump in something that will kill it, like chlorine. You have to keep coming back at regular intervals to make certain it hasn't come back." He shrugged. "But how you deal with a *diatom* I don't know. Wouldn't the little critters be carried off by the current? Shouldn't it be all over the South China Sea by now?"

Sometime's it's possible to be *too* blunt: Chun looked as if he was about to cry, and Pan seemed profoundly cast down, and gave a deep sigh.

"We are dealing with a specific diatom," Pan said, "a bilaterally symmetrical organism that reproduces sexually through the fusion of protoplasts. It won't survive long on its own, but will do well in its colony." He looked at Chun for reassurance. "We don't think the organism will spread far."

"How much plastic sheeting can you get on short notice?" Laszlo asked them.

They looked dubious.

"Oh come on," he urged. "You're in the plastic *business.*"

"That would involve contacting another division of the company," Pan murmured in a subdued voice.

"It would involve *explanation,*" Chun murmured.back.

Pan gave another profound sigh. "So very awkward," he said.

"Awkward," Chun agreed.

I began to suspect that huge sheets of plastic were not in our future.

Which was how, two days later, I found myself the skipper of the 10,000-ton freighter *Twice-Locked Mountain,* a rusting hulk that had been thumping around the bywaters of Asia for the better part of the last century, so ancient and decrepit that it could only have been kept from the breakers' yards in the hope it might successfully be involved in some kind of insurance fraud.

I swung the wheel, steadied onto my new course,

took dead aim at the anchored freighter *Green Snake*, and rang Jorge in the engine room for more turns.

The old reciprocating engines thumped and banged, the propeller flailed water, and a shudder ran along the old ship, shaking off a few hundred pounds of rust flakes. I hoped she would hold together just a few more minutes. It would be embarrassing to sink her prematurely.

"Hurry up," came Laszlo's voice on the radio. "We've got to be in Shanghai by tomorrow night."

"I'm doing the best I can," I said, and reached for the controls of the ship's siren to signal *brace for collision.*

We were probably doing all of ten knots when we hit *Green Snake* dead abeam in a crash of tormented iron, venting steam, and gurgling water. Since *Green Snake* was at least as old a ship as *Twice-Locked Mountain*, and in even worse condition, I half expected us to slice our target in two, but instead we stayed locked together, which wasn't in the plan, either.

"Get everyone on deck," I told Laszlo. "You're about to go down fast."

I reached for the engine room telegraph and rang for full astern, which is exactly what you're not supposed to do when your ship has just collided with another. *Twice-Locked Mountain* backed out of the hole it had torn in *Green Snake* with another shriek of dying metal, and the sea flooded in. In mere moments the *Green Snake* was listing, and the water ballet guys, pausing every so often to flex, began piling into their lifeboat.

Our bow had been caved in, but I wasn't sure how much water was coming in through the bulkhead that we had so carefully punched full of holes, and I called Rosalinda on her cell to find out. The intake seemed insufficient, so I ordered the seacocks opened, and then we began to settle fast. I managed some last maneuvering with the aid of my satnav, then signaled Sancho on the foredeck to trip the anchor, which ran out with a roar and clatter and a splash.

I blew the siren that ordered everyone to assemble amidships, and we watched in some fascination as *Green Snake* rolled over, then plunged to the bottom amid a roil of water and the thunder of collapsing bulkheads. We transferred to our own boats in some haste, as we wanted to get of the area before the sea turned to poison.

In our own lifeboat we followed the Outrageous Water Ballet of Malibu toward Hong Kong, while I got busy on the radio and, in the voice of one Captain Nicholas Turgachev of the *Green Snake*, called in an SOS and issued the first of several environmental warnings, the second followed by the equally fictional Captain Bellerophos Kallikanzaros of the *Twice-Locked Mountain*.

The environmental warning was the only genuine part, as both ships had been loaded with sacks of arsenic originally intended to poison China's substantial population of rats. We had carefully anchored the wrecks so that they would bracket *Goldfish Fairy* when they went down. The arsenic would kill *anything*—man, woman, fish, plant, or mutated diatom—and the heavy metal would be leaking out of the wrecks and drifting over the site for weeks.

In the normal course of events, this would be considered an environmental catastrophe. In fact it *was* an environmental catastrophe.

What I hoped was that it would be preferable to white tetrahedrons growing on the ocean floor from here to Panama, a bleak eerie forest like the setting of some early work by Ballard.

Soon Sancho, impersonating yet another fictional captain (this one a Filipino named Suarez) got on the radio to inform the authorities that he'd taken the survivors aboard the freighter *Ode to Constancy*, heading for Taipei, where they would be made available for questioning as soon as the ship docked. Of course the ship would never dock there, and the crews would never be found, and neither would the owners of all the vessels involved. Over the years the Chinese had got very good at obscuring ship registries, and I was inclined to trust them.

Questions rattled over the radio, but Turgachev and Kallikanzaros and Suarez managed not to find a language in common with the authorities, just scattered words here and there. An emergency helicopter scrambled from Hong Kong got to the wreck site just in time to see *Twice-Locked Mountain* make its final dive.

I, my band, and the water ballet were on their way to Hong Kong, where we'd get a Dragon Air flight to Shanghai to rejoin *Tang Dynasty*.

It was the only gig we had left, after all. Doctors Pan and Chun would soon be on their way back to Taiwan,. where they would attempt to reconstruct Jesse's work from his notes. Even without their female contingent, the water ballet guys had found a new audience here, one that might keep them in Asia for quite some time. Every so often, suitably armored against the arsenic, they might make a dive down to the wreck to make certain that the diatoms weren't making a comeback.

We Hanansayas had become redundant. We were reduced to playing our music and flogging our CDs till the next emergency rose.

Or until the tetrahedrons rose from the sea. One way or the other.

by Gene Wolfe. First published in *The First Heroes: New Tales of the Bronze Age*, Harry Turtledove & Noreen Doyle eds., Tor Books. Reprinted by permission of the author.